Dedicated to Beth and our children, Rebecca, Sophie and Matthew.

The loves of my life. Without you, I would never have embarked on this adventure.

PHILIP J GOULD

THE GIRL IN THE MIRROR

THE GIRL IN THE MIRROR

This novel is entirely a work of fiction. The names, characters and incidents portrayed in it are the product of the author's imagination. Any resemblance to actual persons, living or dead, or events or localities is entirely coincidental.

First Published in Great Britain in 2015
Wildboar Publishing, 3 Ashton Close, Ipswich, IP2 9XY

A CIP catalogue record of this book is available from the British Library

ISBN: 978-0-9934167-0-5

Cover Illustrations and Interior Formatting by Streetlight Graphics
Author portrait © Hayley Waller

PROLOGUE
THE BIRTH

DRESSED IN WHITE SCRUBS, Maksim Alekseev was standing over a microscope, deep in concentration. His hair was tied back and contained unflatteringly within a white bouffant cap. Despite this a few strands of black, coarse hair escaped like spiders legs. White boots concealed his feet, and a procedure facemask covered his face. Latex gloves protected his hands, extra long so that the elasticised cuffs closed around the sleeves of his jacket, creating a seal. He looked every bit like a surgeon about to perform a lifesaving operation or a heart transplant. The laboratory was large and clinical and very *white.* A number of computer flat screens, laboratory equipment, scientific instruments and a variety of recognisable paraphernalia cluttered the cold, brightly lit room. A strong hospital smell of *iodoform*, cloying, almost overpowering, filled his nostrils. He didn't mind the smell – almost liked it.

He was peering down the two eyepieces of a stereo head microscope. Through the ocular lens he was able to view the magnified cell culture, a living organism that was growing and dividing, multiplying and maturing almost quicker than Maksim could comprehend.

"Has the mutation taken hold?" asked Clara, similarly attired, with just a pair of spectacles giving her a differentiating feature. She was across the room studying a video interpretation of what Maksim was viewing. A twenty-one inch screen was flashing a colourful image in front of her; little dots and squiggles in citrine-yellow and malachite-green danced and pirouetted, coalesced and divided; the growth and effect was both dizzying and mesmerising.

There were two others on the research team; George Jennings and Thomas Mundahl.

George Jennings – project leader and head of Kaplan Ratcliff's Biochemical and Life Sciences research facility. He was observing from outside the laboratory, peering in through the large glass wall. The intercom was on so he could hear and take part in their conversations.

Thomas Mundahl was not in attendance, having developed a migraine from a whole night of painstaking microscope gazing and bio-equation number-crunching. Despite his absence, the Norwegian would take an equal share of the credit for the research team's findings, his name eventually appearing on a list that would have serious and dire consequences.

"Woe-w, I've not seen anything like this before," Maksim spoke with a Ukrainian accent; he looked up from the microscope and turned to face George, who could be seen behind him through the glass. "Are you seeing this?" He was smiling and sounded excited.

George's voice was electronically magnified into the room, booming through the ceiling-set speaker system, austere and almost *god*like. "Maksim, answer Clara's question. Has the mutation held?"

Maksim started to laugh like a lunatic. "Hell YES!" His voice came out high-pitched, almost like a girl's.

"Should the cells be dividing like that?" Clara asked in a clipped tone.

Maksim composed himself, becoming serious. "New cells naturally replace old cells as they grow and die, it's no different here with our modified ones, only the pace of dividing and replacement...," he started grinning, "is a bit faster than I'd expected."

"You can say that again. Will that present a problem?" George's voice echoed around the laboratory.

Maksim absently scratched at his head, inadvertently releasing a few more hairs from beneath the bouffant, taking a long moment to mull the question over before answering.

"No," he finally said. "Of course, we will need to do further tests. Just to be on the safe side."

"What about live testing?" George's voice again filled the room, loud and commanding. *I need to adjust the volume on that thing,* thought Clara.

"Soon..." Hesitant. "I think. But more cell testing first."

"No time Maksim, we are on a deadline. Are we good to go now?"

Maksim shrugged. "Without further tests, it might be premature. Just a little longer, a week or two, we'll see."

Unheard by the two research assistants in the lab, George sighed. He was under pressure to deliver the product. The company had given him a blank cheque and already he'd spent tens of millions of pounds. Nearly two years of molecular biology and DNA testing, of endless experiments and countless failings, for what? Nothing! Nothing to show for their money but a lab full of fancy equipment and a few petri dishes of bright yellow sludge. Company heads were getting restless and impatient. Livelihoods were at stake. His reputation and job were in the balance, and worse still, the mission he'd so reluctantly agreed to undertake so many years earlier was a knee jerk away from failure.

"Okay Maksim, do what you need to do. I'll check in later." George did not hide his disappointment and wandered off to leave Clara and Maksim to their work.

The test-tube contained a blastocyst, a single fertilised embryo that had been developed in the laboratory for six days. A year of painstaking research had passed. Hundreds of mice, rabbits, pigs, cats, chimpanzees, and a solitary orangutan, had led to this historic moment. Only a week had gone by since Camilla, the last chimp, had been destroyed humanely after a successful trial. It was sad and had brought Clara close to tears, but it had been unavoidable. It had been a necessary death, but she hadn't gone quietly – far from it. Her strength surpassed anything George had ever witnessed, and her other enhanced abilities made it even more of a challenge to keep her under control and bring about her unavoidable destruction. Nonetheless, Camilla had not gone cleanly, effecting a broken collar bone in Thomas and bloodying his nose and almost killing a student lab assistant who ignored George's instructions to stay well back as they administered the lethal injection.

In the ward, George's wife, Harriet Jennings was lying on a bed, an NHS hospital gown maintaining her modesty. A sheet and blanket was drawn up, hiding her body but doing little to conceal the fear on her face. A nurse was on hand and George entered the private room looking for all intents and purposes like a practicing doctor on his rounds. A white coat and stethoscope draped around his shoulders completed the appearance.

"Are you okay?" George asked his wife.

"I guess," she said. "You sure this is going to be all right?" she asked, a slight tremor in her voice.

"Harriet, trust me. I'm your husband. I'd never let anything bad happen to us." Overemphasising the 'us', he sat down on the bed next to her and placed a comforting hand on her knee.

"You promise?"

"I promise." He leant over and kissed his wife on the forehead in two places.

A knock at the door startled George. His nerves were all jangles. He felt like it was him undergoing the operation, rather than his wife, that he were under the microscope like the cell culture back in the lab more than a year ago. *This was it*, he thought to himself, *the moment of truth*. Time to sink or swim, and any of a hundred other euphemisms.

"Ready?" George's research assistant, Clara had arrived to help escort Harriet to the operating theatre.

"As I ever will be, I guess," replied Harriet.

Accompanying Harriet was a regular hospital porter who, without bidding, had entered the room and began readying the hospital bed for movement, extracting brakes and locking in sidebars, working with the care and attention of someone who'd done the action a hundred-thousand times. She couldn't help flinching from the scraping sounds of metal and jerky movements caused.

The hospital porter wheeled the bed out of the ward and together with Clara, George, and a nurse, they travelled the short distance to the operating theatre. On entering they were greeted by another nurse and a fertility doctor, Dr Phelps.

"Dr Jennings, everything is as you requested. Come this way." The fertility doctor held the double swing doors open to allow entry into a small pre-operating room, and secured them behind George, who was last to enter the room. A further set of swing doors ahead were closed to them, and would remain that way until everyone was clinically sterile and risks of infection were eliminated.

"Now, Harriet. I guess you're prepped for this, but I just want to make sure you fully understand the ins and outs. It's never too late to back down or change one's mind," Dr Phelps smiled reassuringly. "The procedure won't take long, but it is normal to experience a fair amount of discomfort – it can't be helped I'm afraid. It's not too dissimilar to a smear test. For optimum success, we will be using ultrasound for guidance, which is important as we are only transferring the one embryo."

Dr Phelps reached down to a small trolley upon which were a number of medical instruments, supplies and packages. "We will need to use this," he picked up the speculum, and then placed it back down again, "and once we have located the uterine cavity, we will use this soft transfer catheter to load the embryo when ready." The doctor was holding a distress inducing needle-type contraption that brought tears to Harriet's eyes just peering at it. "Once I begin to insert this tube, Hannah our nurse will use the ultrasound to help me guide the catheter home. The rest is easy after that. Any questions?"

Harriet had no questions. George had explained the procedure countless times and she'd been a willing participant, not out of desire to be a mother again, but due to her feeling of duty and marital support towards her husband's work.

"Okay, let's get you pregnant." Dr Phelps opened the second set of swing doors and led the ensemble into the operating theatre. "Okay, let's get the party started. Dr Jennings, you can prepare the embryo ready for transfer. Hannah, when you are ready with the ultrasound, we can begin."

Hannah squeezed some lubricating gel onto Harriet's abdomen and used the ultrasound machine's transducer to spread it evenly. Almost immediately an image appeared on the ultrasound machine. "Okay Dr Phelps," the nurse said jovially, "we're ready."

"Good. Most excellent."

The procedure took less than six minutes and upon transferring the embryo, Hannah nodded confirmation to the fertility doctor indicating the embryo had been placed within the uterine cavity. She watched the catheter on the ultrasound monitor; a white, thin, long object that slowly withdrew as Dr Phelps gently pulled it out from between Harriet's legs.

"Good, job well done. I guess your husband will take it from here." Dr Phelps dropped the soft transfer catheter into a yellow surgical waste bin, followed by the latex gloves that he had been wearing. "George," he affirmed in passing as he vacated the operating theatre.

"Thanks James," George said.

"What now?" asked Harriet, shifting slightly, desperate for comfort. For anyone who's had the misfortune of having spent time in a hospital, one would know that comfort was very low down a doctor or a nurse's list of priorities.

"Well, we just need to wait and see," he said. "Say a prayer or two. Expect the worst... but hope for the best."

Harriet knew the pregnancy wasn't normal – not by a long stretch. After six days her clothes began to feel tight around her stomach, her boobs were bigger and morning sickness was taking her by violent surprise in the most inconvenient of occasions.

"WHAT HAVE YOU DONE TO ME GEORGE?!" she screamed after one such nauseous episode, lurching out from the bathroom of the medical facility where she was staying in a private room. This was during the early observation stages when the risks of failure were at their highest.

"It's all normal, love, I assure you..."

"Normal? I wasn't sick like this with Meredith or Stanley, not even Charlie. Something is wrong."

"Calm down Harriet. I will get one of the team to run some tests."

Within the hour, Clara and Thomas, the big Norwegian, were sitting next to Harriet with an ultrasound machine hooked up and a foetal heart rate monitor whose leads were strapped around her expanding waist. Having squeezed blue lubricating jelly already, Clara ran the transducer over Harriet's extended stomach and stopped, eyes widening in shock. She made no effort to hide her amazement.

"G-e-o-r-g-e," she said his name slowly. "I think you should come and see this."

"What's wrong? What's happening? Tell me... please!" Harriet's voice had an alarmed edge to it having noted Clara's concerned tone.

George crossed the room and peered at the monitor.

"My word, that's a bit different. How curious."

"What's happening George?" Harriet's panic was growing.

George laid a comforting hand on his wife's arm and tried a disarming smile. "The foetus is growing a bit faster than we had expected. It's nothing to worry about Harriet. Apart from that, everything is normal."

"Normal? What do you mean 'normal'? If it's not six days old, how old is it?" she asked.

Clara pressed a few buttons on the ultrasound's keyboard to begin measurements of the foetus. Accidentally depressing the sound 'on' button, the sound of a heart beat began to 'whump-whump-whump-whump' continuously around the room. Unseen on the foetal heart rate monitor was an oscillating dot tracking the unborn baby's heart beat in tandem with the now-audible pulse rate.

"Using the ultrasound, I have dated the scan at," she paused, getting her head around the figure, "twelve weeks."

"That's not possible," muttered Harriet, incredulous.

On the monitor the twelve-week-old foetus could be seen and a light fluttering of its heart could be made out.

"What have you done George? What have you put inside of me?"

"I can explain," he started. "It's nothing more than I'd said."

"Oh, George," starting to cry, Harriet turned her face away from her husband, from Clara and from the other lab technician, knocking the ultrasound transducer away from her stomach, ending the 'whump-whump-whump-whump' sound and the foetal images on the monitor. "I trusted you," she whispered into her pillow, her sobs the only thing those in attendance actually heard.

"It will be all right," he said. He sat down on the bed beside his wife and began to run his fingers through her hair. "She will be perfect."

Clara removed the transducer and returned it to its place on the ultrasound machine. She then detached the foetal heart rate monitor. "I'll leave you two to it," she said, pushing the machine away to the side before exiting the room.

Slowly it dawned on Harriet what George had let slip. "She?" *Was it even possible to know the sex at twelve weeks?*

Thomas Mundahl, who'd been unobtrusive with whatever tasks he'd been set also swiftly disappeared, noting the sharp change in mood and the testiness in Harriet's voice as his cue to vacate the room.

"I meant 'it'," George tried to backtrack, but it was too late. Harriet's look forewarned him to cease any further attempts at transposing his comment.

"What else should I know, George? I assume 'she' will look normal?"

"Well, yes, naturally. There's no advantage to having three legs or two heads. Harriet, you *do* know what I do for a living," he replied acerbically. "We have made some slight tweaks to the DNA – improvements, to say the least."

"You've genetically modified her. You've created *Frankenstein* inside my belly..."

"Actually, *Frankenstein* was the scientist, not...," he went quiet, "...the monster..."

"*Hitler* would have loved *you*." Tears were freefalling down her face. "Oh George, what have you done? You could go to jail for this."

"Don't worry, my love. It's all fine. It's government sanctioned. We are at the forefront of an amazing breakthrough."

Harriet was shaking her head in disbelief. "You are breaking the law. What you are doing George is an affront to humanity. It's insane. You are playing God. Is nothing sacred anymore? You don't have the right."

George stood up from the bed. "People said the same thing about the motor car. Nobody likes change, Harriet."

"THAT'S NOT THE SAME GEORGE!" Harriet was shouting. "If you don't like a car you can send it off to scrap. You can't do that with a human baby."

"Well…" George started but thought better of finishing the sentence. Instead he made strides to the door. "I think I will leave you to calm down," he said, and walked out from the room before Harriet could throw the vase of flowers on the table beside the bed at him.

A little over three weeks had passed since the pregnancy had first been dated and the foetus had been viewed – and heard – on the ultrasound. Harriet still couldn't believe the speed in which her pregnancy had advanced, nor help or contain the resentment she still felt towards her husband, the man she'd trusted and who'd deceived her so impeccably.

How could he treat her like one of his lab rats?

Within the operating room was Dr Phelps, a man she'd thought was younger when first they'd met. In fact he was in his fifties; thick grey hair was hidden within a surgical cap and he wore spectacles that suggested he needed a trip to *Specsavers*. Around him was a team of four medical staff, nurses and midwives, all garbed in blue surgical clothing; caps, face masks; George was sitting at his wife's side, and Clara, also in the room, stood a little out of the way. The room was kept purposefully cold and George shivered.

From outside the theatre, Maksim and Thomas were watching through the large observation wall. Thomas was holding a digital video camera which Maksim thought was a bit odd, but then Norwegians were odd – or was he confusing them with the Swedish?

The operating theatre was fitted with video recording equipment, cameras positioned beneath the ceiling in all four corners of the room. This historic event would forever be remembered, whether it was intentional or not.

"Okay Harriet, just relax. You won't feel any pain."

"I don't want this baby," she lamented. "I mean it George, I'll never love it."

George squeezed her hand reassuringly. "Let's not think about it right now, hey?"

"I mean it. She's not my baby. She's not, George!"

"Now, Harriet, I'm sure you know how this all works." Dr Phelps tried to ignore Harriet's distress and tried to treat the operation like the happy occasion it ought to have been. "I will make an incision down your abdomen, then through the uterus. Once in there we will pop her out in no time."

Harriet turned away from the doctor and faced the side furthest from her husband. "Just get it out of me," she spat.

"Right then." The team of medical staff crowded around Harriet's bed and the doctor began the caesarean. "Let's get this party started," he said with a chuckle. George started to wonder whether this was one of Dr Phelps' annoying catchphrases. He dismissed the thought.

The abdomen was prepared with gentle cleaning and disinfectant to reduce the amount of bacteria and chances of infection following delivery. Sterile pieces of cloth were draped over Harriet, leaving just the section of stomach waiting to be performed on. Using a scalpel, Dr Phelps made an incision to the outer layers of skin, just above Harriet's pubic hairline, approximately six inches in length. Once through, he then cut through some layers of fat tissue, and then through a fibrous layer called the *fascia*. As the doctor worked, Harriet continued to face away, disinterested, numbed to the experience either by the epidural earlier administered, or her hostility towards the baby, towards the situation from whence she came, or towards the instigator – her husband, for whom she'd carried three normal, healthy children.

After a few minutes of more careful cutting and gentle probing, Dr Phelps opened the uterus and reached in; slowly and with practiced ease, he removed the baby, careful not to twist her head, neck, body or limbs – a procedure that isn't as easy as one might think. Reaching for a small medical suction device, Dr Phelps quickly placed the small nozzle in and sucked amniotic fluid from the baby's mouth. A moment later the small child took her first breath and let out a low, guttural cry that brought a tear to George's eye.

"You have a baby daughter," said a nurse who wrapped the baby in a thick blanket as Dr Phelps detached the umbilical cord. After cleaning her, measuring and weighing her (and the doctor had finished stitching Harriet up), the nurse scooped up the baby and carried her over to her mother. "Here," the nurse offered the still crying infant to Harriet. "The first moments are the most precious."

Harriet glanced at the baby, and turned her head on the pillow, facing away. "Take that….*thing* away from me," she said, thick with contempt and utter disgust.

"Here," George came forward. "Let me." The nurse gently placed the small bundle into George's open arms, taken aback by Harriet's vehemence. The baby's cries immediately ceased and a small smile appeared on her lips. George cradled the small child and carried her away from his wife's bed.

"I'm going to call you Sophie," he whispered, "after *Sophia*, the Goddess of Wisdom, who was there at the beginning, the source of wisdom and the keeper of all that was righteous and just."

"Isn't she adorable," Clara was beaming, almost as if, George thought, it was her own child… He shook the thought from his head, correcting himself. In some ways, she was. Sophie was as much Thomas, Maksim and Clara's child, as she was his or Harriet's. "I want to hold her," Clara said eagerly. She looked elfin and childlike. It was the happiest she'd been or felt in her entire life.

Behind them, Harriet huffed. Never had she hated George more than in those mere moments.

The nurse who had cleaned Sophie and who'd moments earlier

handed the baby to George, came over to him, sidestepped Clara and smiled. "She's so special," she said.

George was slow in his response, considering the comment. He turned to the nurse and through a slight smile he said: "You have no idea." George made to hand Sophie to Clara, ever so careful, handling her like a piece of glass.

It was at that very instant the still smiling baby did something extraordinary.

Sophie vanished within George's arms.

One moment she was there...

The next...

She was gone.

CHAPTER ONE

SOPHIE...

FEAR. CERTAINLY NOT THE most genial of emotions, but the one which carried with it more than just a patina of sweat and a flutter of a heart beat. The child – a girl – was experiencing it for the first time, tasting the bitterness of bile that she'd burped up involuntarily, the aftertaste a combination of unpleasantness and a stinging sensation at the back of her throat.

The klaxon – a deep, resonant alarm that drilled deep into her head and threatened to deafen her – permeated the walls and the sealed door, locked from the outside, to her room; her sanctuary, her prison – her home. Quite spacious, there was a bed (a cute kitten-print duvet spread across it), a television (turned on, but mute), a wardrobe, some toys (nothing too fancy – a few dolls, a cuddly kangaroo toy she called *Flopsy* – which she was cuddling for comfort), some books and a computer.

With clinically white walls, it was almost ethereal, shimmering against the glare of the halogen bulbs that burned from various spots in the ceiling; however, the sanctuary was no holy escape from whatever din or disaster that was developing outside, and by the urgent tone of the alarm, whatever it was was immediate and threatening, and – she thought – was heading her way.

A thin tendril of smoke was teasing its way into the room through a crack at the bottom of the entranceway, fingers caressing the cream-coloured *Saxony* carpet that covered the whole living space, normally warm and comforting, now a willing accomplice shedding light on what the exigency was beyond the steel reinforced door.

Pounding feet could be heard running back and forth, up and down the corridor beyond her room. The girl – no more than five or six in appearance – had her hands pressed against her ears, trying with little or no success to blot out the siren and the gradual addition of coughing and muffled screams from somewhere further than the immediate corridor outside her room.

Minutes passed with little or no change to her surroundings when the green LED lamp above the door flashed on and the door burst open, slamming against the wall.

"Sophie, we need to go." George Jennings, the man who had raised her from the moment she had been born, walked into the room, smoke billowing in from behind him like a Victorian gentleman's cloak. He was dressed in white trousers, white lab coat (that was black with soot and singed in places) and black Oxford style, supermarket budget priced shoes. His face was dirty and his shoulder-length hair, usually tied in a neat tail, cascaded in a tangle about the sides of his face, bedraggled and unkempt. "Quick! There's no time!" he hissed.

With the door open the fire alarm was clangourous and hurt Sophie's ears. Dragging *Flopsy* by one of its limp arms, she padded across the room to where her dad stood anxiously.

"I'm scared," she said in a little voice as her father took hold of her hand and dragged her out into the corridor now filled with a light, grey cloud that fogged her sight.

"Try not to breathe... hold your breath." George scooped his daughter up into his arms with little effort, and ran the length of the corridor with big strides, the security door at the end unlocked (as was normal when the fire alarm sounded). Beyond the security door was a set of three elevators (all out of use – as was also normal when the fire alarm sounded). Through a door to the left of the elevators was a staircase, a green sign above the door stating *Emergency Exit*, its little green man running through a white door, illustrating the obvious.

George carried Sophie through it, her arms were wrapped tightly around his neck. Other people were bounding down the stairs, some taking two or more steps at a time; one person barged past George, almost knocking him off balance.

"Sorry," a half-gestured apology as the man, ten years younger than George (who was thirty-seven), disappeared round a bend in the stairs.

Ten flights down the staircase (with eight or nine more to go) the building rocked as an explosion tore through the nineteenth floor, so loud and booming that for a moment Sophie thought she'd never hear anything else again, the sound so intense that her ears were ringing and a thin trickle of liquid seeped from one of them. The sound of glass shattering and metal crumpling was grating against nerves, and the dust of plaster and the shower of brick fragments falling around came laden with the threat of burying them alive. At some point Sophie started to wail uncontrollably and George responded by holding her more tightly, the girl burying her head into his chest, begging for the horror to end. At some point the sound of screaming, haunting and nightmarish, overtook the sound of the devastation that was occurring to the building around them. This terrified her even more than she deemed possible.

Then the last few steps of the stairs were descended and George burst out of the building and ran out into a crisp, autumnal evening, the sky taking on an Egyptian blue as dusk stole daylight in preparation for night. George continued across the car park, passing the congregation of workers who'd converged at the company's designated emergency assembly point, and who now watched the building – their place of employment – burn from a third of the way down, thick black smoke billowing into the air in great sheets of toxic gasses and bright tongues of flame licking out, like a komodo dragons' tongue, searching for more sustenance to devour, urged on by its captive audience.

George continued towards a stationary blue *Peugeot 207* parked in a space designated for the *Head of Scientific Research and Advancement.*

Opening the passenger door, placing his daughter on the booster seat and leaning over her so as to buckle her seatbelt, George stood up for a moment and considered the still-crying girl in front of him. Like most fathers, he considered the child as something more than just a little person. She was special. Unlike most fathers, George Jennings' claim was not just a parent's unconditional claim; Sophie Jennings *was* special. She was different to all the other children in the world. She was – as George often stated within board meetings, with his colleagues, with his superiors and even with his wife, Harriet – unique.

Before closing the door, George ruffled his daughter's hair playfully – reassuringly (he hoped). "I just need to do something then we'll be going."

"We're leaving?" Sophie, still sobbing, was incredulous. She'd never left the confines of the now-burning building, let alone driven off to places yonder.

George didn't reply, instead he closed the car's door and jogged a short distance out of the car park onto the main road that serviced the biochemical research centre and other industrialised buildings peppered along the route. Across the road was a bus stop, and more specifically to George, a black waste bin standing sentinel alongside it, cemented into the pavement, its opening like a large, wide letter box. Fortuitously no one was waiting for a bus as George approached the bin. A quick look from side to side and a backwards glance, ensuring no one was watching before he pulled a small, weighty object from beneath the dirty white lab coat he wore and hastily posted it into the bin.

From inside the car, Sophie had watched, her eyes focusing on the object that her father was disposing of. The shock of seeing the item stifled her whimpering. For a moment her brain could not decipher what her eyes were seeing. Realisation crept in stealthily, blotting out the terrors of just a few moments earlier –

– she bolted upright, a glaze of sweat coating her face and matting her hair to her head. Her heart was thumping like she'd run full-pelt for half a mile and the familiar taste of bile and vomit, cloying and clinging, sluiced around the insides of her mouth and coated her tongue.

She closed her eyes a moment and tried to finish the playback of her dream, willing the item that had caused such distress in her dream state to materialise and give an answer to why her recurring nightmare could threaten to cause the onset of a heart attack.

But the object of her nightmare's obsession would not come into focus and after a couple of minutes trying to make sense of the mental playback, she pulled herself out from under the covers of her bed, turned on the bedside light and swung her legs out over the edge. She sat there for a moment giving the matter some careful thought. Across the small bedroom was a mirror hanging above a desk. She studied her reflection in the dingy light cast by the forty-watt bulb in the lamp. Long blonde hair, sapphire-blue eyes surrounded by deep, dark cavernous sockets, milk-white complexion, full lips courtesy of her father, and a slight, delicate frame – she looked fragile, almost as though a gust of wind could shatter her like a glass bauble on a Christmas tree. Wearing cute bunny-print pyjamas, Sophie shuddered from a sudden chill or from the lingering remnants of her dream memory. *Flopsy* was close to hand and she picked up the stuffed toy and squeezed its tummy without thinking. She found the plush fabric kangaroo comforting in her grip – it soon helped her recover from the replay of that fateful October day when her world changed beyond recognition.

The fire and explosions that had rocked Kaplan Ratcliff's Biochemical and Life Sciences Division. The facility all but destroyed by fire and by the three explosions that rocked the land for one-and-a-quarter miles – eleven staff perishing within the blaze. So intense were the flames that little of their earthly bodies remained, identification rendered impossible on all but one of the unfortunate fatalities.

All of George's team, a couple of interns and a security guard – all dead. By sheer luck – George would attest and confide to his wife – he had managed to escape through a dense wall of flame, miraculously evading injury, except perhaps mental anguish.

Sabotage had been blamed for the incident, and George was very vocal in laying blame on Tom Kaplan himself, the CEO of the company. Though he never looked Harriet in the eyes when he'd voiced his accusations. The reasons for why were not easily explained either, after all, Sophie was 'unique' and more than an asset. Why would anyone want to destroy her father's laboratory and his entire work?

Wrapping a bathrobe around herself and fastening it about the waist with the rope belt, the girl – now eleven years of age in appearance – left her bedroom in the apartment and wandered the short distance to the lounge/dining room, *Flopsy* dangling by one ear at her side.

George was sitting at the table nursing a cup of coffee (steaming), a tabloid newspaper spread open in front of him. The clock on the wall showed the time was 1:08 a.m. Her father was seldom asleep – the pitfalls of a double life and an unhealthy dedication to his work.

Looking up from the newspaper, George studied his daughter as she set herself in a chair opposite him.

"Can't you sleep?" he asked.

Sophie shook her head. *Flopsy* was on the table in front of her.

"The nightmare?" George enquired.

Sophie nodded her head. "The same dream as before."

"Have you had your meds?" The drug Sophie was on wasn't something to aid sleep or prescribed in response to any lingering trauma from the laboratory fire. It wasn't a conventional medicine found in the local pharmacy or one easily obtained, but one which George had designed specifically to counter the side effects of an unusual defect that Sophie had been born with.

"Yes, dad," Sophie replied nonchalantly.

"You know what will happen if you don't take it, don't you?"

"I wish you'd quit treating me like a child," she grumbled.

George chuckled. "You are a child!"

"If you don't believe me... here..." Sophie stood up and crossed the room to enter the kitchen adjoining it, moving directly to the fridge. From the bottom shelf she removed a small glass vial containing an ochre-coloured liquid from a tray tightly packed with thirty-five others. Behind the tray were half a dozen other trays stacked neatly together in two piles. Sophie closed the fridge and reached for a jet injector, a small gun-like contraption in which she slotted the small glass vial into the base of.

"Sophie... you don't need to if you've already had your dose."

Ignoring him, Sophie pressed the tip of the device against her arm and depressed the trigger. Powered by compressed air, the jet injector penetrated the epidermis and administered the drug. She closed her eyes to the sudden effects of her medicine - a slight dizziness and a mild tingling sensation in her fingers and toes – but the feelings were gone almost as quickly as they had come.

"There, satisfied?" Sophie ejected the spent glass vial, dropped it into a small bin that was nearly full with used glass vials, and tossed the jet injector back to where she'd found it – between the microwave and an electric kettle. She collected *Flopsy* from the table and snorted aloud, "Hmpff."

"Sophie..." The name hung in the air as the girl walked out of the kitchen.

"I'll see you in the morning," she said, turning her back to her father, returning to her bedroom.

"Sophie!" He hated quarrels with his daughter. He guessed it came with the territory, though hadn't expected the angst to come for a few more years yet. "I suppose this is just another side effect I'll have to get used to," he grumbled before returning his attention back to the tabloid newspaper.

CHAPTER TWO

...SOPHIE

THE APARTMENT WAS LOCATED in the well-to-do area of Chelsea on the other side of London from where Kaplan Ratcliff had its laboratory building, and just short of thirty miles from where George Jennings had moved his family to a secret hideout in the *less*-desirable location of Stanford-le-Hope.

The fire that had swept through the biochemistry research facility not only took the lives of eleven of his colleagues, it all but destroyed five years' worth of research and intelligence data, setting Project *CHAMELEON* back to its infancy – the saboteur doing a wonderful job in stalling, if not thwarting, the company in its directive of producing its first genetically engineered human being. Every scrap of evidence, every single person involved, was gone – either dead, missing or presumed dead. The stuff of science fiction to remain locked within the realms of imagination – except of course, for whatever details were retained within George's head, his laptop and his personal files kept under lock and key; additionally, you couldn't ignore live specimen number one, who George had named Sophie.

That was four months even earlier, though from the girl's appearance it could have been several years before; against natural order and disregarding millions of years' of evolution, Sophie had aged considerably. No longer a bouncy, flouncy child of five or six, Sophie had the body and face of a ten-year-old. Despite her façade, she still had childlike tendencies, her young brain developing at a slower rate than her physical build – the only hindrance being George's inability to provide learning material to sustain her ravenous mind rather than any innate birth defects.

George marvelled at the way his daughter absorbed information like a sponge, often devouring whole books within a matter of hours - even ones written for an older audience or for academics. No subject too difficult, too laborious or too boring. George provided books ranging in topic; from natural history to modern warfare, from biology to cookery, subtly feeding her with knowledge that could one day save her life.

It was whilst reading a book about torture – not the usual subject for a ten-year-old girl – that Sophie stopped mid-flow, and placed the book down onto her lap, facedown, open at the page she was reading.

"Dad," she said, a strained look on her face. "When can I see mum?"

George was at the dining table typing up notes and theories on a laptop that was open in front of him. He stopped typing, his fingers still poised over the qwerty keyboard, and turned his attention to the girl sitting on the sofa. Absently, he swiped the spectacles off the bridge of his nose and laid them next to the laptop.

"Sophie, we've been through this before. Your mother will see you on your birthday."

"But why can't we live with her? Doesn't she love me?"

George couldn't tell her the truth. He smiled reassuringly and answered: "Of course she loves you, silly. It's just too dangerous for you right now." George waved his hand in the air, searching for a plausible explanation. "It's complicated. You're spec-"

"Special," she finished for him. "I know, I know. Freaking *Frankenstein*, more like."

"You're nothing like *Frankenstein*," George rebuked. He recalled his wife using the same metaphor before she was born. "Anyway, if anyone was like *Frankenstein*, it would be me – he was the mad scientist who *created* the monster, don't you know."

"A'you saying I'm a monster?" Sophie was imitating shock but had a playful smile on her lips that caused a slight dimple in her left cheek.

"Go back to your reading," George admonished, picking up his spectacles, not taking the bait, returning to work.

Sophie continued to smile to herself for a moment longer before allowing it to slip and the memory of what she called her first 'ethereal' moment came to mind – or at least the first occasion she could remember noticing the most extraordinary feature of the genetic alteration that had been made to her DNA.

Shortly after arriving at the apartment, perhaps one or maybe two weeks after, George was called away to his 'other' family – she referred to her mother and the three children who were her siblings as 'the others' – forgetting to administer Sophie's evening injection (it was the event that culminated in George showing her how to inject herself) before leaving.

"I'll be back as soon as I can. There's meats and cheeses in the fridge and plenty of salad. You know what to do," George had said this as he hastened out of the apartment.

Not knowing what the side effect was to missing out on her daily meds, Sophie sat in the living room watching television – an activity she enjoyed unhealthily. She'd never missed an injection before so she was not unduly worried. *Nickelodeon* played throughout the evening, which George allowed her to watch until the alarm went (preset to go off at 8:00 p.m.). It was only just after six and *SpongeBob SquarePants* played out on the giant screen attached to the wall when the strange phenomenon occurred.

Totally engrossed in the farcical antics of *SpongeBob, Sandy Cheeks, Patrick Star* and the various other characters that dwelled in the undersea city of *Bikini Bottom*, Sophie failed to notice the abnormality that began at her extremities (first the fingers and then her toes), and began spreading slowly up her limbs, so slowly in fact that its progress was barely noticeable and totally ignored by the ten-year-old.

It wasn't until she absently went to bat a strand of her long blonde hair away from her eyes that she became aware of the oddity that was occurring to her.

Is this real?

She held her hands up to her face, palm-facing and blinked, turning her hands from back to front, initially wide-eyed in wonder, oblivious to the significance of the metamorphosis taking place – not just in front of her, but actually *to her* – and then the wonderment of the moment evaporated almost as surely as the rest of her limbs. Looking down at her body she jerked up onto invisible legs and watched as the last part of her upper arms vanished and whatever it was that was occurring gradually made the rest of her disappear until all that was left was her head, floating like a balloon in the air.

Then that, she knew, was gone – crossing her eyes slightly she could see that the end of her nose was no longer there.

"Oh, oh, oh, oh..." she started to hyperventilate. "What's going on?" *Am I dreaming this?*

Sophie went to the bathroom and turned the light on using the pull string. An energy saver bulb flickered on and filled the small room with brilliant white. She looked at the mirror above the sink and sighed with relief.

Her image stared back at her. She looked how she remembered.

A two-year-old trapped in a ten-year-olds' body. Her physical age was just a guess really, based on the denominator printed in the labels of her clothing. Her long hair, which fell down straight and ended somewhere at the centre of her back, still appeared in front of her when she twisted her body. Her eyes, like twin-oceans, threatened to drill holes into her as she glared at the image reflecting back.

Running the taps, she half-filled the washbasin with water and went to wash her face. As she went to dip her hands into the water, she stopped with a gasp that turned into a whimper.

Although her reflection was there in the mirror, the origin of that reflection was still no longer visible. It was then that the scream, loud in pitch and long in its intensity, erupted from her lips, unbidden and seemingly endless.

"Are you okay?" George had looked up from his laptop to see his daughter's far-away look.

She shook the lingering memory out of her head. It was as haunting as the recurring dream that still plagued her sleep.

"Sure, why wouldn't I be?" She allowed her thoughts to wander back to the day she discovered her unique talent.

George had returned from 'the others' the morning after the peculiar thing had occurred, finding his daughter sobbing in the corner of her bedroom. To say finding wasn't actually correct; he hadn't seen her there in the corner as he'd entered the room, but instead heard her whimpering, scared and feeling utterly alone. "Oh Soph… I'm so sorry," he'd said, and he looked like he meant it.

"What's happening to me?" she'd cried: "Why can't I see myself? Am I… am I a *ghost?*"

George had tried to reassure her with a smile; failing as he'd looked completely past her. "No, you're not a ghost. Ghosts aren't real."

"Then what am I?" she sobbed.

George didn't know what to say. He shook his head slowly from side to side, searching for something comforting to say, settling on the decision to tell his daughter the truth.

"I will tell you everything," he said. "But first, I think you ought to take your medicine."

The staccato fire as George's fingers struck the keyboard interrupted the tail end of her memory, and she allowed it to disintegrate like smoke from an extinguished candle. Feigning a loud yawn, she stood up, put aside her book atop a pile of others on a coffee table and walked over to the dining table.

"I'm off to bed," she said, planting a kiss on her father's forehead.

"Night Soph... Don't forget your meds."

"Dad! Trust me!" A phrase she found herself often repeating, it was as though he didn't trust her at all. She walked into the kitchen, crossed to the fridge and opened the door.

"Oh, so you don't freak out," George called loud enough to be heard in the kitchen, "I may be gone when you get up in the morning. Just some things I need to do."

"The 'others'?" she sneered.

"They are as much a part of my life as you are, Sophie," he admonished.

"I just wish I could get to see them."

Sophie held the glass vial of ochre liquid in her hand, the jet injector in her other. She studied them both for a fraction of a moment. Peering out of the kitchen into the dining room, she could see the shadow of her father hunched over the laptop and hear the *tat-tat-tat* as he pounded away at the keyboard. Without loading the gun-like injector she depressed the trigger; a quick burst of compressed air sounded – loud enough for her father to hear. Feigning the sound of disposing the empty glass vial (by rattling the small bin that was half-full of other empties), she pocketed the unused serum and scooted off to bed.

From the sanctuary of her bedroom she waited for the consequences of missing her evening dose of the *immunotoxin* to take effect.

George often left Sophie on her own – not an ideal scenario, but one borne out of necessity rather than free will. No one would understand her circumstances, or the work that he did. It wasn't cruel locking her in the apartment to fend for herself; it was a state that she'd been conditioned to since the day she'd learnt to walk. The situation was simple. George spent half his time with Sophie and the other half of his time with his wife and three kids: Meredith, Stanley and Charlie. His life was split in two and spent in a sort of dysfunctional rota system. Usually he would spend three nights at one place, and three nights at the other, alternating between the two where he would spend his days – that way he saw all his family for at least part of everyday.

George had set his alarm two hours early that day so that he could be on the road and out of the city before congestion started. The journey to his wife took a little over an hour on a good day. This would be a good day as he was going to be out early beating the traffic.

Sophie had heard her father's alarm and had dressed quietly in T-shirt and jogging bottoms. It was only the third time she had missed an injection. The first time was by accident. The second – and this occasion – were by intention. As expected, the 'not taking' of her medication had the desired result. The fact that whatever she wore disappeared as soon as it came into contact with her skin, although perplexing, was a useful by-product of her strange genetic disorder. She didn't understand how it worked, or why, but it saved the indecency (and the chill) of walking about in the great wide world naked as the day she was born.

Unseen, she crept out of her bedroom on tiptoe carrying a pair of trainers and snuck out of the apartment. Although at 5:30 a.m. the sun had risen early, its rays not quite warm enough to lessen the chill that was in the air. A short distance from the apartment, Sophie saw the *Peugeot 207* parked up. Using the spare key she unlocked the car, climbed into the back seat and depressed the central locking button to secure it behind her. She crouched down as low as she could, afraid that her father would see her despite being invisible.

A short while later, George unlocked the car and climbed in. He tossed his jacket onto the passenger seat next to him and took a moment to assess his image in the rear-view mirror, sweeping a hand through his hair before attempting to make it neat with a bit of spit which he daubed on a few loose strands. Once satisfied, he started the engine and began the journey to his alternative life – a life that was slightly less complicated but still with its trials and shortcomings.

Just under one hour later, the *Peugeot* pulled into the driveway of a four bed detached modern home. The building had a mock-Tudor style with half-timbering and red brick façade and side-gables that supported a steeply pitched roof. Tall, narrow windows completed the aesthetic, black framed and leaded. As the car stopped in front of the garage adjoining the building, Sophie took a glance.

It wasn't what she'd been expecting.

But what *had* she been expecting?

Having had little or no exposure to the outside world, this building, *this home*, was her first real look at life. Her eyes were wide in amazement at the garden, in awe at the flowers that bordered the driveway; rhododendrons, bright and pink; lavender, purplish-blue, accompanied by its sweet fragrance; bushes of rose – red, yellow, white and pink. Never had she seen so much natural colour. Without realising she gasped aloud.

George heard the noise and, having released his seatbelt, whirled around to see where the sound had come from.

Only empty seats faced him.

"That's odd…" he started, but a small figure jumped up at the driver's side door and slapped two sticky hands against its window.

"D-a-a-d-d-d-d-e-e-e-e-e-e!" Charlie was still chewing half a mouthful of toast that had been coated thick with strawberry jam – the sides of his mouth and chin testament to that, red with a glutinous gel with flecks of crumbs giving him a slight goateed look.

George opened the door and climbed out. "You're up early," he said, ruffling his son's hair. It was close to 7:00 a.m. but the kids weren't usually out of bed before half-past. "Where's your mum?"

"In kitchen," he said. The small boy pivoted round and ran back to the house, disappearing through the front door.

George smiled. It felt good to be home with the family. He slammed the *Peugeot's* door behind him and activated the central locking with the slightest press of his thumb. At the door, he called out the clichéd phrase, "Honey, I'm home," before closing it behind him.

A moment later, Sophie let herself out of the car, closed the door quietly behind her, and then drank in the cool morning air, smelling the mixed garden fragrances for the first time. She especially enjoyed the sweet aroma of lavender.

The bedroom in which Sophie found herself an hour later was relatively small compared to what she expected from its appearance from outside. Sparsely furnished, the room had a single bed (occupied), a bedside cabinet, a chest of drawers, an old fashioned dressing table with a large mirror perched atop it and an array of beauty products placed about it, a freestanding wardrobe (its door half-open but revealing nothing) and a stack of three *Walkers* crisp boxes that were filled with the sleeping girl's personal effects. The curtains were drawn, pink and thin, allowing the early morning sunlight to filter in.

Sophie had crept through the house, exploring the rooms one by one, watching her parents as they interacted with each other, seeing for the first time her brothers, Charlie and Stanley, both sitting at the table in the kitchen eating their breakfast and drinking fresh orange juice.

Charlie, the younger of the two, was talking animatedly about a forthcoming school trip to a zoo. Sophie learnt that his favourite animal was a crocodile. Stanley, the second eldest child, sat and ate quietly.

This was the first time she'd seen other children and she stood transfixed; cast under a spell, she watched them avidly, fascinated with their every movement. It wasn't until one of the boys had suddenly jumped down from the table and collided with her that she snapped out of her absorption and thought better to leave before gaining any unfavourable attention. As it was, the four-year-old was puzzled by the invisible barrier that had partially blocked his progress. Thankfully, his undeveloped mind swiftly moved onto the more important subject of dinosaurs.

That had been ten minutes or so earlier, before Sophie had opened a door that had a small sign *blu*-tacked to its centre, marking the room as belonging to 'Meredith'. A handmade nameplate with the girl's name written in pink, bubble-style writing. Alongside the name was a photograph of a younger Meredith dressed in a school uniform, a souvenir from a previous term at a former school. The whole thing had been laminated, its surface slightly reflective – she could almost see her image on the glossy surface.

Guess it's not just mirrors I need to be concerned about...

Sophie crept in, pushing the door closed behind her and crossed to stand over the sleeping girl. She watched the gentle rise and fall of her chest, listened to the soft rasp of her breathing and the subtlest of whistling sounds that escaped her slightly blocked nose, indicating that the girl suffered mildly from hay fever. So deep in concentration, almost to the point of meditation, she lurched back and yelped aloud in fright when the electric alarm clock on the bedside cabinet - set for 7:30 a.m. - started to bay an unmelodic ringing sound that she felt could bring life to a fossilised Ammonite.

The girl sat up with a start, the alarm continuing its sound: "Who's there?" she muttered, rubbing tiredness from her eyes.

Sophie stood stock-still, unable to breathe. Her heart was pounding from being startled, so loud she thought, she was worried the girl pulling herself out of bed would hear it.

The girl reached out to the alarm clock, punched down on a button, ending the clamour abruptly. After, she reached for a pair of thick-rimmed spectacles lying between the clock and a half-full tumbler of water, and slipped them onto the bridge of her nose.

Sophie quietly stepped away from the bed, backing towards the wall nearest to the bedroom door, backing into a piece of furniture.

Damn!

She'd forgotten about the chest of drawers. The impact caused the furnishing to rattle, halting Sophie's progress. She couldn't help gasping.

"Hello? I know you are there." The girl swung her legs out from the bed and stood up. "I heard you." The girl was wearing a purple nightdress with a *Tinkerbell* fairy print emblazoned across its centre.

Sophie was paralysed with fear and could no longer move.

"So, where are you?" The girl dropped to her knees and peered under her bed. "Well, you're not under there. Hmm." The girl walked to the chest of drawers, and stopped just short of stepping on Sophie's toes. "I know, you must be in the wardrobe!" She strode across the bedroom and flung open the double doors to reveal –

– just a wardrobe full of clothes. She was confused.

I'm sure I heard something.

"Meredith… Come on, time to get up. You've got school, remember?"

Her mother's voice was slightly subdued by the distance from the bottom of the stairs to the bedroom door, which was pushed to.

"I'm getting up!" she shouted back. She closed the wardrobe doors and tried to forget about the unnerving feeling that she wasn't alone in her room.

Hurriedly, she slipped out of her nightdress, found her school uniform (a blue and white checkered dress with a white collar), threw it on and proceeded to the dressing table, where she sat to prepare her hair.

Meredith's hair was blonde, *similar to my own*, Sophie thought; but even longer, cascading down her back like a golden waterfall, ending an inch above the small of her back.

Meredith picked up a plastic hairbrush and started pulling it through her pillow-mussed hair, occasionally wincing from a tangle or two.

Behind her, Sophie sat down on her bed, the springs protesting gently. The girl, too preoccupied, failed to hear the movement, or even see the older girl, staring at her from behind now that she inadvertently appeared within the dressing table mirror.

"MEREDITH!"

"Coming!" The girl quickly tied her hair into a tail and rushed out of the bedroom, her feet thumping as they carried her down the stairs.

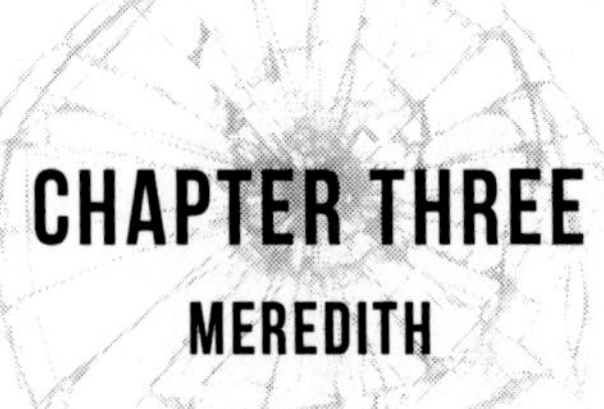

CHAPTER THREE

MEREDITH

MEREDITH WAS NOT SURE why they had moved so suddenly that summer, almost in a panic. Her father had returned from work all sweaty and scared-looking. Normally he was a confident person, radiating an air of control and assurance wherever he went; on this occasion he appeared nervous, agitated. His hands were shaking and his breathing was fast, almost panting. It was as though he'd been for a long run.

Or maybe he'd been chased?

Meredith was playing quietly with a collection of small furry animal characters she'd accumulated from birthdays and Christmases past, especially enjoying a Meerkat family that was more functional than her own. Using a number of play sets for backdrops, she enacted a variety of scenes that were more ordinary than those that existed in reality.

Meredith had heard her father's car return in the driveway, the door of the *Peugeot* opening and slamming hard behind him; heard the stones of the driveway crunch underfoot, and watched as the front door was flung open. He stormed into the house, flinging the front door behind him, stopping with his back against the wooden surface as though his weight would add extra obstruction.

"Harriet, quick," he said to her mother. "We have little time." He was peering out of the window by the side of the door, checking to see whether he had been followed.

"So soon?" Her mother wore a pained expression, but it was clear she understood what was going on, fully in the loop with the turn of events and the urgency of the situation. It hadn't been the first time this had happened, and was not expected to be the last.

In fact, Meredith could remember at least four occasions when they had repeated this same merry dance.

Had there been other times?

Meredith couldn't remember. If there had, she'd blanked it from her memory. It had been two years since they'd lived a somewhat normal life. Though being one of the Jennings had always been far from normal owing to her father's strange work.

"Yes. We must leave tonight. You and the kids need to start packing."

"George... when *will* this end?" her eyes were becoming moist. George looked solemnly down at his feet. He didn't know the answer so said nothing in reply. He didn't like to lie.

Without a word, Meredith's mother reached over to her husband and embraced him. It was the sort of thing she did when faced with fear or the unknown, like a quick hug would make things all better.

"It will be all right," she said. "In the end."

The man composed himself and looked a little less scared. "I know," he whispered, brushing a strand of hair aside and kissing the woman on the forehead. If she'd known him better, she'd have realised this was all an act. He wasn't afraid at all. It stemmed from his past life. A life before he'd met Harriet or had the kids.

Packing wasn't as hard a chore as it might seem. Where most people use all their things and wear all their clothes, the Jennings did not. Having gone through this routine before, they knew to use items sparingly and live out of boxes as a necessity. It was a situation that Meredith didn't enjoy, but not knowing anything different, tolerated without question, or seemingly without question. The fact was she was starting to wonder at it all.

What reason could there be for leaving it all behind, her life, her friends? Another school? What troubles were they in that behooved a sudden, swift exit?

Meredith started to wonder whether her dad was a bank robber or something worse. Perhaps a terrorist? They were all the rage these days and came in all shapes, sizes, colours and creeds.

"Quick, Meredith, go to your room and pack your things," her mother demanded. "Anything not packed by nightfall will have to stay."

"But mum! Do we have to?" she whined.

"Yes. Now do it!" Her mother's face was enough to suspend any further protest.

Meredith went to her bedroom as ordered. In the room next door Stanley played, oblivious to the events downstairs. He was six-years-old and like most boys his age, he was playing with some faddish toy, currently being small monster figurines (which his younger brother was also seemingly mad on); multi-coloured collectables that looked like they'd been designed by pre-schoolers. There was no limit to how odd or obscure the characters could be. Some looked like they'd been sneezed out onto the floor and copied into plastic form. Unconcerned by the urgency of the packing, he carried on noisily within his imagination.

Stuffing dolls, fluffy animals, games and other things into a box, and then starting on her clothes - packing them untidily into two large suitcases - Meredith was finished within ten minutes. Most of her sundry items were already boxed up. In the corner of the bedroom was the dresser; atop was the large, antique mirror. She looked long and hard at her reflection. Beyond her spectacles, dark circles surrounded her eyes, giving them a sunken-in look, and her cheeks were blotchy and red. Her long blonde hair, usually tied neatly in a tail, hung down in an untidy, unkempt fashion. She didn't take much pride in her presentation of late. At school she was teased mercilessly on her appearance – but that never bothered her much, and with the imminent relocation, it wouldn't be a concern any longer.

In the mirror, just behind her, a small face appeared.

An older girl's face; framed by golden blonde hair. She had high cheek bones and a sort of pointed, ratty nose. Although unusual in appearance, she was not unattractive. Completing the look she was dressed comfortably in jogging bottoms and a loose-fitted T-shirt. It was always a shock to see this one-time intruder in her bedroom. It had been five months since she'd caught sight of the girl in her mirror. No matter how many times she had witnessed this peculiar phenomenon, it hadn't stopped Meredith from turning around behind her to see the person to whom the reflection belonged.

But of course, like every other time, there was nobody there.

Meredith had asked her on more than one occasion whether the girl who appeared in her mirror was a ghost. Sophie had smiled knowingly but had never confirmed or denied it. Meredith liked to believe that she was a ghost. Like *Casper*, she was friendly and often made her laugh.

They'd often play together; sometimes leave the house together, always having fun. Both girls getting up to mischief, made easy by Sophie's unobservable appearance.

On the bus into town, for a dare, Sophie tied everybody's shoe laces together; the girls laughed heartily as each traveller stood up to leave only to trip over their own feet, stumbling to the floor of the central walkway. A group of five people collapsed into a heap of intertwined limbs and torsos. The melee was comical. The bus driver didn't know what on earth was going on but knew the girl with the spectacles who'd laugh uncontrollably after each fallen passenger, had almost certainly something to do with it, but knew not what. Throughout the journey he'd glance at the CCTV screen, but not once had he seen anyone up to no good. People would glare angrily at the laughing Meredith, who appeared to be sitting alone at the back of the bus, but no one could suspect that she'd been responsible for the practical joke. No one had seen her leave her seat.

Sophie was Meredith's secret invisible friend; and Meredith was Sophie's only contact away from her father outside of the apartment in Chelsea.

For five months, once or twice a week, Sophie would sneak into her father's car, hitching a lift, so that she could spend some time with someone of a similar age. But that was slowly changing. Somehow, she was growing at a faster rate than anyone else. Meredith had noticed it too, but said nothing.

Meredith looked back to the mirror and the face that belonged to the only friend she had in the whole wide world stared back at her. She looked thirteen-years-old now.

"I'm going to be leaving," said Meredith matter-of-factly. She removed her glasses and rubbed her eyes. They felt heavy, as though laden with tears.

"I know," replied the girl in the mirror, solemnly. "I heard da... *Your* father saying something on his phone..."

"You know my father?" Meredith was surprised. She thought only *she* could see her. It was hard to keep the disappointment from spreading across her face.

"I know of him," Sophie lied. "I smuggle myself in the back of his car from time to time... for a lift," adding, "beats walking. Like today. Not being seen has its advantages."

Slightly appeased, Meredith's features brightened. "You are wicked!" Out of habit, she turned to face her friend, realising as she wheeled round that Sophie wasn't sitting on her bed. "I just don't understand why we have to go. I like it here."

The girl in the mirror looked back at Meredith but gave no further comment.

"I think my dad is in trouble. I think we have to run away from something."

The girl in the mirror smiled knowingly, an eyebrow raised. She looked rather smug, almost sinister.

"You almost look like you know something," Meredith said accusingly at the face that appeared behind her in the mirror.

"I may know something," she admitted. "But I can't say. Not yet. Not now. It would put you in more danger."

Meredith walked away from the mirror and sat down on her bed. "I wish I could take you with me. You are all that I have."

"You are all I have too," Sophie replied sadly, her voice almost a whisper.

Within the hour Meredith's father had returned with a rental van, and in two hours, the van was loaded. All but the furniture that came with the house had been removed. Having practiced this escape meticulously and living out of boxes, the move was swift and efficient. They would be safely relocated and unpacked before nightfall, as was the standard practice.

Meredith and her mother were in her bedroom, the nine-year-old sitting mournfully on the end of her bed, the mattress stripped bare.

"But I like the mirror," Meredith said, "why can't we take it?" In the newly emptied room, her voice echoed against the walls.

"It doesn't belong to us," her mother said, consoling. "And besides, it's ugly. I never did like that mirror."

The girl in the mirror glided across the silver surface, the movement catching Harriet's eye. She jerked up, her eyes surveying the area around her, seeking the source that had diverted her attention.

"What *was* that?" The woman stood up and looked about her, gazing around the room, her attention focused more around the edges of the room, below waist level.

"What's wrong?" Meredith wore a panicked expression which her mother interpreted was from *her* agitation. The truth was Meredith was worried that her secret friend was about to be discovered.

"Did you not see it?" *See what, though?* Harriet couldn't be sure of what she'd seen. It had been a blur, and it had been reflected in the mirror. After circling the room twice, peering under the bed and looking around the sides of the furniture that was being left behind, she shook her head as though clearing out old thoughts and smiled in resignation. "Your mum must be going mad," she said.

Meredith smiled with her, noticeably relaxed.

"Come on. Say goodbye to your room. We've got a new home to go to. Your father's made all the arrangements."

As they left the bedroom, Meredith gave the mirror one last, mournful look before it became hidden from view as the door swung gently closed behind them.

Sophie stepped out from her hiding place beside the wardrobe. The wardrobe had been outside of the mirror's viewpoint, so protected her from Harriet's frantic search, shielding her from the unwanted discovery.

A few moments later, from the window, Sophie watched as Meredith climbed into the passenger seat of a red *Toyota Prius*, with Harriet taking the driver's seat. In the back of the car Charlie was already strapped into the child's seat. Stanley was in the removal van next to her dad. George's *Peugeot* was nowhere to be seen.

Sophie watched him ruffle the six-year-old's hair before setting the van in motion, leading the way out of the drive, a sad convoy that took her family away to somewhere unknown. For now, Meredith was going to be lost to her. She watched as her family drove away, Meredith looking up towards her bedroom one last time from the passenger seat.

For a moment their eyes seemed to lock – an impossibility Sophie thought – and recognition intermingled with a frisson of electricity passing between them before the connection was severed as the car turned out of the driveway, advancing after the removal van which was no longer in sight.

In resignation, Sophie stepped away from the window and walked to the mirror, studying her reflection. She looked older – she knew she aged differently to most people, but was it possible to grow noticeably during the day? She looked down at her hands – still invisible – and couldn't help wonder what had happened between her and her sister. Had they really *connected*? Or was it just a coincidence?

She pondered over the question that evening as she made her way back home using public transport. There was no rush. George wasn't expected back in Chelsea until the following day and his stays away were getting more frequent and for longer periods.

She imagined there would come a day when he would leave her all alone to fend for herself. She didn't know how prophetic that thought would turn out to be.

CHAPTER FOUR

CHARLIE

WILLOUGHBY RISING WAS THE house that George had moved his family into. It was a large detached dwelling that had four bedrooms and stood on top of a hill with panoramic views of the town and a good view of the murky North Sea. The paintwork was flaky and the brickwork crumbly, but the interior was homely. A chimney pot had come down in a storm the previous autumn and still lay smashed in amongst a patch of cabbages. Aside from this, the house was in a reasonable state of repair. Belonging to an aunt, or an uncle, or maybe a cousin (so her father had said unconvincingly) – Meredith couldn't remember exactly, and sort of suspected a slight bending of the truth – at short notice it became the Jennings' home, and for now would be the ideal place to lay low and keep a step ahead of whomever it was who chased them.

That detail was still left unspoken though never far from her enquiring lips.

There was a whole allotment of fruit and vegetables growing, with carrots, potatoes, runner beans, raspberries, strawberries, plums, pears and apples, all cared for and growing in bountiful supply. At the end of the garden was a crab-apple tree that bore fruit growing in its infant stages. The crab-apple tree in the garden became a sort of climbing frame, affording hours of amusement for the Jennings children who cared little for the miniature apples they knew tasted sour on sampling. Standing twenty-five or so feet tall, Stanley and Meredith often climbed it. Occasionally they managed to persuade Charlie to climb up too, though their mother scolded them whenever she caught him in the tree, after all he was only four, his birthday having passed on fourteenth October the year before.

Harriet proved she was right about her decision NOT to allow Charlie to climb the tree early on that sunshine-bright July day. He fell from roughly thirteen-feet up the tree, landing sickeningly awkward, breaking his arm in two places, the crack of bone breaking sounding like a distant gunshot, which Harriet would swear she had heard deep within the house. He was lucky not to have broken his neck!

Who was to know that what was to be an accident, would impact them so greatly – in more ways than just the obvious? Charlie falling from the tree would be the catalyst that would upend their lives and irreversibly change their course forever.

"Come on, Charlie," Meredith had said. "It'll be all right. I'll catch you if you fall."

Charlie had taken her word as gospel and nervously climbed up the gnarly tree trunk, reaching to the low branch first, hoisting himself up to it, shuffling along a foot to further enable him to reach up to the next branch. Climbing a further two branches, he stretched up to his brother who was already sitting two further branches up, almost at the tree's crown. Meredith was standing below him offering vocal support and encouragement and the pretence of catching him should he actually fall, though the way her hands were held out would hardly soften the fall of a barely formed crab-apple.

Charlie was about twelve-feet up the tree, and quite close to Stanley's outstretched arm by now, the older boy's fingers wiggling as a further visual incentive. Being four, Charlie didn't possess the ability to register distances or heights, not yet developing the acrophobia which would manifest itself from this day onwards; or understand his six-year-old brother's limited strength, a failure shared by Stanley, who overconfidently stretched down closer to Charlie, and who overenthusiastically took a hold of his open hand. Neither did Charlie have any awareness of his own mortality; although initially reluctant to climb, mainly from fear of falling (one of two inherent fears we are all born with – the other being loud noises), he'd needed very little persuasion.

Why would he? He hadn't fallen before.

"I've got you," Stanley said reassuringly, his right hand reaching for Charlie, his left hand gripping the branch upon which he was perched, keeping him balanced, maintaining his position in the tree, however precarious it actually felt.

Only, Stanley didn't have Charlie at all. He didn't want to appear weak to his younger sibling, and his false confidence extended the misguided trust the four-year-old had in him. His grip was weak, his hands slippery with sweat, and where Charlie was confident that he was safe and secure, and that his big brother had him protected, with a swift tug to the branch beside him, Stanley suddenly realised that he didn't share Charlie's confidence. All of a sudden, panic entwined with the understanding of what this meant, causing the older boy to scream out:

"Meredith!"

Almost in slow motion, Charlie fell backwards from the branch, his fingers slipping away from Stanley's, falling, falling, the backs of his legs clipping the branch immediately below the one upon which he had been standing only a moment before, turning him so that he was facing downwards, smacking his head on the next branch. He tumbled the rest of the distance, bouncing through the tree, the branches doing nothing to slow his drop, until gravity completed the descent, Newton's law of physics in full demonstration. He crashed into Meredith, who did nothing to cushion his fall, collapsing in a heap beneath him.

"AAAAAHHHHHHH," screamed Charlie. "My arm! My arm! It hurts!" Charlie had rolled off Meredith and was lying on his side, his arm twisted at an impossible angle beneath him.

Meredith was screaming from the pain caused by Charlie knocking her hard onto her bottom.

"I'm sorry. I'm sorry. I'm sorry. Charlie... I'm sorry," Stanley was screaming too; shame, guilt and sheer panic filling his voice. Although worried for his brother, he also knew what the likely consequence was to this. It was him, after all, who had not held onto his brother, who had known his grip wasn't good before his lame attempt of pulling him up.

"Charlie!" Their mother was out of the house and running across the garden, tripping on Charlie's tricycle, maintaining balance, but now with a limp, she continued towards the crab-apple tree, seeing Meredith, now standing over the small, huddled form that she knew was her son who continued to wail in pain. "Oh my God! Charlie!"

"I'm sorry," continued Stanley up in the tree. He was shaking with fear and worry.

"It was an accident," sniffed Meredith, rubbing her bottom. "He fell." She was now crying.

"Why did you let him climb the tree?"

"I didn't," she lied. "He did it himself."

Charlie was still screaming as his mother lifted him up, checking him over. The small boy had a cut to his forehead, a small, thin line of blood trickled to the bridge of his nose. His mother looked at his twisted arm. She touched it lightly, from which Charlie gave an ear-splitting scream.

"I know, petal. Be brave. We'll get you fixed." Turning to her daughter, shaking her head in disappointment, "I need to take him to the hospital. You stay here with Stanley. I will ask Mrs Slocum to sit with you whilst I am gone. When I get back, we are going to have a talk."

Carrying Charlie back to the house, and just before disappearing, she bellowed over her shoulder. "Stanley! You get out of that tree this instant!"

The X-ray showed that the left arm had been fractured in two places. A small, hairline crack was showing in the ulna, a bit above the wrist, and a clean break appeared within the radius just below the elbow.

"He fell from a tree," explained Charlie's mother. It sounded lame, almost like a lie, even to her. "He was quite high," she added, seeing the contempt in the doctor's eyes.

He smiled humourlessly. "I see," he said. The doctor was older than Charlie's mother, with receding grey hair, brown eyes and a very long face, most of which seemed to be chin, which gave his head the shape of a fat carrot. He put the large X-ray picture into the envelope from which it had come. "He will need to have his arm set in a cast, probably for six weeks. *Paracetamol,* to take the edge off the pain, followed by *Ibuprofen*, alternately," he paused, "which will help with the inflammation. You can give him the lower dose of each every two hours." The doctor wrote out the medication order. "Take this to your local GP who will write the prescription."

"Thanks," said Charlie's mother.

"A nurse will come in shortly to apply the plaster cast. It's hospital policy to inform social services of any A&E patients under sixteen." With this, the doctor turned away and left the small examination room through the door with a concealed hydraulic arm. It closed slowly behind him.

With the doctor gone and Charlie lying still on the examination bed, his mother reached into her handbag and pulled out her mobile phone. As the phone was on silent, she was unaware that she'd missed a call until she saw the red 'missed call' icon to the left of the screen. A text message indicated a voicemail had been left.

She keyed 1, 2, 3, followed by the dial button. She then pressed the handset close to her right ear. After a moment, a voice she recognised as her husband, the words spoken fast, his tone urgent.

"*Oh Christ, Harriet, you need to pick this up*," heavy breathing, as though from running. He sounded anxious and spoke hurriedly. "*You don't have any time. They have tracked you. Get out of the hospital. GET OUT NOW!*" The message ended, but before she had time to put the phone away a text message flashed up, it said:

DON'T WORRY. THEY DON'T KNOW WHERE WE LIVE... YET!

On the bed Charlie groaned as he readjusted himself slightly. A moment later a knock at the door, followed by the entrance of a young nurse with short, black hair that Charlie thought made her look like a boy. With little hair to conceal them, her ears looked too big for her head. She wheeled in a trolley ahead of her containing medical supplies; latex gloves, bandages, swabs, cleansing fluid, cotton wool, plasters. On its top a large bowl containing a white mixture sluicing about that Harriet assumed was the plaster.

"Will this take long?" asked Charlie's mother. She tried sounding mildly interested, but failing. Instead, it came out as slightly impatient, the tone registering annoyance in the young nurse.

"It takes as long as it takes," her curt reply. The nurse pulled up a stool on casters, and positioned herself next to the bed alongside Charlie. "Now, who's been a bit clumsy?" She smiled reassuringly. Noticing the blue timepiece strapped to his right wrist, she added: "At least you've not injured your watch arm."

Absently, Harriet checked her own watch. From experience, she knew she had little time to waste. Their pursuers were on their way… could even be here, she thought. But this couldn't be helped. She knew Charlie needed the plaster cast. Of all the stupid things, he had to do this now, jeopardising everything. They'd not even had the chance to settle in their new home or start classes within their new schools.

Just you wait Meredith; you see what happens when I get home she chided her daughter within her mind, her inner voice taking the tone her vocal chords dared not. She knew full well that when she actually saw Meredith she would do nothing at all. Unknown to Harriet, all threats of punishment would be overshadowed by a turn of events that would leave her and Charlie in grave peril.

CHAPTER FIVE

DOMINIC

SITTING OUTSIDE THE CAFETERIA in the heart of Soho, Dominic Schilling traced the outline of the antique diamond pictured within the brochure that was placed on the round, aluminium table set in front of him. Dressed smartly in a dark grey two-piece suit, a white long-sleeve shirt buttoned up to the collar, and polished black leather shoes, he looked – and felt – like an executive straight out of the office; except for the gun, of course. Though concealed within the shoulder holster, it could be made out through the fabric of his suit jacket, if one cared to look; the butt of the *Beretta* semi-automatic poking out every so often playing peek-a-boo. He likened the look to cop shows like *Miami Vice*.

He sipped from a large cup, a frothy cappuccino, cream and powdered cinnamon leaving a residue moustache above his lip. He wiped his mouth with the back of his left hand, ignoring the serviette the waitress had laid beneath a small set of cutlery. On a plate to the left was a Danish pastry which he'd taken tentative bites from, but through lack of appetite had left momentarily discarded.

He'd visited the *Masterpiece London Art & Antiques Fair* the day earlier, roaming through the many rooms and galleries, gazing at the exhibitions and collections brought together from across the globe. According to the brochure, *Masterpiece London* was no ordinary antiques fair, but a 'forum for distinctive design and aesthetic excellence from all around the world'.

Dominic hadn't arrived at the custom-built pavilion set in the grounds of the historic Royal Hospital Chelsea by chance, or through any cultural desire.

He was there for one thing and one thing only.

The *Whisper of Persia*; a vivid yellow diamond cut into a cushion shape, 101.29-carat, with a weight of twenty-seven grams. It was the highlight of that year's fair, on display as part of a sixteenth century Royal jewellery collection. Among other artefacts included *The Mary Tudor Pearl*, once part of a dowry from Philip II of Spain to his new bride, Mary Tudor, for whom the pearl was christened.

Earlier, Dominic had admired the diamond within its secure, glass case, noted the guards standing in close proximity and knew that the display cases were alarmed. Standing just a foot away from it, he'd marvelled at the brilliant cut of the gem, the vivid yellow, the result of nitrogen atoms replacing some of the crystal's carbon atoms. Such a diamond, with more than a hundred carats is extremely rare, and exceptionally valuable. He'd read within the blurb of the brochure that the *Whisper of Persia* had sold for more than three million US dollars in auction in the late 1980s. He estimated its price was now triple that.

This was why he intended to steal it. His days acting as a lackey for Tom Kaplan were coming to an end.

Tom Kaplan, CEO of Kaplan Ratcliff Biochemical and Life Sciences, ordered him around like he was the head of some sort of cartel, and he, *Dominic Schilling*, his personal slave.

But time was running out. The *Masterpiece London Arts and Antiques Fair* only ran for a week, with its last day in just two days time – the third of July.

Stealing the diamond wasn't going to be easy, and the plan that he'd elaborated intended to see the jewel taken in broad daylight under everyone's nose. Audacious or what?

He smiled to himself as he continued to stare at the jewel on the page. He felt himself start to drool and needed to use the back of his hand again to wipe the surplus moisture away from his lips.

His plan involved the services of a person who exhibited some unique and very unusual talents. It involved the person whom he'd been charged with finding and bringing back to the company that had invested heavily in her creation.

It involved the girl: *Sophie Jennings.*

The problem seemed to be finding her. At that moment stealing the jewel appeared easier than finding the one person who could make it happen. It was a little like a paradox.

Every time they'd come close to finding her, or locating George Jennings and other members of his family, they'd up and disappear, always two steps ahead. It was like someone from inside was warning them; someone from inside his own organisation?

It had to be.

But then luck intervened.

A waitress dressed in a white blouse, black skirt, and white apron draped down her front approached his table. She had auburn hair tied into a bun.

"Is everything al'right?" She had a thick cockney accent, like she'd walked straight off the set of *EastEnders.*

Before he could respond, his *Sony Xperia* mobile phone began to vibrate on the metal table, his large cup rattling in its saucer.

"Y'ello," almost shouted into the handset, making the waitress jump. She turned on her heel and wandered to another customer who was waving spasmodically to get her attention. "Aha, that's good. No, follow her, but keep your distance. It's taken six weeks to find them again; we don't want you scaring them off before I've been able to put together the extraction team." Without saying goodbye, the call was terminated and Dominic stood to leave, pulling out a billfold wallet from which he slipped out a ten pound note and anchored it to the table using the side plate on which his Danish was sat, barely touched. He picked up the brochure, folded it shut and tucked it under his arm.

"Keep the change," he said louder than necessary towards the waitress, not waiting for any acknowledgement before leaving the premises.

The waitress observed the man as he crossed the street to his car.

Dominic Schilling was in his early thirties, well above average height at six feet two inches, and muscular. When not dressed to kill in his *Armani* suits, he could be found in a vest and shorts, either at the local fitness centre pushing metal or out in the park pounding the earth over a ten mile run, an iPod hooked up and strapped to his waist. As a former Marine, he knew fitness was the key to success out in the field. The saying 'healthy body, healthy mind' wasn't coined for nothing. He believed it, and it was a mantra that he believed gave him an edge over those he worked for, and for those he sought, or pursued.

Starting the engine of the metallic grey *Mercedes SLS AMG*, Dominic took the car out of the disabled space, enjoying the disparaging looks from passersby who noticed he had absolutely no impairments, and drove the car away from Soho towards the one-way that would lead him out of the city and towards the location he'd just been given.

Depressing a button on his mobile phone, a telephone number rang out and the ringing tone began to sound over the Bluetooth, coming through the car stereo speakers. After eighteen seconds a voice with a slight American accent sounded, filling the car's interior.

"*Hello*."

"It's Dom."

"*Dominic. I thought I told you not to call me*." The voice sounded slightly agitated, annoyed.

"I don't care; I just thought you should know. The corporation has found them. The youngest child was taken to a hospital; a nurse spotted the likeness of the mother from the wanted poster."

"*You sure it's them*?"

"It's a lead, nothing more."

"*Not another headless chicken chase*?" Not waiting for an answer, "*Is the child okay*?" disinterested.

"Apparently, yes."

"*That's a pity. What of the others*?"

"Marlon is following, and a team is being assembled, but they have orders not to intervene. I will have the advantage – it'll be too late before anyone gets wise to the deception."

The phone went silent for a moment, and then the American voice came through, thick and fast.

"*Good. Let's not screw it up this time, hey Dominic*? *We are running out of time, our sponsor is getting a bit impatient. Do what you have to do, just make sure the girl and her father are kept safe. It's important that we take delivery of the package*."

"What of the others?" Dominic asked.

"*Do what you have to do, but you know how we operate. See no evil, hear no evil, and speak no evil. Probably best to tie off those loose ends, if you get my meaning*."

Dominic smiled; he became aware of the *Beretta's* weight against his chest, almost like it knew it was almost time to shed its deadly load.

"Okay."

"*Now, if you don't mind don't bother me again until we have her in holding. That should give our friend enough incentive to do what we want*," and with that, the American voice disappeared and the line went dead.

Yes, that will give him an incentive – George will do more than what the American intended. A lot more.

"Jerk," Dominic muttered under his breath, an ominous smile spreading out across his lips, unable to stop the duplicitous thoughts that filled his head.

On the passenger seat, the brochure from *Masterpiece London Arts and Antiques Fair* folded open at the page of most interest; the *Whisper of Persia* glaring up at him. Tangible, it felt almost like it belonged to him, as though he could reach into the page and grasp it in his hand.

Soon, he thought.

Soon.

CHAPTER SIX

GEORGE

"YOU DON'T HAVE ANY time. They have tracked you. Get out of the hospital. GET OUT NOW!" George had left the message and all he could do was hope and pray that he'd done enough to warn them.

Two minutes earlier a call had come through to his mobile, which in itself alarmed him. No one but his family had his number. He changed mobiles often, disposing of phones and SIM cards as often as some people changed underwear.

The voice at the other end of the phone had claimed to be a friend. But who was he? Could he be trusted?

"Who are you?" he had asked; his voice exasperated. Now he felt stupid even to expect an answer.

"*Just a friend, but that's not important. You need to get your wife and child out of that hospital as soon as you can.*"

Hospital? What was he talking about? "*An extraction team is on its way to them as we speak. Your wife and child don't have much time.*"

"How-" *did they find us? How did you get my number? Who are you?*

"*It's not important,*" sensing all the unasked questions. "*Just keep them safe. Your home has not been compromised...* yet. *Lie low. We'll meet when the time is right.*"

That had been six minutes ago, and since then he'd followed up his call to his wife with a text message:

DON'T WORRY. THEY DON'T KNOW WHERE WE LIVE...

But who was this mysterious caller? How did he know that he could genuinely trust him? Importantly, how did he get his mobile number? Was he being watched, even now?

Paranoid, he crossed the room to the window and peered out through the gap at the edge of the curtain, glancing furtively from one side to another. A large, black car was parked across the street, stately, possibly a *Bentley*. Had it been there before? When had it arrived?

"Dad, what's wrong?" The voice was female and echoed in the room, concern and fear intermingled. Sophie was standing in the doorway. She'd heard her father talking on the phone; had heard the anxiety in his voice.

"I hope it's nothing," he replied absently, still looking at the parked car, contemplating his next moves.

"Have they found us?" She knew about the corporation, about the sabotage at the laboratory, and the blame that had been pointed squarely at her father. He protested his innocence and feared for his life and the life of his family; rather than face up to the charges that included the murder of eleven co-workers, he'd taken them on the run; fugitives, not only of the law, but also from the corporation itself. Kaplan Ratcliff had placed a bounty on their lives. Although it didn't make much sense to the girl in the room, George had said that the corporation had wanted to end his project, and anyone or anything related to it.

George didn't immediately answer her question, but after a long twenty seconds he said: "No. Sophie, try not to worry about it." He tried to reassure her with a smile, allowing the curtain to fall back into place. He decided that the car across the street was empty and posed no threat. He returned to his laptop on the dining table, though did nothing but stare at its brightly-lit screen.

The room was part of a purpose-built ground floor apartment, with two bedrooms, a bathroom and a laundry room off a short hallway that connected the living/dining room. Adjoining this room was the kitchen, currently situated behind George who had his back turned to it. Since the 'incident' at the laboratory, George had spent half his time living at the apartment with Sophie in Chelsea, and the other half of his time with his family (currently in Seabrook at the house affectionately titled Willoughby Rising).

Of course, only his wife (and Sophie) knew of this arrangement. As far as his three kids knew, he was away at work, like most fathers. This wasn't altogether a lie. Despite being away from the lab, his work continued. He owed Sophie that much if she was ever to live something of a normal life.

But his work was more complicated than his children could ever know. As far as they were concerned he was a biochemist at a hospital, his work involving the study of chemical processes in living organisms. He rarely talked about his job and never took work home with him. It was easier to carry on with the lie. Plus, his children were too young to be really that bothered. Apart from Meredith, but she knew not to ask.

Before the fire and explosions that culminated in George taking his family into hiding, his occupation was far greater than a mere biochemist - even more than he'd ever divulged to Harriet. On the face of it, his work, although linked to biochemistry, was more with genetics and the study of DNA and RNA molecules. Over the past five years he'd been actively involved with a top secret programme, codenamed *CHAMELEON*. The actual details of the programme were classified, but his involvement was more with genetic engineering, and looking at ways to improve the human condition.

George was head of the *CHAMELEON* project, and his concern

was with five components of improved ability: Strength; Intelligence; Endurance; Longevity and Visibility.

Heading a team of three scientists (all now dead), George had first used mice (hundreds of them) to experiment with, moving onto larger animals with each phase of success; rabbits, cats, pigs and chimpanzees. Even an orang-utan. Two years ago things had advanced much further than he'd ever imagined and he'd done something unethical. Something he wished he could turn back and undo.

A scientist's dream is to see his life's work come to fruition, turn a theory into reality, help to make things better. What he and his team had done was more than this, it had been a miracle. It was as close to godlike as you could imagine.

Now, his team was dead. Thomas Mundahl. Maksim Alekseev. Clara Barber. His laboratory destroyed. Anything (and everything) linked to the *CHAMELEON* project had been destroyed. He was all that was left – plus his laptop (and the backup flash drive which he was never without – kept on a keychain around his neck).

What had been hailed as a scientific victory had been debunked by his superior, was now viewed as nothing more than a madman's whimsy, and he, George Jennings, a despot conman, now a fugitive, a wanted *murderer.*

But there was more at stake than surviving capture or continuing his pretence of innocence. His work, his unsung success, needed perfecting. He knew its full potential, the benefits, the pros, the cons. In the wrong hands a superhuman being could do untold damages. What he had created was something more heinous than that.

But was *heinous* the right word? After all, his daughter was beautiful…

"Will you go to her? Your wife? *My mother?*" The question almost sounded like an accusation.

In answer, George deflected the question with his own often-repeated question. It was almost a catchphrase:

"Have you taken your meds?"

"Yes, dad!" Sophie walked into the room and sat down onto the leather two-seater. "Now answer *my* question."

George stood up from the dining table, crossed to where his daughter was sitting and sat down beside her. The two-seater faced the window where moments earlier he'd been spying from. Because the curtains were drawn, a corner lamp illuminated the room.

"Later." Dismissive. George was agitated. He was concerned how someone knew his telephone number; also knew where his family was staying. Claiming to be a friend he did not know. He didn't have any friends... not any more. That was a luxury from a long-ago past, and if he were honest, probably from a period long before he'd ever met his wife. From a time when loyalties were not brought to question.

His instincts were to not trust this stranger. Trust was something that had to be earned, not given like a tacky gift from a Christmas cracker.

George flinched as Sophie wrapped an arm around his neck, aware that her small frame was pressing up against him. He closed his eyes and inhaled deeply, smelling lavender, reminding him of the house they'd been forced to leave in Stanford-le-Hope; freshly cleaned hair and other soft fragrances assailed his nostrils. With his eyes closed she seemed like any other sixteen-year-old, something he wished with all of his heart were true. She was growing up fast.

Too fast, but that was the way Sophie had been designed.

"Do you love me, no matter what?"

"What sort of question is that? You know I love you – unconditionally."

"What about if I didn't take my meds?"

"But you did, right?"

"It's not the point."

"Well, it wouldn't matter. I'd still love you. You're my daughter."

Sophie went quiet and pulled away from her father. She drew her knees up to her chest and wore a forlorn look.

"What's wrong?" George asked softly. For someone with advancements in strength and intelligence amongst other things, she often exhibited such vulnerability and weakness.

"I wish I was normal," she said timidly. "I wished I could have grown up like any other kid," she paused to contemplate. "I wish I was more like Meredith."

"Meredith? What d'you know about Meredith?"

"I know she's free to live a normal life," she sidestepped, avoiding the direct question.

"Well, she's not exactly 'free'," he said, dismissive. "But I take your point. That's why I insist on you taking your meds. So you can live more or less normally."

"About the meds, dad – I think they're becoming less effective."

George looked quizzically at his daughter, not needing to press a question, for she continued, "I've had to step up the dosage. The effects wear off between four and six hours."

"I see," George mulled over what Sophie was saying. "Why didn't you tell me?"

"I AM telling you. It's only now beginning to become a problem."

"How many doses are you now on?" He could do the math but wanted to hear his daughter tell him for herself.

"I'm up to four injections. I had to increase the dose from three last week."

"I see." George looked down, trying to think. The answer was in his laptop. He jumped up and crossed to the dining table and sat in front of the open computer. He typed in a couple of commands and waited for a file to appear.

"Dad?" Sophie had stood up from the sofa and followed the man into the other half of the room.

George raised a hand in a stop sign. "I'm thinking," he said.

"Dad… that's not all." Sophie grabbed George's attention.

"Oh?"

"Despite the medication I can will myself to… change."

"What d'you mean? Change? How?"

"I'll show you." Sophie closed her eyes and concentrated hard. A small vein pulsed in her head and she could hear her heart beat pumping hard, deafening and drowning out all other noises. Less than ten seconds later George almost fell backwards off his seat as he watched the young woman disappear almost as suddenly as she had the very first time when she'd been born. Sort of 'now you see me, now you don't'.

Sophie had vanished like no parlour trick ever witnessed.

"Astonishing," he said. "Can you change back?"

"I'm afraid not. Only another shot of meds counteracts the symptoms."

"Fascinating," George said. He started typing some notes.

"Dad, I'm scared. What if the inhibitor starts to fail? I don't want to live like a ghost, where others can only see me through my reflection in a mirror?"

George sighed. "It won't come to that," he said.

"You don't know that!" she shouted back. "Why is this happening to me?"

George didn't know for certain, but he'd feared the drug he'd created would lose its potency in time. A bit like an antibiotic, its effectiveness was only guaranteed through limited exposure. "At a guess, your body is becoming immune to the serum. But Sophie, time is on our side."

"Really?"

"Sure. I will continue my research and eventually I will find you a cure. In the meantime, I will increase the dosage of your meds." He sounded confident, and for a second he believed it. As Sophie was invisible he was unable to gauge whether or not she was convinced, though a pair of lightweight thermal imaging goggles were easily located should he have wanted them. They lay at the bottom of a backpack filled with evacuation supplies hanging from a hook on the back of the kitchen door. They looked no different to a pair of ski goggles – with the altogether distinct advantage of allowing the user to see either in the dark, or to see heat signatures of objects, people and other sources in very low light, or even through brick walls. Currently not available outside of the laboratory, this pair was just one of five pairs created – an accessory purpose-built for the task of observing his daughter before the antidote had been developed. Before then, the only way to have seen Sophie was through the reflection of a simple mirror.

From behind him, through the kitchen's serving hatch, George heard the sound of compressed air as Sophie pressed the jet injector against her arm and depressed the trigger, releasing the ochre liquid. Almost instantly Sophie began to softly swell into appearance, an act that was almost as amazing as disappearing was in itself.

Returning from the kitchen, Sophie was restored to her 'normal' condition.

"When can I see mum again?" She'd not seen her mother since her birthday. April sixteenth. There had been three candles on the cake.

"I don't know." George was being honest. It wasn't his choice, but Harriet's. She'd willingly donated an egg, even acted as a surrogate for George, but despite sharing her and George's genes, she refused to accept Sophie as her daughter, knowing that science had been used to manipulate her genetics, changing her in more ways than the obvious.

She spared as little time as she could with the girl, ultimately refusing Sophie any interaction with the other, natural children in her family.

Harriet agreed to see Sophie only at Christmas and on her birthday – this was more to appease George than out of any desire to see her.

George didn't have the heart to tell Sophie this. Life was hard enough as it was without learning that your own mother didn't want anything to do with you.

Deep down, Sophie knew much of the truth. After all, she *was* a freak, an experiment with extra features, despite what her father often said. Although George had never spoken of the children, she knew everything about Meredith, Stanley and Charlie. She'd visited them often at the old house, sneaking into her father's car and using her invisibility to slink into the house unseen, observing them as a fly would from a wall.

That was before they had moved to the detached house in Seabrook; before, when there was a large mirror in Meredith's bedroom, a looking glass for the rest of the world to see her – well, the nine-year-old Meredith who lived in that bedroom at least – the only way she'd been able to see Sophie.

Sophie sighed. She felt like an animal caged up in the apartment she'd lived in for the past two years. Very little human interaction, nothing but the isolation and her father's 'lessons.' They varied from the foundation studies, the basic numeracy, literary, history, science and geography to other, mentally stimulating exercises, honing stratagem and problem-solving abilities; adding to this physical training, building upon her strength and agility, she mastered the fighting techniques and skills of *krav maga* and *kali*, martial arts that equipped her for close range fighting, and weapons training; she'd had extensive instruction whilst cooped up during her short life at the apartment.

For a fleeting second she remembered her fight and weapons

teacher, a man her father claimed was found in the backstreets of Soho, but someone who'd hinted a closer connection; Malaxi Bacaunawa, or *Maxi* as she called him, a little Filipino man much shorter than her slender, but moderately built frame. Standing at five feet two inches, he was the shortest and skinniest man she'd ever seen. And totally bald, with not a single hair on his body, not even eyebrows. He'd been hard on her, very disciplined, and the training had been bruising and relentless. Yet, with the exception of her father, he'd been the nicest, kindest person she'd ever known... She allowed the image to dissolve as her dad interrupted her thoughts.

"You know I said I was going to have to go 'later'," he started. "The time's now." He glanced nervously at his watch.

Sophie was used to her father's comings and goings. He had two lives. One involved her; the other inextricably didn't.

"It's to do with your mother," unbidden, "she's in danger." Sophie already knew this from the telephone call she'd overheard.

"Let me come with you," a note of pleading in her voice. "I could help."

"No. Sophie, it's too dangerous. There's too much to risk."

"I'm not a child anymore," she challenged. George begged to differ. Although sixteen in appearance her cardiac and respiratory systems had pumped blood and absorbed oxygen for only a handful of months more than three years, a realisation of the genetic modification that had taken place – the manipulation of which would continue its aggressive rate of aging until her body had developed to its peak at twenty-one; this would be well within the next year. From her physical age of ten (all so long ago... back in February!) Sophie's body had aged at the genetically enhanced rate of one-and-a-half years per month. At the synthetic age of twenty-one her body's growth would slow dramatically to less than a tenth of a normal person, the benefits of which were countless, especially for, but not limited to, the military, for which these genetic alterations were originally designed for.

In theory, by the age of seventy, Sophie would have the body and appearance of a twenty-six-year-old woman. Who at seventy wouldn't give all they had and more for the health and strength of a supple, agile, twenty-something, with the prospect of many more years ahead of them?

With the laboratory destroyed, his colleagues dead, and all the data, the notes, his entire research, annihilated, all that remained of his work stood in the room in which he was about to leave (and on the laptop computer which he stowed in a safe hidden beneath the floorboards; and of course the flash drive which he hung around his neck).

"Lock yourself in the safe room until I get back." George crossed the room to his daughter and kissed her on the forehead. "I'll be as quick as I can." Turning away, he walked to the window and peered out through the curtains again. The *Bentley* was still parked across the street. It was hard to tell, but he thought he could see something glinting inside, as though reflecting the sun...

A camera?

A rifle scope?

"Bye dad..."

He gave it no further thought.

Sophie disappeared from the room. Before he left the apartment, George heard the sound of the safe room door closing, the high security locking system latching into place and the bleeps and warbling sounds as the alarm activated. A quick check on his android phone confirmed his daughter was secure, the safe room 'app' pulsating a light green. She was secure, protected, and knowing he could check on her at any time by touching the 'app' on the screen (which would produce a live video feed of the room at any given moment) helped him relax a little; but not by much.

And not for very long.

CHAPTER SEVEN
HARRIET

HARRIET USHERED THE SMALL boy out of the treatment room, picked him up and carried him the length of the corridor. Already she felt like they'd overstayed longer than they could afford, a burning fear grappling inside her. She felt sick, her heart pounded fast. She had a headache that stabbed from above her eyes. Ignoring all these feelings she knew she had to act now, get herself and her son to safety. Once safe, return home for Meredith and Stanley. And George. Her family. These were her concerns; her priorities. Family was all that mattered.

You don't have any time. They have tracked you. Get out of the hospital. GET OUT NOW!

The call had been over half an hour ago. The nurse casting Charlie's arm had noted Harriet's agitation, but said nothing. It was none of her business. Harriet had repeatedly checked her watch; kept glancing at the door. All these mannerisms indicated something was wrong. Was she guilty of something? The nurse continued to apply the plaster, unrushed. She would only finish when the padded arm sling had been placed.

Harriet glanced at her watch again. How had only half an hour passed? It felt more like an hour or even two. Every second that crept by she expected to see their pursuer. She didn't know much about him, but she'd recognise him should he appear. She'd seen him before when he'd turned up at their first house before they'd 'disappeared'.

That had been a little over two years ago now. There were others on their trail, but he was her main concern. *The Man In The Suit,* she'd called him. He'd been unflagging in his pursuit. Harriet likened him to *Robert Patrick* in *Terminator 2,* the cop made from liquid metal. *The Man In The Suit* was worse. He was assiduous, a constant threat.

Dominic? That had been his name. He'd claimed to work for Kaplan Ratcliff, the corporation where her husband had spent most of his time doing his 'research'; but she knew there was something not quite right about him. It was something about the man's eyes. She'd also glimpsed the gun beneath his jacket, peeking out ominously, itching to breathe, to exhale its deadly breath. There was also something about his whole demeanour which warned her that *Dominic* (if that was his name) wasn't afraid to use it.

Since then she'd learnt to keep low and be ever vigilant, always watching, checking behind and ahead of her, nervously glancing this way or that.

She never knew why *The Man In The Suit* had let them go, but Harriet knew that he wouldn't be that charitable again. In truth, the man had regretted that single action more than anything else in his life, often playing back the moment in his mind, the moment that he'd let them slip away.

They'd eluded capture ever since – almost like they'd been alerted to the danger, always one step ahead.

Leaving the hospital was easy and uneventful. *Too easy*, Harriet thought. It was still warm and the early afternoon sun was bright, making her squint, her eyes adding to the pain that throbbed in her head. She'd left her sunglasses behind in the mad panic of getting her son to the hospital. The time on her *Seiko Sportura* chronograph watch, with its white leather strap: 2:21 p.m.

"I want to go home," Charlie griped, not for the first time, and certainly not the last. Four-year-olds didn't appreciate that life didn't revolve around them.

"Soon," Harriet replied. She scanned the surrounding area, watchful, more attentive towards the car park and any cars that might look out of place. She looked for vehicles with dark, tinted glass windows. She searched for men loitering suspiciously on corners or in doorways.

Seeing nothing that aroused uncertainty, Harriet carried Charlie across the car park, passing three rows of parked vehicles and jogging across a road in front of an approaching *Mini Cooper* receiving a blast from its horn. Despite the haste, she was careful of his broken arm, and soon found herself standing next to the red *Toyota Prius*. From her pocket she found the key and unlocked it with a quick press of a button.

Quickly, she strapped Charlie awkwardly into his seat in the rear, careful of his broken arm dangling within the sling tied about his neck.

Climbing behind the steering wheel, she took a moment to compose herself, took a deep breath, keyed the ignition, and then put the car into reverse.

Before reversing, Harriet spied two black cars fast approaching, tyres screeching as corners were taken too tightly, clouds of dust kicking up behind them. The vehicles pulled up outside the hospital in the spaces outside the Accident and Emergency entrance marked with a large yellow grid - designated for emergency vehicles only.

Three men jumped out of the first vehicle followed by two from the other. All five disappeared into the hospital, oblivious to the glares of patients and passersby who stared at the less than discreet manner of their arrival.

They're here, she thought to herself, watching and waiting. She had seen these people before, though they all looked the same, she mused. Black suits, black ties, black sunglasses. Wannabe FBI agents, or extras from the *Will Smith* and *Tommy Lee Jones* Alien movies, *Men in Black*. They were *Dominic's* people working for Kaplan Ratcliff.

Calmly, Harriet reversed the *Prius* out of the parking space and drove slowly so not to arouse suspicion. Out of the hospital grounds she drove, round the roundabout and onwards to the dual carriageway, her nerves still jangling but beginning to relax as distance began to build between her and her foes. She exhaled noisily, checking her rear view mirror, risking a glance to her son strapped in the child seat. Satisfied she focused her concentration fully on the road ahead. Taking the next roundabout, she turned right, heading for the road that would lead towards the coastal road.

Towards safety.

Towards the house that – for four weeks – she had called home.

"That was close," she whispered to herself, though Charlie's ears pricked up. She dared to increase the speed, wanting to put more distance between her *Prius* and the danger she'd left behind at the hospital. She knew it wouldn't be long before her pursuers realised that she had taken flight and resume the chase.

Cars occasionally passed from the opposite side of the road, though it was relatively quiet for most of the way ahead; although winding, there was a speed limit on the road of sixty mph, occasionally reducing to forty when passing a stretch of housing or entering a length of road notorious for road traffic accidents. Harriet took the car closer to seventy, feeling the speed with every twist and throw of her body. The road's surface was in a little disrepair, marred by divots and potholes overlooked for repair by the local cost-cutting council adhering to a strict spending budget. Charlie was being pitched from side to side, the child seat rocking with the car's momentum; Charlie groaned and winced from all the jerky movements his arm was being subjected to.

"Mummy, I feel sick."

"Close your eyes sweetie," Harriet continued at the same speed, undeterred. "The feeling will pass. We're nearly home."

Charlie made retching noises and though he tried hard not to, he vomited noisily into his hands; yellow and white liquid bubbled from his mouth, chunks of breakfast cereal and a makeshift lunch of sausage roll and *Pringles* overflowed and trickled through his fingers, splattering his top and pooling around his lap. He started to cry.

Great!

Coming up, the road sign to the side of the road advised of a junction that joined, creating a crossroad. Harriet maintained her speed though could not deny that she wasn't distracted by her son's distress and discomfort. Charlie's retching and vomiting had stopped, but his crying had turned into thick, wracking sobs; tears were streaming down his cheeks, a snot-bubble was forming at his nose.

"It's okay Charlie. Mummy will fix this when we get..." the sentence was unfinished. From the corner of her eye, Harriet saw something moving fast through the trees to her left, something metallic, heading towards the junction she was fast approaching. She wasn't concerned, vehicles approaching had to stop; she had right of way. Sunlight sparkled and reflected from the silver-grey shape through the trees, not slowing as the crossroads were about to meet.

That's not right, she thought.

Playing out in what appeared to be slow motion; Harriet continued to watch the movement through the trees of what turned out to be a silver *Mercedes*, not taking her eyes off it as she drove the car up to pass the crossroads. She could see everything clearly; the car, the driver of the fast-approaching vehicle, the determined look upon his face, and the recognition of it as it dawned on her.

She knew him.

"Oh no!" She screamed, the moment of dread, of fear, and of intermingled realisation of what was about to happen, flashed before her eyes, halting only when –

CRASH!!!!!

The impact hurled her body forward, her seat belt digging deep into her shoulder and pulling tight across her stomach, winding her. It felt like her lungs were about to explode.

The sound of glass shattering and metal scraping as the *Mercedes* hit Harriet's *Toyota Prius* at the rear, crumpling and buckling the metal wheel arch above the left alloy wheel, forcing the car to careen out of control ten meters before flipping over, the car rolling like a toy – first to its side, then over onto the roof, then to the other side, then back on its wheels – before rolling a further 360°; sounds of smashing, of exploding glass, of chinking metal, of scraping, of loud bangs as tyres blew, of more glass as the windscreens, front and back, and the windows to the sides all shattered, and the crumpling of more metal, together with the sound of the engine as it continued to whirr, an accompaniment as Harriet absently continued to press the accelerator pedal down to the floor. With this cacophony of sounds, she watched the horror play around her in magnificent HD3D, watched as her car rolled two times, felt every impact as it flipped over the embankment and heard the tremendous SMASH! as the vehicle came to a sudden halt upside down in amongst a heavy brush of brambles, nettles and wild grass.

Dazed and confused, her vision was impaired, blurry. A cut across her forehead leaked blood past the corner of her left eye, dripping down the ridge of her nose.

What had just happened?

Gradual realisation crept in.

"Charlie?" Harriet struggled free from the seatbelt, pressing the release button; gravity did the rest. She dropped like an oversized stone, landing heavily on the underside of the roof, shattered glass crunching under her weight. She scrabbled under the upturned seat to where her son hung, strapped to the child's car seat, fragments of glass piercing the pads of her hands. He was staring out ahead, eyes wide, catatonic. Initially she thought he had stopped breathing, or maybe it was because time was frozen still. He looked like a china doll, not a mark on his upside-down face.

"Charlie," she repeated, and at first the small boy, whose good arm hung downwards, all limp, all *lifeless*, failed to reply. Harriet, fearing the worst, started to howl hysterically. Then Charlie inhaled sharply, a panicked intake of air akin to that of a near-drowned victim breaking free from the watery depths. Oxygenated, Charlie began to scream, the sobs and the vomit from just a bit earlier long forgotten.

Dispersing the histrionics, Harriet reached out to her son and stroked his head. "Shush, baby, we're okay," she reached to the seat belt and released the straps. "It'll be okay," the reassurance was more to herself. As the belt was released, Harriet caught her son. He winced from the sudden drop and the pressure on his arm. He continued to cry, fat tears falling down his cheeks.

Composing herself, Harriet glanced through the webbed glass of the windscreen behind her, the rear-view mirror, though still attached to the glass, was also cracked (that's going to bring bad luck, she mused); then to her left and right, out through the empty windows to the sides.

She half-expected to see the man who'd caused this devastation to be creeping up on them. It was just a matter of time, or slender moments, she thought. He was most definitely out there somewhere, casing out the situation, biding his time, preparing his next move. She knew none of this had been an accident. They'd found her somehow. She was in immediate danger; her and her son. She had to get out of the car and get to safety. The car could explode, she knew this. There had been countless fatalities where cars had burst into fireballs after a collision or RTA. The smell of petrol was strong in the air – all it needed was a single spark to set things off and they'd be identifying her and Charlie via their dental records.

Still holding Charlie, Harriet edged backwards to the front of the car; she twisted round and shuffled onto her back. Now with her feet facing the windscreen she aimed a powerful kick at the shattered glass, kicking it again, larruping it repeatedly, smashing it free from the buckled frame. She clambered round and with Charlie she climbed out of the car, reaching, as an afterthought, for her handbag that lay amongst other personal debris that littered the upturned roof of the car.

The strong stench of petrol was thicker as she crawled out from beneath the vehicle, adding to the urgency, through the brambles and the nettles, barbs piercing and slicing and bloodying her bare arms and face. She was aware of the pain lancing through every inch of her body but did not feel it – adrenaline anaesthetising and subduing the pain receptors in her brain – but only momentarily, just enough to see her out of immediate danger.

Once clear of the wreckage, Harriet made to stand, and screamed, dropping Charlie as she collapsed in a heap. Her left leg beneath the knee was swollen to twice its size. Probing it she felt the contusion and winced from the slightest touch. A second touch elicited a curse.

It just gets better and better! She screamed in her head. She dared a look over her shoulder, going past the ruined *Prius*, scouring the area for her pursuer. She could hear the telltale sounds of a car accident; the continuous trumpet of a horn filled the otherwise serene summer's afternoon.

Where was he?

Then she spotted the smoke and could just make out the rear of the *Mercedes*, the tree that had halted its progress having shed a sizeable branch atop its roof, crushing it beneath.

She needed to know what had happened to her pursuer. Against all reasoning she picked her four-year-old up and then limped across the road a short distance, to a small clearing that provided relative safety from the threat of either the wreckage of the *Prius* or her pursuer's car exploding.

"Charlie, I just need to check something. Wait here for a moment. Don't you move!" Harriet inched away, her left leg screaming bloody agony with each and every footfall.

"Mummy, don't go!" Charlie cried behind her. "Don't goooooo...!"

"Shush, be quiet," she hissed. "I'll be back in a minute," less chiding, the pain in her voice notably worse.

"Promise?"

Harriet tried to smile. To Charlie it looked more like a grimace.

Approaching the car, Harriet stooped and armed herself with a club sized branch. She tested the weight of its swing and then carried on shuffling forward, momentum helping her to ignore the pain.

The front of the *Mercedes* was concertinaed from the impact against the large oak that stood in its way, the windscreen, like the *Prius',* was shattered, a small branch having punctured through the screen at driver's eye level, surprisingly missing its coincidental target. Music boomed from the speakers, discordant in its accompaniment to the horn that blared continuously. *Born to be Wild,* by *Steppenwolf.*

Yeah, darlin' Gonna make it happen... Take the world in a love embrace... Fire all of your guns at once... And explode into space...

Harriet remembered the song from her teenage years. Even then it was an old song having been penned in 1967 – it was around 1990 she'd regularly heard it on the jukebox at her local pub, The Swan – she was seventeen at the time. She would meet her eventual husband George there listening to that song. Some regarded it as the song that gave birth to *heavy metal.* She tried to ignore it and peered through the passenger side window.

Through the cracked glass she could see that the driver's seat was empty. Peering closer, she could see from across the vehicle that the driver's side door was open. Hobbling around the back of the car, stooping below the branches that overlapped the car's roof, and continuing around further, she stopped only when she saw the prone form of the man who'd caused the mangled, smoking mess that had cost Dominic the better part of two years' wages.

He was lying still. *Was he dead?*

He'd shuffled about thirty-feet away from the wreckage, his virgin white shirt was a little stained with the maroon liquid that continued to leak from a wound to the side of his face.

At her feet, Harriet found Dominic's handgun. She picked it up, felt its dangerous weight, thumbed the safety and pointed the semi-automatic weapon towards the decumbent man, barely registering thought.

Hearing the gun, Dominic lifted his head up and stretched a look over his right shoulder. On seeing Harriet he relaxed and dropped his head to the dusty ground.

"You," he half-croaked almost in a whisper, ending in a cough. He started to laugh at how absurd the woman looked. Her appearance was dishevelled, her face was coated in blood from a small cut above her eye and one of her legs looked either badly bruised, or maybe broken, so swollen it looked like she had substituted it for a balloon. The way she held his gun, she could have been the heroine from a 1980s action movie, *Cynthia Rothrock* in *China O'Brien.*

Harriet levelled the gun so that it was aimed at Dominic's head. She felt sick to her stomach and her heart thumped so hard that she half-expected it to wear itself out and explode beneath her chest.

"You'll never get her!" Harriet spat. The gun in her hand was now shaking – more from her body's reaction to shock than justifiable nerves.

Dominic chuckled. "How do you know it wasn't you we wanted?" he rasped. "Poor deluded Harriet. Do you think it will really *ever* be over?" He smiled sinisterly, "Killing me won't change a thing." It was a knowing smile that almost bordered a lunatic's grin.

"You're probably right." Harriet sneered as she aimed the weapon and squeezed the trigger of the *Beretta* –

Click!

Dominic laughed harder which turned into a fit of coughs.

Click! Click!

Harriet squeezed the trigger desperately but nothing happened. No explosive discharge. No bullets punching holes into the man who'd pursued her and her family relentlessly for so long. She pressed it again. Over and over.

Click! Click! Click! Click!

"Oh dear…" *tut tut*, "no bullets." He was shaking his head as he stood up, composing himself. He opened his left hand that contained a dozen shells and allowed them to fall harmlessly, as though it were a fistful of sand. They jingled and chimed against the ground, ending their descent in a puddle of boxer-primed brass shimmering in the sun. "I can assure you, Harriet, that this one isn't empty." Hidden from view, Dominic pulled a gun - his spare - from behind his back, raising and pointing it ominously at the injured woman.

Harriet reluctantly dropped the *Beretta* and raised her hands up in surrender.

"Okay, what now?"

"We wait for the cavalry to arrive," he said.

Born to be wild had made way for *This is the end*, by *The Doors*.

How prophetic, Harriet thought.

CHAPTER EIGHT

RYAN

LIKE THE VCR, TAPE decks and *7UP* shandy, phone boxes were now a thing of the past, or fast in decline. Finding one that wasn't conspicuous was like searching for a book in the local library that didn't contain the word 'the'. A victim of the mobile phone age, phone boxes were all but extinct, located now in a few isolated spots around shopping districts or in busy shopping centres, or placed in tourist hotspots for their 'intrinsic' value, but, sadly no longer on every other street corner.

Only *one* could be found that suited Ryan's needs and he'd had to travel for over an hour outside of London to find it. Nestled at the end of a road in a discrete, dozy village he'd stumbled upon the phone box by chance, as far removed from the noise and bustle of the city that he could ever have imagined.

Reaching into his pocket, Ryan removed a small scrap of paper. It had been folded in half, and upon opening he noticed the deep crease of the fold obscured one of the numbers written therein.

He felt nervous, his palms sweaty. He looked about him before entering the phone box, only setting forward once satisfied he hadn't been followed. Closing the door of the phone box behind him, he picked up the handset and carefully studied the scrap of paper clutched in his hand.

Punching in the telephone number, guessing that the obscured digit was a 'two', he waited for the ringtone before inserting a pound's worth of change. Judging the obscured number correctly, the line's expectant pre-dial-up tone was replaced by the keener ringtone as the call was connected.

The ringing sounded for longer than Ryan would have thought possible. He was used to hearing recorded messages before now, offering the excuse that the receiver wasn't available; please leave a message. Instead the ringing tone stopped with a click, abruptly followed by unearthly silence.

Using a folded handkerchief, Ryan spoke in a disguised voice.

"George?" slightly muffled. He pressed the receiver tight against his ear. He could hear the slight exhale of breath. "George?" he repeated. "I know you can hear me. Listen, I know about your son's accident."

"*Sorry… I can't hear you.*"

"George?"

"*You're terribly muffled...*"

Ryan removed the handkerchief and spoke into the handset undisguised.

"George Jennings? Is this better?"

George sighed, ignoring the question. "*Who are you*?" he demanded.

"Just a friend, but that's not important. There is no time. You need to get your wife and child out of that hospital as soon as you can," he paused, hoping George was listening. "They are in danger. An extraction team is on its way to them as we speak. You have to hurry, they don't have much time."

"*How-*"

"It's not important," he repeated. "Just keep them safe. Your home has not been compromised yet. Lie low. We'll meet when the time is right."

Ryan pressed the cut off button, ending the call. *I hope I'm not too late*, he thought.

Ryan Barber stepped out of the phone box and hurried back to his car. Despite being in a quiet, sleepy village where no one was in view, the roads being empty; the silence was deafening. He couldn't help feeling exposed; couldn't help feeling countless eyes spying his every step and every muscle movement. Maybe it was the guilt. After all, had he not just given warning to Britain's most wanted man?

But wasn't it for the greater good?

It wasn't guilt, he decided, it was the shame he felt at *having* to betray his employer. He had worked for the corporation since leaving school – which on latest count would make it twenty-one years now – and since the beginning of his career he'd had nothing but admiration and respect for his boss – and for the work undertaken by the business. However, the killing of innocent men and women, and now the hunting down of children, was not something he had ever signed up for, no matter how just the cause may appear to be.

Besides, he was motivated by something else closely linked. Irrevocably, it had become personal.

He closed his eyes to the emotions which threatened to engulf him. Now wasn't the time to dwell on past losses or succumb to grief.

He knew he was taking great risk in doing what he'd just done, hence the precautions. Before now he had only helped from a safe distance, never speaking to his quarry, always keeping well back, his identity retained, his involvement barely noticed. What he'd now done exposed him to almost as much danger as that which George and his family experienced on a daily basis. His employers wouldn't understand his rationale; they wouldn't care for his reasons. Duplicity and betrayal would be all they understood.

What to do, he thought. He couldn't run or just leave the organisation; that would arouse suspicion. He had no alternative but to return to his post at Kaplan Ratcliff Biochemical and Life Sciences, despite the air of foreboding that surrounded the idea. Besides, from the inside, he was George and his family's best chance of survival, and *his* only advantage of acquiring retribution.

From his position as the firm's Assistant Intelligence Officer, it was his job to know what was going on. Until two years ago, his role and single objective was only interested in what his competitors were doing. Since then, he had been enlisted into a whole different programme, a programme that had spiralled out of control, involving designs that he did not agree or wish to be a part of; it was also one that was maligned by his own personal ambitions. He knew what Samuel had planned for the girl and what he meant to do with the loose ends that stood in his way.

Ryan couldn't in good conscience allow the fate that was reserved for Sophie. And the punishment to be meted out to George? Honestly? That would NEVER compensate Ryan for everything that he'd lost.

An hour's drive found Ryan back in the command centre, which was just a fancy name for a large office where intelligence operations were controlled and in which he and a number of other agents carried out their mundane jobs and sundry tasks. It was also where Samuel Jackson could be found, mostly sitting in his office on the mezzanine floor, drinking vending machine coffee and eating macaroons; he, who could be seen through the glass wall of his office that overlooked the command centre, locked away within his ivory tower, a false sense of power. In truth he was just another puppet being guided by Tom Kaplan and his cohorts.

The command centre had a high ceiling, and was illuminated mainly by the large video screen that took up most of the wall at the front of the office, as well as the many swing arm desk lamps that were bolted to the desks, a variety of different colours making the desks less clinical. There was no natural light as the room was deep within the building and devoid of external walls or windows. Analysts and intelligence operators dressed in sharp suits and razor-thin ties sat at desks, computers flashing up data and video images ahead of them, some on telephones, whilst others were on laptops or smart phones. Most were in various stages of consuming lunch or drinking coffee; half-eaten sandwiches, bagels, jacket potatoes and cheese toasties lay amidst the clutter of papers and the disarray of operators' desks. To the uninitiated observer the place could easily have belonged to the financial services industry or a busy stock brokerage trading in shares and securities. The command centre was abuzz with activity and noise levels were at a crescendo.

Despite the hubbub the acoustics of the room allowed Samuel's voice to carry, booming like thunder and momentarily subduing the hysteria bubbling around.

"Ryan Barber. My office," barked Samuel. The way he spoke lacked decorum, almost akin to a parent berating an unruly child. He was standing a short way from the metal staircase that led to the mezzanine floor, to the conference room and more specifically to the office of the Security and Intelligence Director.

Samuel Jackson was the tallest man Ryan had ever seen, stocky and built like an American footballer or a wrestler off *WWE*. Like the actor of the same name (minus the 'L'), he was also black; unlike the actor, he didn't have an inimitable, tough, ruthless voice or punctuate every sentence with a swear word. Nonetheless he was someone you didn't torment or dally with.

"Yes, sir," Ryan muttered to himself sarcastically, moving slowly and heavily towards the Director's office, full of nervous apprehension. Suddenly he became aware of how dry his mouth felt as he climbed the stairs to the mezzanine floor.

Ryan entered the office and closed the glass door behind him.

"Ryan, take a seat." The Security and Intelligence Director was sitting behind a large mahogany desk. A laptop was open in front of him, its screen facing him. Behind his back was a large LCD television affixed to the wall. A screensaver displayed the Kaplan Ratcliff company insignia and logo, flickering across the visual display unit on a continuous loop.

Despite the heat of the office, he wore a black suit that radiated authority, white shirt and an electric-blue tie pulled taut to his neck. The air-conditioning was turned off. Almost, Ryan considered, to make any visitors sweat no matter what their disposition was. One was ALWAYS uncomfortable when in the presence of the Security and Intelligence Director.

"Do you mind if I grab a glass of water?" Ryan asked before taking a seat. Not waiting for a reply he made for the pewter-coloured *Primo* water machine and poured himself a glass. Taking a deep mouthful of water he immediately felt refreshed by the ice-cold H2O. He refilled the glass.

"Better?" Samuel asked as Ryan took the seat in front of him.

"Yes. Thanks."

"Good. Listen Ryan, there's been a development. Police are reporting a roadside accident near Seacrest. Quite nasty apparently. We've got a make on the vehicles involved," he paused for effect. "One's Dominic's car. Christ knows what happened, or what he is doing, but he's gone off the grid. The other car belongs to Harriet Jennings. A red *Toyota Prius*."

"Jeez, what happened?"

"Your guess is as good as mine. You're probably aware, Dominic's team were acting on a tipoff that Harriet and her youngest son were at the hospital. It's the closest we've been in a long time. It should have been a simple extraction. A snatch and grab. I guess things don't always go to plan... especially when it comes to the Jennings."

Samuel stood up and crossed to the glass wall that gave him an overview of the command centre. "Damn it, Ryan!" The outburst startled the Assistant Intelligence Officer. "Why can't they just come quietly… or just lie down and die? Haven't we gone through enough?"

"George is smart, Sam. Hell, it's his daughter we're targeting, who wouldn't go all out to protect their children?"

The Director grunted, returning to his seat.

"George isn't *that* smart, Ryan. For two years he has managed to keep one step ahead of us, always avoiding us, missing the traps or outrunning our field agents. We're always close, always within a whisker, but somehow... he knows." Samuel steepled his hands in front of him, his elbows on the desk "I've had my suspicions for some time now, Ryan. I've been in denial, but I can't deny it any longer. He's got help, he must have. I believe we have an internal problem." He sighed sullenly. "We have a mole in our midst."

"But that's impossible, Sam. I vetted all the applications; I can vouch for every single analyst and every agent," Ryan genuinely sounded incredulous, hiding his fear and the inner turmoil behind his act. "We did countless checks; they've all been polygraphed."

The Security and Intelligence Director looked sternly at his deputy; a worrisome thought clearly troubling his mind. "That's what I fear the most Ryan, someone is determined and... very skilled at lying." He then visibly relaxed, exhaling deeply. A reassuring smile surfaced. "Do me a favour; see to it that you find him. Or *her*," he paused again for emphasis, "and when you do, you know what to do."

"And what is that, Sam?" not entirely needing the answer spelt out to him, but wanting to hear his intentions.

"Exterminate this… *scourge*. I want them burnt. Set the fire so hot that even his soul gets incinerated."

CHAPTER NINE

GEORGE

GEORGE EXITED THE BUILDING through the back entrance, looked furtively from one side to the other, peering suspiciously through the gap of the open door; satisfied there was no one watching (*Was there someone out front?* A nagging thought), that he was unobserved, he darted across the small green, a sign staked to the ground warning:

ABSOLUTELY NO BALL GAMES.

On his left, a small play area designed for the local pre-schoolers with half a dozen apparatus upon which three children (a toddler and two robustious four-year-olds) currently played, their mothers sitting in a gaggle, talking animatedly, not watching nor caring for the man running away from the apartment block behind them; on the right were half a dozen washing rotary lines, metal trees bearing laundry for fruit. He cleared the green and vaulted a low wall that bordered the gardens, scant protection in such an exclusive area of the nation's capital; should anyone have wanted to use the rear as a means to break in, it would have been child's play. George thought there ought to have been a sign fashioned to rival *ABSOLUTELY NO BALL GAMES.* This one reading: *Thieves: THIS WAY!*, hand pointing helpfully should the property's mediocre defences not be clear enough.

He made his way through a series of alleyways that eventually led to his car, safely parked in a neighbouring road, and (he hoped) far enough away to avert the attention of any would-be pursuers. To further avoid detection he often changed number plates, the latest having been screwed into place just two nights previously.

Bursting out of an alleyway, he reduced his speed and slowed to a more leisurely, less conspicuous pace. He felt bad about leaving Sophie in the apartment by herself - though it was only natural - paternal instincts deep-rooted and borne out of fear. He needn't have worried, she was no ordinary kid. She was more than capable of taking care of herself - thanks to him. Better equipped, in fact, than most sixteen-year-olds. Better even than men twice that age!

His car was a small *Peugeot 207*, blue in colour. Being a common car with a common colour helped camouflage his comings and goings amongst the ordinary everyday folk that travelled into and away from London. Additionally, it was economic to the wallet with low carbon emissions, a concept not shared by his pursuers who erred towards brash, bold, gas-guzzling vehicles favoured by government agencies (and narcissists) the world over.

Desperate for news about his wife, he reached for his mobile phone, and pressed the shortcut dialler for Harriet.

The ring tone played out for twenty seconds before going to voicemail.

"Hi, you have reached the voicemail of Harry, please leave a message and I'll get back to you as soon as I can..." It was her voice, so familiar, so clear – it was like she was sitting next to him.

"Harry, call me when you get this message. I hope to God you and Charlie are all right." He ended the call, but before replacing the phone in his pocket, he typed a short SMS message:

OKAY... I'M COMING HOME.

He pressed send. A moment later the delivery receipt 'dinged' on the phone, a confirmation message envelope flashing up on the screen.

Behind the wheel of the car, George reached to the glove compartment, unlocked it with the ignition key and pulled out a small leather case. Unzipping it he revealed a tablet computer, the sort readily available in most supermarkets. A *Google Nexus.* He switched it on. Upon loading – it took thirty seconds to go through boot up and presentation of 'unlock' screen – he keyed in a five digit password (*4-2-0-1-0*) and opened up an application that enabled him to track his wife via the GPS signal transmitted from the electronic device he'd insisted she wore. It was strapped discretely to her ankle and acted much like a tag on a criminal serving out a sentence under home curfew. In fact, it enabled George to view the whereabouts of anyone whose GPS coordinates were installed, whether it be on an ankle monitor (like his wife), or from a simple mobile phone. If he had the number and keyed it into the search facility within his programme, he'd be able to see whomever and wherever any one was at any given moment.

His children all had a GPS tracking device strapped to their wrists. Looking like an ordinary wrist watch, these simple to use gadgets enabled George to maintain a watchful eye, despite being far away for a greater part of the time. Meredith wore a pink one, the boys had blue.

Likewise, he wore a similar gadget attached as a pendant to a gold chain Harriet had bought him for his fortieth Birthday. This was mainly for Sophie's benefit, helping her feel 'close' to him when he was away; she could also spy his movements and gauge when to expect his return. These devices all came about after the first 'attack', around the time the laboratories were destroyed and Thomas, Maksim and Clara died.

On the screen a map powered by *Google* appeared. He zoomed in on the map and counted the five pulsating blue dots that indicated GPS traces. It was reassuring to know where his family was – it gave the illusion that they were within 'touching' distance.

By pressing any of the dots with a finger he could see details of who it was being tracked, and exactly where the GPS coordinates were located.

George did exactly that, lightly tapping each dot in turn. All, except for Sophie, were within forty miles of each other; he could see that Stanley and Meredith were still both at the house, Willoughby Rising. Sophie was obviously closest, her signal was emitted from a transmitter she was unaware of, surgically planted inside her brain, situated just behind her left eye, deep within the ocular cavity. George had had it planted there before she was a calendar month old. Although unaware of its existence, very occasionally she would feel the slightest twitch behind her eye. It was mildly irritating, though she put the sensation down to tiredness and it would always be gone after a night's sleep.

The GPS locators he was most interested in were currently stationary on a road eight miles west from home. The two signals had merged into a single pulsating blue dot.

George softly touched the tablet's screen with the pad of his right index finger and saw the confirmatory information, two speech bubbles colliding with each other:

Charlie Jennings: Location, Seacrest Road.

Harriet Jennings: Location, Seacrest Road.

George sighed, slightly relieved, but perturbed by a nagging doubt. His wife and child were okay, that he was certain. He hadn't been too late. His earlier warning to Harriet - provided by a mystery tipper - had been enough to get her and Charlie clear of the hospital, helping them to safety.

He put the tablet computer down onto the passenger seat, turned it so that it was facing him, allowing him to view the map every so often without taking his eyes off the road.

Starting the engine, George made the decision to move; only when Harriet was in his arms and the kids were seated around his feet would he feel completely at ease – no matter what his obligations were, or how deep his troubles may be, first and foremost came family. He allowed his imagination to conjure an image of the five of them sitting together, no longer anxiously turning at every corner or in fear of each stranger that ever approached. How long had it been since the time when they had laughed easily together, an act most families took for granted?

A couple of Christmases ago? *Easter last year*? He couldn't remember, it had been so long.

Had it been two years already since the explosion at the laboratory?

He couldn't be sure, but one thing was certain. He'd do anything to keep his family safe and return them to the idyllic days when they'd been a proper family.

Soon... There was something he needed to do first.

The image in his head melted away as the tablet computer next to him started to emit a slow, oscillating bleep, an indication that one of the GPS signals was moving. A sideward glance indicated it was Harriet. The dot had changed colour to red, a disclosure further heightened by its rapid pulsation.

"That's good, Harry," George muttered, "keep on moving."

George steered the *Peugeot* away from the residential street and his home in Chelsea, and made his way towards the one-way system that would eventually take him out of the city and to a bypass that would indirectly route him via a couple of A-roads to *Seacrest Road*, approximately one hundred miles east; he would soon be heading in the direction of where his wife currently travelled.

The tablet computer, continuing its bleeps and pulsing dot, did not immediately deliver the information that George needed to know.

He wouldn't realise that his wife was no longer heading towards Seacrest or *home*, but instead away from it *towards* a destination unknown. Neither would he notice that Charlie was not moving *with* Harriet, that *his* GPS signal was still blue, pulsating only and unmoving.

These facts eluded him and would go unnoticed for twenty-one minutes, by which time it would all be too late.

CHAPTER TEN

SOPHIE

SOPHIE WAITED ALMOST FIFTEEN minutes from the time her father had left the apartment and the moment she decided *to hell with this*, before letting herself out of the panic room.

From the confines and safety of this room, she'd watched her father on one of the nine surveillance screens fixed into the farthest wall; images transmitted from cameras located in and around the property, strategically placed, flashed up on the colour monitors, all being recorded digitally. She'd watched George from the camera hidden outside of the apartment as he left by the back door of the building; watched further as he exited the building and crossed the lawn at the back of the apartment, passing the small play area and the rotary washing lines, jumped over the small boundary wall, making his way to the car she knew was parked in a neighbouring road. He disappeared altogether once entering the first of a small series of alleyways.

Allowing time to put distance between them, Sophie had waited patiently. Whilst waiting she petted the stuffed toy kangaroo – *Flopsy* – her comfort toy from when she had briefly been an infant, a gift that George had presented to her after taking the rest of his family to London Zoo, small consolation for missing out on a day out with her father, mother and siblings. She had never been to the zoo herself – but she'd seen the photographs with Meredith, Stanley and Charlie, their faces beaming in delight from the array of animals that paraded within their enclosures. Sophie had wished she'd been able to go.

Sophie especially liked the photographs of the gorillas. How large and powerfully built they were, a species not too distant from our own. She'd studied the photograph and could read the sadness within the gorilla's eyes. It was a sadness she felt akin to – after all, was she no different to the caged animal, trapped behind closed doors?

Once certain she was safe to do so, she deactivated the alarm, turned the wheel that locked the safe room's steel door, and stepped out into the more comforting surrounds of the living room. She left her stuffed toy, momentarily discarded. This was a routine, an action she'd performed countless times since her body had developed into teenage proportions - as soon as she'd been left alone.

Sometimes she'd forego her meds to bring about the onset of her *heteroclitic* form, so as to venture out into the world, go to places many could not - unnoticed, unrestricted and unobserved. Free to do whatever she wanted. Like the first time she'd left the apartment to visit her family, unbidden, it was initially out of curiosity. Towards the end it was simply from love and out of human need for contact.

The last such time had been over four weeks ago. She'd sneaked into the car when George hadn't been looking, lying low in the back seat. For the whole journey she would concentrate on being as quiet as physically possible, trying to breathe as silently as one could. As always when trying to be quiet, she found a sneeze trying to foil her act of concealment, but always she managed to hold it in.

At the house she'd climbed out of the car and ventured into her father's second home unseen. She'd often done the round trip, returning to the apartment either by reversing her initial actions and stealing a journey back via George, or by being adventurous and taking the bus, surprising travellers with subtle pushes and shoves, having a giggle when she took a fancy at being mischievous; knocking hats off passersby and tripping up lecherous youths when their antics had gone beyond that of a joke. There had even been the times, she often reflected, that she took great pleasure from tying the laces of shoes; sometimes, when feeling ultra wicked, she'd take greater amusement from tying the laces of two different people's shoes together, watching with unrestrained hilarity the resultant calamity, of limbs falling into an intertwined heap.

In the house, away from the apartment, she'd spend a lot of time with the children. At first she hadn't known who the three children were. Two boys: Stanley and Charlie; one girl, Meredith. It didn't take long to realise that these children were her siblings, how they looked so much like her; and after coming to terms with it, she embraced her newly discovered family from a distance, stealing a family photograph from a photo album, which she'd doctored by adding a cut out of her own image amidst the sibling portrait. She kept it hidden beneath her pillow.

Things had gone on like that for two or three months, but then she made the mistake of falling asleep in Meredith's room.

The first she'd known that Meredith had discovered her was when she was woken from her slumber with a start.

Meredith had screamed. It was as though she had seen a ghost.

In point of fact, this was indeed exactly what Meredith had thought. Standing in front of the antique mirror that stood atop the dresser, its wooden frame gilt-edged and carefully carved in a wild English garden style with roses, thistles and brambles, the image of an older girl appeared deep within the glass, lying strewn across her bed. When turning around and looking towards the place the girl was being reflected, all that appeared in front of her was an empty bed.

Meredith had scratched her head, puzzled. Nothing in her nine years had prepared her for the experience of seeing someone in a mirror who wasn't there.

The only conclusion she could come to was thus: her bedroom was being haunted by a rather scary looking girl.

The scream that followed was ear piercing and long, alerting and alarming everyone in the house and waking the sleeping girl as though she were *Goldilocks*.

"Meredith!" her father shouted up the stairs, his voice closely followed by his lumbering strides as he ascended the stairs two at a time.

"Shhhhhh. Please!" Sophie had sat bolt upright and was trying to calm Meredith, appealing to her to quieten down. "Meredith, stop screaming. Please... don't be alarmed." She was begging and was now standing next to her, an invisible hand laid gently upon her arm. "Your father must not know."

Meredith stopped screaming, at first puzzled by the feel of the hand pressing against her arm, the indentation appearing in the sleeve of her shirt; she became further startled as her father burst into the bedroom puffing and panting from the exertion of running up the stairs, a knee bruised having taken a stumble at the second last step.

"What's wrong?" George had demanded, breathy. His cheeks were bright red.

Meredith shook her head. She was confused. What she saw in the mirror could not be possible, and yet there she was, still standing there in the reflection, a finger, poised, held to her mouth in a 'shushing' gesture. Meredith turned to face her dad, glancing over to where she knew the girl in the mirror was still standing.

"Meredith?" George pressed, concern still etched across his face. "What's happened?"

Meredith shook her head and tried to smile reassuringly. "A spider... I saw a spider, big it was," she hesitated, "the size of a grapefruit! Completely freaked me out!" She followed the lie with a nervous chuckle. "Sorry dad. I didn't mean to scare you."

"Do you want me to hunt it down and get rid of it for you, honey bunny?"

Meredith feigned a look of embarrassment. "No, that's fine. It wasn't *really* that big. She's gone now..."

"She?"

"I mean 'it'," she corrected.

"Okay, love," suspicious. "As long as you are all right. I'll be down the hall."

After that, once George was gone, Sophie introduced herself, leaving out many of the details that were difficult to explain - which was most of her life story. There after a seed of friendship had grown between the two of them.

That seed had been planted and nurtured some six months earlier. She had been much younger, the aggressive ageing process that had been genetically manipulated having added four years to her appearance, and breasts to her slender frame.

Things had been more enjoyable with Meredith. In her company she'd felt like a normal kid. Playing with dolls and makeup and talking about her favourite boy band. In Meredith's company it had been so easy and carefree. Now, she hadn't seen Meredith since George had the urgent need to uproot the family and move them to a detached house 120 miles east to the coast; though she had wanted to, she hadn't dared to smuggle herself away in George's car again. Their new home was much further than before, and the air in which George carried himself seemed more maligned and fearful. It was as though he carried the weight of the world on his shoulders and every inch was burdened with a sense of foreboding and danger.

"I miss them," she whispered to the empty room, wishing she'd brought the fluffy kangaroo with her from the safe room.

At times when she felt most downcast and melancholy, Sophie would comfort herself by watching her family's movements on her iPad, using the same application that George was currently using to track his wife and Charlie, discretely gazing upon their whereabouts.

It also enabled her to be prepared for when George returned so she could safely secure herself back in the panic room and to re-engage the internal lock and alarms, a trick she'd often employed.

What her father didn't know, didn't hurt him.

Watching the screen now, Sophie could see four stationary dots that belonged to herself, Meredith, Stanley and Charlie. They were blue and pulsating. There were two red dots that were moving and flashing more urgently; unlike her father, she didn't have the sound on, so the accompanying oscillating bleeps were muted. One of the red beacons belonged to George, who by now was in the one-way system that led towards the bypass that took him in the direction of the house in Seacrest; the other red dot belonged to her mother.

"That's strange."

Her mother and Charlie were separated, and Harriet was moving *away* from Seacrest in completely the opposite direction.

"Where are you going?" she whispered to herself. Using her index finger she gently probed the red dot that belonged to her mother, and followed it, willing the subtle act to conjure the answer to her question. Harriet's details appeared on the screen in a speech bubble; her name, the exact location, including latitude and longitude coordinates flashed up. She went to touch her dad's dot, and stopped –

– a noise... from outside the apartment. Her ears pricked up, picking up on the sound, ever so slight and almost inaudible, but Sophie heard it nonetheless. Her training had taught her to notice the unnoticeable and her heightened hearing ability allowed her to hear the merest sound. It was unmistakeable. Her senses were as keen as a razor blade; a couple of clicks followed by a louder crack – it was coming from the entrance to the apartment.

Sophie put the *iPad* down and with stealth, crossed the room to stand beside the living room doorway, her right dominant ear lifted towards the hallway. The door was pushed to. She allowed it to open just a crack, peering through.

She sensed the entrance door opening, could see a silver swath of light creep into the hallway and wash over the threshold of the living room; further, she could feel a soft breeze puff through, dappling her skin and ruffling her hair.

The safe room now seemed rather appealing to Sophie, now that she was on the wrong side of its defence system. She felt vulnerable, but then she countered; she didn't fancy being held under siege in a small room no bigger than a glorified wardrobe either... she'd seen the film starring *Jodie Foster* and a very young *Kristin Stewart* – it hardly glamorised the situation.

A shadow belonging to the first intruder fell across the threshold, extending into the room. Slowly and silently, each step measured, he came into view. Sophie quickly assessed the situation, calculating her options. She considered the foe in front of her and the risks involved with any form of contact. It didn't take a nanosecond to realise that chances of survival would be greatly increased were she to employ her greatest defence mechanism:

Invisibility.

Closing her eyes for just a moment, the onset of deep concentration engulfed her. Almost immediately, without preamble or ceremony, Sophie's petite frame vanished in an eye blink. Sometimes it was gradual, though more often it was sudden. Blink – now you see me – blink – now you don't!

The man was dressed all in black, in full combat clothing: outer body armour; two-piece balaclava; trousers with additional hard shell knee pads, and black *Magnum Spider* assault boots, heavy duty footwear that provided comfort and reliability, laced up tight to above the shin.

Concealing his eyes he wore night vision goggles secured to his face by a head mount. An earpiece was visible and wrapped round his right ear and a small microphone was clipped to the inside collar of his jacket. In his hand, pressed against his shoulder, he carried a *Colt*

M4 rifle. He meant serious business. Sophie doubted he'd be shooting blanks.

"Control, this is Alpha One... I'm entering the living room."

From behind the man a second similarly attired person had entered the building and was slowly progressing down the hallway towards the bedrooms and the safe room, floorboards creaking beneath him. Unlike the intruder entering the living room, he was much taller, almost a giant. Standing nearer to seven-feet in height, he was a colossus of a man, having to stoop to pass through the apartment's doorways.

Behind the door, Sophie was poised for action; though trained in various forms of close quarters combat, she had no live experience of using *krav maga,* or indeed with *jujitsu* or any of the other forms of martial art she'd learnt under Malaxi Bacaunawa's tutelage. Her heart was pounding; she could hear it loud within her ears almost drowning out all other sounds.

Whump. Whump. Whump.

The intruder placed a hand on the door handle and gently pushed it as he entered slowly into the room, carefully with concentrated force, his other hand remaining on the rifle, a digit touching the weapon's trigger, a muscle contraction away from releasing its death spray.

Coming into view, Sophie stilled herself to take stock of the situation, to contemplate the best course of action. The first rule of combat is to have a plan, or more specifically a *backup plan.*

"Screw it," she muttered to herself. She didn't have time to think. That's the one thing training never prepares you for; what to do in reality.

The intruder was now entering the room; she noticed the night vision goggles. She cursed inwardly – invisibility would not gain her much advantage – no doubt the glasses were equipped with heat-seeking capabilities. Without a doubt, they'd come prepared specifically for her.

As intruder one stepped past the door, Sophie took the moment to react, and with the youthful agility you'd expect from a fit, lithe, sixteen-year-old girl, and with the margin of surprise on her side, she thrust out a clenched fist to the armed man's face, knocking the night vision goggles out of position, and leapt to the furthest side of him, sprinting across the room to take the barest cover behind the leather sofa.

Caught unawares and suddenly without the ability to see his prey, the intruder reactively squeezed the trigger of the *M4* rifle, a burst of automatic fire spraying the room with deafening booms and muzzle flashes with each discharge, smashing bullet holes the size of Galia melons into the walls, pulverising plasterboard stud walls, disintegrating the window that overlooked the street and ripping through the fabric of one of the sofas, tossing up hunks of foam and leather fragments into the air like expensive confetti.

"Cease fire!" screamed the second intruder, charging into the room. "You idiot, she's to be taken ALIVE!"

"The bitch jumped me," intruder number one spat, as though it vindicated him. He removed the *M4*'s magazine and replaced it with a full one, click-clunking as the magazine engaged, echoing within the living room. It took him a further moment to replace the night vision goggles, restoring his ability to see their quarry.

Sophie was lying flat behind the bullet-riddled sofa, panting hard, her heart thumping louder than before. Plaster dust, leather confetti and foam chunks rained down on her. Smoke and the smell of cordite hung in the air, suffocating to breathe through. Sophie fought the urge to cough, not wishing to expose her position.

"You'd better pray she's not dead." Intruder number two was surveying the room. He swept the area with his visual aid, his *M4* aimed ahead of him. So far, there was no sign of the girl.

Where is she?

Intruder one was walking around the side of the leather sofa behind which Sophie was lying in hiding, in wait. Sensing and hearing his approach, she shuffled towards him slowly, crouching slightly. She formulated a plan and played out the key elements within her head. It was true what they said. Attack was the best form of defence.

As his dark frame came into view, Sophie kicked out, sweeping his legs out from under him. An erratic burst of gunfire peppered the ceiling as intruder one fell onto his back.

With inhuman speed and significant dexterity, Sophie grabbed his rifle hand (still clutched to the weapon) and pummelled it hard against the floor, twisting the hand at the same time. After a short tussle, she heard the sickening crack as his trigger finger broke; in pain, the grip on the gun was relaxed, intruder one screaming out: "My hand!"

She pushed the rifle out of reach, and then struck the man forcefully with both her hands, one at a time, against each side of his neck, carefully aimed for pressure points she knew would momentarily paralyse him. She followed up with an inexplicable elbow punch to the bridge of the fallen man's nose, hearing a satisfying *CRACK* sound, as of a cricket ball glancing heavily against willow, of further bone breaking, rendering intruder one semi-conscious.

Intruder two, watching the melee as he entered the room saw the girl - though just a blur - through his night vision goggles, the thermal signature his only way of tracking the invisible teenager. He advanced, in awe of what he had witnessed, his partner felled and incapacitated in less than four seconds, the girl now leaping over the bullet-shredded leather sofa, seeming to fly towards him.

He was transfixed. Never had he seen such finesse in a combatant. He raised his weapon seemingly in slow-motion and found Sophie bearing down on him, kicking him solidly in the head, knocking the night vision goggles clean from his face, the force flinging them to the floor, and bloodying his nose.

No longer able to see, Sophie's advantage was absolute. From the kitchen, she armed herself with a carving knife usually used for serving up the Sunday roast, pulling it free from the wooden block next to the microwave.

Intruder two scrambled to the side of the room, looking for cover, finding none. He brandished the *M4* menacingly ahead of him. He spoke into his microphone, his nose streaming blood. He sounded bunged up, like he was suffering from sinusitis.

"Control, this is Alpha Two. Alpha One is down. Our target is not coming easily. We need backup... over."

A sudden gash to his left leg brought his seven-foot frame crashing to the floor; a second cut appeared to his right wrist. He dropped the *M4* rifle, his other hand clapping to the bleeding wound to his wrist, pressing down hard.

A vase sailed through the air and smashed against the side of his head, unbalancing him.

"Stop!" he yelled, clambering to his knees.

Sophie kicked the kneeling man, knocking him backwards with such force that he was lifted from the floor to crash heavily onto and smashing the coffee table in the centre of the room.

"Please," intruder number two burbled, blood dribbling from his mouth, the fleshy remains of his tongue lolling out. "No more. I'm done."

Sophie was now standing in front of the fallen soldier. He slowly reached up to his ear and removed the earpiece, electronic voices continuing to whisper commands and instructions, oblivious to what had concluded in the apartment. He pulled the microphone out from his jacket and tossed it aside.

"I'm done," he repeated hoarsely, then spat a globule of spit and blood out.

Sophie reached down and picked up the ear and mouth piece, holding it up to her ear.

"Alpha Team, what's going on? Report? Back up team will be with you shortly. Do you copy?"

Sophie walked over to the place where the window had been, the curtains billowing in like an unfurled flag. She peered out just as her father had done earlier.

"Why won't you leave us alone?" she asked into the microphone. "We've done nothing to you!"

At first the radio went silent.

In the distance the sound of sirens wailed as they fast approached in answer to all the gunfire and an elderly neighbour who'd been crudely woken from a nap in his armchair from all the hullabaloo. A small gathering of nosey onlookers had gathered at a safe distance down the road, their macabre fascination for blood, death and destruction fuelled their appetite to watch, no matter the risk to themselves.

"It's not what you've done... Sophie. It's what you are programmed to do." An electronic voice secreted from the earpiece now held in the palm of Sophie's right hand.

"You should stop. Whilst you have the chance. Stop now, I'm warning you."

A police car appeared at the end of the road, tyres screeching, siren blaring, flashing lights splashing blue translucent colour urgently as it drew closer, coming to a halt outside the apartment block. Another police vehicle arrived moments later and still more sirens sounded in the background.

"Sophie... It doesn't have to be like this. We could be friends, you and I."

Sophie knew the voice at the end was playing with her, stalling for time, time which she didn't have. She had to leave, and leave immediately, but before she did there were things she had to retrieve, things essential to her (and her father's) survival.

Speaking as she worked, Sophie replied: "I doubt that very much."

Retrieving a backpack and a large sports holdall, she filled the backpack with things she absolutely needed; spare clothes; provisions, water, food; the iPad which had miraculously survived the gunfire and violence; a mobile phone; a torch; her fluffy kangaroo from the safe room. What she couldn't fit into the backpack, she placed into the holdall. She then emptied the refrigerator of every vial of serum, not forgetting to pack the jet injector.

From one of the fallen soldiers she unholstered a handgun and collected all the ammunition she could find (from them both), six magazines in all.

"We need to meet Sophie. I'm sure we can come to a mutually beneficial arrangement."

Lastly, Sophie located the place where her father's floor safe was, hidden beneath a section of carpet that was easily lifted. She pulled up the floorboard, exposing the digital combination lock of the safe. She keyed in her date of birth – a combination, or version thereof favoured by her father:

1-6-0-4

The latch clicked as the door from within was released. Sophie opened the door and reached in; removing her father's laptop and two thick A5 envelopes which she knew each contained a thick wad of fifty pound notes. These last items she dropped into the holdall without much ado, and zipped it closed.

"Nice talking to you creep. Let's do it again... *not!*" Sophie dropped the ear and mouth piece back to intruder number two, and unseen she left the apartment carrying the big holdall in one hand and the backpack over the shoulder of her opposite arm. She passed the policemen who were busy marking their territory, some armed and taking up strategic positions, rifles aimed ahead of them; others cordoning off the area at a safe distance, trying to assess the situation.

She passed further the group of bystanders who'd gathered into a very large force of spectators, busily gleaning and gloating at the theatrics now playing out ahead of them. Ignoring them, she continued at a pace putting distance between her and the Chelsea apartment, passing the black car that had gained her father's attention but which hadn't quite convinced him that there was an occupant staking them out, despite the possible sighting of a riflescope or the glass from a pair of binoculars.

She paid the car little more than a sideward glance, deep in concentration as she tried to make sense of what had just happened and formulate some ideas as to what next to do.

Sophie knew there was only one place she could really go, one place where the people who lived therein she could honestly trust. Although angered to be leaving all her worldly goods and her home behind, she was equally excited at the prospect of seeing her sister again, the only friend she knew.

The rear window of the black car, now behind her, electrically wound down. The passenger watched from a safe distance, night vision binoculars held against his eyes. For all intents and purposes he looked like a Peeping Tom. He watched the girl religiously, unseen by all she passed, her dishevelled appearance and determined look concealed to all except one. The man picked up a walkie-talkie and spoke into it.

"Bravo Team, stand down. Do not engage; repeat, DO NOT ENGAGE."

CHAPTER ELEVEN

HARRIET

IN THE DISTANCE, A lone vehicle appeared on the horizon, the hood of the car shimmering in the intense July sunshine, its mirrored surface reflecting the sun as if it were a fiery beacon, momentarily dazzling. Dominic had ushered the woman away from the crippled *Mercedes*, his *Beretta* aimed at her back, and together they stood by the roadside like a couple of hitchhikers thumbing for a ride; only their ride wasn't to be with some good *Samaritan*-passerby helping a motorist in distress. Their lift was pre-arranged and fast approaching from the east on Seabrook Road.

"What about my son?" pleaded Harriet, aware that Charlie was watching from a safe distance, camouflaged by deep shrubbery and prickly bushes. "He's only four, he's not safe out here all alone."

"Harry, Harry, Harry..." he spoke slowly, "you mistake me for someone who gives a crap. Your son will be all right, I'm sure. Someone will be here for him soon enough. If not, I'm sure his suffering won't last too long. You should worry more about yourself."

The silver vehicle drew closer. Harriet could identify the make of the car by its four ring insignia. An *Audi*. Through the windscreen she made out the dark outline of two figures seated within the front. Less than a minute later, the silver *Audi Q7* slowed down, pulled over to the side and came to a halt by the edge of the road.

The driver's side door slowly opened and the driver, a portly man in his fifties with thinning hair and a moustache, climbed out and walked forward a few feet, surveying the scene. Wearing a light blue long-sleeved shirt, the collar was unbuttoned, the sleeves rolled up to his elbows. Sweat coated his tanned face, and dark round circles highlighted how hot he was beneath his armpits. Carelessly, he wiped his forehead with the back of one wrist before drying it on the thigh of his trousers.

"Well done, Dom. I never did like that *Mercedes...*" He had an American accent, nodding towards the smoking wreckage behind the man and his captive. "I guess insurance will cover it."

"I expect so," nonplussed.

"I shouldn't bother replacing the music though." *This is the end* had played out, followed by *Chris Rea's The Road to Hell* and now *Bon Jovi's Living on a Prayer.* Dominic ignored the insult towards his choice of music. He believed his taste in music was eclectic. Besides, the CD compilation was mood music handpicked for the occasion.

Harriet barely heard the exchanges between the two men, focused instead on the plight she found herself.

What to do?

Everything had gone totally wrong. She feared for what this man and the newcomers intended to do to her; more than this, she was scared for her son. Looking across the road she was sure she could see Charlie's small form through the trees; his ruffled mop of hair, his little face full of alarm, his cheeks, tear strewn.

A sideward glance indicated that her captor still aimed the gun her way, though his attention was more directed towards the newcomer than it was on her.

What to do? The question urgently plagued her thoughts. She was panicked, she felt desperate. Never had she felt so scared, so hopeless and so defenceless.

She needed to escape; not for herself, but for her son – although that was a given – the question was, how?

"I guess you'll need a lift."

"You Americans don't miss a thing," Dominic replied sarcastically, his English over accentuated and noticeably plummy.

To the side of the road, not more than a couple of feet away from where Harriet was standing, debris from the car lay scattered amongst a mess of stripped foliage, torn shrubbery, broken-down trees and fragmented remains of a border fence, all demolished by the relentless *Mercedes* as it crashed out of control off the road, its progress finally halted by the sturdy oak which now wore the German car like a Christmas bauble.

Considering the debris scattered close by and the potential for one or two of the items, she formulated half an idea in her head.

"What are you staring at?" The American had noticed Harriet's fixed gaze towards the ground. "Com'on, let's get going." He turned and led the way, a mobile phone suddenly pressed against his ear. He started talking into it.

Harriet took a pained step forward, Dominic behind her, gun still aimed at her back, and deliberately tripped on nothing substantial, stumbling a couple of steps before falling to her knees with a thud, then falling forward, as though felled by a pro-wrestler weighing 300 lbs. She grunted from the impact and cried out exaggeratedly, the entire act carried out within a couple of seconds. She lay sprawled out on her front – her face hidden from view. She was crying loud and dramatically.

"There's no time for a rest… get up!"

"I... I think I've broken something, " wailed Harriet.

Dominic stood over her, the *Beretta* lowered, his guard dropped. He spoke calmly, "It's probably a sprain. Here..." grudgingly, he offered his free hand, reaching down.

Harriet slowly pulled herself up, her back still to her pursuer, her right hand wrapped around the base of a splintered wooden support post approximately three feet in length. It was part of the fence that had collapsed from the *Mercedes*' impact. A rusty nail jutted out from it menacingly like a crudely fashioned mace.

Looking over her shoulder, she made eye contact, and smiled. "Thanks," she whispered. Ignoring the offered hand, she stood up fully, turning awkwardly, pain continuing to burn within her swollen left leg; from the shielded vantage point granted by her outthrust chest she swung the piece of wood in an arc from behind her body, the makeshift club not registering with Dominic until it was too late.

The club connected squarely with the side of her pursuer's face, narrowly missed by the sinister looking spike protruding from it –

CRACK!

The force propelled the man backwards, the hand which had only moments earlier been poised with the offer of help, now clutching at his head, blood trickling between his fingers.

Not waiting to see what damage she'd inflicted, with barely a heartbeat passing, Harriet charged after the American as he readied himself to get into the *Audi*. Coming up behind him at great speed, she brought the makeshift club crashing down, smashing his arm and knocking the mobile to the ground, following up with a hefty wallop, clouting the fifty-something driver on the side of the head hard, grounding him with the one, nasty blow.

"Youngs? Youngs? You still there?" The electronic voice, also American, emitted from the *Samsung* mobile talked into the tarmac, its intended lying on his side next to his car, a thin line of blood leaking from a gash to the side of his forehead.

"Youngs, can you hear me?"

Harriet stepped over the unconscious man and peered into the driver's side of the car, glanced to the ignition and noted with relief the small bunch of keys dangling from the ignition key slot.

"Thank God," she said, about to climb in.

Before she could, a sudden burst of electricity stabbed into her back as the forgotten passenger from the *Audi* crept up from behind the trees and fired the *Taser* from fifteen-feet; two electrode darts hitting her square in the back, the barbs attaching to her blouse. The sudden electric charge caused a neuromuscular incapacitation that she was powerless to overcome. She fell to the road, her limbs twitching spasmodically.

"Mitch, you okay?" Brayden reached down to the driver and felt for a pulse at his neck. A strong heartbeat could be felt from the carotid. Almost immediately the man felled by Harriet stirred and opened his eyes. He winced as he gingerly touched his head.

"You chose a good time to take a piss," he grunted, slowly raising his head.

"Youngs?" The mobile was still twittering away.

"When you gotta-go, you gotta-go," Brayden, the passenger shrugged. He was younger than the driver, but taller – six-feet-two-inches, towering above his partner. He was muscular and ruggedly handsome; two day's worth of stubble had grown making him look older than his thirty-six years. He was dressed stylishly in a white shirt and light tan-colour trousers. Brown shoes completed the look. Unlike the *Audi*'s driver, very little sweat coated his skin, with no perspiration marks staining the shirt under his arms. He reached into the *Audi* and pressed a button that released the boot door. Turning his attention to Harriet, he reached down and effortlessly picked her up and carried her to the boot, dropping her in hard with a thud and closing the door after with a slam.

The *Audi*'s driver retrieved his mobile phone and put it back to his ear. "I'm here," he growled.

"*About time, thought you'd been killed or something...*"
"Almost, but Brayden came to my rescue, a proper knight in shining armour," he muttered.

"*So... you have Harriet Jennings? You sure it's her?*"

"Yes, positive. Dominic's photo doesn't do her justice. She looks prettier in the flesh. A real peach." Mitch was holding up a crumpled photograph for comparison.

The line went quiet for a long moment. When finally the voice at the end of the mobile returned, his voice was chill and icy hard: "*Good. Excellent. Bring her in and set the plan in motion. It's what he wanted.*" The electronic voice was suddenly gone and Mitch dropped the mobile into his trouser pocket, returning to the *Audi*.

Brayden had trotted off to where Dominic was lying semi-conscious from where Harriet had clobbered him. He crouched down and shook the fallen man gently.

"How you doin'?"

Dominic sat up gingerly and forced a smile.

"Just dandy," he replied. With Brayden's help, Dominic stood up, but being proud and *too* British he shrugged off the American's continued support and staggered a couple of steps independently before dropping to a knee.

"Guess you need my help after all." Brayden picked Dominic up and guided him to the rear passenger seat of the *Audi*, opening the door and pushing him through.

"I have unfinished business," Dominic slurred. He shuffled up on the back seat and slouched across so that he was half-lying and half-sitting. Lightly, he touched where Harriet had used the side of his head as a rounder's ball, wincing as he caressed the swelling.

"Tell me what to do," Brayden had stooped down and was peering into the rear of the car.

"This was going to be my retirement party," he said sardonically. "In the boot you'll find the poor schmuck who volunteered to be my stand-in."

"Volunteered?" In the driver's seat Mitch had turned to look over his shoulder, an eyebrow raised.

"Well, let's just say he passed the audition stage and was fast tracked to the judge's house," Dominic chuckled at his idle reference to *The X-Factor*. Brayden missed the jape having never watched the *Simon Cowell* presented talent show. He much preferred *The Voice*. "Put him in the driver's seat then douse him with petrol – you can find a couple of cans of the stuff with his body in the boot.

"Then let one of these two-inch fellows do the rest." Dominic handed a small cardboard book of matches - a famous London Soho nightclub advertised on its packaging - to the six-foot-two-inch man and chuckled again. "They'll need *Temperance Brennan* for identification after these pyrotechnics. I just wish I'd brought a couple of steaks and a beer for the barbecue."

"Tsk!" Mitch was shaking his head at the Brit's attempt at humour.

Brayden nodded understanding, then his face changed to a slight look of consternation.

"Just one thing – who's *Temperance Brennan*?"

"Don't you watch any TV? *Bones*?" Dominic glanced at Mitch, his eyes asking the older man to back him up but instead received an equally blank look. "I thought you Yanks liked that crap. Jeez! Call yourselves Americans." Dom turned away in resignation, failing to notice the sly smile appearing at the corners of both the Americans' faces.

Brayden closed the *Audi*'s door and made off towards the *Mercedes* to carry out Dominic's macabre fabrication.

A thick billowing cloud of black smoke was stretching into the midafternoon sky. The *Mercedes* was by now a dense ball of fire when Mitch started the engine of the *Audi* and drove them back in the direction Harriet had originally come from.

Charlie, though concealed by the thicket in which his mother had placed him, had watched in silence through a small gap that allowed observation. Stifling a cry, he witnessed his mother's capture and sudden fear enveloped him as the car in which she'd been unceremoniously stowed in the boot of, drove away. After a moment, he crawled out slowly from his hiding place, careful of his arm, snagging his clothes on thorns and bracken but not scraping his skin.

"Mummy!" he cried, clambering unsteadily to his feet and toddling up the slight embankment to the road's edge. "Mummy," he repeated more urgently, tears beginning to spring from the corners of his eyes. "MUMMY!!"

He watched as the *Audi* shrunk with distance, becoming a shimmering, silver disk. The heat of the sun had started to become overshadowed by the heat emanating from the blazing vehicle just a short way through the bushes across the road.

BOOM!

The explosion caused the ground to shudder, the backdraught lifting Charlie clear off his feet for what seemed longer than a nanosecond, and propelling him backwards three feet to land in a heap deep in amongst the thicket. Once again he was hidden and shielded from the dangers or the deliverance that Seabrook Road begrudgingly offered.

Before unconsciousness spared him from further fear or distress, temporarily taking the pain of losing his mother and the dull ache that was growing in his broken arm, he heard the distant siren of the first emergency vehicle rushing to the scene.

He hoped that the nightmare which he now found himself in would be over when he awoke. Maybe his mother and father would be there and he'd find himself tucked up in bed surrounded by his favourite toy dinosaurs and monster playthings, and the smells of cooking wafting up from the kitchen.

In retrospect, the nightmare wouldn't be over; this was just the first of many events that would shape an unsettled future for Charlie and his siblings.

CHAPTER TWELVE
MEREDITH

BY WAY OF PUNISHING herself Meredith had locked herself in her bedroom and refused to leave.

Not even for lunch.

Mrs Slocum, the house sitter, had hammered on the door relentlessly for what seemed like ten minutes, made threats and even resorted to the undignified position of begging for her to come out – all to no avail.

Meredith felt terrible, felt more guilty than had she have pushed her small brother out of the tree herself. After all, she *had* encouraged both her brothers to play in the crab-apple tree in the first place, whilst she, herself, had stayed safe out of harm's way on the grass down below.

"I'll leave your lunch by the door," Mrs Slocum had called through the double plywood that kept her at bay, her voice tinged with a slight undertone of annoyance. Meredith didn't realise that had Mrs Slocum wanted she could have easily forced the door with the slightest elbow punch, or kicked it in with a mere toe punt to the right place.

But she didn't, resisting the urge that burned inside her, an accomplice to her anger. Instead, she slowly retreated down the stairs biting her bottom lip and cursing silently.

That had been over half an hour ago. Though in the act of self punishment, starving herself was not part of the plan; it was not something she was keen to maintain, seconded by her stomach, which protested noisily with rumbling and gurgling sounds. She admired those people who went on hunger strike in their fight for some noble cause. Meredith Jennings wasn't one of them.

Once sure the house sitter was no longer outside her door, she unlocked the barricade and accepted the cheese and salad sandwich that sat on the side plate taking centre piece on the tray presented before her. An apple, some raisins and a *Cadbury's* chocolate mini roll completed the meagre offering. It took her less than three minutes to devour the lot.

Stomach full, Meredith returned to lying on her bed, self-pity once again consuming her thoughts. The scene of Charlie's fall: the run-up, the incident, the aftermath, playing over and over in her mind like a broken DVD, stalling at the bit where she had lied to her mother:

"Why did you let him climb the tree?"

"I didn't. He did it all himself."

She knew better than to lie to her mother. Besides, what did it serve? It didn't change the fact that Charlie was hurt, regardless of her protests of innocence; she knew her mother had the truth. What's more, she *was* responsible for her brother whilst playing outside. She was the eldest – the *responsible* one!

How stupid of me to allow it, she chastened. Would the feeling ever end? Would remorse consume her thoughts for eternity?

At some point sleep had taken her hostage, though not allowing her the sanctity or respite from her guilt. She dreamt of that morning, reliving the incident over and over again; different scenarios, differing perspectives but exactly the same final act and calamitous conclusion.

A knock at the bedroom door sounded like thunder in her dream before startling her awake, temporarily halting the movie playing within her mind. Knuckles rapped the wood a second time – three quick taps followed by one big 'bang!'

"Meredith. Meredith, I need to talk to you." It was her six-year-old brother.

Like Meredith, Stanley had taken refuge in his bedroom. Although relatively new to the house and the area, all three of the Jennings' children immediately took a dislike to the neighbour of Willoughby Rising. Mrs Slocum seemed overfamiliar with their father, almost as though she'd known him for a long time. Looking old beyond her years, she had the frame of a jolly, plump grandmother, without the demeanour or the tendency. With grey curly hair and a pudgy nose that bore a mole the size of a five pence coin and which was ugly enough even without the three thick white hairs sprouting from it, she looked the more menacing by the sheer size of her hands. Meredith had nicknamed her *Manhands* from the beginning, for they weren't too dissimilar in size to her father's and equally as hairy.

Following Mrs Slocum wherever she went, worse than a bad smell, was an eerie cold draught that sent goose bumps up their arms and shivers down their spines. Although she skulked around the place, often creeping with the stealth of a leopard out on a hunt, her presence was often realised just by the chill that swept close behind.

Stanley had joked that Slocum was a ghost.

Meredith had remarked that she thought perhaps Slocum was something entirely worse, maybe DEATH itself in disguise. They'd laughed after that, though nervously; none of them ever felt comfortable in her presence.

"Go away," said Meredith sulkily. "Leave me alone."

"It's important. Please Meredith, let me in."

Knowing that Stanley would never leave her alone, she sat up and climbed from her bed. Crossing to the door, she glanced at her reflection in the mirror on the wall. Her face, she noted, was blotchy from all the crying she'd done since that morning and her hair was dishevelled from lying in bed.

Meredith withdrew the bolt on the door and turned the handle, allowing access.

No sooner had the door swung open, Stanley had charged in boisterously. The door slammed behind him, a gust from the window helping it shut, rattling the frame.

"Well?" demanded Meredith, her arms folded across her chest. Stanley had leapt up onto her single bed and had started to use it as a trampoline.

"Do you know what time it is?"

"You badgered me into letting you in just for the TIME!" she emphasised the word in a shout.

"No silly," he continued to bounce. "It's mum and Charlie. They should have been back by now."

Meredith looked at her watch. It was after four. They'd been gone over six hours.

"Perhaps there's a long wait at the hospital. It is the *NHS* after all."

"Mum would have called. Something is wrong," he hadn't noticed, but he was whining. "Meredith, something has happened to them, I know it." He stopped bouncing and fell to the bed where he lay still, sullen.

"Stanley, calm down. Stop being silly," Meredith had taken on the role of the reasoning parent. In the absence of their mother and father, and not accepting Slocum as a reliable replacement, somebody had to.

"It's the bogeyman," Stanley continued. "He's finally caught us, after all this time."

Meredith thought to argue further, saw her brother's wild-eyed look and thought alternatively. Maybe he was right. Maybe the bogeyman *had* finally caught them.

"What did Slocum say?"

"She told me to shut up and stop being silly."

"Well, there you go then. If grownups don't believe you, why should I?" Meredith often resorted to sarcasm; it made her feel more in charge. Others thought she was just being smart-alecky; some though, like her old school teachers, considered her a pain in the *derriere*.

"Don't you think it odd us moving so suddenly recently, and not for the first time," he continued. "Something is wrong."

Meredith had to agree with Stanley that their hasty departure from the old town house had been questionable, but trusting her parents she'd never dared to ask. Instead she'd accepted the move to Willoughby Rising, embracing it even, loving the vastness of all the rooms, the corridors and enjoying the surrounding beauty at the top of that hill; the crab-apple tree and the great North Sea it overlooked made it even more magical. The only thing she didn't like about the place, she thought, was Mrs Slocum herself.

Why her dad trusted her was beyond reason. She was an ogre.

Accepting that something might be amiss, Meredith put on a show of calm and tried to comfort her brother.

"What do you want me to do?" she'd snaked an arm around Stanley's shoulders, hoping to placate him.

"Phone dad, he needs to know that mum is missing. We need him here to take care of us."

"But Mrs Slocum is looking after us. Dad trusts her."

"Fat use she is," Stanley retorted. "Too busy emptying our larder and biscuit tins to notice us. I don't even know why dad suggested using her, the old witch."

"Shhhh. She might hear you. Besides, she's our nearest neighbour and dad reckons she was once a friend of our grandmother."

Though we never knew our grandmother, she mused. The observation was meaningless, though the comment momentarily quietened her brother. It did little to lessen her own anxiety.

Meredith got up and walked to the window. The double-glazed unit faced eastward, towards the sea allowing spectacular views. She could see the outline of a container ship in the distance, small like one of Charlie's bath toys as it sat on the edge of the world, its cargo destined for Zeebrugge, Belgium. Outside, the July sun was warm, its rays continuing to glisten and sparkle upon the sea's constant murky-grey surface. Meredith turned her back on the outside world and crossed to her brother, sitting back next to him.

"We can't just do *nothing*, mum and Charlie could be in danger... or *worse*." Stanley was whining again and was fidgeting on the bed, the springs creaking noisily.

Meredith couldn't think about what was worse than just mere danger. She was just nine-years-old, not ten until December. In her young mind only death was worse than danger, and she couldn't – *wouldn't* – think or comprehend that.

"What can we do, we're just kids?"

A sudden gust of wind forced the bedroom window to open wider, the curtain billowing out like an opening parachute, knocking a framed photograph, a *Cabbage Patch kid* doll, and a couple of ornaments off the window sill to the carpeted floor. One of the ornaments – a porcelain ballerina – broke in two.

Meredith jumped from her bed and crossed to the window, closing it altogether. A glance across the garden showed little movement of the trees.

There was not the slightest breeze or the whisper of a draught. Not noticing, she bent down and picked up the broken ornament.

"Oh no, look at my ballerina Stanley." She took the two pieces to her bedside table and lay them down. "It was Nan's. Mum will kill me."

"Maybe dad can fix it."

"I'm already in enough trouble," bemoaned the girl.

A sudden movement from her right tugged her attention, ending for the moment all thoughts of the broken ballerina and the woe that beset her.

Meredith sat alert on the edge of her bed.

Stanley continued, oblivious to Meredith's look of alarm: "Or maybe if we get some superglue ourselves, we could mend-."

"Shoosh." Meredith waved her hand at her brother to quieten him; she was straining to hear the slightest noise or movement.

What did I just see?, she asked herself.

Had the movement come from the mirror? She started to analyse the situation. If the movement had come from the mirror, it must have been a reflection, perhaps Stanley or herself? But this was not the case. A look across to the mirror confirmed it – neither of them had moved, and besides from where she was sitting any movement either of the children would have made could not possibly have been captured by the silvered glass, not from the angle of its wall placement.

What did that mean?

"What's wrong?" asked Stanley, slightly frightened. He was watching his sister who in turn, was looking about herself wildly.

A thought sprung to Meredith's mind.

Could it be? *Was it at all possible*?

"Meredith?" Stanley was alarmed. Replicating his sister's actions, he too started to look around the room, though not sure what he was looking for.

"Hello," Meredith called out. "Are you here?"

"Who are you talking to?" asked Stanley. He continued to look about the room, following the direction of Meredith's darting gaze.

Ignoring Stanley, Meredith listened hard. Nothing but silence followed. She had stood from her bed and had walked across to the mirror. Once again, she looked at her appearance, her blotchy complexion, and the rings beneath her eyes. She looked – and felt – exhausted.

"Meredith?" Stanley didn't like being ignored. "What's wrong? I'm scared."

Meredith sighed. She felt like she was going mad. "Nothing's wrong Stanley. I'm seeing thin-," she'd started to turn, and then stopped, paused mid-sentence, her eyes returning to the mirror, widening – not in fear – but surprise.

Reflected in the mirror, standing behind Meredith a blonde-haired girl stepped into view sheepishly. Aside from her dishevelled appearance (almost matching Meredith's), she was just as the younger girl remembered; or maybe not - she seemed a little different. She looked taller, her face a little fuller. She appeared older.

"Hello Meredith," said Sophie, a smile stretching out across her elfin face. "So this is where you've been hiding."

CHAPTER THIRTEEN

GEORGE

George had been listening to the radio, not from any desire to learn of the current top ten chart hits or even to enjoy the pointless banter volleyed back and forth by the station's witless DJs (currently discussing their favourite jacket potato topping amongst other inane things), but keen to learn of any traffic delays or reports of accidents that may or may not blight his journey. A short time later, the DJs had ceased talking, giving way to a rare song or two, an old hit from the 1980s: *Too Shy* by *Kajagoogoo*. Before that *Feargal Sharkey*'s *A Good Heart* played and after the DJ promised *Kids in America* by *Kim Wilde*.

It brought back memories from his school days in the 1980s and a time that harkened back to another world and another continent; but that was just for a fleeting moment, the bleeping from the GPS tracker muscled in on his attention, extinguishing thoughts of a more peaceful, less complicated, less duplicitous and somewhat happier time.

Ten minutes had passed since he'd realised that Harriet was no longer travelling towards home; instead she was moving in completely the opposite direction. Currently she was heading towards him, but this did not immediately cause concern. What troubled him was the fact that Charlie's GPS location had him pinpointed to a spot along Seacrest Road, unmoving, where he'd remained since at least the moment he'd first climbed behind the wheel of the *Peugeot 207* – just over half an hour had passed since leaving Sophie at the apartment. It led him to two theories of conclusion. One, Charlie had removed his tracker from his wrist and had accidentally 'left' it behind, thus transmitting an incorrect location for his father to see. Two, Harriet had left Charlie behind to fend for himself, on his own, alone, the signal concise and correct, the only method from which anyone would find him.

Only one conclusion vied for full attention and it was the one he feared and dreaded the most.

What was Harriet thinking leaving Charlie alone like that?

"He's four-years-old for heaven's sake." His voice was louder than he'd meant, almost startling himself. He thought he'd only said the words in his head.

Unless something had happened to him...

Terrible thoughts started to steal into his head, gruesome and macabre. Images flitted through his mind of Charlie in various poses half-imagined and half-feared. He was dead or dying in each of the pictures gate-crashing his thoughts.

Please God, no. Not Charlie...

Taking a series of roundabouts, George eventually joined the start of Seacrest Road by which time Harriet's GPS marker was no longer bearing towards him, having turned off at a junction to the right (George's left as he made the approach), heading northward in the direction of the Midlands. Here onwards the Seacrest Road would continue unhindered for the greater part of forty-eight miles, less than half the distance between the apartment and Willoughby Rising. He'd already put thirty miles between him and Sophie. According to the satellite tracking system and Charlie's GPS coordinates, he was just nine miles west of his son's location.

The TA on George's radio interrupted the airplay, cutting short *Too Shy*, replacing it with the dulcet tones of a traffic reporter who spoke with a broad Norfolk accent, from the local BBC radio station.

"...traffic is moving steadily in and out of Norwich, with no reports of delays or major incident. Some road works on the Caister Road leading into Great Yarmouth are causing motorists some difficulties, so expect a little build-up of on-peak traffic if you're heading that way...."

George spotted a column of smoke in the distance ahead. From behind, a fire engine, sirens blaring and blue lights flashing, forced George to pull in to allow passage, speeding off towards what he guessed to be the source of the burning. It wasn't unusual for field fires during hot spells so George paid it little notice.

"...reports are just in of an incident on the Seacrest Road. Two vehicles involved, one is understood to be on fire. Emergency vehicles are on the scene, with air ambulance also in attendance...."

A glance at the tablet computer still on the passenger seat continued to display his family's' positions. His wife was steadily moving away northward, which concerned him, but Charlie's marker remained unchanged. Fear and preoccupation had blinded him to noticing a second GPS marker slowly moving (at the London apartment); his fixation deafening him even to the additional bleep that had begun. Instead, George assumed Harriet's movement alarm had sped-up, rather than consider that another member of his family – Sophie – was on the move.

"Oh no, Charlie..." Once again fear was ignited, eating into his thoughts, gruesome images flashing behind his eyes. He tried to ignore them, instead asking himself a series of questions which he hoped would highlight an alternative point of view.

Why would Charlie not be moving with his mother?

After much deliberating his rational mind could only come up with one answer: he was critically injured... or... or... worse.

He wouldn't, and couldn't consider this option. Nothing untoward had happened to his son, he was certain; but the thoughts continued to plague him. His heart was pumping hard. He felt sick with worry. He hadn't realised it, but his hands were quaking and slippery with sweat; he was gripping the steering tight, trying to lessen his shaking. Despite the July heat (it had already been a hotter-than-normal summer) an icy chill had crept over him.

The TA report ended and was abruptly replaced by the original radio station. *Kids in America* was now playing.

A minute later, George drove past the junction that a little earlier had been taken by his wife. For a second he thought to follow her... but no, he couldn't. He needed to know what had become of Charlie. Harriet was old enough to take care of herself, and although it may appear it, with the tracking device strapped to her ankle, she was never truly alone. Charlie was just four and all by himself. He was the higher priority.

Traffic ahead was slowing down to a crawl. Usually Seacrest Road would be empty perhaps save for a couple of cars every few minutes, or a tractor ambling by. Because of the car accident, as reported on the TA, vehicles had begun to queue and a short time soon after George found that his vehicle had drawn to a complete stop.

Through the windscreen he counted a dozen or slightly more cars ahead of him. Quickly unfastening his seatbelt, he opened the door and climbed out from behind the wheel. Now standing, a hand resting on the top of the open-door, he was able to view the spectacle clearly. An ambulance was parked up; three police cars and the fire engine that only a short time earlier had forced its way past him, were positioned in various places, blocking traffic and managing the incident. The air ambulance that had been detailed on the traffic report was preparing to take off, its rotors whirring noisily, sending up a gust of road dust, grit and dry air to buffet those bystanding.

George returned inside the car, leaning over to retrieve the tablet computer from the passenger seat. Using the zoom in feature within the GPS tracking programme, he used it to pinpoint his young son's position. Charlie's beacon continued to glow. He was still here (or the watch was), close by. He had not (yet) been found.

As the helicopter took off, George half-expected Charlie's GPS signal to change to red and begin to move away.

Closing the door, George advanced towards the scene of the accident. Within one hand he held the tablet computer, using it as a guide.

A policewoman noticed him approach and came forward, barring his progress. "Sir, you need to return to your vehicle."

"It's my son," started George. "I need to find my son."

George pushed passed the young policewoman and bounded around the emergency vehicles that were parked disorderly, successfully blockading the road. To his left he saw the smoking wreckage of his wife's *Toyota Prius*. To the right, the focus of six firefighters' attention, the burning wreckage of a car, its make and model beyond recognition due to the ongoing destruction from the intense flames. He shielded his face against the heat, not wishing to add to the human barbecue.

"Sir, you can't come through here. It's too dangerous!" shouted the woman police officer from behind, making a grab for George.

"CHARLIE!" he shouted, shrugging off the policewoman's clutches, who, unbalanced, fell to the road. A quick scan of the tablet computer indicated Charlie's location was thirty yards away. He trotted in the GPS coordinates direction and then broke out into a full sprint. "CHARLIE!" he bellowed. "CHAR-LIE!!"

There was a moment's pause when the Earth seemingly stood still and for all around there came an eerie silence, almost expectant with foreboding, like the sound sometimes reported before a volcano erupts – cacophonous noise at an ear-splitting level – to absolute nothing...

"Daddy?" Breaking the quiet, a small figure crept out from the underbrush, his face wet from crying, the sling harnessing his arm blackened with grime and his clothes bloodied, vomit coated and torn in places. The Earth suddenly began to move again in tandem with all its surrounding brouhaha.

"Charlie!" George was just twenty-feet away from his son, a smile spreading upon his face. It was such relief to see his boy safe and well after fearing and agonising the worst. It had been less than twenty-four hours since the boy had last been in his company but the feeling of elation was easily akin to that experienced by fathers and sons reunited after a long parting. To those observing, George might well have come to collect his son after five years in Australia.

"Daddy!"

Slowing down as he came within six feet of his son, the sudden locomotive of a man charged into him from the right side, taking him completely off guard, knocking him hard and painfully to the ground, his tablet computer clattering to the tarmac, its screen becoming a spider's web of inky-black cracks. A burly policeman straddled him.

"Now, sir! You were told to return to your car." The policeman was applying handcuffs.

"But it's my boy," George was struggling with the large policeman sitting on his back. "Just my boy..."

"Please, don't hurt him," Charlie started crying again. "Please!"

The policeman took one look at the four-year-old, saw his banged up features, his arm in a sling and sighed. Using a key, he removed the handcuffs from George's wrists.

"Okay, sir. Return to your car and wait. This is no place to let a child out to play." He didn't give the boy's cut and bedraggled appearance a second look.

"Thanks." George stood up, retrieved the tablet computer, winced in dismay from the sight of the damage and drew Charlie close to him, a protective arm resting over his shoulder. Together they headed back to the car.

The policewoman said something angrily to her colleague as George passed. The policeman shrugged and walked off unperturbed. Within a couple of minutes they were safely confined within the *Peugeot*. Charlie was safe and secured at the back behind the passenger seat.

George threw the broken tablet into the glove compartment. The damaged LCD screen rendered the gadget useless. Currently he had no way of tracking his wife. He hit the steering wheel hard with the heel of his hand, frustrated. He resisted the urge to curse, the loss of his tracking ability akin to losing eye sight or the ability to walk. He sighed and put things into perspective. His son was a little battered and bruised, but he was okay. He was now safe.

"Charlie, I was so scared," he started, "tell me what happened. Tell me what's happened to mummy."

At first he acted as though he'd not heard the question. "I don't want to talk about it," replied Charlie finally, reticent. He turned away to the door and closed his eyes just as a tear leaked out beneath one of the lids. Behind closed eyes his mind conjured the scene of his mother's abduction, her capture and stowage within the boot of the big, shiny car.

"They can't hurt you Charlie, and I want to get mummy back. I promise I *can* get her back. But I need your help."

After a long minute Charlie's resolve caved in. He re-opened his moist eyes and turned from the side of the car to face his father. He juddered involuntarily from the memory. "They took her," he whispered. "The bad men took mummy away."

A car horn blared from behind aggressively, three loud bursts. Ahead of George traffic had started dribbling forward once again and the driver of the car immediately behind (*BMW*) was loath to have his journey delayed any further despite progress moving at a sloth's pace. Now that the air ambulance had departed and debris had been cleared from the carriageway, a policeman had opened up one side of the road and was directing traffic alternately using hand signals and curt gestures, slowly dispersing the tailback that was spreading up and down either side of Seacrest Road.

The policeman who'd rugby tackled George to the ground was beckoning him forward with a hand signal.

George keyed the ignition and set the vehicle into motion. A moment later he was passing Dominic Schilling's smouldering *Mercedes* carcase and the wreckage of his wife's car. He tried to blot the images out and concentrate on getting his son home to safety and reuniting his family. Dwelling on thoughts of his wife and what her captors might be doing to her had to be put on hold – for the moment at least. His son had experienced one RTA too many in his young life, an ordeal that would haunt Charlie's dreams for many years beyond his childhood; he didn't want to expose him to that again by being distracted and not paying enough attention on the road.

CHAPTER FOURTEEN
RYAN

SATELLITE IMAGES WERE PLAYING on the large screen that took up the wall. For once there was little sound filling the room, all analysts and operatives were sitting motionless, voices hushed, lulled by the events captured on the wall where all eyes were directed. It wasn't ever this quiet, not even when the planes hit the towers on 9/11; not even at night when only a handful on late shift occupied the operations room, nursing cups of coffees to fight intruding sleep and the unavoidable boredom, where the cleaners kept them company, pushing their *Henry* vacuum cleaners and emptied the bins.

Samuel had descended from the mezzanine level and was standing next to Ryan's desk. Ryan had stood up so not to feel so intimidated. Nothing he hated more than having someone tower above him whilst seated at his desk – it made him relive the ordeal that had been school. Even standing he was dwarfed by the not-so-gentle giant.

"When did this happen?" demanded the Security and Intelligence Director. His tone was not friendly and urged caution to any who dared to answer.

A timid man in his forties raised a hand to speak. Sweat had stained his light-blue long-sleeved shirt dark and had spread beneath his armpits, a by-product of his heightened nervousness and anxiety. "Ahh, ergh… Just before the police arrived at the scene, sir," he said.

"Who are you?"

"Ja-Jason, s-s-sir," he stammered.

"How *was* this missed, Jason?" Samuel demanded. He whirled around the room: "Anyone?"

A bespectacled young woman dared to speak. She looked more like a stereotypical secretary than an intelligence analyst. Naturally blonde, her golden locks cascading to just below her shoulders, slender of frame with a delicate, triangular face, her chin prominent but not unattractive; most the men in the room often found themselves distracted by her pleasing appearance. The name plate placed beneath her monitor identified her as Emily Porter.

"Our focus was on Grampian House," she ventured, "George's 'not so' secret apartment. We stumbled upon it completely by accident two days ago and believed we'd located the girl. We were following up on our leads."

"What? All of you?"

Behind them, on a loop, the large screen continued to play footage from the overhead spy satellite; images of Harriet Jennings attacking what appeared to be a man on a mobile phone with a club-like weapon. Obsessively, they watched the overhead images of a man appearing from the cover of some trees, creeping up behind Harriet.

"Are you seeing this?" Samuel was shaking his head as he watched the scene play out. Harriet was then overpowered from the use of a *Taser*, falling to the road, paralysed, visibly shaking from the electric shock. The second man, talking to the subdued mobile man, probably checking that he was all right, before manhandling her into the boot of the car. Then the image became distorted, the picture bouncing up and down, becoming snowy, the image fading into ghostly shadows, then a small warning box popped up on the centre of the screen:

SIGNAL LOST

"What did we just see?" demanded the Director.

"Opportunists?" prompted Ryan, baffled by what he had witnessed.

"D'you think?" answered Samuel abrasively. "What about the events before the *dynamic duo* showed up?" He walked away from his assistant, fighting the rage that was bubbling beneath the surface and the urge to punch something (*or someone).*

"The satellite wasn't in range – this was all we've been able to see." Ryan sat back down, earlier fears of feeling intimidated overshadowed by the feelings of inadequacy heard in the Director's voice.

"Okay people, I want to know who they are. I want to know how come they were able to do what Blighty's finest was unable to." He started up the flight of stairs to his office. "Simply, I want answers. A bottle of *Moet and Chandon* to the person who can answer: how the bloody hell did they know to find her there when we'd missed it?"

No sooner had the door of the Director's office closed behind him the noise level once again grew to a crescendo. Ryan tossed his pen down and let out a deep breath. He hadn't realised it, but he'd been nervously chewing at it, bits of plastic were still in his mouth. He spat them out discretely, becoming aware that a number of people milling around were watching him, waiting for instructions.

"What?!" The 'millers' scattered like a flock of birds disturbed from pecking the ground by a Tom on the prowl. He turned to the bespectacled woman seated close by.

"Emily, what question is more important than any asked by the Director? Your thoughts?"

The woman in the glasses stepped over, thought lines creasing her brow. Despite her secretarial appearance, she was Kaplan Ratcliff's most senior Intelligence Analyst, someone Ryan trusted more than any – and it wasn't just because of a longstanding private connection they'd kept secret, a fact that, if known, would lead many to believe her position within the company was out of favouritism. She took a long moment to consider the question, mulling over it deeply before conceding defeat. The puzzled look gave way to one of resignation.

"Let me answer that with another question: Where is the boy?" Ryan stood up, taking control. "Our focus has been on George's wife... but the boy... where is he?"

"He must still be out there," she interjected, excitedly. "Unless... those two (indicating Harriet's abductors by jabbing a finger towards their fuzzy images on the screen on the wall) found him after the satellite feed failed."

"Possibly, but it's worth looking into don'cha think?" Not waiting for a reply, Ryan continued. "Get a team out there looking for him."

"I'm on it boss." She trotted back to her desk, picked up her phone and made an outgoing call, her voice high in pitch and full of urgency.

"You two... Crocket and Tubby," Ryan was picking on two assistants who acted like a double act from the 1980s – hence the nicknames (a nod towards the vintage show *Miami Vice*) – they were two of the less offensive monikers bandied about. In truth he'd never bothered to remember their names, thinking he'd rather save the memory space. One was called Matt Homer, the other Jacob Bowers. "I want you two to find out who these clowns are who have taken Harriet Jennings, and where they have taken her to. Start looking at CCTV footage on all roads leading to and from the satellite location. Get a make and model on that car, then get registration details." *Tweedle Dum* and *Tweedle Dee* stood nodding furiously like a couple of *Churchill Insurance* dogs. They made notes as they went. "Time is money, guys. When you have this information," Ryan smiled, "give me a holler."

Ryan crossed over to another bank of desks where a man wearing a wireless headset was standing looking agitated. Moments earlier he had been shouting into the mouthpiece of the digital radio transmitter jutting out like a single vibrissa to the side of his face, a cat with one whisker. Before the Director had come down to the lower floor, all faces had been turned in his direction, eaves dropping his co-ordinated operation of attack. The Grampian House operation had been directed by this man, a former commander with the SAS and Alpha Team's in-house team leader. He was stocky and seemed not to have a neck, his square head perched centrally upon his thickset shoulders. A second, willowy man sat next to him looking decidedly fragile in comparison.

The smaller man looked up. "Alpha Team are down, sir. Bravo Team are on standby, but orders have just been given to stand down."

"Orders? What orders, by who?" Ryan did nothing to hide the agitation from his voice.

"Tom Kaplan, sir. He took charge as soon as Alpha Team were hit." Ryan took a step back mentally and physically. *What was going on?*

Tom Kaplan was the CEO of the company. To most he was a phantom, a ghost, nothing more than a name to scare young children at night or threaten with to combat unruly behaviour. To his knowledge, no one, not even the Board of Directors, had ever seen Kaplan in the flesh – though that was just a rumour circulated to add an air of mystery and foreboding to his reputation – a sort of *Emperor* from *Star Wars* sort of character trait. Very few had even seen his photograph, so elusive and reclusively obsessed he was.

"Why wasn't I told?" Ryan was second in command and yet things were happening beyond his knowledge or influence.

"You just were, sir," replied the team leader sarcastically.

Ryan shook his head in disbelief, muttering a curse and walked off.

What the hell was going on? Why was Kaplan interfering? So much had happened in so little a time – could some blame be apportioned to him? After all, almost immediately after warning George earlier that afternoon about the hospital strike, events had snowballed way out of control.

But did they ever have control?

Needing to clear his head, get some fresh air, he walked out of the room, opening security doors with the electronic pass that hung around his neck on a blue lanyard, the words *MAKE A DIFFERENCE* printed continuously on the fabric. His picture embellished the pass with an image that would have better suited a cadaver on a mortician's table. His eyes were shut, his lips purply-blue, his face appeared ashen-white. He couldn't remember the circumstances surrounding that picture but thought it must have been taken on a day when he'd been ill.

Exiting the building via a side door – a services entrance – he walked down a short alley that took him to a busy road. Large commercial bins (black with green hinged lids) lined the passage, one overflowing with full black refuse bags, spilling its rubbish to the ground where the wind distributed it the length and breadth of the path. At the end of the alley he joined a sprawling commercial avenue with shops and businesses lining either side; he crossed the road, darting through a break in traffic and entered into a small coffee shop nestled between a newsagents and a dusty old empty shop, boarded up and decorated grotesquely with bright spray paint graffiti.

A small bell 'dinged' as he stepped into the coffee shop, the telltale aromas associated with such establishments assailing his nostrils and causing his stomach to do a 360° somersault. Fresh coffee relaxed and helped him think. The smell alone had soothing properties, immediately calming his nerves. He ordered a regular sized black coffee, refusing any attempts of upgrade or cross-selling ("No, I don't want a choc-chip banana side salad with that.").

"Do you have a phone I could use?" he asked the coffee shop attendant who'd taken a few moments to prepare his drink; a skinny, pale youth of indeterminable age, his greasy black hair reflecting an overhead fluorescent light, who looked blank, as though the question had been posed on *Mastermind*. Ryan exchanged a fiver for his steaming beverage, though it could easily have been for the answer to his question. A good cop bribing an informant for an illicit tip.

"No," was the curt reply as he reached into a cash register. He handed Ryan a handful of change. It was service without a smile. The youth was more accustomed to washing his hair than exchanging pleasantries, the Assistant Intelligence Officer mused - which would be saying something.

Taking a seat in a dark, quiet corner, Ryan reluctantly removed his mobile phone from his pocket.

He was loath to use his own mobile – he knew better than to do it – but there was little time. If he was to ever get close to *him* he needed the man's trust.

Reaching into his trouser pocket he retrieved the slip of paper that he'd used earlier. He considered what he was about to do for a moment. Gut instinct was warning him against what he was contemplating. He knew better, but couldn't help himself.

Ignoring years of experience and better judgement, he took a leap of faith and with it, an enormous risk; he proceeded. Using stubby fingers, he carefully keyed the number into his mobile phone. Once the number appeared in its entirety on the screen, Ryan took a moment to reflect, considering his actions.

What are you doing? his conscience demanded.

Then – hesitantly – he pressed the green 'call' icon.

The digital ringtone reverberated through the mobile's small speaker almost immediately. *Is it me*, he thought, *or did it sound louder than normal?*

A long moment passed and Ryan felt nervous. He felt like a man cheating on his wife or partner. In some respects this was no different. After all, it was just as great an act of betrayal, with some arguing that it was even worse.

"It's for the greater good," he whispered to himself, answering his conscience, trying to appease the guilt and settle those nerves.

"*Hello?*" Like before, the voice sounded tinny, distant. Interference crackled on the line, raspy and whistling.

"It's me George." Despite his nerves jangling his voice never betrayed him. He sounded confident, in control. Almost authoritative.

At first, the crackle of interference on the line was all Ryan got in reply, then the person at the other end spoke. "*Wait a minute,*" he said, "*I just need to pull over.*" A long silence followed before George spoke again, this time more clearly. "*Your warning was too late. They got her. They've got my wife...*"

Ryan exhaled noisily. This wasn't as easy as he thought it was going to be. "I know George, but 'they' are not who you think. It's not us. It's not the corporation; it's someone else."

"*Who?*"

Ryan took a moment. How could he reply? He didn't know. Unseen, he was shaking his head; his free hand was turning his hot coffee absently on the table in front of him, the steaming beverage scolding his fingers ever so slightly. He was looking around the room nervously, over his shoulders and occasionally glancing out through the large glass window. "We don't know." He sighed.

"*We? Who are you? Do I know you?*"

Ryan sighed. "I work for Kaplan Ratcliff. We've never met George, but you knew my daughter." Ryan found his throat constrict. The memory of her brought a lump to his throat. It was over two years but the loss was still raw. It still tore at his heart. How beautiful she had been. How kind and wonderful; everything one would want in a daughter. She was on the level, hardworking and very clever. He remembered her when she had been just a kid, going on holiday, fun days in the park; or just messing about in the garden. He remembered Penshurst Place, west of Kent, on a bright midsummer's day, looking radiant. It was at Penshurst Place he'd first taken his daughter with the other girl who he'd go on to treat and love almost as much as his own flesh and blood. The two playing together came to mind, a myriad of images flashing up, long ago memories. They often came, and like Christmases, went – superseded by the abundance of regret and loathing that he felt.

He didn't think he could say her name, but then surprised himself when he heard the syllables pass his lips:

"Clara." He fought back the tears and the anger that burned within the pit of his stomach.

"*Ryan*?" George whispered it. Clara had mentioned him often. The ups and downs between them; how she provided him with an easy ear when things in their life had soured, or the turbulent times when she had been rebellious as a teen, making things near impossible between them. Clara had regularly opened up to him. A regular shoulder to cry on; he'd learnt it all, rough and smooth.

"Listen George, I'm sorry about Harriet." Composing himself, "We are looking into it. You need to find Charlie. From what we know, he wasn't taken."

"*I know. I have him here.*"

Ryan audibly sighed with relief.

"You need to get off Seacrest Road. We have agents en route even as I speak."

"*What about my family*? *Meredith and Stanley*?"

"We don't know where they are… yet. They'll be safe whilst it stays that way."

"*Okay.*"

"You do have a problem though. Your project piece is on the loose. I'm sorry, George, there's only so much I can do without blowing my cover. We made for her as soon as you'd left your apartment."

"*How did you know*?"

"That's not important. I just didn't want anything to happen to you..." *yet*! "...your wife and son gave me the perfect reason to get you out of harm's way."

"*You have... Sophie?*"

Ryan caught sight of two big, burly men on the other side of the road. In black uniform, suited with matching blazers, both parading the KRBLS Military Division insignia badge stitched to their breast pockets, and ties that could have doubled at a funeral; they waited at the road's edge, itching to cross. They stood out on this hot, July day in their uniforms, though despite this neither man perspired. Most passersby wore loose T-shirts and shorts or thin, strappy tops and thin, billowing skirts. Sandals and flip-flops were the order of the day or trainers worn without socks.

"George, I've got to go." Ryan stood up fast, the top of his right leg jerking the table, knocking the coffee over, hot liquid spilling across its surface.

"*No Ryan, tell me what's happened to her*!"

Ryan was running for the door, his mobile pressed against his ear.

"She got away is all I know; but she's being followed. It gets worse. Tom Kaplan is now involved. He's taken charge. Listen, George, I'm out of time... if you don't hear from me again... good luck!" Ryan hit the cut off icon on the Smartphone as he hurried out of the coffee shop; startled faces watched him exit (including the coffee shop attendant), the bell on the door jingling excitedly from the force.

The two burly men on the opposite side of the road did not fail to notice Ryan leaving in a hurry; one raised a wrist and started talking animatedly. Ryan knew he was talking into a concealed, wireless microphone attached to a cufflink. He'd often worn them himself. They were standard issue and all security personnel wore them giving them instant communication to the operations centre. He glanced at them as he started to run away. Both were now hurrying across the road, neither looking nor heeding the traffic that sped by, confirming that they were indeed coming after him.

Horns blared and tyres screeched. Ryan continued regardless.

One of his pursuers was clipped by a taxi; he tumbled to the road hard, skidding on his knees. Further horns sounded from angry motorists forced to break hard and stop. No one liked their journeys delayed, no matter the cause or however fleeting it would be.

Momentarily the chase was over for the felled security man, however not for long. Chancing another glance, Ryan confirmed that he was still being pursued by both security personnel, albeit one was limping and hanging back a good few yards.

Turning the next corner, taking an alley beside a *Nandos* restaurant, Ryan hoped to lose his pursuers through the maze of narrow passages, the myriad of back alleys and dead ends that he knew were sprawled around this side of the city.

What he hadn't expected was to find the very first stretch of alley – which he'd decisively hurtled down, and which extended for about forty meters – to abruptly end around the next darkened corner.

He couldn't help cursing: "Damn it!"

Ahead, he found to further his chagrin, two large steel refuse bins, a number of empty plastic crates and a dozen beer barrels stacked up ready for collection, and the back entrance to a *Conservative Social Club* (locked from the inside). The smell of stale beer and alcohol drifted over him, intermingled with the odours exuding from the *Nandos* restaurant. He barely noticed.

Whirling round desperately, Ryan sought a way out, another direction to take, an escape route. Anywhere to avoid being collared.

Wildly he looked up, and then back to the direction he came, his eyes darting all over. He trotted back to the original alley, and stopped.

Finding no escape – there *was* no escape – he could see that to go on was futile, the chase was up; he looked down forlornly. It was hopeless. Out of breath and out of luck, he bent over, gasping for air; hunkered down, he watched the two security personnel as they approached; one half a dozen meters ahead of the other, running towards him, beginning to slow to a jog.

One of the big men, the one limping who had been knocked to the road by the taxi, had laid a hand on a *Taser* gun that was attached to his belt. His eyes were willing Ryan to try something – anything – to make him want to use it.

"Mr Barber," started the first security guard, slightly breathless. "It's over. The Director wants to see you."

Ryan said nothing and just nodded. He stood up straight and walked forward. He recognised him. He was someone he knew. He'd used him on occasion when things needed to get 'messy'. He was almost someone he'd previously counted on as someone he could trust. He even had his number saved on his mobile.

The second security guard had pulled up beside his colleague, an angry look plastered across his face. Ryan was under no illusion that he was being blamed for the injury causing the second man to limp.

Ryan didn't know the second man; he was one of Samuel's recruits, probably a former soldier or marine. They all tended to be ex-military – better equipped to deal with any eventuality, and more disciplined. He looked him up and down, his eyes stopping at his knees. He cleared his throat:

"I think you need to get that looked at." Ryan was indicating the man's leg. His trousers were torn at the knee and Ryan could see crimson through the shredded black fabric.

The security officer grunted, stepping forward menacingly.

"Okay," Ryan said nonchalantly, half-smiling. He raised his hands in surrender. It was almost comical. "I'll come quietly."

Together the security personnel flanked the Assistant Intelligence Officer and escorted him back to the command centre where Samuel Jackson steeled himself for the confrontation, bitterly disappointed.

CHAPTER FIFTEEN

HARRIET

HARRIET AWOKE TO FIND herself seated and in complete darkness. Initially she thought she was blind, before she realised that by opening and closing her eyes she could feel the soft material of a scarf or blindfold wrapped around her head. It was tight and allowed no light to penetrate.

Wherever she was, it was silent, like death, she imagined. She started to worry that she had been buried alive, though she soon dismissed those ungrounded thoughts.

As her faculties started to tune in, awareness of her situation began to filter through; a gradual feeling returned as her senses began to awaken. Pain receptors screamed throughout her body, highlighting her many injuries – mostly minor, considering – sustained during the accident earlier that day. Aches, stiffness and soreness lanced all over.

Blocking out the many discomforts, she tried to focus on her situation and surroundings. In addition to her covered eyes, she was gagged and her hands bound behind her back. An attempt at moving confirmed that her ankles were also secured together, tied to the chair legs.

She was completely restrained and trapped.

Cable ties or cuffs and gaffer tape had been used in good measure and with her sudden burst of agitation and straining she realised that there would be little, or no movement… not without either help or a sharp implement in her hand that may have given her the slightest chance to work the ligatures from her wrists and ankles.

She was breathing hard she found – made harder by the tape obstructing her mouth. She tried blowing against the adhesive swathe, her cheeks expanding like a hamster's, the exertion hurting her face to bursting point; her laboured breathing causing her chest to ache.

She screamed against the roof of her mouth and through her nose as loud as she could muster; a long, constrained noise that sounded like a high-pitched klaxon; it was loud in her head but barely filled the room. There was no echo or resonance bouncing off the walls. The room that she was in was small – she could sense that – but it wasn't a coffin, for that she was grateful.

Several more vain attempts at working the restraints loose were to no avail. It was no use. The shackles around her ankles confirmed that she was powerless. Fear clawed at her. She started to panic and sob.

WHERE AM I? She screamed in her head. Fear gripped her further when she started to remember the events of that afternoon, playing out like an extended episode of *EastEnders* within her memory. Realisation swept over her like a tsunami:

CHARLIE!

Oh my God... my son... my baby boy... what of my Charlie...?

Harriet sobbed harder, her body shaking from the convulsions, like she was having a fit, having what her own mother called an 'episode'.

"Harriet Jennings. Calm yourself." The voice filled the void, amplified by internal speakers built into the ceiling. She heard it coming from above, loud, clear – almost godlike. "Don't fight it and you'll be okay." The voice had a slight accent. *Australian? Canadian? American?* She couldn't tell for sure. She tried calming herself by breathing slower through her nose.

It was little or no use. She could not calm down, not under these circumstances, not whilst trussed up like a turkey and not knowing what had happened to her son.

No matter her own tribulations, thoughts of her son prevailed, all alone in the bushes and trees along Seacrest Road – they overpowered everything else. She was scared, but only for her son's safety.

Just four-years-old.

FOUR-YEARS-OLD!

How long had he been on his own? An hour? Two? Ten hours? A day? A week? The concept of time was lost. A minute on his own was too long and the fear of what might have happened to him started to bite from within her chest, like a hungry rat chewing an exit from a place of entrapment.

Panic began to well up again, threatening to engulf her. She fought against it without success, the urge to vomit was too much. Blocked by the gaffer tape across her mouth, her cheeks once again ballooned out and she began to choke. Thin tendrils of liquid sprayed from her nose. She began to asphyxiate, her body convulsing. She had the appearance of an epileptic having a seizure, another instance of what her mother would have called an 'episode'.

The door to the room burst open and a man in a tan suit ran to where Harriet was restrained, ripping off the gaffer tape in one swift, deft movement. Vomit sprayed out across the room, some splashing her saviour's trousers and shoes.

Harriet coughed and spluttered, tears leaking from her eyes.

"Here." The man poured a small cup of water from a jug placed on a corner table and was gently tipping it against her lips. Harriet gulped it down, the aftertaste from the retching and nearly choking strong in her mouth. Before it was able to settle she threw it back up, emptying her whole stomach across the floor.

The man crossed the small room to the corner table and poured a further cup of water. He waited for Harriet to relax and offered the cup again. Harriet accepted it, taking smaller mouthfuls, sipping slower.

"Better?" His voice was soothing, like a placating parent.

Harriet nodded. The screaming and the retching had made her throat sore. She didn't trust any sound to come from her mouth even had she tried speaking.

"Good." Using a cotton handkerchief, he wiped Harriet's mouth. Flecks of upchuck clung to her chin. The man, continuing his paternal role, smiled. "There," he said. "We took the liberty of patching you up. You were a bit banged up after..." he trailed off.

Harriet became aware of a dressing taped to her forehead – when she furrowed her brow she could feel it pull taut, aggravating the cut beneath it. Also, she thought she could feel bandaging wrapped around her hands below the cuffs (which she'd now assumed as the restraint of choice, owing to the cold touch and weighty feel). Involuntarily, Harriet heard herself ask: "What have you done with Charlie?" Her throat was hoarse and it hurt to talk, so the question came out in more of a rasp, almost a whisper.

The man didn't reply; instead he untied the black scarf that blotted out the world. He dropped it to the floor. Harriet closed her eyes from the immediate blinding white intrusion, wincing and blinking back tears from the intense light. Bright fluorescent tubes burned above, dazzling further by the brilliant-white walls that enclosed her.

After a couple of minutes she found focus. Harriet allowed herself to look upon her captor. In his early to mid-thirties, he carried the looks and stature of a famous catwalk model. Chiselled jaw line, blue eyes. His blond hair was neat and short, combed with a left side parting. She could tell from how he stood that he worked out and took care of his appearance, though he was over a day unshaven. She could also tell by how he looked that he was American. Without even talking, she could tell, but his voice had all but confirmed it.

"I'm sorry you've had to go through this Harriet," he said. "Really I am." He was perched on the edge of the table where he'd returned the jug and Perspex cup.

"Who are you? Where am I?"

"All in good time Harriet." He made to leave.

"Please don't go!" she begged. "Where's Charlie?" pleading, "he's just a little boy."

A hand on the door handle, the American stopped and turned to Harriet, a puzzled look upon his face. "Mam, we don't have *Charlie*," he said. The look dissolved as he added, a hand gesturing towards the mess around the seated woman, "I'll get someone to clean this up."

"Hello!" she shouted. "I need a toilet! Can anyone hear me? ARE YOU LISTENING?" Harriet was rocking back and forth on the chair. Her bladder screamed for relief, her body was willing her to go but her mind told her to keep it together, urging her to retain her dignity. They may have taken her freedom, but they'd never take her dignity... you could only give that away.

Time seemed to be passing slowly to a point where she was convinced it now stood still. She'd been left on her own in the room for over an hour, maybe two, she wasn't sure. Time had lost all meaning in this room. No one had visited since the American, despite the offer of getting someone to clean up the vomit spattered floor. The smell was unbearable.

Paranoid, she had thought she could feel eyes on her, a feeling that was confirmed when she spied the small surveillance camera placed in the furthest corner of the room, above the door. A small red LED lamp indicated that it was in operation. It winked at her rhythmically, almost hypnotic as she studied it.

"SOMEBODY LET ME USE THE BATHROOM!" she screamed.

The sound of keys jangled and the door opened. The American appeared once again. He carried in a bedpan and placed it on the corner table alongside the half-empty jug.

"This is the best we can do for the moment," he replied. Using a flick-knife the American removed the cable ties securing Harriet's ankles to the chair legs and then from his pocket he retrieved a small key. Walking behind the restrained woman, he inserted the key into the hand cuffs and removed them.

Harriet turned and watched him leave the room.

"Well that's just perfect!" she spat, standing up on unsteady legs. Her limbs felt numb and wobbly from sitting for so long, her muscles weak and pulpy as though made from *Play-Doh*. She staggered across to the table, almost fell owing to the injury to her leg sustained during the accident, and used the table's edge to hold herself up. She picked up the bedpan with her other hand, a look of disgust on her face. She glanced up at the glowing LED light above the door. "Go ahead and watch for all I care!"

Across a short hallway, within a small box room that was no larger than a utility cupboard, dark in contrast to the cell where Harriet found herself, sat Dominic, sporting a bandage wrapped around his head. With him was the older American, Mitch.

Mitch had a matching dressing to that on Harriet, secured to his head, thanks to the woman they now watched. Unlike Harriet he also paraded a purply-blue bump. Slightly concussed, he'd sought medical attention (together with Dominic) as soon as he'd secured the target at the safe location.

In front of them was a bank of a dozen CCTV monitors, each display about fourteen inches in diameter. Most of the screens were off, but one was on. Harriet was preparing herself to go to the toilet. Mitch was too busy making a cup of soup to be interested. He emptied a sachet of tomato flavouring into a steaming mug of hot water, using a pen to stir it.

The younger American stepped into the office a moment later, tossing the handcuffs onto a table.

"Well," Mitch licked the excess soup from the end of his pen and placed it back into the breast pocket of his shirt, "d'you think she'll play along with our game?"

"She'll play along. One way or another."

"You know Dom… you should have told us her son was with her. It's a shame we left him behind. It would have made things a lot easier and given us more leverage."

"Well *DERR*! Maybe the concussion had something to do with my lapse of memory!" Dominic stood up, grunting: "I'm going to go and get some air." He pushed past Brayden muttering: "Prat," under his breath.

The door to the surveillance room closed and Brayden smiled towards his colleague. "I love the British," he said. "They have such a knack with words... such a great vocabulary."

Mitch shrugged indifferently.

Harriet was still standing – one leg taking most of the weight whilst the other hung loosely – when the American walked back into the room. At least ten minutes had passed since he'd left her to her business.

"I trust you feel much better," he said wrinkling his nose at the cloying smell of vomit and the fragrance of urine in the room. "Sorry that housekeeping hasn't been by to clean this up," he indicated the mess about the floor. "Staffing shortage."

Harriet stood quietly, impassive.

"My name is Brayden Scott. I work for, shall we say, an interested third party. I have it under good authority that you may have access to, or information about, something that is very valuable, very dangerous and very useful; if in the wrong hands, it poses a very real security threat to my country."

"I don't know what you are talking about Mr Scott." Harriet limped back to the chair that she'd woken to find herself attached to and sat down. On close inspection, the bruising sustained in the car accident to her left leg, just below the knee, was swollen to twice its normal size; a bubble of fluid had appeared just below the surface of the skin and threatened to erupt. Ignoring the pain she diverted her attention to the American in the room. She felt a little intimidated by him, like a naughty school girl sitting in the headmaster's office.

Brayden considered the woman for a moment; her banged up features gave her the look of a mugging victim. "Harriet, I think you do. And you are going to tell me what you know... and do a little something for us," he walked around the room slowly, "... one way or another."

"Are you trying to frighten me?"

Brayden smiled and shook his head gently from one side to another. "Not yet – this is nothing - but soon. First, I need you to understand something. The organisation I work for is not afraid to use whatever it takes to get what we want. We are quite resourceful."

"And what organisation would that be, Mr Scott?"

"Well," he chuckled, "we're not the *WWF*, let's put it that way... but that's beside the point. The point is we usually get what we want. Now, Harriet, if you don't mind me calling you that, let's put all unpleasantness behind us."

For a long moment there was silence. Brayden walked to the other side of the room, his back to the woman, allowing her time to consider her options.

"What is it you want?" she asked finally.

Brayden walked back and stood in front of the seated woman. "Before I answer that, you should understand that I know all about your husband's work, about the girl Sophie, and *her* abilities. I know that you've been on the run for almost two years, and that there are unanswered questions surrounding the explosion at your husband's research laboratory."

"How do you know all this?"

"I've already said Harriet, we are quite resourceful."

"My husband had nothing to do with that explosion. We are innocent."

"If that was true, why do you run?"

"Because they mean to kill us like they killed his lab team."

Brayden shrugged. "I think your husband has been liberal with the truth. If what you say was right, then I can understand your reasons. But I don't believe he's been honest – in fact I know he hasn't – but that's all by the by. That's not why we're here."

"Okay, so what then?"

"So, Harriet... you have the ability to persuade someone to help us in procuring something very valuable."

"George would never give Sophie up."

"Calm down, calm down," he ushered her with lowering hands, as though he were urging her to put something dangerous down. "Harriet, hear me out." Brayden crossed to the corner table and leant against it once again. "We don't want Sophie," he said earnestly, thinking: *Not yet!* "But we do need her help."

"What is it you want?"

"We want her to steal something."

"Something?" she quizzed.

"Just a diamond."

"A diamond? All this is about a robbery?" she sneered. "You're nothing more than common criminals?"

"I assure you we are more than that," Brayden chuckled.

"George would never agree to it."

"Well, I guess that's where you come into it." Brayden's smile disappeared and his tone turned serious. "Your husband will either help us liberate this diamond we so very much want, *or* he will collect your body parts, piece by piece, in the mail until either he eventually complies, or there's nothing left of you to send back."

Harriet allowed the gravity of what the American had said sink in before speaking. Half a minute passed.

"How do I know I can trust you?"

Brayden smiled again – he was always smiling – and shrugged. "You can't, but you've little choice." Reaching into his trousers he removed a mobile phone and handed it to the seated woman. "Here. Call your husband. Let him know you are all right, then tell him what we want. Make sure he understands the severity of the situation."

"Okay. What then?" Harriet rolled the handset over and over in her hands for a moment.

Brayden smiled ruefully. Reaching into his trouser pocket he retrieved a tube of *Extra Strong Mints* and pressed one out. He offered the sweets to Harriet. She waved them away.

Sucking on a mint, he returned his attention to Harriet. "Tell him to meet us in *Ed's Easy Diner* in the London *Trocadero* tomorrow, 12:00 p.m. He can order lunch, they do a fantastic burger. We will give him further instructions there."

Harriet righted the mobile and pressed a button to illuminate the screen. She proceeded to key in her husband's mobile number and then hit the green 'call' button. A few seconds passed before the ringing tone started. She imagined her husband's phone ringing, the opening chords of a *Queen* song filling the void wherever he was currently located. The ringing tone continued for longer than she expected and when she had all but given up on it being answered, the ringing tone was replaced by silence. Then:

Hello? The voice was distant and tiny, also somewhat metallic. The line was crackling with interference.

"George? It's Harry," she said.

Mitch and Dominic sat in the small surveillance cupboard glancing every so often towards the bank of monitors in front of them. Still only one was currently activated. Through a set of speakers they listened to the telephone conversation between Harriet and her husband George, Brayden having configured the surveillance equipment to tap into the call being made on his mobile. Not only did the equipment play the call for all to hear, it also recorded it for future playback and analysis.

Despite the significance of the call, Mitch showed more interest in his cup of soup which was now cool enough to drink. He slurped at it noisily; a thick trickle of dark orange liquid ran a line down his chin.

Dominic gave the balding guy a disgusted look.

Undeterred by the Englishman's look of contempt, upon finishing the soup he belched loudly. "That's better," he said, before using the back of his hand to wipe the residue that ran down the lower part of his face.

"You're disgusting, d'you know that?"

"All part of the package deal," Mitch replied airily, silent satisfaction at how easy it was to get under the younger man's skin.

CHAPTER SIXTEEN

SOPHIE

"HELLO MEREDITH. SO THIS is where you've been hiding."

Meredith was stunned into silence, overcome by the emotion that came with seeing the friend she thought lost when her father had uprooted and moved them from the old house. She broke out into a big cheesy 'clown's' grin that threatened to split her whole face in two.

"Wo-ah, this is not real," Stanley said sceptically. He was looking at the blonde girl that appeared in the mirror as though seeing the coolest illusion in the world. "Is this some kind of magic trick, like in *Snow White*?" he started to laugh a lunatic's cackle. "Mirror mirror, on the wall, who's the *ugliest* of them all..." then putting on a girl voice, he ventriloquially mimicked the girl in the mirror: "Meredith," starting to laugh hysterically.

Meredith punched her brother in the arm.

"Hey! That hurt!"

Meredith scowled at Stanley before turning to the mirror. "I'm sorry about him... my brother is an idiot half the time, and a complete moron for the rest."

"Hello Stanley," Sophie said, walking closer to the mirror so that she stood more in prominence. "I've heard a lot about you."

Taken aback, Stanley shook his head, as though trying to clear a dream from his mind. He spoke slowly: "You... know... my... name?"

"I know all there is to know about you Stanley Theodore Jennings."

Stanley looked sternly at his sister, his eyes stabbing daggers at her. He hated his middle name and now Meredith was sharing it with the entire world. Why did he have to be burdened with an old fogey name like *Theodore*? Just because it was the name afforded to his grandfather, whom he was named after, and who he had not seen since before all the moving and hiding, he thought it a bit cruel of his parents to burden him in such a way.

Meredith began to laugh. "Stanley. Meet Sophie… she's a *friend*."

"Actually, Meredith… Stanley… I am a bit *more* than a just a friend," she went sheepish. "You see, I've not been entirely honest."

"What do you mean? Are you saying you're NOT our friend?" Meredith spoke solemnly, articulating each word deliberately.

"No, silly. Meredith…" Sophie was smiling and began to beam. "I'm not your friend because... I'm your sister."

The two siblings were stunned to silence.

"Sister?" Meredith finally whispered. She was shaking her head slowly, in disbelief. "But… how…? I mean… when…?" Lost for words. "Does my mother know?"

Sophie nodded.

"I'm sure you have lots of questions Meredith – *both* of you – but I'm too exhausted to explain. It's a long story."

"You can't drop something like this without at least telling us *something!*"

Sophie sighed theatrically, reluctantly conceding. "Very well, go on then, just the one question."

Meredith considered her options for a moment, mulling over what question to ask. She was deliberating in such a manner that Sophie thought that maybe she'd asked the girl to name her final request before being executed. After a moment, before Meredith had time to speak, Stanley blurted out:

"Why do you live in my sister's mirror?"

Sophie laughed. It was genuine, full of mirth.

"Seriously?" Meredith thumped her brother in the arm again. "I'm gonna kill you!"

"Owww! I'm telling mum!"

Sophie chuckled at the sibling rivalry, at the petty squabbles, at the overreactions, the idle threats and the actual lashing out. She was almost unable to stop laughing. She felt a wave of envy, wishing she'd experienced her brother and sister's relationships instead of being locked away, a virtual prisoner.

"I don't 'live' in Meredith's mirror, silly! It's just easier for you to see me when I'm... like this. Here-," Sophie rustled about and reached into her backpack, retrieving a pair of special glasses and dropped them onto Meredith's bed. To Stanley and Meredith they just appeared from nowhere, like an apparition. "Please, put them on... you'll see... literally."

Stanley gasped: "Are you like *Harry Potter*?" he asked, overawed by what appeared to be more magic.

"If you put the glasses on Stanley, you will be able to see me."

"What, like magic?"

"Yes, Stanley," impatient, "just *like* magic."

Stanley picked up the glasses. They were heavier than the *Spiderman* sunglasses he wore outside, and a bit too big for his head, but he tried them on and held them into place with both hands.

"Whooa... this is *soooo* cool!" He raised the glasses above his eyes, then lowered them, raised them, then lowered them again, watching as Sophie would 'appear' then 'disappear', 'appear' then 'disappear' before his very eyes. He did this three or four more times before Meredith snatched the glasses from him, removed her spectacles and looked through them herself.

"So you ARE real!" Meredith reached out to the young woman

and, taking Sophie by surprise, embraced her. "I thought you lived in the mirror, or that I'd imagined you," she started to cry. "I thought you were gone for good," she sniffed dramatically, "I've missed you so much; I've missed you terribly, but I don't understand... I don't understand *any* of this. How've you gotten SO big since last time?"

Sophie returned the hug, running her hands through Meredith's long, blonde hair, touching the nape of her neck, feeling her slender shoulder and the subtle contours of her back. *I've missed this,* she thought to herself; the love and affection afforded to most children growing up was something that she'd never experienced. A simple hug had very rarely been offered to her, not even by her father. Being isolated from the world was more than just lonely, it was desperate – ostracised for no reason other than being different; a science experiment where no one had cared about the repercussions. Even *Quasimodo,* a freak of nature, had an inkling as to why he was forced to spend his life in the bell tower of the *Notre Dame.*

"I will answer all your questions soon enough," she said wearily, "but first I am famished. Can you get me some food? I've not eaten since breakfast and growing up is hungry work."

"I will try," said Stanley. "That's only if Slocum hasn't eaten it all."

"Who is Slocum?"

"Mrs Slocum, our dad's idea of a babysitter; an ogre of a woman with the appetite of a silverback gorilla," answered Meredith.

"She looks like one too," joked Stanley. "She gives me the heebie-jeebies," he said, pointedly. "Ghosts are not as scary as she is."

"I'm sure she isn't half that bad," Sophie mused. "But be careful all the same. My being here, keep it a secret, I have enough problems as it is without freaking out some strange adult?"

"Well, derr!" Stanley disappeared from the room, closing the bedroom door behind him. The sound of his feet echoed as he stomped down the stairs.

"I envy you all," Sophie said sadly. "I wish I could have been part of your family."

"But Sophie, you are. You're our sister."

Sophie shook her head slowly. "No," she muttered, "it's not the same." She sniffed and wiped the moisture from her eyes. She felt tears were threatening to come. "We are different, you and I – and not just because people can't see me. You were lucky; you've had a mother's love and a father's closeness. All I've ever known of love is what our father has given me, and most of that has been part time – that's all he could ever spare."

"Our mother is a kind, loving person. She would have loved you had she known about you," Meredith reasoned.

Sophie closed her eyes and fought the urge to tell her nine-year-old sister the truth, but how do you? How do you tell a child that their mother had carried out the shameful act of abandoning their sister in the delivery room? She couldn't. Instead, Sophie just gave a reassuring smile and lied: "I guess you're right."

Stanley returned with a plate of food and a bottle of *Dr Pepper* shortly after; a slab of bread, a selection of cheese, meats (mostly ham but a little chicken), and fruit, together with a big family size bag of tangy cheese flavoured *Doritos*.

Both girls looked at Stanley, confounded by the amount of food he'd pilfered from the larder.

"I guess Slocum didn't eat it all," giggled Meredith.

"I don't think any of this will get missed," Stanley said. "If it does, we'll just blame her."

"Where was the old bat anyway?" asked Meredith.

Stanley shrugged. "I wasn't looking for her. I think she was in the living room on the phone; probably making a long distance call on our parent's phone bill. Probably Australia. I would."

"Thanks Stanley, I think this will keep me going for a few hours."

Sophie started to feast, tearing chunks of bread and cheese and eating them unabashedly without a care. "I'm SO hungry," unapologetic, she spoke with a mouth half-full. She opened the *Doritos* and pulled out a great, big, dirty handful of orange tortilla chips. Opening the *Dr Pepper*, she followed her mouthful of food down with a deep swig from the bottle. Meredith was glad to have taken off the glasses, excusing her from her sister's loathsome eating manners.

The *Dr Pepper* was very gassy and it wasn't long before Sophie apologised for emitting the longest, loudest belch a girl could ever expend.

Meredith and Stanley both laughed.

"Excuse me!" she sniggered. "Better that end than the other." She followed it with a smaller burp, giggling. "So sorry!"

CHAPTER SEVENTEEN

COOPER

THE CAR WAS VERY nondescript, a small *Ford KA*, graphite-grey, parked at the start of the cul-de-sac between a *VW Golf* and a *Vauxhall Zafira*. The *Ford* looked *ordinary*, no different to any of the other town and family cars parked along either side of the road. This was how it was intended, a camouflage to allow maximum advantage of surprise – unlike the big black armoured SUVs favoured by the corporation and government agencies. A green *Magic Tree* air freshener dangled from the rear-view mirror, its fragrance long faded – as had its colour, now sun bleached.

The sole occupant of the *KA* looked like a leaflet distributor or a window cleaner, scruffily dressed in faded jeans, an off-white T-shirt and *Converse* trainers. He was young – early twenties – and clean shaven. His hair was swept back and slick with gel. In one hand he held a mobile phone to his ear, in the other a small, but powerful, pair of night vision/thermal signature binoculars. The man was looking through the twin eyepieces towards the house at the end of the cul-de-sac at the top of the hill. Having arrived over an hour earlier, his job was nearly done.

"I followed her into Seacrest to a house called Willoughby Rising. It's a nice place at the top of a hill, big garden out back, a good view of the sea. A sort of well ta-do kinda place." He spoke airily and cheerful. He was a man who enjoyed his job.

"*I'm not looking to buy the place, Cooper,*" the voice cut in testily, "*is she there?*"

The *KA* driver continued: "I can't be sure, but I think so. It looks like our host's hideout. A very good location with a good view of the approach." He did nothing to mask his genuine admiration towards George Jennings' choice of refuge.

There was momentary silence, then: "*Good work Cooper.*" The voice at the end of the phone was sandpaper rough. "*Bravo Team is en route to you as we speak – and I'm not far behind either. On their arrival I will give you your next orders. For now, just sit tight and keep watching. Let me know if anything changes. If the girl starts moving, keep your distance, but follow – do nothing to panic or alert her. This is the closest we've ever come to capturing her.*"

The *KA* driver sighed. "Understood sir."

"*And Cooper – she's very talented and dangerous. There's no promotion or advancement in pay for heroics, just a hospital bed or pathologist's meat counter.*"

The news of Dominic Schilling came to mind, a man who, though two or three pay grades higher in status, through either ill-informed judgement or stupidity, was no longer in the game. Word had filtered through that the former marine's charred remains had been found in his car a little earlier that day.

Still, good for me, Cooper thought, the voice in his head as cheery as his own; *had Schilling not been barbecued inside his car, he'd be sitting here instead.*

Before Cooper could reply further the mobile connection was lost, the call concluded. He tossed the *HTC* Smartphone to the passenger seat and continued to watch the house at the top of the hill through the binoculars. Occasional movement could be seen beyond the upstairs' windows, a few silhouettes and shadows flitting just within view, but little else.

Patiently, he continued to monitor and observe, awaiting the arrival of Bravo Team. The sun was still hot despite its rapid descent down the sky, the early July afternoon nearing its end. Until that moment, Cooper hadn't noticed how much he'd perspired and how sweaty his T-shirt looked. Were he to climb from the *Ford KA*, his appearance would certainly be noticed and probably commented upon, despite it being a natural look for someone so hot and uncomfortable. He raised his free arm and sniffed beneath his pit, ruffling his nose in disgust at the stale body odour and rueing the decision not to keep a can of *Lynx* in the glove compartment.

"I must remember to change when I get back to the office. Maybe a cool shower," he muttered and returned his attention back to the house at the top of the hill.

Bravo Team wouldn't arrive for another hour. Cooper was growing more and more bored by the second. Half an hour passed and he heard himself yawn. To keep awake he removed a chocolate bar from the glove compartment (and tore it open), taking his eyes off the house for a split second.

A door at the rear of Willoughby Rising opened and a woman, largely built, not very pleasant to look at and fairly old, trudged out falteringly. She stopped a short distance from the building's exit and stood surveying the surrounding area, searching, her eyes penetrating every square foot within the vicinity, combing the land, looking for something. *Or Someone...*

What's that she's holding? Cooper asked himself. He twisted a knob on the binoculars, adjusting the focus and changing the setting from 'thermal' to 'normal'; the images initially blurred, and then clarity; he gasped and jumped as from an electrical shock or a poke in the eye from a needle.

The woman was staring right back at him, a small telescopic lens – the sort attached to high-powered rifles – held to her eye. Defying her large frame and Cooper's belief, the woman hastily disappeared back into the house.

"Darn it!" Cooper thumped the steering wheel. He thumped it a second time. He didn't know for definite but he was sure he'd been sighted. He was positive in fact. "And who the HELL are you!" he wanted to know. At no time had he seen her face featured within the dossier of images of George Jennings' known associates and cohorts.

His one chance, his greatest moment to shine, was all but over – he'd blown it. He dared a further look through the binoculars. No one was outside – yet, but inside, he could make out movement; hurried, urgent shambling. From his standpoint, the Jennings' appeared to be readying themselves to move. His carelessness had alerted them of his presence and now the mission was in jeopardy. He had to do something; he had to think of something… something – *anything* – fast.

What would Schilling do?

Cooper knew the answer to that question, but by following in Dominic Schilling's footsteps not only would he be contradicting a direct order from Tom Kaplan, but also run the risk of a comparable outcome to Dominic's.

But what else could he do? They were so close to nabbing George Jennings' daughter; so close to ending a two yearlong pursuit; so close to having the ultimate weapon in their possession, a weapon that would revolutionise modern warfare. With Sophie on side, the enemy quite literally *wouldn't* see her coming.

Not thinking a moment longer, Cooper climbed from the small, nondescript car, and jogged round to the boot. Popping the bonnet, he reached in and pulled from a dark green canvas holdall a *Browning* 9mm semi-automatic pistol, black in colour with a brown handgrip. Reaching further, he removed a pair of thermal imaging heat seeking goggles with head strap and flip up ocular attachments, a couple of thirteen round magazine clips for the *Browning* and a small plastic box, red in colour, which opened on a hinge and was fastened by a spring button catch. The magazine clips he placed into the pocket of his jeans, the goggles he would carry until he got to the house. The *Browning* itself, he slipped beneath the waistband at the front of his jeans, tucked beneath his loose hanging T-shirt. He studied the small red box for a moment before slipping it into the back pocket of his jeans.

Inside the box were a hypodermic needle and a small vial of *Propofol*, a drug commonly used by anaesthetists or medical professionals to induce sleep at the beginning of surgical procedures. *Propofol* was also infamous for being the cause of *Michael Jackson's* cardiac arrest and subsequent death; Cooper solely intended it for use on Sophie, though only to subdue her for a short while until she was safely restrained. He couldn't take any risks. He'd heard about how ineffective Alpha Team had been.

"Okay, I guess the party is going to have to start without you, Bravo Team," he whispered beneath his breath as he slammed the car boot closed and started the short walk up the slight hill towards Willoughby Rising.

A woman in her early thirties walked towards him pushing a stroller, her child slouching down in the seat, a bag of sweets (*Haribo* jelly babies) in one hand, his other feeding a fistful of confectionary into his sticky mouth. Casually, Cooper walked past her, averting his eyes so not to make eye contact. The woman appraised him fleetingly then carried on, taking no further interest despite Cooper's sweaty shirt and dishevelled appearance; her priority was getting home, getting her son his dinner, then getting him to bed. Evening was fast approaching.

At the top of the hill, Cooper stopped and peered back down the road towards the *Ford KA*, watched the back of the woman as she pushed her child around a corner out of sight, and then took a deep breath.

"Let's do this," he muttered, suddenly feeling bold, almost

invincible. The speed of his steps increased with his heartbeat as he closed in on the house at the top of the hill, his right hand wrapping round the butt of the *Browning* in anticipation, appearing to any who looked as though he were clutching his stomach in pain, the illusion shattered upon a look at his face. A sinister grin stretched across his features, dark and menacing.

No one looked, and no one watched as he opened the gate and walked into the garden that belonged to Willoughby Rising.

CHAPTER EIGHTEEN

GEORGE

A QUARTER-OF-A-MILE AWAY FROM HOME, George pulled the car in hard to stop alongside a kerb a short distance from the entrance to a community sports' centre. A van following close behind needed to brake decisively to avoid colliding, the driver blasting his horn and hand gesturing rudely his agitation.

George paid no notice, his mind and thoughts elsewhere. His mobile phone had just started playing the opening music to the *Queen* hit, *The Show Must Go On*, a ringtone he'd converted from a track he'd lifted off *Innuendo*, an mp3 album saved to his computer.

George accepted the call, ending *Freddie Mercury's* singing. He waited mere seconds for the connection.

"Hello?"

"George? It's Amanda," the voice sounded hurried and breathy, as though the caller had been running. She sounded agitated.

"Mrs Slocum?"

"You told me to call you if I noticed anything or anyone strange around the neighbourhood, no matter how big or small."

"Go on," urged George, he peered over his shoulder to take a look at his son. Charlie was lying across the seat, sound asleep.

"I've seen someone strange. A gangly looking fellow is watching the house through binoculars from a car at the end of the street."

"Have you seen him before?" asked George.

"No. In fact, he's only been there a short time. He wasn't there an

hour ago – I've been deliberately carrying out perimeter checks and the way he's scrutinising the place strikes me as rather suspicious. George, what do you want me to do?"

George thought for a moment. So much happening, so many things going off plan – it was just *knowing* what best to do – for himself, for his family, *and* for Sophie.

"Can you get the kids ready to leave?" George had started the *Peugeot*'s engine and was once again moving.

"Yes, sure – but there is another thing George, I think he saw me."

George cursed. "Amanda, I'm less than five minutes away, keep the kids safe until I get there. Do what you have to do, I don't need to tell you your job, or how important it is that nothing happens to anyone in my family." He was now unconsciously driving, preparing himself for whatever he was likely to face on arrival at Willoughby Rising. The mobile was on speakerphone. George continued to talk:

"Another thing, I need my black suitcase. You know the one I told you about. It's already packed, it's in my wardrobe."

"Okay George. We'll be ready."

Taking a corner too fast, the tyres of the vehicle screeched loudly, startling passersby and a small dog tethered to a lamppost outside a corner shop, which started barking excitedly, its little mouth snapping viciously at an invisible aggressor.

Behind in the back seat, Charlie awoke with a start. His father's driving had gone from careful smooth to fast erratic, and the jerky-jarring movements of the steering wheel had begun to throw him from one side of the car to another, jolting his broken arm. Had he been in his mother's car, he'd have been strapped into the child's seat, safe and secure. Unfortunately, his father didn't have any child seats in his car – never needed them for the trips to and from his Chelsea home. The kids did all their travelling in the *Prius*.

Crying, Charlie started to complain: "Slow down daddy, you're hurting my arm!" he sobbed.

"I'm sorry. Just hold on Charlie, we're nearly there."

Turning left at the next junction, George steered the car into the cul-de-sac, at the top of which stood Willoughby Rising, dominant and majestic on the immediate skyline, paying no attention to the cars that flanked the road, not noticing the *Ford KA* parked on the right at the bottom of the slight hill, and seeing nobody in the street, George floored the accelerator pedal and sped up to his family's residence.

Bringing the *207* to a halt outside his house having already released his seatbelt, the engine still idling, George jumped out of the car. He turned hastily and peered through to the back where Charlie was sitting.

"Charlie, you wait here. I won't be long." He flung the door closed behind him and centrally locked it (two warbling bleeps accompanying it), not looking back as he hurried ahead, running up the three steps that ascended to the front of the property, taking the first two with one big stride. Charlie sat forward apprehensively, his face pressed against the glass watching his father hurry away.

At the top of the steps, George faltered, not sure of what he was doing. He couldn't help thinking that perhaps he was about to enter a lion's den armed with just a feather duster. Before he could contemplate his next move, from inside the house two sudden explosions cracked deafeningly, the double boom resounding around the cul-de-sac.

BANG! BANG!

Followed by three more:

BANG! BANG! BANG!

George instinctively dropped to the ground, and crawled towards the front door, shuffling beneath the window, out of view from any who may be peering out from inside. His heart was thumping, he felt sick with fear and worry for his children and for Mrs Slocum holed up inside, but then training from long ago kicked in.

Getting to the front door, he stood up and reached out to the door handle, flinching as the handle jerked down, out from his grasp before he'd managed to touch it. The front door was pulled open sharply and a dishevelled and rather bloody woman stood barring his path. She was holding a pistol, its barrel pointing harmlessly towards the ground.

"Amanda?" George gasped, alarmed and shocked at what faced him.

"Help... me... George," she choked, blood trickled from her mouth and spattered out with each word she uttered; a little spraying George's T shirt.

"He got me, George... I... I... I tried to stop him..." Slocum slipped to the floor at the threshold, her right hand clutching a spot on the front of her blouse that was bright red, a dark patch of crimson spreading.

"Where is 'he'?"

Slocum shook her head. The gun slipped from her grasp and clattered loudly to the hallway floor. "I tried to stop him... he... he... he was too... fast." She winced from the effort and the pain and closed her eyes, blinking back tears. "I'm sorry George, the agency taught me better..." she whispered and slumped over.

"No Amanda, don't you die on me," George shook her violently, her head snapping back and forth. The action had the desired effect and Slocum fluttered open her moist eyes, though they maintained their distant glaze.

"I'm... so... tired," she said drowsily.

"Amanda, I need to know where he is. Are my children safe?"

Slocum fought hard against the darkness that threatened to steal her away. Finding some energy she faced George, and spoke for the last time:

"He's gone up the stairs, looking for the children. He's hurt, I put a bullet in him, but it didn't stop him. I didn't... have... time... to warn the..." she trailed off, and this time George allowed unconsciousness to take her.

"Hold on Amanda, just a little while." George stepped over the woman he'd assigned, not only as a babysitter for his children, but as a lookout and protector for his whole family. Under the guise of a friend of the family, he'd never let on where he'd first come across Amanda Slocum. The truth would have been a hard pill to swallow. It was better for all concerned that they never know. Had Harriet or the children known of her colourful past, more questions would have been asked, it was inevitable; things would then naturally get complicated. He wasn't yet prepared to reveal the hard facts of his past life, knowing that his wife wouldn't understand and the kids were too young. He was also afraid.

Afraid that they wouldn't forgive him for what he'd done and what he was soon going to do.

Reaching out for the handgun, George released the clip of bullets and saw that the magazine was still half-full. Using the heel of his hand, he pushed the magazine back into the gun, chambered a round, and quietly entered his house.

Passing into the hallway he could see the staircase a dozen or so feet ahead of him. Droplets of blood speckled the wooden flooring, and a trail, like breadcrumbs, spattered a path to follow up the stairs. George stealthily moved forward, taking a larger step over the first stair, knowing that the board was slightly loose and creaked under the merest weight. He didn't want to give away his position.

From upstairs, George heard laboured movement. Floorboards creaked and heavy feet fell.

"Where... are you... you... BITCH?" The words sounded close... pained and embittered. A few seconds later the sound of a closed-

door was smashed open. Light spilled out at the top of the stairs, highlighting both the way ahead and the location of Slocum's attacker.

Quickly, and quietly, he climbed the rest of the way one step at a time. Although difficult, he tried to put thoughts of the dying woman lying across the entranceway to the back of his mind. His primary concern was now for his kids.

Reaching the stairs' landing, George levelled Slocum's gun ahead of him and steeled himself to use it. Standing stock-still, he strained to hear where exactly the intruder currently was, poised to react should he appear in front of him. A long time ago, he'd been taught to shoot first and ask questions after; it wasn't very diplomatic, but this didn't appear to be the occasion. His finger was steady on the trigger. The safety was off.

He was calm. He was ready.

He was waiting.

CHAPTER NINETEEN

COOPER

COOPER HAD NOT EXPECTED any resistance as he'd crept into the house via the back door. Sure, he knew the girl everyone had been talking about was here – after all, he'd watched her alight the bus in the town's centre after getting off the train, then pursued her from a safe distance, watching her through the binoculars, the heat signature mode in place – but he hadn't expected the housekeeper to be armed and waiting for him in the kitchen, standing by the hallway door. Had he not had his wits about him, he was certain he'd now be dead.

"Hello laddie," she said as he'd gently, quietly closed the back door behind him, the element of surprise he'd intended totally backfiring. She was curious as to why he was wearing night vision goggles strapped to his head considering it was broad daylight and there was next to no darkness within the detached house. "Are you after somethin'?" In her hand was a small handgun. A *Sig Sauer 1911* .45 calibre pistol, its magazine capacity was eight bullets.

Cooper jumped, quickly regaining his composure. He smiled reassuringly and offered his hands in supplication, his own weapon concealed beneath his baggy but rather sweaty T-shirt.

"Easy," he said soothingly, "I think I've made a mistake."

"Damn straight you have sonny. You have no idea!"

Lightning quick, Cooper reached down to the *Browning* tucked beneath his waistband, thumbed the safety catch, raised the weapon and was diving for cover behind a pinewood dining suite, all in one fluid movement. Righting himself, he brought the handgun down to bear on the woman, ready to pull the trigger, finding that she'd retreated into the hallway, the door swinging closed behind her. He cursed aloud at his misfortune.

I bet Dominic Bloody Schilling never had this luck, he thought to himself. He then remembered: Dominic Schilling had been reported dead.

Standing up, he slowly crossed the kitchen-diner to the doorway – beyond which the woman had disappeared – and pushed the door open.

The way appeared clear. *Where was she?*

Making to step through, his progress was immediately halted by a double staccato burst of gunfire:

BANG! BANG!

Pain flared in his stomach as a .45 slug tore into his abdomen, the second shot smashing into the doorframe, just missing his head, raining wood splinters and fragments about his face like rice thrown at a wedding, mingling with his hair. Managing to retain his balance, and seemingly of its own accord, the *Browning* was up and three quick bursts echoed around the hall, sending its deadly loads in seemingly random directions, but Cooper knew differently:

BANG! BANG! BANG!

Two bullets gouged holes harmlessly into the wall, kicking up a cloud of plaster, dust and debris; the other took the woman to the centre of her chest, knocking her off her feet cinematically. She flew three or four feet backwards and smashed into the wall beside the front door, slumping to the floor.

Feeling exposed and unexpectedly weak from the gunshot wound, but wanting to salvage his mission and his integrity, Cooper laboured up the stairs two at a time; a sideward glance down the stairs saw the woman regain her feet and go to the front door.

Go for help, see if I care. I'll finish you off in a bit. By the time anyone comes it'll be too late.

On the last step, Cooper stopped and surveyed the stairs' landing ahead of him. It was unnaturally dark for the time of day. All the doors were closed and he faced five of them.

Edging above the last stair, he took a furtive step towards the first door that stood to his left. He faced a short corridor on which two doors were set to his left, two on the right, and one at the end – he could make out their outlines through the goggles (set to night vision with a subtle touch of a button).

Multitasking with his right hand (he was still holding the gun), slowly, awkwardly, he squeezed down the handle on the first door and applied a little downward pressure. The door opened with only a little protest, the hinges creaking with a pitchy whine.

Beyond the door there was just a bathroom, white porcelain wash basin, matching toilet and a bathtub with a combined shower unit placed above in the corner, a glass shower screen enclosing it in. Water dripped from the showerhead – *drip drip* – spaced out by a few seconds, echoing in the small room. The walls were tiled, also white. Cooper found the brightness of the room intense through the night/heat seeking goggles, the window above the wash basin was west facing, and the sun now receding slowly down the afternoon sky made the room glow ethereally. Cooper shielded his eyes, turned away from the room and closed the door behind him. He blinked to readjust his vision to the gloomy hallway once again.

"Sophie!" he called, his voice echoing in the enclosed hallway. "I know you're here. I only want to talk."

The next room on the left wasn't as bright to Cooper's relief. The curtains were drawn, but like the bathroom, it was void of life.

A single bed was made up along the furthest wall. No other furniture cluttered the room, but Cooper could tell that its inhabitant was male, probably the youngest child going by the toys strewn across the floor. A variety of toy cars, dinosaurs, action dolls, cuddly toys and other pre-school play things cluttered the room. Cooper retreated swiftly from the room, unaware that he continued to leave a trail of blood behind him; crimson droplets spattered the bedroom's carpet and marked the wooden flooring within the landing area.

"No one else needs to die, Sophie... I promise I'll let the children live, just come out. Cross my heart... I will spare the boy and the girl. It's only you I want. It's up to you."

The door at the end of the landing was the master room, so large that it was unmistakeable. Cooper could tell by the king-size bed, the type of furniture and the clothing he spied through the gap of the fitted wardrobe that this room belonged to George and his wife. The bed was made and the smell of a woman's perfume still lingered. Something inexpensive, he reflected, though in truth he couldn't tell the difference between a good bottle and a cheap one (an ineptitude he shared with wine tasting) having never purchased such items, not for a girlfriend, sister or his mother; he had none of them to coddle or spoil. A quick glance to the dressing table made him none the wiser. Bottles of *Chanel No.5* and *Vera Wang* sat amongst deodorant sprays, moisturisers and other feminine beauty products.

Tommy Girl, he considered, having not a clue. It never ceased to amaze him how the smallest of details overwhelmed his thoughts, no matter how utterly wrong or incongruous his thoughts actually were. He was sure the fragrance so strong, so cloying, was *Tommy Girl* though.

Upon a bedside cabinet an electric alarm clock displayed the time: 5:21 p.m.

The curtains were open, but as the window was north facing, the sun was not causing him any issue. A quick scan confirmed that this room, like the two before it, was empty.

Knowing that his options were reducing, he started to feel a tingling sensation in the fingers loosely wrapped round the butt of the *Browning*.

Anticipation, or excitement, he could never tell the difference, pumped adrenaline around his body – but despite his excellent sense of smell, intuition, sight and hearing, he failed to comprehend that the feeling in his hands and circulating his body was the result of the blood that he was steadily losing from the hole that gaped in his stomach. His left hand was still pressed to the burning agony that ripped at his abdomen; thick, mucilaginous, warm blood coated his hand, oozed between his tightly pressed fingers and continued to drip-drip-drop to the floor, leaving a slightly larger puddle whenever he stopped, even momentarily.

Running out of choices, he kicked open the next door - what would have been the second door on the right (now the first to his left). Cooper readied himself to take a shot at whoever it was he faced first. His concentration was starting to wane; the reasons for this mission were beginning to sound fuzzy in his head and less important, almost like it were part of a dream he'd fought hard to retain memory of. Through the goggles his vision was beginning to go a little distorted, a little blurred, and somewhat doubled. It took all his concentration to maintain focus, albeit unsuccessfully for the most part. He was starting to feel weak and increasingly tired.

Staggering into the room he was irritated further to find that, like the three rooms before it, this one was also deserted.

"Where... are you... you... BITCH?" his voice was laboured and high pitched, breathless and almost desperate.

He took a moment to take in the room's effects but was losing interest fast. In addition to a single bed there was a desk and a few boxes stacked up in the corner. Some toys lay about, but the room was much neater than the previous child's room. Cooper no longer cared who the rooms belonged to but could tell simply by its contents that the older boy slept in here. There was a telescope aimed towards the sky and other sundry items easily associated to a male child.

"Where are you!" he screamed like a lunatic, not bothering to shield his annoyance. "You can't hide forever!" Exiting the room he concentrated on composing himself. He closed his eyes and willed the pain burning in the pit of his stomach to go away.

Just one room left. Nowhere left to run. The job was nearly done. He took a deep, jagged breath and closed his eyes to the blurry images. He tried to forget the bleeding hole at his centre that pumped his life fluid effortlessly between his fingers despite the effort extended to stem the flow; he knew medical attention was desperately needed. Grimacing, he tried to ignore the excruciating pain.

Tightening his grip on the *Browning*, Cooper backed out of the bedroom and quickened his pace towards the final room, expectation and wanton success giving him renewed energy.

Using a booted foot, he kicked the last bedroom door open and extended his gun arm, moving it shakily from left to right, concentrating with even more effort to focus, sweat now adding to his visual impairment, dripping beneath the straps of the goggles, into his eyes, further encumbering his mission.

The bedroom door creaked closed to just a crack behind him.

"I know you are in here Sophie, so let's not do anything rash – you wouldn't want me to kill anyone on purpose!" Cooper spoke through gritted teeth.

At first glance the bedroom was like all the others, void of life, unexpectedly empty, but something told him otherwise. He could tell that a girl occupied this room; pink bed linen, flowered curtains,

Barbie dolls and other sundry items that clearly defined the room. It was without a doubt Meredith's room.

Although not seeing anyone, not hearing the slightest of sounds, Cooper knew they were in here – somewhere. Call it instinct, gut feeling (what was left of his gut!), hubris, or just a keen aptitude for knowing these things, Cooper was almost never wrong.

And then, there it was, the telltale moment that he was waiting for. Ordinarily it was all that he would need. Like an act of God or call it a sign, confirmation was granted. There came a sound... or a movement.

It was both. Cooper's attention was drawn to the most likely hiding place in the bedroom. The place everyone chooses to hide.

Meredith's bed, or specifically *underneath* it.

"Come out, come out… wherever you are," he said in a playful, singsong voice, though it sounded sinister, malevolent. "No one is going to get hurt," Cooper stooped for a better look beneath the bed, wincing as he did from the pull and crease of the bullet wound. "I promise."

Behind him an ornament fell to the floor from the window ledge, disturbed by the curtain, smashing against the floor.

Startled, Cooper whirled round and fired a single shot blindly, tearing a hole in the wall beneath the window. He cursed at himself, at his nerves, at the waste of a bullet and the uneasiness he felt, and returned his attention back to the bed, the place Sophie and the other children were most likely hiding, this he knew with growing certainty.

"Okay, I lied… someone IS going to get hurt."

Stanley let out an audible whimper. Cooper smiled.

"I know you are under the bed little ones. The question is: is *Sophie* there with you?"

Cooper started to crouch down again, grimacing from the pain that burned in his stomach and began to peer under the bed.

With his back to the door, he failed to hear its gentle creak as it ever-so-slowly opened. He didn't even notice the silhouette of a man enter into the bedroom behind him, his gun silently pointing to the back of Cooper's head.

CHAPTER TWENTY
SOPHIE

"QUIET! DID YOU HEAR that?"

Sophie had stopped eating; her mouth half-full with the remnants of chewed *Doritos*, cheese and a piece of bread; she stood up with a start from the bed – not that Meredith or Stanley had noticed. For the moment, Stanley had removed the special glasses for the umpteenth time and was oblivious to the invisible girl's whereabouts, a feat which he would never tire of.

Sophie crossed unseen to the bedroom door. She pressed her ear up against its wooden surface and listened carefully, blocking out all other sounds that threatened to impede her concentration.

There were voices, though muffled. Two of them. She heard:

Easy… I think I've made a mistake. Male voice. Calm and exacting.

Damn straight you have sonny. You have no idea! A woman; Slocum, Sophie surmised. She looked over her shoulder at Meredith and Stanley. Both were obediently quiet but their breathing was loud. Meredith had retrieved the glasses from Stanley and had placed them back atop the bridge of her nose. She was now watching with keen interest.

BANG! BANG!

Sophie flinched but remained at the door, listening intently. Meredith gasped, cocking her head up in alarm. Stanley's eyes widened.

BANG! BANG! BANG!

Something akin to a yelp was heard from below them; then silence. Sophie slowly turned the key in the lock, weakly securing the plywood door with the two-lever mortice sash lock. She turned around fast, a look of concentrated effort etched across her face. It was soon gone as her genetically enhanced intelligence grappled with a plan – not a grand scheme that involved an elaborate offensive, but one which would help them evade detection. Spending little further time to think, Sophie returned to her backpack, which had been left by the side of Meredith's bed alongside the large sports holdall. Reaching in, pushing *Flopsy* to one side, then knocking it to the floor altogether in her haste to reach the item she sought, which had inconveniently wormed its way down to the bottom, she retrieved the handgun she'd liberated from one of the attackers at the apartment. A full magazine of bullets was already loaded; all she had to do was remove the safety and she would be ready.

"Sophie?" Seeing the gun, Meredith was suddenly frightened.

"Shhh," Sophie admonished, followed by a whisper, "don't be afraid. I know what I'm doing. You need to hide. Quick, beneath your bed! Both of you!" She spoke with authority, like a parent or a teacher Meredith considered. Like most kids, she hated to be told what to do. Nonetheless, she was soon off the bed, on her hands and knees, crawling within the narrow space beneath the bed frame. It was a tight squeeze and, no sooner was she under, she felt nauseous from claustrophobia – she'd always had a fear of confined spaces. She was also afraid of spiders. And heights! Hence why she had stayed at the bottom of the crab-apple tree instead of climbing it. *Had Charlie been the same, would things be any different right now*? she wondered.

Stanley gave no fuss and was under the bed no sooner had Sophie demanded it, close behind Meredith's heels. He pressed up close to his sister, making her feel further confined, hot and soon damp with sweat.

Outside the room Sophie heard the slightest of movements,

of someone trying to be quiet but failing terribly. Someone was ascending the stairs one stair at a time, each step betraying the man's footfall with a creak of objection. Looking for somewhere to hide for herself, Sophie scanned the room. With just one blink she was able to ingest the entire scene, storing it to memory like a fast frame camera.

Behind the curtains? No, not enough cover and the first place he'd look.

The wardrobe? Too obvious.

Under the bed? That's just ridiculous!

Think! There was nowhere. The bedroom was sparsely furnished, so options were limited. Looking above her head, first surveying the coving bordering the walls, she noticed how high the ceiling was, and pondered an idea.

She also glanced at the window and considered escaping – dismissing the idea no sooner than it had sprung to mind. That just wouldn't do; she couldn't leave Meredith or Stanley... under the bed was scarcely a hiding place. They had absolutely no chance of surviving on their own.

Outside the door, Sophie heard laboured breathing and the creak of a door from opposite the bedroom.

He's here.

Time had run its course. Sophie crossed the room and took a silent run up towards the door. Nimbly, she leapt up like a ninja, using one wall to propel her upwards, twisting mid-flight, and utilising the other wall to help wedge herself in above the door, into the corner itself. Her head was just below, pressing against the ceiling. The movement was fluid, as though a well rehearsed manoeuvre. In truth, Sophie had never attempted such a thing before, and had she given it any thought, she doubted she'd have managed it successfully. It was just another by-product of the genetic tinkering and the tailored training provided by her father.

Meredith risked a peek from beneath the bed and through the

glasses (which she'd kept on) she spied Sophie pressed up against the ceiling in the corner of the room. She looked like *Spiderman* without the spandex. Somehow she was holding herself in place just by the outward pressure of her feet. In her hands she held the gun, the barrel pointing ahead of her, aimed slightly downward.

A couple of minutes passed and the sound of a door banged loudly, forcefully kicked open. The vibrations were felt through the seat of Sophie's jeans, indicating that the forced and splintered door was very close by. Sophie knew that the intruder was in the room next door. She could almost hear his laboured breathing through the stud walls.

"Where are you!" His tone was angry, but there was more to it Sophie noted – she sensed a hint of desperation and something else... pain? Pain was clearly in his voice. Pain, she reflected, indicated that their foe was hurt, possibly shot – she'd heard five gunshots after all, so it stood to reason that he may have taken a bullet. If that was the case... *who could have shot him?*

Taking her by surprise, the door just beneath her balanced body burst open, threatening to make her slip. Part of the frame shattered in a shower of splinters where the lock was feebly bolted, disintegrating from the force of the sharp, booted kick applied by the intruder, the lock giving no resistance or security at all. The man who'd moments earlier been clamouring from room to room had entered swiftly, his *Browning* 9mm aimed ahead of him, his left hand clutching a dark crimson patch that continued to spread across his off-white T-shirt.

"I know you are in here Sophie, so let's not do anything rash – you wouldn't want me to kill anyone on purpose!"

Sophie's breathing had all but stopped. Calmly she watched... and waited, a feline poised to pounce. The man had hurried into the room without care or heed, the door swinging closed behind him, his back to the carefully poised girl pressed above the door against the ceiling. She had a clean shot, she felt compelled to take it, but not yet. She couldn't shoot someone in the back, that was the coward's way. She wanted to see the man who was hunting her; wanted to see his face, to see his eyes, before she closed them forever.

Although not seeing anyone, not hearing the slightest of sounds, the man sensed he was in the right room; he knew they were in here.

Sophie watched Cooper as his attention was drawn to Meredith's bed. A most obvious choice of hiding place. She knew he would find Meredith and Stanley, after all she could see them clearly herself even high up from her vantage point. Subconsciously she'd known this would happen all along and part of her would argue that it was part of an elaborate plan. She'd used them as bait.

"Come out, come out… wherever you are," the man in the bloodied shirt said in a playful, singsong voice. "No one is going to get hurt," he started to stoop to look beneath the bed, "I promise," he added.

An ornament fell to the floor from the window ledge, disturbed by the curtain, smashing against the floor. It was the second of Meredith's ornaments to receive such a fate.

Abruptly, Cooper whirled round and fired a reckless shot in the direction he'd glimpsed movement and heard the ornament crash, smashing a hole in the wall beneath the window, quickly concealed behind the still billowing curtain.

"Okay, I lied… someone IS going to get hurt."

Sophie heard Stanley let out a small, nervous whimper.

"I know you are under the bed little ones. The question is: is *Sophie* there with you?"

Beneath her, the door slowly creaked open and the silhouette of a familiar person holding a gun walked into view just as the opening chords of *The Show Must Go On* began to play on his mobile phone.

CHAPTER TWENTY-ONE

GEORGE

THE SOUND OF THE first bedroom door being kicked in quickened George's pace as he climbed up the stairs, though he continued to move quietly, barely making a sound, using his knowledge of the family home to his advantage.

"Where are you!" The voice came from one of the rooms up ahead.

George inwardly sighed relief to hear that the man who, only a couple of minutes earlier had shot his house sitter and friend, had not found his son or daughter.

George was nearing the top of the stairs, but ducked down as he watched the man who, even in the dark murky shadows, looked a wreck in his blood coated T-shirt with lumbering gait; blood was now staining the front of his jeans and continued to spatter the wooden flooring about him, a trail of stippled crimson following him in and out of each room. George observed the man take a swinging kick against another of the closed doors, splintering the frame under the force, bursting the door inwards.

"I know you are in here Sophie, so let's not do anything rash – you wouldn't want me to kill anyone on purpose!"

What does he mean? Sophie isn't here. George was puzzled, mentally scratching his head.

George climbed up the last of the stairs and stopped short of entering the first bedroom on his right – his daughter, Meredith's room.

"Come out, come out... wherever you are... No one is going to get hurt."

George was now standing outside his daughter's bedroom door, peering in through the small gap. Ahead of George, Amanda Slocum's aggressor was standing with his back to him. As he stooped down, he said, mischievously: "I promise."

George aimed the gun and made ready to fire, his index finger wrapped round the trigger, applying slight pressure.

An ornament fell to the floor from the window ledge, disturbed by the curtain, smashing against the floor.

At blinding speed, the man turned and fired a shot towards the ornament, smashing a hole in the wall beneath the window.

"Okay, I lied... someone IS going to get hurt."

George heard Stanley let out a small, nervous whimper.

Stanley! George took a step forward and silently entered the bedroom.

"I know you are under the bed little ones. The question is: is *Sophie* there with you?"

George watched the man crouch down by the side of the bed and make ready to use his weapon.

Before George was able to act, the opening chords of *The Show Must Go On* began to play from his trouser pocket.

No!

The man, still crouching, rotated from the hip and fired his gun.

BANG!

"Nooooooooo!!!" George heard the howl of rage in his head, not realising that he had started to shriek it.

Not waiting to find out whether he was hit or not, George fired Slocum's pistol just as he became aware of another being discharged above his head.

BANG!

BANG!

George's shot took the assailant high in the arm, winging him sideways; the shooter above his head was more lethal, more accurate. She'd taken a kill shot and placed the bullet into the centre of the intruder's forehead, blasting a hole through to the other side, decorating the wall behind him with globules of blood and brain chunks, the spatter dripping and sliding down the paintwork. The man dramatically slumped to the floor, his hand still clutching the gun, spasmodically twitching.

The mobile phone continued to ring, Freddie Mercury's voice, though muffled, escaped from George's pocket: *Empty spaces – what are we living for…*

"Dad!" The voice carried down from above him and George looked up. "Are you hit? Are you all right?"

"Sophie?" He could not see her but the voice was unmistakeable.

She dropped down from the compacted position which she'd maintained between the two walls above the door, landing in a squat beside her father.

Does anybody know what we are living for… The ringtone continued.

"What are you doing here?" exasperated, he aimed the question in the direction he thought his daughter was now standing, unable to see her without the aid of special glasses and being in the wrong part of the room to see using the wall mirror.

"Dad!"

George looked himself up and down, and smiled reassuringly. "I'm fine, love. Look, he missed." George pointed to the bullet that had punched into the wall just inches away from his head. But it had been a close call.

Behind the curtain, in the pantomime…

"Just!" Sophie saw the shredded material in the sleeve of her father's shirt. The bullet had missed him by the narrowest of margins.

"Sophie, I want you to tell me why you are here... but first..." George pulled out his mobile phone.

The show must go o-o-on!

He pressed the green connection icon, ending Freddie Mercury's dulcet tones. "Hello?"

"George? It's Harry." The voice sounded distant, the line very faint. She could have been in Alaska or on the moon for all George knew.

"Are you okay?" concerned. "Where are you?"

"I'm okay George, I've not been harmed – not yet. But I've lost Charlie... When I was taken I left him by the road..."

"It's okay, Harry. I have Charlie. He's safe with me, just a little banged up and bruised."

George heard Harry sigh.

"Thank God." Harriet went quiet for a moment, absorbing the news that her son was all right. She then went on: *"George, listen – they will let me go if you do something for them."*

"Harry, I can come for you."

"Don't do anything stupid. They said they will kill me if you don't do exactly what they ask."

George fell silent. Stanley was crawling out from beneath his sister's bed, followed by Meredith, struggling a bit, due to how limited and oppressive the space had felt. Her face was slick with sweat.

"Okay, Harry. Who are they, what do they want?"

"Who they are, I haven't a clue. One of the guerrillas, though, I recognise. He's been after us for a long time."

"Dominic Schilling?" he offered, almost knowingly.

"Yes, that's him. He nearly killed us with his car."

"What do they want?"

"It's something to do with a diamond. They said for you to meet with them at Ed's Easy Diner in the London Trocadero tomorrow, 12:00 p.m. where they'll give you further instructions."

"Let me guess, they want to use Sophie?"

"Just do what they ask. I want to come home." Harriet was crying.

"Okay my love. Stay strong. I'll get you out of this. Trust me." Before he could add, *I love you*, the line had been cut off.

"Oh dad! Why was he trying to kill us?" Meredith had bounded over to George and had wrapped her arms around his waist. She was crying silently, tears rolling down her cheeks. "And where's mum? I'm scared!"

"Meredith, later I will explain everything, but right now we need to help Amanda."

"Who's Amanda?" Stanley had been quietly sitting in the furthest part of the room.

"Your house sitter, Mrs Slocum – she's downstairs. She needs medical attention."

"That old witch," blurted Stanley.

"Hey!"

"Dad, please tell me what's going on?" Meredith was now standing up; the glasses perched atop her nose allowing her to see Sophie, who was standing next to their father.

"There isn't much time. Go get some things, we're leaving." George turned and left the bedroom, a moment later was bounding down the stairs to check on his friend from the distant past. Opening the front door he found Amanda slumped over. He placed his right hand against her neck, feeling for her carotid artery, searching for a pulse.

Meredith and Stanley had soon followed George down and hung back, watching from a safe distance. Obviously, Sophie was nowhere to be seen – but she was there also, standing not too far behind the children.

"Is she going to be okay?" asked Meredith, remorseful, regretting the nasty things she had called her.

George shook his head and looked down to the ground gravely. Before standing he closed the dead woman's eyes. For a long moment he quietly considered what next to do. He sighed with regret and stood up.

"Come, you two wait in the car, try not to upset Charlie, he's in a lot of pain with his arm. Sophie, I assume you are still with us; you can come and help me get some of our stuff."

"Yes, sure dad."

"Oh, and Sophie… thanks for shooting that guy in the head. I think you may have saved me."

"I don't know, dad. I'm sure your second shot would have been better…"

If I'd been able to take a second shot; I got lucky, he thought to himself. *Jeez, I am so out of practice…* His thoughts changed direction when something occurred to him.

"There's just one question, Sophie: where did you get the gun from?"

"Um..." like a guilty child, she tried to think up something plausible. Instead she avoided it tactfully, going with: "It's a long story dad. Just don't expect to get your deposit back on the apartment..."

CHAPTER TWENTY-TWO

RYAN

"SO YOU'VE BEEN THE rat, all this time. My very own assistant… conspiring, colluding, conniving against the Company… helping THEM get away. I've trusted you. Why? Why'd you do it?"

Ryan's hands were cuffed behind his back and his feet were manacled in chains. He was sitting on a wooden chair, it was uncomfortable and the only piece of furniture within the holding cell.

Samuel Jackson was pacing the room, wafting a draft as he manoeuvred back and forth. Despite the air con he was perspiring profusely and a dark patch had spread rings beneath his armpits and stained the lower back of his shirt.

Ryan's face was bruised and bloodied from a pummelling received, his tongue was swollen and bleeding, a thin trail of blood running a line down the left side of his chin, a consequence from having bitten a chunk from it and the result of a vicious punch from one of the heavies that had collared him; furthermore, it had fractured a tooth and uprooted another. His mouth was a throbbing mess which did nothing to help encourage him to talk.

Resolutely, Ryan sat in obdurate silence. He'd acted like this since the corporation's goons had hauled him in and trussed him up like a common criminal. Despite the threat of torture and violence he'd been unfazed and uncompromising.

"Why, goddamn it!?"

"You wouldn't understand," Ryan croaked hoarsely, barely loud enough for the Security and Intelligence Director to hear. *It was because of my daughter,* he said in his head, unable to say it aloud because he knew the senior man wouldn't get it. His daughter was dead, and someone was accountable. In his mind, George was the only one who could help him see retribution and justice for Clara.

"Still, no matter Ryan. Say what, or as little as you want; you can stay stubbornly silent for all I care, all will be known soon enough," he paused for emphasis. "I have your phone, Ryan. We know that you used it to contact George before we grabbed you. You've been careful, I grant you that, up 'til then. Making that call was your only failing, your *downfall.* Stupid, stupid man," Samuel shook his head in mock disappointment. He smiled a huge grin, like the joker in a pack of cards. "I really should thank you for it though, Ryan. We now have George's telephone number. We are now triangulating his exact position as we, well, as 'I' speak." Samuel turned to the door and rapped his knuckles against the toughened glass panel.

A couple of seconds later the door opened and in stepped one of the security men who'd chased Ryan Barber down and who'd dragged him back to the operations centre.

Turning to the newcomer, Samuel spoke sternly:

"Cullum, see that our guest here...," hand gestured towards Ryan who had turned his head slightly away, "repents for his actions. Afterwards, do what you will with whatever's left of him."

Cullum raised his eyebrow with an unspoken question.

Following with an unspoken answer, Samuel laid a loose hand on the burly security guard's shoulder and nodded affirmation, patting him gently. Samuel made to leave, hand poised to knock the door, signalling his wish to exit the cell. He turned to look over his shoulder. "Oh, Cullum. Can you bring me a little trophy?"

"Sir?" Confused.

"Nothing too fancy, just bring me... oh I don't know... his heart. Or his head. Whatever's easiest."

The Director rapped the door twice, quickly disappearing as soon as the way out was unlocked. The door closed slowly behind him.

Cullum considered the instruction for a moment before addressing Ryan. The Director had left him with the job to do, never dirtying his own hands. It was often the way with the most senior in organisations. They issued the orders, no matter how decidedly dirty the task, leaving a *lesser* man to carry out the deed or *misdeeds.*

"I'm sorry Mr Barber. You know, it's a shame because you were always kind to me. I like you," he spoke sincerely. "Because of this I promise to make it quick. Despite what the Chief wants, you will hardly feel a thing." He looked up towards a surveillance camera pointing down from a corner in the room, a small flashing red light confirming that it was in full operation. The interrogation was being digitally recorded for future reference and Samuel's perverse sense of amusement. Cullum exhaled noisily, shaking his head.

Ryan looked down at his cuffed hands, at his restrained feet and felt resignation at what was about to happen, accepting the inevitable.

"It's okay Ricky; I know it's not personal."

Cullum walked behind Ryan's chair and without further word or warning, enfolded an arm around the sitting man's neck, applying pressure to the restrained man's carotid arteries and jugular, depriving his brain of oxygenated blood, causing what, in the medical profession, is called a *cerebral ischemia.* It was commonly called *a sleeper hold,* often faked in wrestling matches. Cullum wasn't faking. Swiftly, Ryan went limp within Cullum's grasp and slumped over, blacked out within the chair. It took less than five seconds. Using two fingers to the neck, Cullum checked for a carotid pulse.

Good, he thought. Ryan wasn't dead, just unconscious. When doing the 'blood choke hold' properly, the desired affect would always result in the subject blacking out. Cullum was a practiced expert having used the method many times, especially when he was younger and worked as a bouncer for a local night spot, diffusing situations and ending patron disputes. He'd earned the nickname *Sandman* because he was so successful at putting people to sleep.

"See, Mr Barber, I said it was going to be painless. It's better this way. Now you won't feel a thing."

Cullum cracked his knuckles using one hand over the top of the other, and left the room momentarily to locate a black body bag (a stock of them were kept in the utility cupboard on a shelf next to bottles of all purpose cleaner and a large supply of toilet rolls), the sort that's watertight and has a zipper down the centre, regularly used by pathologists or medical staff when transporting dead bodies.

CHAPTER TWENTY-THREE

EMILY

SAMUEL WAS ONCE AGAIN in his office having been absent for more than an hour – a peculiarity that had not gone unnoticed. The door was closed and the blinds at the windows were all drawn making the room unnaturally dim. Seated in front of him was a small, bespectacled woman with elfin features, long blonde hair and piercing blue eyes.

She'd follow at the Director's beck and call, though truth be told this was the first occasion she found herself sitting ahead of the most senior man in the building. In her hands was her security pass card, a younger version of herself looking up at her. She fiddled with it nervously, turning it over and over, shuffling it from one hand to the other like it were a pack of cards.

"How are you holding up Emily?" the Director asked, seeing the fear in the intelligence officer's eyes. He didn't wait for a reply, adding: "I know it's a shock to learn that someone we all trusted and all held dear has betrayed us. Ryan was more than just a colleague to me – he was my *friend*."

"I'm fine… sir. I just can't believe it, not Ryan. He was like a father to me." Literally! Emily felt weak, starting to weep. She couldn't believe what had transpired that afternoon. The day had gone from bad to worse.

"Here." Samuel offered the young woman a bright white handkerchief he'd unceremoniously produced from a pocket, his initials *SPJ* embroidered into the cotton. Emily took it and gently dabbed at her eyes. "It will be all right," said the Director. He stood up and walked round to the front of his desk, circling behind the small woman and placing two large hands on her shoulders, massaging them. "So tense, let me help you."

Emily relaxed and felt the strain begin to ebb away. She closed her eyes and murmured from the pleasure the massage gave her. The Director stopped, knowing his boundaries and returned back to his seat at the head of the table.

"Better?"

Emily nodded. Despite this she still felt moisture leaking from the corners of her eyes.

"Now, Ryan was special – not someone we will ever be able to replace, not easily – but," he waved a hand theatrically, "the Assistant Intelligence Officer position is now up for grabs. I look at the challenges we come across in our lives, not as problems but as *opportunities*; Ryan turning out the way he has, presents us with a very difficult challenge."

"I know, sir."

"On the other hand, it also gives someone unique an enormous opportunity." Samuel smiled. "Emily, I'll be straight with you. I need someone I can trust... more now than ever before. You've been with the company what, two – three years?"

"Four years, sir."

"Quite. Well, if I can be so bold, I think you're good for the part."

"I'd be honoured, sir. But aren't there better qualified analysts?" she asked, a flattered lilt to her voice. "There are others who've been here longer."

"Maybe," he shrugged, "but who worked closer to Barber? Besides, managing that lot," indicating the people downstairs with a sweep of his hand, "should be easy – half of them idolise you already."

Emily blushed. “Okay. Thank you, sir.”

“Enough of the ‘sirs’, Emily, call me Sam.”

“Okay. Thank you... *Sam.*”

“Good, that’s settled then. Your first job is to glean as much information as you can from this.” The Director conjured Ryan’s mobile phone from some place out of view and placed it onto the table in front of him, slipping it across the shiny surface towards the bespectacled woman. “Ryan used it to call George Jennings earlier today. It shouldn’t present someone of your ability too much difficulty in helping us find the fugitive once and for all.”

Emily smiled uncertainly. She reached for Ryan’s phone and palmed it, trying not to think of the man to whom she owed everything.

“And Emily. Utmost discretion. You don’t need me to tell you that we are under the spotlight. Tom Kaplan has gotten himself involved because there is an external pressure to deliver the product the corporation promised. It would be satisfying if it were us who brought George and his daughter to heel.”

“Understood, sir,” Emily chose to forgo the informality as she stood to leave. “Thanks again. I’ll crack on with this,” indicating Ryan’s mobile phone, before hastily retreating from the room.

CHAPTER TWENTY-FOUR

RYAN

RICKY CULLUM DRAGGED THE body bag from the white Mercedes van, only slightly guilty that he allowed it to fall to the hard forest ground with force that had the potential to break a bone or two. The occupant was lifeless and in no position to complain.

Devoid of insignia or markings, the nondescript vehicle he'd driven had gained little, or no attention as it made the hours' long journey from the garage at the rear of the Kaplan Ratcliff control centre and ended up deep within a heavily wooded area.

Parked in a small clearing at the end of a winding dirt track that was overgrown in places, he'd traversed for ten or so minutes and found the perfect place to bury the body.

He knew it well, having used it before. Hell, he'd used it more than once, the site was a regular potter's field. He'd never pretended to be a good boy, or that he enjoyed his job, but someone was being paid to do it, and at five-thousand a pop, he was loath to turn down the money. He had a mortgage and a wife with an expensive habit (Josephine collected *Swarovski* crystalware, which she displayed throughout their four bedroom home).

Far off the beaten track, the security man knew that this area of forest was rarely used, except, on occasion (sometimes more often), by him. Deep within the forest, once called Waltham forest, a tiny area flanked by *silver birch* and *pedunculate oaks*, was pinpointed by a mound of freshly excavated dirt, a shovel poking out from the large heap awaiting his arrival, a half-empty bottle of water and a backpack lay close by. The hole was deep – approx seven-feet – deeper than a standard grave, and crudely fashioned; long and wide enough to fit the remains secured within the body bag. In truth, it could probably fit two or three bodies. Cullum wasn't taking any chances, not wanting the cadaver unearthed by scavenging critters looking for an easy meal.

By the time he got there, Cullum was panting from the exertion of dragging a body and sweating profusely. Arriving at the prepared site, he stopped, dropped the body bag at the site's entrance and wiped his forehead with a *Kleenex*, taking a mouthful of water from the small bottle he'd placed there.

A crow cawed noisily from a tree close by. Cullum looked up at it and shivered. He hated the sight of the carrion crow – black and sinister. He wasn't superstitious, but wasn't it bad luck to see a single crow?

Picking up a stone, Cullum tossed it like a missile towards the bird.

CAW-CAW-CAW

The crow was unmoved by Cullum's act of hostility, cawing louder.

CAW-CAW-CAW

Setting his mind straight, ignoring the crow, Cullum walked over to the body bag and dragged it closer, bringing it to a halt once it lay alongside the hole. Stooping down to his knees beside the bag, the security man shoved the body into the grave and watched it fall the seven-feet to the bottom. Peering down, he smiled; satisfied the job was nearly done.

With the shovel, Cullum refilled the hole from the pile of dirt, and afterwards camouflaged the area with forest debris he'd carefully collected before digging earlier. He was nothing but meticulous in his work. The soil that was leftover he put into a garden refuse sack – he didn't want to leave any clues behind.

Once finished, the clearing looked almost how it had appeared on his arrival. To the casual observer, nothing appeared to be outside of the ordinary. Satisfied, Cullum retrieved his backpack, emptied the bottle of water with one, long pull, and with the refuse sack full of dirt, the backpack on his shoulder, and the shovel in his other hand, he wandered back to the Mercedes van, hearing the crow caw one last time.

Cullum was exhausted. He sat in the driver's seat of the Mercedes van, dabbing his brow with another *Kleenex*. Using the rear view mirror he studied his reflection. Face was dirty, lined with streaks from where sweat had run; his hair, though short, was greasy and untidy. His eyes were bloodshot and rheumy. In short, he looked a total mess and his body fragrance further compounded the urgent need for him to take a shower. Maybe two, so bad he looked. He felt no better.

"Well, that's done," Cullum straightened the rear view mirror and composed himself for the journey back to Kaplan Ratcliff, away from the forest, away from the burial site. He started the *Mercedes'* engine and shifted the gear from neutral. The passenger in the seat next to him had been impassive, contemplative and quiet. He finally broke the silence:

"I appreciate you doing this Ricky; I owe you a debt of gratitude." In the passenger seat sat a man whose face was swollen, bruised and bloodied, and whose shirt was stained with drying crimson. He tried his best to conceal his appearance beneath a *West Ham United* baseball cap. In his hands he held a plastic container with an airtight lid sealing within its macabre contents. Just thinking about it made the man gag reflectively every so often.

"We'll never be even, Ryan. But I owed it to Clara. She was always sweet to me. I miss her."

The atmosphere in the van turned subdued.

"Me too, Ricky. Me too."

Talk of his daughter now had that affect on the former Assistant Intelligence Officer. After a couple of moments he shook himself out of his melancholy and risked some small talk.

"Who was the organ donor?" he asked, indicating the plastic container by lifting it slightly from his lap, curbing the urge to heave.

Cullum laughed. "The word 'donor' implies there had been a choice or support in the giving of this heart." He shook his head. "The benefactor had and did little of either."

"Was he someone we knew?" Ryan asked anxiously.

"No one who *I* will miss," replied the security man cheerfully. "Let's just say I carried out an act of kindness for society."

Somewhere in London a homeless guy, dishevelled from head to toe, grimy all over with lank dirty grey hair and a matching beard that was almost as long as *Dumbledore*'s, stumbled upon an empty sleeping bag and scant belongings left strewn in disarray behind a waste bin not far from the city's busy shopping district. A quick, furtive glance from one side to another – to check that he wasn't being observed – before he scavenged the few items for himself (the sleeping bag, a photo frame with a picture of a child with her father, a small suitcase containing some old clothes, and a half-empty bottle of *Glenfiddich*, concealed within a blue plastic carrier bag) placing them in an old *Waitrose* shopping trolley, one of its wheels squeaking noisily, which contained all of his worldly goods (amounting to very little) and a small Norfolk terrier dog, curled up amongst a bundle of clothes – every successful beggar's obligatory friend.

"Here we go Jasper, something to keep us warm in the winter," the homeless guy rasped. "And a new wardrobe!" he chuckled. He tossed the picture frame into the trolley with barely another glance. The brown dog looked up absently, made a little sniffy-whining sound, then curled back up again, preferring sleep to the company of the smelly old homeless man who now pushed the trolley away.

CHAPTER TWENTY-FIVE
HARRIET

"George? It's Harry."

"*Are you okay*?" he sounded distant, almost distracted, but the poor connection did not fail to convey the note of concern in his voice. "*Where are you*?"

"I'm okay George, I've not been harmed – not yet. But I've lost Charlie… When I was taken I left him by the road…" She sounded a little panicked, her voice going up an octave.

"*It's okay, Harry. I have Charlie. He's safe with me, just a little banged up and bruised.*"

Harriet sighed, closed her eyes and blinked back tears. "Thank God," she said, before going quiet, absorbing the news that allayed her deepest fears. After a moment she dared to speak again, trusting her voice not to crack.

"George, listen – they will let me go if you do something for them."

"*Harry, I can come for you.*"

"Don't do anything stupid. They said they will KILL me if you don't do exactly what they ask."

George fell silent. "*Okay, Harry. Who are they, what do they want*?"

"Who they are, I haven't a clue. One of the guerrillas, though, I recognise. He's been after us for a long time."

"*Dominic Schilling?*"

"Yes, that's him. He nearly killed us with his car."

"*What do they want?*"

"It's something to do with a diamond. They said for you to meet with them at *Ed's Easy Diner* in the *London Trocadero* tomorrow, 12:00 p.m. where they'll give you further instructions."

"*Let me guess, they want to use Sophie?*"

"Just do what they ask." Harriet had begun to cry, her words wracked by sobs. "I want to come home."

"*Okay my love. Stay strong. I'll get you out of this. Trust me…*"

She wanted to tell her husband that she loved him, but Brayden had snatched the mobile from her hand and had disconnected the call.

"Thank you, Harry… That wasn't so hard now, was it?"

"Screw you…"

"That's not nice. Do you kiss your children with that mouth?"

"I've done what you want. Just leave me alone. Please..." She spoke quietly… almost at a whisper.

Brayden nodded slightly, turned and left the room.

Mitch and Dominic were still in the small surveillance booth when Brayden returned, having listened to the entire telephone call and analysed the voices using Voice Stress Analysis software, recording the psychophysilogical stress responses present in the two-way conversation. Though the software could not highlight any lies or deceptions told, it could determine whether either person being monitored had suffered any physiological stress during the exchange. Unsurprisingly, there were spikes of psychophysilogical distress for Harriet – under the circumstances, it was quite understandable. However, through close scrutiny and judgement, it was in Mitch's opinion that Harriet and George Jennings had been sincere in their questioning and answering, and no signals or mixed messages could be deciphered.

"Do you think George will play nicely?" Dominic, not an expert in using the VSA technology, genuinely wanted to know. He was swinging from side to side on the office chair.

"There's nothing to suggest otherwise. We will just have to wait and see if he shows up tomorrow." Mitch absently rubbed at his bandaged head, the swelling had heightened and felt tender to the touch.

"What if he tries to rescue his damsel in distress?" Dominic, always thinking, always looking at the alternatives pressed the American agents.

"Well, that IS a possibility," Brayden drawled. "Especially as his damsel *does* have a GPS tracker strapped to her ankle," he added.

"Oh... why on earth did you not take it off her?!" Dominic was annoyed and stood up fast, making for the exit, his mind set on disarming the GPS signal.

"Wait! Dominic, it's not a problem. Really, I mean, I know something that you don't."

"What's that, Brayden? Do you believe you can trust them? Well, I've been chasing after them for two years, and I can tell you something, *Yank*... they are very clever. More clever than you could ever think."

"I don't doubt their intelligence, Dom. But, that's not the point. The point is I know for a fact that George will be at the *Trocadero* tomorrow."

"And there you go again, such certainty and assurance. What is it you're not telling me?"

"Okay, Dom. Let's just say we know George a lot better than you think YOU do."

Locked in the white room, Harriet was pacing awkwardly again, her swollen leg sending pain up and downwards with each clumsy footfall.

She was relieved that Charlie was safe, but she didn't know the half of it. Unaware that her home had been attacked and that her husband had almost taken a bullet in the arm whilst rescuing their children, she just hoped that her captors kept to their word and released her once George had done what they demanded.

But she couldn't help thinking that maybe things weren't going to be that simple. Sure, they intended indirectly to use Sophie through George, to gain an item of value using her unique abilities, but what's to say that it would stop there? What if this was all just a ruse to get access to Sophie? George had kept her location hidden even from her, so what better way of finding the girl than by luring her out using subterfuge, a tact often employed by spies and covert government agencies. Agencies such as… the *CIA*. She was certain that was who her captors were. How Dominic fitted into it, she couldn't second guess.

Oh God, what have I done? It's a trap! Wracked with guilt and anxiety, she stopped pacing and tried to think. *What to do? I told George not to come for me. How stupid!*

Sitting back down, her hand strayed absently to her ankle, as if to scratch an itch. A hard protuberance bulged beneath her loose and light summery trousers just above her ankle bone. She stroked it as she remembered. The GPS tracking device was small and strapped discreetly to her leg. She'd worn it for so long now that she'd completely forgotten about it. A small LED flashed subtly every forty seconds indicating its functioning. She felt the small button to the side of it, which she knew when pressed, signalled a panic warning.

Maybe I can give George a warning… she thought.

Trying to look inconspicuous, she gently pressed the panic button. The LED continued to flash, just slightly faster – every twenty seconds it pulsated, indicating a change in Harriet's state of mind and wellbeing.

Okay George, you were right – you insisted on these gadgets and toys. Don't let me down. Harriet sat back down in the room's solitary chair, closed her eyes and willed her predicament to go away.

CHAPTER TWENTY-SIX

GEORGE

THE THREE KIDS WERE cramped in the back of the *Peugeot*, elbow to elbow, Meredith on the right behind the driver's seat, Charlie on the left side (in pain and looking utterly miserable) and Stanley in the middle, whilst Sophie (unseen by any passersby, but very much present), sat in the passenger seat in front. George had loaded the black suitcase and a large sports holdall that Amanda had managed to prepare before being shot, into the boot and was back in the driver's seat. Sophie had retrieved the backpack and her own, slightly smaller sports holdall and had collected a bag of personal possessions belonging to the kids, and had placed them alongside George's. The boot was now as tightly packed as the back seat was, like they were about to embark on a summer vacation rather than making a getaway to preserve their freedom and lives.

In one hand George held a *Nexus* tablet computer, replacing the one smashed out on the Seabrook Road, GPS tracking app already installed and activated; in the other hand were a couple of ordinary looking sunglasses. Deactivating all but Harriet's signal, George placed the *Nexus* onto the dashboard, secured in place by Velcro fastening tape attached to both the back of the computer and the dash, and positioned the screen so that he could watch it without taking his eyes off the road. A faint signal flashed to the north of the screen.

"Put these on," George handed Stanley and Meredith the glasses, both donning the innocuous looking fashion accessory; once again, aided by their unique spectacles, they were pleased to see their newfound companion seated in front of them. Charlie looked at his brother and sister with a puzzled look.

"They help us see," said Stanley, seeing the question about to spring from the youngest child's lips.

"See what?" asked Charlie. Seeing the passenger door open and swiftly close of its own accord had barely registered with him.

"You wouldn't understand..." replied Stanley, dismissively.

"What's going on dad?" asked Meredith tersely. She'd not spoken since her father had closed Slocum's eyes. Instead her mind kept playing the nightmare that had invaded her bedroom over and over. She'd watched her father, her gentle parent, the man whom had sat her on his lap, read her bedtime stories, played 'row, row, row your boat, gently down the stream', who'd sung her lullabies to sleep, shoot a man without thought or contrition. *Who IS my father?*

George started the engine. The sound of sirens wailing mournfully, complaining in the distance, a protest against the urgency and the speed in which they intended to travel, hurriedly approaching.

"Let's get away from here, shall we. I will tell you as much as I can along the way... once we are safe."

George drove the small vehicle out of the close, Willoughby Rising shrinking behind them, the small, ruffled heap that was Amanda Slocum, lying dead outside the front door, almost out of sight, her blouse undulating beneath a slight sea breeze grazing her lifeless body.

I'm so sorry Amanda, he thought. How many more people were willing to die to keep Sophie and his research from getting into the corporation's hands?

Intuitively, he guessed a lot more.

Turning right at the junction, George took the vehicle in the opposite direction to that from which he had come. Their pursuers no doubt would be coming from London; fortunately the destination most in his thoughts was more north-easterly rather than southwest. Using the *Nexus* like a Sat-Navigation system, George followed a course that would place him somewhere not too distant from where his wife was being held captive.

Keeping to single carriage roads with speed limits alternating between sixty mph, fifty mph, forty mph and thirty mph, passing through villages varying in size, constantly checking the rear-view mirror for signs of being followed, George drove in silence. The kids in the back travelled for the best part in silence, subdued by the events of that afternoon and anxious owing to their mother's abduction.

"Dad, I assume you have a plan?"

The voice surprised Charlie, who, until then, had been oblivious to Sophie's presence (and existence) in the front passenger seat; Sophie's sudden speaking also startled George, jolting the car into a slight swerve. Not wearing the special glasses, George had forgotten Sophie was seated to his left. Like him, she had been quiet, either deep in thought or through ponderous worry.

George was gripping the steering wheel so tight the skin over his knuckles were stretched white. "It was planning, Sophie that landed me in this mess," he said. "I've found improvising has been serving me better just lately."

"Don't forget, there are three kids back there."

"Damn it Sophie, don't you think I know that?!" George shouted, the vehemence in his voice taking, not only his children by surprise, but shocking him. *Where had that come from*? He took a deep breath, calmed himself. *It's the stress*, he told himself. It was getting to him, penetrating his skin as though it were made from porous sandstone. "I'm sorry, it's just..." he trailed off.

"I know," Sophie said, laying an invisible hand on his left arm (his fist was currently closed around the gearstick), offering comfort.

"My wife – your mother – has been taken, and they could be doing all manner of untold things to her." He couldn't mask the pain or hide the anguish in his voice.

"What's this all about dad?" Stanley broke the silence at the back of the car. "Who has taken mum?"

"The bad men took her," exclaimed Charlie matter-of-factly, the first words his traumatised brain permitted since being reunited with his siblings.

"I don't know who has your mother; it's not the same people who have been… you know, chasing after us… not all of them."

"And who are *they*?" chipped in Meredith.

"People I once worked for. You see, I have something that they want, something very dangerous if put in the wrong hands." Another furtive glance to the mirror showed the road behind was clear of any vehicles for at least a mile back. So far, no one was following behind.

"Why don't you just give it to them?" Stanley asked the same question Harriet had asked many, many times. George almost heard her voice reverberating in his mind.

"Because Stan, it's *Sophie* they want. She's as much a part of our family as you are. If faced with another choice, would you want us to consider handing *you* over to them?"

Stanley went quiet.

Sophie sat in silence, embarrassed that she was the reason their mother was missing. She was to blame for her brothers and sister now squashed in the back seat of a small car, driving away from the sanctuary of home to an unknown and potentially dangerous future.

"What about the others, who are they, what do they want?" Meredith was desperately missing her mother. If anything happened to her, she feared she could never forgive herself. She wished she could time travel and go back to that morning and never h Stanley to climb into the crab-apple tree. Everything was

"I don't know who they are *Mer*, probably some govern agency with a similar agenda to my ex-employers; I don't know what they want for sure, but I'd hedge bets on it having to do with Sophie. They want to meet me in London tomorrow."

"What about Sophie?" demanded Meredith, protective of her friend – her only friend, whom until that afternoon she'd thought was left behind at the old house, trapped within that old antique mirror, a ghost or a figment of her imagination.

"I think it's time I told you everything," sighed George. "Let's take a break. You must be hungry. There's a place just ahead."

As the car pulled into an almost deserted pub car park, George noted that the afternoon had made way for the evening. The sun was still in the sky, though now making a hasty retreat towards the western horizon.

How long had they been driving? One or two hours?

As George stopped the car he checked his watch; a quarter-past seven. They'd been travelling for nearly two hours, the realisation bringing forth an achiness to his legs and numbness to his backside.

Doesn't time fly when you are having fun?

Glancing at the tablet on the dash, he observed that his wife's GPS signal continued to pulsate, though with an additional symbol, a flashing (!) within the red GPS beacon. The panic button on her GPS tracker had been activated. Harriet had set off the alarm indicating she was in danger.

George was confused. She'd told him *not* to do anything stupid, so why the change of tact? Despite the panic symbol, George's mind was set. He intended on doing what his wife had been coerced into instructing. He would meet with her captors in London the following

;ay. It was all part of an elaborate plan. Sometimes you had to consider the bigger picture before acting out.

The Pig and Whistle was a village pub, and was housed in a modern brick building belonging to a popular brewery chain. According to the board screwed to the wall to the left of the main entrance, the proprietor promised cooked meals from '11am to 11pm – families welcome!'

George and the children relished the opportunity to leave the car, to walk off and stretch dead, tired legs, and return some life to their aching limbs. So as not to elicit curiosity, George opened the passenger door to let Sophie out making it appear as though he was retrieving something (he took the *Nexus* from the dash board, carefully reaching over Sophie so not to knock her). Once Sophie was out of the car, he closed the door and centrally locked the vehicle.

"How quaint," she said, eyeing up the structure. It was a relief to get out of the car, and almost a novelty to be joined with her family. Had the events of earlier not weighed on her mind, she might have convinced herself that this was just a family outing, the rarest of rare treats. She'd often dreamt of such an occasion, frequently wished that she could live a normal life and be treated and cared for like any other child… or teenager. Within the space of a month her body had aged closer to adulthood. Some days it was like waking after a long period of being trapped within a coma, so utterly different and surprising her appearance would be from the night before. And her clothes! There had been several times she had awoken only to find that she'd moved up a dress size, her pyjamas having stretched ridiculously to the point that they needed to be cut free from her body to enable their removal. Just another mere by-product of Daddy's little experiment…

Meredith had thrown a protective arm around Charlie's shoulder, careful of his fractured bones. He winced from the slightest hint of a touch, uttering "Ow!" every-so-often just as a reminder to elicit sympathy from any and everyone in hearing distance.

"I'm sorry," she whispered to her brother.

Charlie shrugged with one shoulder. "That's al'right," he said in a small voice, looking down at his feet.

"Okay folks," started George. He turned off the *Nexus* and led his kids towards the pub's entrance. "We need to be careful here. No one will be able to see Sophie – and we don't want to draw attention to that fact under any circumstances. It goes without saying kids, but I need you to be on your best behaviour." Ahead of the family, arriving at the entrance door, George turned and reemphasised in a low voice: "No shenanigans of any sort... from *any* of you."

For many village pubs, trade was often slow or decisively nonexistent. The Pig and Whistle was no exception, having become a victim of a change in culture where cheap supermarket booze, sky-high taxation and a deep recession, had driven its regular customer base to stay at home, all but forsaking the place. The only saving grace was its restaurant, the nearest premises serving food for nearly twelve miles in any direction.

The bar/restaurant had tables laid out for as many as 150 patrons, but on this weekday just four people took up places within the colloquial setting; a young professional couple, man in collar and tie, woman in a light, summery dress – empty plates pushed aside as they enjoyed the last dregs of a pint of *John Smiths* and a wine spritzer; two lonely men sat at either end of the bar nursing glasses of beer or spirits, a newspaper in front of one, a mobile phone in the hand of the other.

Behind the bar stood a giant of a man, six-feet-eight-inches in height and built like a Chieftain tank. Smartly dressed in black shirt and tie, a white apron was tied about his waist. His hair was jet-black and tied neatly in a tail. He had a mole on his right cheek which did little or nothing to diminish his looks. He was a handsome man with the look of someone of Spanish descent. On first glance, George was intimidated and felt that the man would still tower over him even were he to sit down on the floor.

"Ah, welcome," the barman greeted in a deep, resonant tone, heavily Norfolk accented. "And what can we be doin' for ya todi?" Meredith imagined him to be a pirate, further encouraged by the large hooped earring that hung from his left ear like a perch for a budgerigar.

"Can we have five large cokes please?" George ordered.

"Five?" The barman counted just four people in front of him. His look was baffled.

"Yes... it's thirsty work driving," George replied without thought and without further enquiry. It was a warm day after all.

Putting the five pints of *Pepsi Coke* onto a tray, the barman completed the order with a flourish, dropping a black straw into each.

"Can I get ya anythin' more?"

"We'll order food shortly, if okay?"

"That be fine," he shrugged. "Jus' come up t' bar when ya ready with ya table number." He rung up the drinks order on the cash register in front of him. "That'll be nine-pounds-fifty for now."

George paid the behemoth with a crisp ten pound note and told him to keep the change. He then carried the tray to a table that had been setup for eight, located to the furthest part of the room that, until then, had been completely empty. On sitting, he was satisfied that he could talk relatively easily in no danger of being heard or listened to, and pleased with his seated position (facing the entire room with his back to a wall), allowing ample sight of all comings and goings and a vantage point that afforded him a view of the car park through the sheet windows to his left.

Meredith and Stanley were starving and having quickly discovered the menus stashed in a tidy stand to the centre of their table, were perusing a fair selection of cooked meals and tasty snacks.

Settling into his seat, distributing the drinks around the table, George looked at his children and sighed. *Now to keep a promise*, he thought.

"I guess you want to know what this is all about?" he started, "why we have been running for so long like fugitives or terrorists, and from whom?"

Meredith nodded enthusiastically; Stanley and Charlie just sat and stared. George couldn't see Sophie preferring not to wear sunglasses indoors, not wishing to draw undue attention. As it was, the big Spaniard kept glancing his way.

George nodded in affirmation. "I promise to give you all your answers, though it's not going to be easy and might not make much sense to you. But first, we must eat."

A little over an hour-and-a-half later, refreshed and rested, George and his brood returned to their car. The barman interrupted serving a new patron to bid him with an unfriendly smile, "Fare y'well," as George and his children hastened past, the car outside no longer a solitary fixture within the car park. A dozen more vehicles had arrived bringing forth some much needed custom to the village pub. It was edging closer to nine o'clock and dusk was almost upon them.

After dinner, George had made a call to the only person left who he could trust; Harriet's father. He didn't live too far away in a home he shared with a much younger woman. The man was now in his seventies and hadn't had contact with his daughter in more than a decade – not since becoming estranged from Harriet's mother after eloping with Harriet's best friend, Camilla. The shame and the feud had split the family, and everyone knew that the damage done between father and daughter was irreparable. It was for precisely that reason he'd chosen to leave his children in their grandfather's care. Simply, his house would be the last place anyone would think to look for George or his family.

Once again the *Nexus* tablet was switched on and placed on the dashboard, a dot continuing to pulsate; the (!) still flashing; the captive woman's location remained unchanged. George put his wife's plight out of mind and started the car's engine.

During their meal, George had attempted to explain the situation with regards to Sophie, though sketching over her abilities, the 'whys' and 'wherefores' of their regular house moves, and the recent display of violence and murder they'd borne witness to. Meredith, who had known of Sophie's existence for some time, took it in her stride, though the prospect of more danger as they sought reuniting with their mother daunted her. Stanley and Charlie, being very young, were a little harder to convey the more extreme details of their situation, but George tried, and by the end of the two courses (burger, pizza, lasagne, gammon steak and roast chicken for main and chocolate brownies, sticky toffee pudding or ice cream for dessert), they all understood the severity of the situation and the undeniable risk of danger they all faced.

Buckling his seatbelt, George took the car out of The Pig and Whistle's car park, counting fourteen ordinary vehicles scattered around, none arousing fear or suspicion. He drove onward. According to the GPS app, Harriet was located just a little over twenty miles away. Harriet's father, George knew, lived less than five miles to the west.

The time according to the digital clock built into the dash corresponded exactly with his wrist watch:

8:59 p.m.

They'd been at The Pig and Whistle for longer than George had intended, and despite the speed with which they had all eaten and the short time it had taken George to recount the abridged version of events that led to them being on the run AND culminating in Harriet's capture, and the consequences of it, George couldn't help worry that he was exposing his family to too great a risk. He should have taken them directly to Theodore's, got them out of danger.

As the car bobbled over the rough, uneven surface of the pub's gravelly car park, no one noticed the tall figure of the barman watching them leave from the window alongside their recently vacated table, dirty plates and empty glasses left strewn in their wake. He wondered about the fifth dining place, the fifth dinner and dessert and the fifth set of cutlery. He was certain he'd counted only four of them on arrival, and only four of them at the table. He scratched his head, deep in thought, his mind wandering to what this all could mean, how significant it was. A small queue forming at the bar distracted him from his pondering and thoughts of the stranger and his children were soon forgotten. They were now just empty dinner and dessert plates, waiting to be washed up ready for the next paying customer.

CHAPTER TWENTY-SEVEN

TOM KAPLAN

THEY WERE PARKED A couple of cars behind the now abandoned *Ford KA,* which, although Cooper had believed inconspicuous, stood out like an alcoholic at a tea party. From his vantage point, the old man in the back of the black *Bentley Mulsanne* could see the ambulance and the fleet of police cars crammed into the bottleneck of the cul-de-sac. Tom Kaplan had arrived at the scene to witness the removal of the first of two body bags on a trolley, loaded unceremoniously into the back of an ambulance. From the rear seat of his chauffeur driven car he couldn't make out who it was, and even had he been closer to the trolley's unresponsive passenger, *his* or *her* identity would have still been unknown, shielded from the public scrutiny inside zippered white bags.

A throng of (shamelessly) curious bystanders had congregated on a corner, as close as one could get to the excitement without crossing the yellow barricade tapes, the words: POLICE LINE DO NOT CROSS printed repetitively over and over on one side of the tape.

Tom looked at the house at the top of the hill. Willoughby Rising looked like a nice sort of family dwelling, he noted. Cooper had been right in his description.

Overlooking the sea, it was the kind of place he imagined would have captivated his ex-wife in the days when children were an option, before his affair and the ensuing divorce put paid to that. A string of failed relationships later he found himself in his sixties, embroiled in a pent-up loathing for the female species, and all alone. He sighed. Family, and the type of house at the top of the hill was just fool's gold. That ship had sailed past into choppy waters.

Through binoculars he spied a cauldron of activity; men in white coveralls traipsed around the house, some within the grounds, others going back and forth within the building. SOCO, or Scenes Of Crime Officers, carrying out their procedures for what appeared to them to be a double murder, and detectives dressed like those in British police dramas roaming the streets, speaking to potential witnesses and searching for clues, their little note books held in one hand, constabulary issued biros in the other.

Tom glanced at his watch. The time was now edging closer to seven o'clock. The sun was descending the western sky, still warm and pleasant.

All Cooper had to do was wait, he grumbled inwardly. He shook his head at the waste of another of his team, and the seemingly impossible task of catching the girl they simply referred to as 'S'. Just half an hour was all Cooper had to wait and Bravo Team would have been there with extra support. Instead he had to do a *Bruce Willis* and take matters into his own hands. Unlike the *Die Hard* action hero, there was no triumphant third act, no *Yippee ki-yay!* and a barrage of expletives; just cold, hard as stone, death.

On arrival Tom had seen the flashing blue lights and knew instantly what had transpired, especially as radio contact with Cooper had not been re-established since he had warned the young agent against making a move without backup. Prophetic words he now realised. He could've been a saint or Nostradamus.

Cooper indeed wouldn't be getting his promotion or pay rise. Although lady luck did favour the brave and the bold in equal measure, it rarely endorsed stupidity.

The mobile phone started to ring, the opening chords to *Beethoven's Fifth Symphony* played:

Dah, dah, dah-daahhh; dah, dah, dah-daahh…

Tom snatched up the handset from the seat beside him and ended the classical orchestration. "Give me something," he barked. He was desperate for news of the Jennings family after the day that he'd had. At the end of the phone Bravo Team leader Jack Wyatt audibly cleared his throat. It sounded like a smoker's hacking cough.

"*My sources indicate that there were two bodies found at the scene. One was unidentifiable. A woman, in her late forties, large build, took a bullet to the chest, found across the threshold of the front door. The other body was found upstairs in one of the bedrooms. It was Cooper, ID was found in his wallet. He'd taken two shots, one to the stomach, the other, the head – a dead centre, expertly carried out, precision kill shot. Someone with experience.*"

Tom considered the news gravely. Not only had he lost an aspiring agent, he faced yet another setback regarding the capture of the girl. He cursed aloud.

"Do you have any good news?" he demanded.

"*Um, no, afraid not sir. Not regarding S or the other occupants of the house. They're gone without a trace.*"

"They can't be far."

"*Command centre are reporting something interesting that might be useful, mind…*"

"Go on…"

"*An analyst thinks they've located the mother. Apparently a good satellite was passing overhead providing a visual of a vehicle in the area where Harriet was abducted; they managed to follow it to a warehouse on the outskirts of Norwich.*"

"Interesting," Tom interjected.

"*Yes,*" he continued. "*Using traffic cameras they have identified the vehicle used; a silver Audi Q7, the plates are registered to a Martin Hamilton from Inverness, but he's not our guy. The plates were stolen a week ago from a Nissan Quashqai.*"

"Have they checked out this *Martin Hamilton* fellow properly?"

"*No need, Martin Hamilton isn't who we are after. Traffic cameras gave us a pretty good image of the driver and forward passenger of the Audi. There was someone else in the back of the car, but it was too dark to see, so no ID has been possible. They ran the image of the two faces we do have through their facial recognition software and came out with a couple of names.*" The voice at the end of the phone paused. "*You're not going to like it.*"

"Wyatt, I don't take to intrigue or suspense, so quit with the histrionics. Just get on with it and give me the names."

"*Brayden Scott and Mitch Youngs… travelling salesmen on the face of it, working for a large pharmaceutical enterprise based in Fort Worth, Texas, with offshoot branches all over the globe, including here in the UK. Further digging reveals they aren't exactly what they are supposed to be. Both have US military backgrounds, serving in Iraq and Afghanistan; Mitch also fought in Somalia; both have history in Clandestine Services, and their frequent air miles and irregular travel patterns indicate they work for the American government.*"

"What are we dealing with: Homeland security, NSA, CIA, FBI, or something entirely different?"

"*Best guess is they are CIA, or an offshoot of the agency.*"

"So our American cousins are operating in our backyard, looking, I guess, for our girl."

"*It would seem like it sir, bloody Yanks.*"

Tom paused to watch the second body being wheeled out of Willoughby Rising towards a second waiting ambulance. The first had moments earlier driven past with little pomp and no fanfare.

"You say you have the location of where they took the Jennings woman? You're sure?"

"*Yes, a supposedly disused warehouse.*"

"Very good Jack, all's not lost. I'm not a betting man, but George Jennings is quite resourceful. I'd stake my wealth that he will mount a rescue operation. He loves his family more than life itself, so it's a bit of a no-brainer. Of course, he'd be no match for two hardened war veterans and whoever else they might have there... but the girl..." Tom trailed off, deep in thought, considering the possibilities. Two decorated war veterans, with Special Forces training and years' of covert operational experience would pose little or no challenge to Sophie, after all Alpha Team had succumbed with the least of pressure, and they were ex-Marine commandos.

"*Sir?*"

Tom snapped out of his reverie. "Take your team to this warehouse and be on standby. Stake it out. Your orders are to observe and report only. Not like our dead friend Cooper over here. If we play our cards right the Americans will do most of our work for us – all we need do is hold our nerve and, most importantly, put the *Moët* and *Chandon* on ice."

CHAPTER TWENTY-EIGHT
SAMUEL

SAMUEL JACKSON FELT LIKE a spare cog in a well-oiled machine, surplus to adding any real value to proceedings, dejected and suddenly unsure of what was going on. Overlooking the command centre from the mezzanine floor balcony, he watched the throng of activity and unmitigated excitement, unaccustomed to being precluded from such high brow proceedings. News had cascaded that an agent in Tom Kaplan's charge had stormed a hideout thought to be where the Jennings family were residing, ignoring direct orders to wait for backup and ending up dead for his troubles.

Samuel had also kept abreast of developments closer to home, like where Harriet Jennings had been taken, and who her abductors were, but stayed aloof. He was still reeling from Ryan Barber's betrayal – the pain from this knowledge felt like a stab in the chest with a rusty sabre.

It hadn't been a complete surprise to learn that the CIA were muscling in, also in search of their quarry; after all, the human technology they'd developed and the by-product they had stumbled upon could change the game of war for any in possession of it. He was in no doubt that there were others – government agencies *and* terrorists – all seeking the girl borne from project *CHAMELEON*.

Despite being detached from the core of proceedings, Samuel received regular updates to the status of Kaplan and his team from one of the analysts sitting close to the action; as of yet, nothing noteworthy had come up except the satisfying news that Tom Kaplan had gained no better luck thus far than he had.

Stupid old fool trying to go this alone. Samuel was bitter. He still felt that he had more than a fair chance at apprehending George and his *oh-so* special daughter… But until Tom had finished playing out his hand, he was powerless. Like Cooper, he was under strict orders to 'hold fire' by the corporation's CEO. Unlike Cooper, he was adhering to the instruction to the letter.

I just need to bide my time…

He felt he had more of a chance at success now that the mole in the organisation had been flushed out. He still couldn't believe the turn events had taken. Had he been rash with his decision to have him terminated?

Too late now, he reflected sadly. What was it his mother used to say? *Sleep on any big decisions you have to make, and never carry out something in haste – especially in anger – because more often than not you'll only regret it…*

Samuel heard her voice in his head. Nine times out of ten she was right. And now he was starting to wish he'd been more lenient with Ryan.

Ryan… I'm sorry. It had hurt the Director enormously to learn that his most trusted and loyal colleague had betrayed him. He'd also been a close friend, which made the deception all the more unsettling. If you can't trust your friends, who can you trust?

A short time passed as Samuel continued to watch the fifty or so analysts move about with purpose like worker ants, all oblivious to his spying from above or the depression that was burgeoning his soul. A moment later he pulled himself out of deep thought.

Coming through the entrance was one of the facility's security officers, a man he immediately recognised from the interrogation room. He was carrying a plastic container, the sort that looked like it contained a cake or some pastries. Tupperware. His mum had collected the stuff. It had been all the rage once.

Samuel's mood lifted slightly at the man's arrival, despite his grimy and mussed up appearance. Those hustling around the room closest to the door gave him an apprehensive look and a wide berth, as though sensing danger or seeing a dark aura about him that radiated doom and death.

Another long-time associate who'd shared more than a position at Kaplan Ratcliff Biochemical with him. They'd served in Iraq together during the *Desert Storm* conflict. He was another 'trusted' friend.

The Director stood watching the security officer from the balcony as he approached the metal staircase, then mounted it noisily; each footstep clanged upon the steps, ringing out for everyone's attention.

"Cullum?" Samuel startled the man, momentarily off balancing him. He'd not seen the Director looming above like a gargoyle. And just as ominous, he thought.

"It's done, sir," he said, breathless and a little shaky, making for the second last step on the stairs leading to Jackson's personal floor. "Ryan's dead."

"Good," responded Samuel miserably. He looked down in resignation, avoiding the security officer's eyes. "In the box, is that…?" he left the sentence trailing, unfinished. He couldn't say it even if he'd tried.

Cullum nodded quickly. "It is. What do you want me to do with it?" He was now on the metal balcony overlooking the command centre; stopping in front of the Director he suddenly felt overwhelmed by fatigue and muscular pain, his body aching from the exertion associated with hard labour, which was unsurprising. The fact was that a little earlier he'd dug, and then refilled, a grave. Although not unused to carrying out this type of task, it wasn't one his body had ever adjusted to and never would.

Samuel guided the man into his office with a wave of his hand, hanging back for the bedraggled officer to move deep into the room before closing the door. He waited for him to sit at the large conference sized desk before sitting himself at the head of the table, his back to the video screen hanging from the wall.

"You know, in some cultures, it was thought that to eat the heart of your enemy enabled you to consume their spirit and absorb their strength. Some even believed it would make you immortal, can you believe that?"

"You plan to eat it, sir?"

Samuel laughed, loud, hearty, almost false, his voice booming and echoing around the large room. "Do I look like a savage lunatic to you?" Not waiting for a reply, the Director continued, "No, I don't mean to eat it. I will pickle it instead and keep it on display as a permanent reminder to me, and a deterrent to others. This is the fate that befalls those who mean to deceive me. If it wasn't so barbaric, and murder not so *illegal*, I'd have had you bring me his head and place it on a spike like the Kings of old." Samuel sighed. "I belong in a different age," he said whimsically, before returning his attention to the security officer.

You belong in a nuthouse, Cullum thought distractedly. For a moment Cullum worried the Director was seeing through the pretence, and his guilt from the fabrication caused his cheeks to flush. He felt hot and sticky all over. Like the woodsman in *Snow White and the Seven Dwarves*, he was going to fool the master with a decoy – only his *dupe* did not come from a pig. Samuel misread Cullum's demeanour, thinking it more to do with the security man's exertions than anything duplicitous or untoward.

"I'll leave it on your desk then." Cullum placed the Tupperware box onto the desk and pushed it towards the Director. Ridding himself of the grisly prize gained him a little confidence.

"Tell me... did Ryan suffer a horrendous ordeal?"

Cullum was slow in his reply. "I can tell you that, sure," he said, comfortable with the lie but taking no chances with eye contact. Instead he stared at the Tupperware box. "Ryan screamed like a baby throughout... until, that was," he paused for effect, "I cut out his heart. He watched it beat its last then just slumped forward; bled everywhere - even on my shoes - and then died." He had rehearsed this in his head - over and over - so the lie sounded quite natural by the time he needed to recite it.

Samuel didn't suspect a thing.

"Good... good." He sounded sad, withdrawn even. His thoughts were in turmoil.

"I'll be off then..." Cullum stood to go. Samuel was deep in thought and hadn't heard the security officer. Neither did he notice Cullum hastily retreat out of the office and disappear back down the stairs, exiting the room with barely a second glance.

But somebody else did.

The secret to successful spy work was having a heightened skill of observation. Being able to see and hear things most people barely register was essential; and it was a talent the newly appointed Assistant Intelligence Officer had been born with.

CHAPTER TWENTY-NINE

THEO

GEORGE HAD BROUGHT THE *Peugeot* to a halt outside the semi-detached house which he knew belonged to Harriet's father. It had been her family home, the place where she'd grown up, the place where Harriet had lived before George had whisked her away like the prince in every young woman's fairytale.

The house had a short driveway on which a black *BMW* was parked in front of a garage, the mahogany 'up and over' door of which was pulled up to reveal another car; a silver *Porsche Boxter* convertible, its roof retracted.

Although it was still warm, the overhead light had faded as night closed in. A new moon sidled up the eastern sky, pale and discrete like a tiny cloud. The time was edging towards half nine and full darkness was an hour away.

"Kids, you wait here. I'll come and get you in a moment." George turned the ignition key, killing the engine and the radio (which had been on a Norfolk station playing rock tunes).

"Where are we?" Stanley stifled a yawn, peering out of the car at the house alongside where they'd parked.

Ignoring the question, George climbed out of the car, poked his head through the driver's side and reassured his children:

"I won't be long. I just need to check everything is alright."

George turned, strode forward through the gates leading into the driveway, then continued further towards the front door of the house, passing the *BMW* on his left and a well tended garden to his right, the short lawn vibrant green, lush and ornate – it would not have looked out of place on day one of Wimbledon.

At the door, George depressed the doorbell placed below the number 'seventy-three', and listened to the subtle chime from within that 'dingdonged' just the once, slightly muted by the double-glazed white PVC door. A moment later a shadowed silhouette could be seen shuffling forward through the frosted and stained glass, the twin roses adorning the twin set glass panels allowing light to filter through but minimal sight of the interior from the outside.

A key was turned from inside and the sound of multiple security bolts within the double-glazed unit clicked and grated as the man inside unlocked the door. It opened up fully to reveal a tall, lithe man in his late sixties, though his appearance belied his age. Standing six-feet high, he appeared much taller to George, owed partly to the way he stood and the thick soled slippers he wore on his feet; he was confident and projected virility as though trying to impress, his chest thrust out. Though his hair was white, it was cut short and his craggy face appeared youthful despite some obvious wrinkles, masked by the deep tan that could only have been gained from an exotic or extended vacation abroad. George would later learn that Theo had a week earlier returned from a cruise around the Caribbean, and from the way he was dressed he looked like he was still in holiday mode. He wore a loose cotton shirt buttoned up to halfway, and three-quarter-length stone-white trousers. The dark blue slippers looked odd to say the least.

"Well, well, well… George Jennings." Despite living in Norfolk, the man's upbringing was in the East End of London. His voice had not lost any of its cockney accent. "You've got a bloody nerve showing up 'ere," he said, folding his arms resolutely across his chest. "A bloody nerve."

"Theo," George said by way of acknowledgement.

"So... Why have you thought it prudent to break you and your wife's vow of never seeing me again? Despite me offering an olive branch before my wedding... and another before the 'basin of gravy' arrived." Theo had thrown in some cockney slang, 'basin of gravy' meant 'baby'.

"Can I come in?" George asked.

"No, you bloody can't! You tell me what has your knickers in a twist at such an hour."

"All right, Theo. Alright. It's about Harry."

"What about my daughter? She isn't dying, is she?" A look of concern flashed across the older man's face. He dropped his arms to his side.

"No... no," George quickly reassured, throwing his hands up in a gesture that meant 'forgive me'. "She is in danger, though. I need your help."

"Tell me, George Jennings. What of my daughter? Where is she?"

George proceeded to outline the day's events, making light of the whys and wherefores, but laying on the plight as thick as one could without mentioning the attack at Willoughby Rising, or the fact that since Harriet had emancipated all ties to her father, Sophie had been born and that she was... *different.*

"Why haven't you gone to the police?" asked Theo reasonably in response to George's outlandish claim that his daughter had been kidnapped and held for some sort of bizarre ransom.

"It's complicated," George replied earnestly. "We are being pursued by others – *resourceful* others – we don't know who we can trust."

"So you came to me. Not because you want to, I see… but because you have no choice." Theo wasn't a stupid man.

George shrugged, intimating agreement. "Sorry," he said. Theo took a deep breath and sighed.

"Where are the children?"

George glanced over his shoulder as he spoke. "In the car, back there."

"I see," Theo took a moment to consider the situation, deliberating over the moment. "What *exactly* do you want from me George?" he finally asked.

"Just… sanctuary. For a couple of days." It would turn out to be longer.

"Okay, despite all else, you are family. Just for a couple of days mind. Let me go tell Camilla that we are having guests whilst you round up your brood."

"Thanks Theo." George meant it and half smiled to his father-in-law. Without emotion, the older man turned away and pushed the front door to, leaving it slightly ajar, an invitation to come in when ready.

A quick trot out of the garden, George returned to the car and climbed back in, the door he left open.

"Dad, where are we?" Stanley asked again, his tone anxious, slightly pitchy. He'd watched his father disappear behind a row of conifers, placed in such a way to the front of the house it afforded the property an illusion of remoteness, privacy and security. It gave little and none.

George smiled warmly, noticing similar looks of apprehension on Meredith and Charlie, squashed up together in the back of the car. Sophie was still invisible to him without the glasses.

"I've brought you somewhere safe. These people we can trust. We can stay here a couple of days until things have settled and I've got your mother back. Come let me take you in, introduce you to your grandfather."

The click of Sophie's seatbelt sounded as she unclasped the restraint. She started to open the door.

"Not you Sophie. I think you ought to take your medication first. Theo is in for enough surprises without you turning up like that."

Without speaking, Sophie pulled the door closed again. Meredith noticed the look of annoyance on Sophie's face in the reflection of the rear-view mirror but chose to say nothing.

"When you're done love, lock the car and come and join us." George tossed the car keys in the direction of his daughter, always amazed to see things just 'disappear' within thin air. He closed the driver's door behind him. "And Sophie... don't be too long."

Escorting the three children, George took them up the driveway, past the *BMW* and the open garage, and stopped at the front door, peering through the opening.

"Theo? Is it okay to come in?"

The older man reappeared, followed by a much younger woman in tow. Camilla, Harriet's former friend, was holding Theo's hand, being led like a prom queen to the dance floor. She was how he remembered her, stunningly beautiful, painfully thin with a complexion that was pale, almost milky-white – like that of a porcelain doll, giving no indication that she'd only a week earlier returned from a trip to Saint Lucia, Barbados and the Cayman Islands. Standing within Theo's broad shadow, she appeared just as fragile. Her hazel-brown eyes, delicate nose and bright red lips were accentuated by the mousey bobbed hair that framed her face. Wearing a floral print dress that hung from her shoulders on thin, bootlace straps, and white slip-on sandals, George could see how easily Harriet's father would have been charmed by her. She was an attractive woman.

"Well, well, well. Don't you three look a sight for sore eyes?"

Meredith, Stanley and Charlie stood together in a huddle behind George, almost cowering away from the tall old man standing at the door. Their appearance was ruffled, sweaty and grimy – and with Charlie's arm in a cast, they indeed looked a motley crew, bringing to mind images of children from an old Charles Dickens novel, maybe *Oliver Twist* or *Great Expectations*.

"Kids… meet your grandad, Theo."

"Grandad? Mummy said he was…" Stanley stopped abruptly; a sharp elbow to the stomach from Meredith suspending the sentence.

"Theo, your grandchildren: Meredith, Stanley and Charlie," George presented each child with a pointed finger.

"Pleased to finally make your acquaintance."

"There is one other, but she is making herself more… presentable. It's been a long journey."

"Well, don't just stand out there. Come in, come in. Make yourselves at home." Theo, still holding his wife's hand, led George and the three children through the hallway into a sparsely furnished living room. "Are you hungry? Stupid question – kids are always hungry!"

George couldn't fail to notice the many photographs framed symmetrically on the main wall above a grand fireplace, surrounding a wall mounted flat screen television.

Theo noticed George's quizzical look, and followed his son-in-law's gaze. A particular photograph had caught his eyes.

"Aren't they beautiful? Twins – Josephine and Henry! They are both abed, but I'm sure they will be delighted to meet you all in the morning."

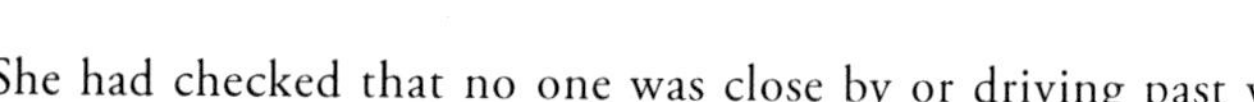

She had checked that no one was close by or driving past when she opened the car door and climbed out. Unseen, she walked round to the boot, popped the catch and reached into the deep receptacle for the sports holdall. Unzipping it, she revealed within its guts the jet injector and the many vials of serum that countered the unique physical side effect to her genetic modification. With the injector and a vial of the ochre liquid, Sophie returned to the passenger seat and sat down. Preparing the injection was simple. She loaded the jet injector like an automatic gun, pushing the vial into the butt of it, applying pressure until the small bottle 'clicked' into place, its foil seal breaking.

"Here we go again," she muttered, holding the jet injector in her right hand. She reached round to the top of her left arm, pressing the injector's gun-like muzzle to the side of her bicep. Once in place she depressed the trigger, releasing the gas pressure with a jolt, injecting the serum in a quick burst that was so fast she barely had time to register the stinging sensation. What she *did* feel was the immediate warmth that always followed the injection, spreading up and down her body just beneath the skin but flowing throughout; the tingling sensation was almost like pins and needles, though pleasant, it was also mildly irritating and always made her want to go to the bathroom.

Placing the jet injector on the driver's seat, Sophie sat and waited for the serum to take effect. Holding both hands, palm facing in front of her, she watched with bated breath as her transformation began. Starting at her extremities, first her fingers and toes reappeared, then fluidly visibility spread up her body in tandem with the warmth flowing through her; her arms; her legs; her torso; finally her head.

"There I am," she whispered, then using the mirror, she tidied herself up by combing a hand through her hair, which she then tied into a tail with a hair band she'd kept in a pocket.

No longer any need for care, with no threat of shocking or surprising anyone, she opened the car door without thought –

narrowly avoiding a passing cyclist, who teetered for a few yards but managed to retain balance.

"Look what you're doing! Jerk!" yelled a furious woman in luminous pink cycling shorts and a dark ill-fitting T-shirt, her balance still slightly wobbly as she closed in on the junction at the end of the road.

"Sorry!" called out Sophie. The woman replied by flashing a one fingered hand gesture behind her as she rode away, a sign universally accepted as 'go away'. Clearly she hadn't accepted Sophie's apology.

Sophie closed the car door behind her and returned to the boot, replacing the jet injector unceremoniously back into the sports holdall, and zipping it back up before removing the bag from the car in its entirety together with her backpack and the bag she'd collected containing items belonging to her siblings. Her father's bag and suitcase (which Amanda Slocum had prepared), she left in the car, once again concealed with the closing of the door.

A slow walk round the car, through the open gate into the driveway, past the *BMW* and the open garage door, then the short distance to the front door; Sophie soon enough found herself outside the house within which her father and her recently acquainted siblings were now holed up. The white double-glazed door was closed. She reached for the doorbell and depressed the button. The subtle 'dingdong' sounded, soon followed by a gentle rapping against the glass as a dark silhouette came to the door.

"You made it, I see?" George said slightly concerned at the time it had taken her, allowing his daughter to enter. Seeing her *after* what he called an 'SVA' or *Sophie's Vanishing Act,* he always thought he noticed a subtle change in her appearance – it was almost as though she was getting *older* before his eyes.

How old are you now, Sophie? This morning she was sixteen – now she could have passed for eighteen, or almost. Before she was able to read his thoughts, George smiled, genuinely pleased to see her.

"Come, I have someone I'd like you to meet." Entering the living room, from the doorway George announced his youngest, but *eldest looking*, daughter, as though broadcasting her arrival in the court of a King or Queen of old. "Theo, this is my other daughter... Sophie."

As Sophie stepped into the living room the three younger children gasped.

"You're real?" Meredith's eyes were wide, stunned. She looked up at her father, her eyes imploring, begging for some sort of explanation.

Without uttering a word, using just his eyes and a subtle shake of the head, he told her to be quiet. He said more in that one look than he'd said in the whole of the car journey.

"I thought you were a ghost," laughed Stanley.

Putting the children's strange comments down to tomfoolery, Theo waded from the other side of the room to where Sophie and George now stood, just ahead of the doorway.

"Welcome my dear..." Theo took hold of Sophie's hand and gave it a gentle shake. "So beautiful." Turning to George, the older man said: "Tell me, is she adopted because I can't recall you having children BEFORE you and Harry disowned me."

CHAPTER THIRTY

EMILY

LEAVING THE OFFICE SUDDENLY had gained some unwanted attention, but Emily Porter hadn't cared. She had to get out; had to get away. Things were snowballing out of control.

Hitherto, she had been watching the security man and her boss exchange words from her work station before they disappeared within the Director's office. To any casual observer or those passing she appeared to be engrossed in her work, the flat screen in front of her flashing video images and sundry items that gave the pretence that she was working on something important (an Excel spreadsheet open with many lists of stats and data, boring to glance at and unintelligible to those passing – reinforced the charade).

The two men had been standing on the mezzanine floor overlooking the command centre; the security man who'd just arrived was holding a plastic container. *Had he brought Samuel a cake*? she wondered.

The newcomer was dishevelled and weary looking, and after a laborious climb up the metal staircase, stood in front of the corporation's senior intelligence office like a prefect in front of the headmaster. The way he stood interested the newly appointed Assistant Intelligence Officer; the way he held the plastic container intrigued her further as to its contents.

Emily had closed her ears to all the background noises and all distractions that were a constant hubbub around her and focused on the faces that loomed above the floor, reading their expressions, their mannerisms. Using her little-known skill, acquired as a child to help communicate with her deaf mother, she pried into the conversation taking place above her, reading their lips.

Cullum? Samuel Jackson was facing the security officer as he climbed up the remaining steps.

It's done, sir. Ryan's dead. The security man turned just enough so Emily could read his lips.

Good. He paused. *In the box, is that...?* Emily tried to see what it was the security officer carried.

It is. What do you want me to do with it?

The Director turned and showed the security officer called Richard Cullum into his office, ending any further intrusion by Emily into their conversation.

Ryan's dead...

Emily jerked back in shock upon realising what she'd 'lip-heard', the sudden movement of her elbow knocking a half-full cup of coffee over, fortunately spilling liquid away from her computer, the dark brown sludge sluicing across the desk, over its edge, and dripping to create a puddle a couple of inches away from her chair's castors and not far from her handbag.

"Oh sh..." she had stopped herself in mid-curse, pulling up a wad of tissues from a box hidden behind the computer monitor and half-heartedly mopping up the mess. By the time she'd finished swabbing up coffee from around her workstation and starting on the puddle on the floor, the office door on the mezzanine floor above had re-opened and the security man was hastily retreating back down the metal stairs, making his way out of the command room. It looked to Emily that his legs could barely carry him out fast enough.

"No," she whispered to herself, pulling up the bunch of brown, sodden, glob of soggy tissues. She dropped them into a waste bin situated between her desk and what had been Ryan's. His name plate was still positioned atop his computer's base unit beneath the *Dell* VDU screen.

He can't be dead, not my mentor. Not my...

She had left the building in a hurry, driven out of the underground car park erratically, her steering all over the place, her tyres screeching as she took corners too fast – it had been a miracle that she'd arrived home in one piece.

Turning her phone off, closing the curtains at all the windows, and keeping the lights off as darkness slowly descended, Emily had closed the world out and sought refuge in sleep. Taking above the 'recommended' dose of sleeping pills her doctor had prescribed, she'd drifted off to sleep soon after lying her head down on the pillow. Until the morning, the nightmare that was yesterday had momentarily gone away, blanked out by medicinally induced slumber.

But all the memories, the grim abysmal truth and the grief and sadness, all returned, multiplied a thousandfold as Emily had slowly awoken. At first she was bedraggled, then slightly hungover from the side effects. After a short while the subdued memories gradually reformed in her mind, superseding all other feelings.

Now, twenty-four hours later, she was sitting back behind her desk, her ill-gotten promotion did little to compensate the immense loss she was now feeling. Ryan, his desk left as it had been the day before, was gone. Not only from his job, but from life itself. He had been like a father to her. He was the entire reason why she had joined the company in the first place, straight after university, shunning the advances of several corporations all offering employment to the academic starlet, choosing instead the dark and shady mysteries of a multinational biochemical company that spied on the activities of its competition almost as feverishly as it pursued its own affairs.

Shock and grief threatened to destabilise her so she locked her computer, picked up her *Gucci Hobo* handbag (containing everything a woman needed) and left the chaos of the command centre to seek solace in the washroom, passing through two security doors (which she unlocked with her key card) and locking herself into the third of the small toilet cubicles placed in a row like stalls at a horseracing meet.

Behind closed doors she fought back the tears that had leaked almost continuously since she'd learnt the terrible news that Ryan Barber was dead. Taking her completely by surprise, an agonising cry escaped from her lips, echoing within the rest room. Sitting on the toilet lid, she clasped her head in her hands and started rocking back and forth.

The pain of loss was like nothing she had experienced ever before in her twenty-six years. She'd been three and too young to comprehend what death really was when her actual father had died suddenly from a brain tumour. Her mum had often spoken of him as though he was some sort of saint, but the young woman never knew him. The only father figure to feature in her life was Ryan, a kindly man who lived across the street and who had taken her under his wing when she'd become friends with his daughter. A single parent himself, she'd often fantasised that he and her mum would get together; it was similar to a whimsy that Ryan's daughter, Clara, had often talked of, but knew it could never happen. Ryan had been hurt too much by his ex-wife, the scars running too deep to ever heal.

When Clara had died in the explosion at the hands of the very company that her father had helped build, Ryan sought solace from the woman he'd treated almost as kindly as he had treated his own daughter. He had been in bits, his whole world all but destroyed. If it hadn't been for her she knew he would have had nothing.

Now *he* was dead.

Why had Ryan done it?

He'd known the type of people he worked for; knew he could not play games or attempt anything untoward, no matter how noble his thinking – had he not learnt this from the death of his daughter?

Emily's tears were streaking mascara down her face as she came to terms with the truth of the matter.

"It was because of what *he* did to your daughter, that was why you did it, wasn't it Ryan?" The question was barely whispered. She wished he was there to answer her. Had she known, she might've been able to help – she felt her loyalty was more to him, not to her employer who often resorted to dubious means and nefarious practices in getting what it wanted.

The discordant *Pizzicato* chime came from her handbag lying just ahead of the toilet, the accompaniment to a text message's arrival. Sniffing, she reached down to the light pink/grey crescent shaped bag and retrieved the *Samsung Galaxy* phone from deep within. Whilst her hand was in there she pulled out a tissue from the travel pack of *Kleenex* she always carried with her. It was almost empty.

Sniffing back tears, she unlocked the phone with a swish of a finger, lightly tapped the small yellow envelope on the screen and waited for the message to flash up. She removed her spectacles. In the microseconds of waiting she blew her nose and wiped some of the moisture from her eyes. This action did little to improve her appearance. The mascara tracks made her look like someone from a *KISS* video.

The text message was from someone familiar. But it had to be a trick she reasoned, for its sender was someone she'd learnt just the afternoon before was deceased.

She read the message and deciphered its meaning:

Hi Em,

Know that I'm safe.

Remember Penshurst Place.

R. x

The text had been sent from a number she did not recognise,

but the authenticity of its author was unquestionable. The only other person who knew of Penshurst Place and its significance to Ryan and her was Clara – and she was dead.

She could hardly believe it and couldn't help breaking out into a big, cheesy grin.

Of course Ryan isn't dead. How could she have believed it? The man was resourceful and something of an enigma. He would never have put himself into harm's way, not without a means of escape well established. A regular *David Blaine* was Ryan Barber.

Relieved to learn that the former Assistant Intelligence Officer was still alive, she picked herself and her handbag up and unlocked the toilet door. Using the large full-length mirror that supplied a backdrop for the half dozen *Royal Doulton* wash basins that bordered the wall across from the toilet cubicles, she cleaned the mascara streaks and fixed her tousled appearance. Emily replaced her spectacles and readied herself for the return to her desk, and a pretence that everything was all good and dandy.

Although obviously relieved she pondered over the source of her torment: Samuel and the security guard.

Had she misread, literally, their lips?

She doubted it as it was the only means of communicating with her mother, and she'd had a lifetime's worth of experience. No, there was nothing contextual in what they had been saying. The security guard had been specific in his description of Ryan's demise.

Emily applied makeup (from her tardis-*like* handbag) and mulled over what she had lip-read, and what was indicated in Ryan's text.

"Know that I'm safe," she repeated for herself. "Sort-a implies that I may hear otherwise." *Ryan means for everyone to believe that he is dead.* "The person saying that he WAS dead is the security guard who stated that he did it." *It was an elaborate story concocted for the benefit of the Security Director, who no doubt had given the order.*

But what was going on? Why had Richard Cullum told the Director that he had killed Ryan? Unless...

"Unless he was working with Ryan." It made no sense, but she was willing to entertain the idea. "The security officer was lying to protect him. He knows that Ryan is still alive." She whispered it but the acoustics in the ladies' washroom amplified her voice and she flinched from the echo of it.

Emily relaxed and smiled to herself. In her head she heard Ryan, a note of praise in his imagined tone:

Well done, Emily. Well done.

"I have to find him. I need to know what is going on." She barely whispered this time as she reapplied her ruby-red lipstick. She smacked her lips together and a moment later left the washroom, hoping her short disappearance from the command centre hadn't been noticed, not that she needed to care. She was the second-in-command, after all.

Re-entering the command room she couldn't help feeling guilty. Paranoia embraced her as she took to her desk; she imagined everyone was watching, whispering behind hands about her. She was convinced they had all seen that she was gone from her desk for what may have been an inordinate amount of time – much longer than a wee or a poo would normally necessitate.

A glance up to the office on the mezzanine floor calmed her momentarily. The Director was in his office, probably marvelling over the container which the security man had brought him, salivating over its contents, whatever they were - she didn't dare to think.

Without thought she picked up the phone's handset from its cradle and pressed the Directory key on the base, keying in the surname of the security guard:

C U L L U M

There were two *Cullums* stored on the phone's database. The first was Alison who worked in human resources, a pencil-thin woman with an oily complexion, short black hair and a stud in her nose. The second *Cullum* was who she wanted.

Richard Cullum – or *Ricky* to his friends. She didn't know him at all and had never really acknowledged him, but now she found herself pressing the dial button alongside his name and waited to be connected to his extension or for the call to be forwarded to his mobile.

A moment went by with just the sound of the ringing tone filling her ear and the conviction that the man she was calling was not going to answer; unexpectedly the ringing tone stopped, replaced by a man's gravelly voice.

"Security Desk, Cullum speaking."

At first Emily couldn't speak, her mouth was so dry she thought the ability to form words was going to fail her.

"Hello?" Cullum pressed.

Just silence was all Emily offered as she struggled to regain control of her mouth. *What's wrong with me?*

"Hello, who's there?"

Emily was looking around the control room now convinced that people were listening in to her.

"Okay, whoever this is it isn't funny. I'm going to hang up now!" Agitated, Cullum was about to cut the call.

"Wait!" Emily made herself jump by the sound of her voice and all of a sudden she found the restraint that had impeded her speech was gone. "I need your help."

Now it was Cullum's turn to be quiet. He gave no indication that he'd heard her.

Undeterred by Cullum's silence Emily continued: "I want to know where Ryan Barber is."

Emily heard the security man sigh. *"Who is this?"*

"Emily Porter – Ryan's replacement."

"I don't know how to tell you this Miss Porter, but Ryan's dead."

Emily removed the handset from her left ear and placed the cold plastic earpiece to her forehead. Until then she had been unaware of the headache that was starting to form and the plastic provided a microsecond of relief. She placed the handset back to her ear and resumed talking.

"Richard. Quit lying to me. We both know that he's alive," she paused, nervously glancing about her. "I want you to take me to him."

CHAPTER THIRTY-ONE

GEORGE

ED'S EASY DINER WAS located just off Piccadilly Circus on the ground floor of the Rupert Street side of the *Trocadero* opposite The Blue Posts pub.

George had arrived a good half-hour early for the pre-arranged appointment. Leaving the kids back at Theo's, George had driven into the nation's capital together with Sophie, but had ordered her to stay in the car whilst he met with his wife's captors alone. Driving into the city had been slow but they'd allowed enough time.

"But I can help," she'd pleaded.

George shook his head. "It could be a trap. I can't risk losing you." With that he'd walked away from the girl who seemed to be changing and growing by the day, ignoring further protest and heading towards the point his wife had instructed him to meet.

At Ed's Easy Diner George had ordered a 'Just Outta Bed' breakfast and an Iced Coffee Frappe and sat by the window to wait for his order; he watched the hundreds of everyday folk walking by, the many tourists easily identifiable with their foldout maps and their cameras hanging round their necks like medals from the 2012 Olympics and the local businessmen, sharp suited and rushing about their lives in search of their next pound, euro or dollar. He tried to gauge as to whether any of them were potentially heading his way to meet with him. Although *Ed's* had only been open half an hour a steady number of customers had entered into the eatery and by the time the waiter had presented his 'Just Outta Bed' breakfast and Iced Coffee Frappe, most tables around him were full – a basis for why a number of patrons stepping through the doors glared disparagingly at him – George was seated by himself at a table that had been laid for four.

Nearing the end of his meal, a man George recognised stepped into the diner and crossed confidently towards him. He was a bit banged up but avoided too much attention by hiding the bandage (still wrapped around his head) beneath an Oxford University baseball cap, blue in colour with the university logo embroidered to the front. George was mopping up snotty egg yolk from his plate with a broken piece of bread. The man striding towards him had an A4 sized manila envelope and the way he walked indicated that he was packing a concealed weapon beneath his shirt.

"George," the newcomer greeted, taking one of the two empty seats opposite the dining man.

"Dominic," George acknowledged, talking between mouthfuls. "I'm guessing you're not working for the corporation anymore on account of the exaggerated report of your death last night." When the kids had all been tucked up in bed, George had searched the internet for information regarding his wife's earlier accident. In little time he'd read that the media were reporting a two car collision in which the driver of a silver *Mercedes* had been killed. He recognised the number plate despite its mangled, warped and singed condition. Details regarding the occupant of the other car were not known, but George knew. She was being held hostage until he did whatever ill designed plan her captors were shortly to lay down on him.

"What can I say? Reports of my demise were slightly exaggerated."

"Still... it's good to see you didn't go totally unscathed." George had noticed the bandage and accompanying cuts and scratches to the newcomer's face.

The waiter who'd served George his meal appeared at the table and asked the newcomer if he could get him anything.

"I think I'd like one of your premium shakes. The mint chocolate is…" Dominic looked George straight in the eyes, "… to die for," he finished.

The waiter smiled, wrote down the order and disappeared.

"To tell you the truth George, I've grown weary of all the running around. It was beginning to feel a bit like a *JJ Abrams* TV show, or one of those things on HBO. I fancied a change. I'd heard the money is in going freelance," he said with a smile. "But my new business venture takes a bit of financing."

"I guess you've not won the lottery, then?"

"Alas, no… That brings us to you."

George finally finished his meal and laid his cutlery down on the centre of the plate, pushing it to the side.

"Go on," urged George. "Get it over with."

"Here." Dominic handed the manila envelope across the table to George, who accepted it reluctantly and pulled open the flap that was loosely sealed. Inside the envelope was a brochure for the *Masterpiece London Art & Antiques Fair.*

"What's this?" George hadn't known what to expect inside the envelope, but a brochure for an antiques fair was a complete surprise.

"Open it up. I've bookmarked the page."

George flicked through the thin publication and stopped at a page upon which a *post-it* note had been stuck to highlight the article Dominic was drawing his attention to.

George's look initially was nonplussed, before it melted into one of amusement.

"A diamond?"

"Not just any diamond, George. The *Whisper of Persia* is one of the largest diamonds ever cut. 101.29-carats! Its value could set one up for two or three lifetimes."

"It's very pretty." George agreed. He handed the brochure back to Dominic just as the waiter returned with the former agent's order. Dominic closed the brochure and pushed it to the side.

As the waiter placed the premium shake down on the table, Dominic smiled gratefully, directing a "Thanks," his way.

"So, what's this got to do with me?"

Dominic drew a mouthful of mint chocolate milkshake through the straw and grinned.

"Isn't it obvious? I want you and your girl to steal it for me. You do that one thing for us; we'll give you your precious Harriet back."

"What if I refuse?" George didn't want to hear the answer, but Dominic gave it anyway.

"Well, let's just say, you won't have a very long Christmas shopping list this year."

George snorted and shook his head incredulously. "All of this to steal a diamond. Why don't we rob a bank while we're at it!?" His voice was slightly raised drawing one or two heads to turn his way.

"Shoosh, you fool!" Dominic growled. "I don't think you understand that your wife is going to die if you don't do this."

George couldn't believe that his wife had been kidnapped for such a ridiculous reason. All along he'd been expecting that they were going to want to trade her for Sophie. Instead it was to draw her out, to use her in an elaborate scheme that reduced them to nothing more than common criminals.

As the glares and interest from other restaurant patrons subsided, George sunk back into his chair, his demeanour relaxing as the gravity of what was being asked filtered in. After a long, uncomfortable moment of silence had passed, punctuated only by sucking and slurping sounds from Dominic who continued to drink his premium shake, George threw up his hands in surrender, and took a deep breath.

"Okay. Okay," he said. "I'll do it. When?"

Dominic put down his milkshake and theatrically glanced at his wrist watch, a *Seiko* analogue, silver and gold bezel with matching strap; more a functional timepiece than a fashion statement.

"Oh... Shall we say in two hours? Should be enough time for you to plan the heist and get Sophie onboard. I assume she isn't far?"

"She's here," George confirmed. "But two hours... that's not enough time to plan this."

"Don't cry George, I've got it covered. I've cased the place out already. I've been planning this a long time," Dominic finished his milkshake. "Meet me at Chelsea Embankment Gardens at two-thirty; I will fill you in on the details then. Make sure you bring Sophie with you." Dominic stood up, pulling out a black leather wallet from his trouser pocket. Opening it, he pulled a crisp twenty pound note out and dropped it to the table. "I'll shout lunch. They can keep the change," he said. "I'll see you later." Turning, he left George and walked out of the now buzzing restaurant that was Ed's Easy Diner.

George slid the brochure that Dominic had left from the opposite side of the table, and opened it up again to the page on which the *Whisper of Persia* was pictured. He studied the vivid yellow and brilliant cut diamond, wondering what it would feel like in his hands.

Well, won't have to wait long to find out, he thought, finishing what was left of the Iced Coffee Frappe.

CHAPTER THIRTY-TWO

HARRIET

HARRIET WAS GETTING DESPERATE. It had been almost a day since she'd been separated from Charlie. She wondered how he was getting on with his broken arm, wishing that she was there to comfort him. She sniffed back tears, berating herself and willing herself to 'be strong'. If not for herself, for her children.

It seemed like such a long while had passed since the previous morning when she was back at Willoughby Rising with her two sons and daughter, overlooking the North Sea and enjoying the splendid view afforded her from the hilltop. They had been safe, or so she had foolishly thought. With her son falling from the crab-apple tree her world had metaphorically shattered, almost like Charlie's arm had.

But who was she trying to kid? They'd never been safe, not in the truest meaning of the word. When she'd agreed in assisting George with his research, carrying the child through to birth, she had never dreamt of the pain and hardship that would soon follow. If truth be told, she wished she'd lost the damn thing. Life would have been far less complicated had Sophie never existed.

A sudden electronic sound buzzed from the corner where the door was. Harriet allowed her thoughts to drift away, like smoke in a breeze. The door opened and the smooth American with the male model looks reappeared.

"I'd started to think you'd forgotten about me," said Harriet, the emotion and fight from the previous day having departed.

"No, no, Harriet. We've just been biding our time. Watching. Waiting. Waiting for the right moment to present you with this." Brayden held out the ten-inch iPad to the woman and played the video.

"What's this?" she asked.

"This... Harriet... is insurance. You see, if your husband fails to deliver his part of the bargain, not only will he never see YOU alive again... he won't be burdened with having to look after your children any longer either."

On the tablet's screen a video played showing an image of two kids running around in a garden that Harriet vaguely thought familiar, although the sound was turned down low, she could just make out the playful sounds of screaming and laughing children – her children – as they enjoyed a game of 'it' or some such pastime. Another – smaller – child sat on a patio chair almost out of camera shot, but Harriet could just make out the telltale sign of a bandaged arm elevated in a sling.

"How...?"

"How did we know to find them there? Well, we had a little help, Harriet, to be honest. But that's by the by. The fact is we know that your children are at your father's house, and we are watching them. Closely. Don't worry. They are perfectly safe. For now."

"Why are you doing this?" Harriet pleaded, dejected. She continued to watch her children playing, oblivious to the intrusion posed by two men stationed in a silver van parked across the road, the video camera attached to a telescopic lens pointed into the garden.

"Well, it's one thing for your husband to carry out a robbery for the safe return of a loved one, but an entirely different ballgame altogether to give up something as precious as his beloved *Sophie*. One wonders whether he'd be willing to sacrifice one child for the lives of three."

"You're crazy!"

"No Harriet, we're just following orders." Brayden snatched

back the iPad. "When the time comes, I hope I can trust you to help your husband make the right decision. For you AND your children's sakes." With that, the American turned and left the woman to absorb what he'd just said.

Harriet felt terrible, fear grappling at her mind, tearing at her heart. She felt sick to her stomach, acid reflux gurgling just out of vomit reach but she retched all the same.

Calming herself, Harriet took slow, deep breaths. Whilst trapped in this temporary prison, she was powerless to help her children. If she was going to survive she needed to think positively.

Where was her husband? The GPS tracker strapped to her ankle would pinpoint her exact location. George would not forsake her. He had insisted the whole family wear such devices – despite all her vocal protestations – so why *hadn't* he come to the rescue?

Then a thought occurred to her. Well, actually two thoughts sprung to mind, one colliding with the other for greater prominence, both vying for overall attention. It was almost like she had a split conscience, one positive, and one negative. Like in a cartoon she imagined an angel whispering into one ear and the devil the other.

Maybe George hasn't come for you because he was not able. He was after all responsible for three young children in addition to Sophie.

Thought number one sounded logical in her mind, and though she knew he wouldn't want his wife to come to any harm, she knew that there was more at stake than just saving her.

The other voice was less encouraging, an all but certain mood killer.

Perhaps George has no plans on rescuing me because he is complicit to their plans. She considered this momentarily, and then it was gone – dismissed, the angel winning the contest. She knew how resourceful

George had become, how determined he could be. He'd sheltered and protected them no matter how close their pursuers had been. For more than two years he had been their saviour. George would not forsake them. Not now… not ever.

"But hurry up George, do something. We don't have much time," she whispered to herself, beginning to fear for her safety. It was just a matter of time, she knew, these men holding her captive would resort to *other* methods to get what they want, and George would not be giving up *Sophie* easily.

Sophie Jennings wasn't just a kid with a special talent; she was a weapon that would be more than useful in a world where wars were no longer fought by armies, but by civilians in everyday clothing using everyday things.

The great war effort could do with a person with Sophie Jennings' abilities. How the tide would turn if the enemy faced a similar obstacle to that of the civilised western world, that they were no longer able to see the soldiers of the west as they advanced and annihilated them mercilessly.

Harriet had no doubts that Uncle Sam would do absolutely anything to get his hands on Sophie. With Sophie, the possibility of a burgeoning new army could be developed; an army that was not only stronger, would never get old and be near invincible; also, having the added benefit of being invisible.

"I know you have your priorities George. Just don't forget about me."

CHAPTER THIRTY-THREE

SOPHIE

SHORTLY AFTER 2:30 P.M. within the confines of the Chelsea Embankment Gardens, George wandered across to a memorial bench upon which Dominic was already seated looking casual as he watched the world go by, enjoying the midafternoon sun and hiding behind a pair of designer *Aviator* sunglasses and the same baseball cap he wore earlier at Ed's Easy Diner. A folded newspaper lay to the side of him providing him with a more innocent look to any passerby who gave him a casual glance; just a guy out for a stroll, taking a rest to read his newspaper in the tranquillity of a small recreational facility, a temporary sojourn from the bustle of the city and the well sought houses and apartment blocks that enclosed it. The river Thames was within view just a look over the shoulder.

"Where's Sophie?" Dominic asked, watching a woman pushing a double buggy, a girl of seven or eight months in one chair, a boy of two in the other. "You know, she *is* integral to the plan..."

"She's here," George cut in. He sat down next to the man. He still looked pretty banged up to any who bothered to inspect him closely.

"Where is she?" Dominic demanded.

"Around," George replied, nonchalant. "But you won't see her. Unless she wants you to."

Shortly before arriving, George had parked the *Peugeot* in a neighbouring street a corner away from the Royal Hospital Chelsea, within whose grounds the *Masterpiece London Art & Antiques Fair* was nearing the end of its annual exhibition. "Okay Sophie, do your thing," he had said to the teenage girl, having briefed out the details of the task that Dominic had set out for them.

"I'm not happy," she had replied hawkishly before following it with a sigh.

Within a moment he'd watched his daughter vanish before him, slowly at first, then absolutely as the change passed over her limbs, up her body and finally cloaked her face and head. It always amazed him to watch, reminding him of being the kid at a magic show. On arriving at the park, George had ordered her to keep her distance.

"I was rather hoping to meet this 'special' child of yours, George."

"I'm sorry to disappoint," George grunted. *Trust me, you don't want to meet her*, he thought, ominously. "Now, if you don't mind let's cut to the chase."

"Very well. Here," Dominic handed George a floor plan of the exhibition. "The *Whisper of Persia* is being kept in a glass showcase at A-five on the plan. We will be entering the building via the London Gate on Royal Hospital Road."

"Okay."

"The glass case will be alarmed," he continued, "and on sounding police will be on site within two minutes – standard response time. There are two guards hovering around close by and another half a dozen loitering around the main corridors in various places, but these I assume will pose no problem for Sophie – after all, they won't be able to see her."

"True."

"There are a number of other things worth stealing. That exhibit alone has a dozen items worth upwards of a million pounds each. Your girl is to just focus on the diamond – nothing else. I'm not a greedy man."

"Don't worry, she's not at all interested in stealing and is doing this with the most reluctance."

"Good. Also, I don't want her to be cocky. She shouldn't get involved with any of the guards if she can help it. There should be no fatalities. They are just doing their job after all."

"They won't see her, so there'll be no reason for any nastiness."

"Exactly. Your job is to ensure she gets it done. Here," Dominic offered George his folded newspaper.

"I don't read the tabloids."

"It's not the newspaper I'm giving you; it's what's hidden inside."

George took the newspaper and peeked to be certain. A folded knife was concealed within.

"A knife? Isn't that contradicting what you just said?"

"Sure, but it's also a glass breaker. Sophie might find it more useful than trying to break into the display case using her bare hands."

George closed the newspaper tightly around the carbon steel object. "Okay Dominic. When do we start?" he asked, nervously.

"Now you're keen!" Dominic laughed. "Under different circumstances we could've been friends."

"I doubt it," George muttered under his breath.

Ignoring him, Dominic went on: "I've judged it that the exhibition is at its busiest from three onwards. So, around now. It's open until nine p.m. So I'll let you take the lead here."

"How generous," said George sarcastically.

"You're welcome," not taking the bait.

"Once you're in possession of the diamond, call this number." Dominic handed George a scrap of paper with a mobile number scrawled across it. It was barely legible due to the creases. It looked like it had gone through the wash and been tumble dried. "I'll let you know where to meet me."

"Will we do an exchange for my wife then?" George pocketed the scrap of paper.

"In good time we'll talk about that. First you need to get my diamond." With that, Dominic turned to go.

"Where are you going?" George enquired.

Dominic didn't stop or give a reply. He just gave a slight wave of his hand, his back to George, dismissive and disinterested.

Dominic had been gone less than ten minutes when Sophie deemed the coast was clear and sat next to her father. He had remained on the park bench that Dominic had vacated; a waste bin in close proximity and a bed of flowers behind providing enough of an attraction to ensure a dozen wasps buzzed threateningly nearby. George hated wasps with a passion. Bees he could live with; they had a purpose pollinating the flora and producing honey. But wasps? What use did they have other than be a menace to society?

"So we ARE going to go through with this?" she asked in disbelief. The voice seemed to come from thin air, startling George. He'd been a world away for a few minutes, daydreaming about happier times, of his family. He wondered if there would ever be happier times again. Sophie was invisible (as he'd expected) and having left the glasses that enabled him to see her back in the car, he was oblivious to her whereabouts. He looked about him nonetheless.

"I guess we are," George sighed, his voice barely a whisper, glancing at his watch. No more than five minutes had gone by since he'd last checked the time. He sighed again, shaking his head as if he were trying to clear fuzziness, almost cartoonlike, as though he'd been bumped on the head and he was trying to rid the birds flying about it. He stood up and grabbed the newspaper lying by his side. "I guess we are," he repeated, a little firmer, beginning to walk towards the Royal Hospital Chelsea within which *Masterpiece London* was in full swing and the *Whisper of Persia* diamond, quite literally the jewel in the exhibit's crown, was on grand display, a throng of visitors milling about for a glimpse of one of the world's largest cut diamonds.

Sophie pushed herself reluctantly to her feet and followed her father, jogging for five yards to close the gap. "So, how is this going to work exactly?"

George stopped and turned to where he heard Sophie's voice. Shrugging without commitment, he tried to reassure Sophie with a soft smile. "It should be simple. You go and do *your thing* and enter the exhibition hall unseen. Think of it as a test. The diamond is on display in a secure glass case in the exhibit marked 'A5' on this floor plan," George held out a folded pamphlet to his daughter, who snatched it. Almost immediately upon taking hold of the leaflet, the document vanished. "There are two guards close by," George continued. "Try not to engage them where possible."

"And how, dare I ask, do I get the diamond out of the glass case?"

"Smash and grab. The alarm that sounds should offer enough chaos to enable you to escape without much of an issue – your invisibility will do the rest. Here," George removed an object from the inside of the folded newspaper he was carrying. The blade was folded within the handle but Sophie instantly knew what it was.

"A knife?"

"Glass breaker," he said matter-of-factly. "Use it to break in to the glass case." The knife vanished in much the same way as the floor plan had. George looked about nervously to check that no one had been watching or close enough to hear him talking seemingly to himself.

Sophie studied the weapon-cum-glass-breaker with her fingers as she walked alongside her father. "Neat," she said, measuring it out within the palm of her invisible hand. "I like the weight."

"Just use it for breaking the glass. Nothing more," George muttered.

"Yes dad," she replied mordantly.

George ignored her. "Come, let's get this done with."

At precisely 4:00 p.m. George was standing a short distance from the entrance to the austere *Masterpiece London Art and Antiques Fair*. Sophie, close by, had said very little for the ten or so minutes they'd walked from Chelsea Embankment Gardens. Because she was invisible, George found himself asking: *Are you there*? countless times, just for reassurance. After the first half a dozen times of giving verbal responses, Sophie had resorted to punching her father in the arm.

"Okay, be careful. No fancy stuff, just go in, smash the glass, grab the diamond, then get out."

"Dad, I know what to do. You've already told me the plan. TWICE! This will be a breeze. Too easy in fact. Maybe you should do it!"

"Don't be cocky!" George admonished. "Remember; don't engage with the security guards, they're only salaried. And don't get greedy. It's just the diamond we want. Nothing else."

"Dad!"

"Okay, okay! I'm just saying. I'm going now." George felt invisible arms wrap around his neck and the lithe, athletic body of his teenage daughter press up against him in an embrace.

"I'll meet you back at the gardens."

"I love you Daddy," she whispered before pulling away.

"I love you too," he said. But she was already gone.

A long red carpet was laid out ahead of the entrance and leading around the front of the building, black velvet roped queue barriers lined either side, a further one in the middle splitting the area in two, a barricade that pretended to give order to the assembled throng entering or leaving, shepherding the masses who paid the exhibition a visit in either direction. Currently a large mass of people were shuffling a couple of inches forwards every few seconds as attendants dressed in matching black suits allowed admittance after giving each patron a cursory security check. One waved a hand-held metal detector about each person before stepping aside. Forgiving the obvious security delays, Dominic had been right about one thing. It definitely got busier after 3:00 p.m.

Sophie bypassed the regular order of things and the ninety or so people waiting patiently in line, the great British pastime, making her way to the front of the building walking alongside the red carpet and queue barrier, and crouching beneath the roped cordon just before the large entrance doors. She pushed past one or two startled guests at the head of the throng, knocking one who had been clutching a champagne flute, to the ground. Cries of alarm and shock filled the air but none were the wiser to the cause of the disturbance.

"How rude!" exclaimed one (a friend to the one who'd fallen), a woman in her mid-fifties, deathly thin, her skin hanging off her bones like a baggy dress on a hanger, her head jerking round to face the offending culprit who'd barged her and her friend – only to face absolute nothing. The attendant manning the door nearest looked her way to see what the bother was, at first puzzled but then slightly concerned. He started to weigh up whether he should allow this woman entry in view of her bizarre behaviour. He glanced across to a second attendant on the other side of the large double doors (the attendants stood sentinel on either side of them) and gave a signal with a glance and a slight turn of his head. The other attendant nodded his head in affirmation. An unsaid decision had been communicated. Mid-fifties woman and her friend's day out was about to be curtailed.

As Sophie walked past the two attendants through the large gulf the open double doors afforded, she stepped into the vast opulent room that was filled with over 150 exhibits and four exclusive restaurant areas. Behind her began an argument between the women she'd regretfully pushed aside and the two attendants, both of whom had stepped in front of the two women, the victim of the fall was a slightly younger, terribly officious woman wearing a leopard print dress that ill-fitted her ample, unattractive body.

"...I've NOT been drinking. I hardly took a sip from the champagne you know..." The shrill voice of the woman began to fade behind Sophie as she walked deeper into the exhibition hall, now passing the information desk situated first and foremost in the room; the bright lighting above, although soft, gave the place an almost ethereal feel to it – it was how she imagined the reception to heaven would feel if she believed in such places.

Unfolding the pamphlet her father had given her, Sophie placed the printed matter onto an empty seat (allowing it to reappear) and studied the floor plan of the exhibition centre, an invisible finger tracing a line to the location of most interest: Exhibit A5. To get to the *Whisper of Persia*, Sophie needed to walk to the centre of the vast room and pass two corridors, from which four rows of galleries (or streets, as they looked like a row of shop fronts) and exhibitions showcasing art, antiquities and jewellery of varying age, branched off. With the information desk directly in front of her, Sophie glanced to her left. Each gallery front had lighted signage above the threshold, the name of its benefactor and its exhibit number clearly marked. The first row correlated with Sophie's floor plan and the numbers were prefixed with the letter "C", starting with C1. Like a residential street, the galleries were started with odd numbers one side and even numbers the next. Although she could see that within each individual unit unique works of art were on display, Sophie held very little interest. The paintings, the statues, the ancient tomes and the modern art, meant little or nothing to the young woman.

There were many people milling around – too many – and despite the camouflage of invisibility, she felt out of place and almost naked within their company. They were all well-to-do, *avant-garde* types;

men in suits, women in cocktail dresses. All talking in stilted tones, lips and noses turned upwards.

Sophie retrieved and refolded the floor plan, making it vanish once again. She moved on, passing the information desk and heading towards Scott's Seafood and Champagne bar directly ahead. She walked alongside the restaurant towards the next corridor of 'street fronts' that were identified with numbers starting with C29, and opposite C30. Like before, showcased within each gallery were art and antiques. Sophie paid no further notice than she would have had they contained garden tools or spare motor parts and moved on deeper still. According to the map, she needed to take the next corridor on her left. 'A5' was the third gallery along on the 'odds' side.

Before turning, nerves hit her hard and she faltered at the junction, her body twitching to go back. It was a relief knowing that no one could see her indecision or the look of guilt that she knew was etched across her face. In such circumstances others would steel themselves with a stiff drink, a drop of 'Dutch courage', but she wasn't others and had no experience of intoxicating liquors. Instead she calmed herself by way of concentration and a form of meditation. She closed her eyes, breathed in deeply and exhaled slowly. A couple of minutes did the trick. She forced herself forward.

As Dominic had informed George, who had then imparted the information crucially to Sophie, there were indeed two security guards standing close within the unit identified as A5.

It didn't take many seconds for her to see the glass case within which the yellow diamond was being displayed. In fact, it wasn't the display itself that had drawn her attention, rather the horde of people flitting around it, like ants atop a sugary treat. Four or five people were looking at the item admiringly from around the glass case that took up a square meter of space at the centre of the small gallery. No one was showing any interest in the other items situated around the room. It occurred to Sophie that most of the items placed were just 'gap fillers' so that the gallery didn't look so cold and bare.

With a steady flow of visitors going to and from the exhibition, Sophie started to wonder how on earth she was going to be able to get close enough to the diamond without having to trample, jostle or hurt someone.

Then, without much thought, it occurred to her.

She needed a diversion.

But without her father on hand to help, and no others party to the plan, the only option was for Sophie to cause a disturbance herself, something close by – enough of a distraction that would give her the space needed to do what was necessary and enough of an attraction to clear the room of as many bystanders as possible.

The gallery on the other side to A5 (A6), was home to an exhibition of eighteenth and early nineteenth Century English furniture and Asian and Continental decorative arts. Sophie walked over to the gallery and looked at a table upon which a large *Ming* vase was on show. She looked about her, worried that she could be seen despite knowing that she was invisible, and without thinking further, picked the vase up and hurled it across the gallery against a far wall.

The vase, worth several thousand pounds, shattered into two dozen pieces and brought cries of shock and alarm from those in the small room. Others passing close by joined in on the act of being surprised.

Turning to go, Sophie gasped, momentarily frozen – a pair of George II period *Chinese Chippendale* carved gilt wood mirrors adorned the wall – her reflection was blatantly staring back at her from within the wooden framed looking glasses.

Behind her, people had come out of A5 (as she'd hoped) and had started to crowd round the opening to the adjacent gallery, curious to what the fuss was. Taking the opportunity, Sophie started to leave, only to hear a lone voice cut through the babble of noise that you'd expect with a gathering crowd.

"In the mirror? Did you see her? A ghost..." It was a man, in his sixties, pointing wildly towards the twin mirrors, a look of sheer terror upon his wrinkly face, the glare of the overhead fluorescents shining from his bald head.

Sophie did not hang about and fled, barging people out of her way and running into the almost deserted gallery opposite (the two guards remained in close proximity to the object of interest, constantly professional). She withdrew the glass breaking knife from inside her trouser' pocket as she went, moving swiftly to the glass cabinet and swinging a hefty blow to its furthest side, not stopping to catch a breath, barely keeping herself from falling over, off balanced.

Sophie expected the glass to shatter on impact and thought she would be able to just stick her hand into the case and retrieve the diamond effortlessly, like she were helping herself to a friend's punnet of popcorn at the cinema.

This most definitely wasn't the case.

Instead, the glass breaker bounced harmlessly off the glass as though it were merely made from rubber, and her closely following hand, prematurely making for the diamond, cracked painfully against the toughened clear surface, sending a bolt of agony shooting up her arm and a sharp spasm to her elbow.

"Sh...!" she started to curse, biting back the expletive. Because of the brouhaha her smashing the *Ming* vase next door had caused, her attempt at breaking into the glass case with the *Whisper of Persia* displayed had miraculously gone unheard. Although the pair of security guards were still close at hand, their interest was directed to the throng massing across the way, their attention momentarily curbed. One spoke into a mouthpiece alerting other security members, calling for backup.

"It's absolute pandemonium..." Sophie overheard him say. She tore her focus back to her objective. Recovering herself despite the pain in her hand and wrist, she prepared to aim a second, harder blow against the glass. This time, she intended to strike it like a hammer against a nail, designing a quick follow-up whack, hoping sustained force would shatter the clear obstacle where a single strike had failed. A quick, nervous glance around reassured her that attention from those in the gallery was still directed elsewhere, that the window of opportunity was still open; she followed through with her plan.

The carefully directed blow glanced off the glass in much the same way as the first attempt, but the second caused a slight chip in its surface, just a tiny dot of a hole; a third hammer strike caused the glass to crack in a spider web but still remained intact, the diamond secure within. Buoyed by the signs of success her fourth (and final) aim was more forceful and decidedly, as Sophie half-expected, smashing the entire glass wall of the case, the glass imploding in a shower of barbed shards to fall around the *Whisper of Persia* that sat, undisturbed, on a velvet pillow that helped transcend the diamond's unquestionable beauty.

Immediately on shattering, the alarmed display case set off a shrill, strident ringing sound that alerted everyone near (and far) of an assault on the contents within gallery A5. The two security guards in close proximity turned their heads to the place where the alarm blared, expecting to see a thief (or thieves) in the act of robbery but instead puzzled to see the area around the display case was still empty. Where the diamond had been placed, visually pleasing to the many thousands who'd entered the gallery that week, there was nothing but the velvet pillow, the slight indentation from where the *Whisper of Persia* had been placed, and a surprising amount of broken glass (more than seemingly possible from just one broken side panel) strewn dangerously about the case like stalagmites in an ancient cave, razor-sharp points and barbed edges looking to cut or slice any who dared to poke a hand in.

"What's going on?!" Security guard number one shouted to his colleague who was momentarily stunned, like a transfixed animal in the path of an oncoming vehicle. He needed to raise his voice to be heard over the din of the alarm, deafening in its urgency, and the renewed excitement amongst the ever-expanding group of visitors, voyeurs eager to see what the commotion was all about, not realising that their absolute presence aided the perpetrator's cause and escape.

Sophie, not wasting any time, jostled through the swell of people, pushing and shoving forcefully her way past, unavoidably knocking one or two people to the ground in her haste. Words of shock and confusion intermingled with the babble of excited voices, all receding behind her as she left them in her wake. As the crowds of people thinned out, Sophie increased her speed, putting distance between herself and the scene of her crime. Security reinforcements ran past, totally oblivious to her, unaware and unable to do anything to stop or thwart her escape.

Striding by the information desk she started to slow down as she fast approached the exhibition hall's exit. As she expected, the doors had been closed and the two attendants, ordinarily happy to allow patrons entrance (except those two earlier women), now stood in front of the double doors, barring access. More importantly, their new task was to ensure no one got out.

"This will be easy. A breeze in fact," she recalled how blasé she'd been earlier. She shook her head, looking about for an alternative point of exit. Pulling out the floor plan again and placing it on the floor, Sophie scanned the layout of the room and noted the exit points. She counted eleven fire escapes.

Through the glass doors of the entrance the sight of two black transit vans appeared in the distance, pulling into the grounds of the Royal Hospital Chelsea.

"That's not good," she muttered to herself noticing the approaching vehicles. Having consigned the map to memory, she folded up the floor plan and returned it to a deep pocket. Backing up a bit, she walked by the information desk and turned left at the first corridor. Above the door of the first gallery on Sophie's left was the unit number C1 and the name of the gallery, Wartski. On the opposite side was C2, Tomasso Brothers Fine Art. Sophie hastened past not caring to look at any other galleries; her attention focused on the fire exit that she knew was at the end of the cul-de-sac situated to the rear of the location marked as '13'.

Behind her a cacophony of shouts and orders filtered through as the front doors were thrown open allowing a small army of men garbed all in black, all holding rifles with handguns strapped at their waists, and all fitted out with night vision eye pieces strapped to their heads. Attached to their body armour was an array of close combative weapons, various knives, smoke grenades and spare ammunition. Without any warnings or reassurance, the dozen or so soldiers burst into the exhibition hall, giving the many guests and exhibition staff a fright, sending patrons sprawling for cover and causing them to scream in alarm and confusion, running in various disorderly directions overshadowing the chaos that Sophie had generated back at the unit opposite to where she'd taken the diamond.

Sophie turned the corner at the end of the row of galleries and stepped behind the stand marked '13', Ruinart Salon's stand showcasing handmade champagne boxes, each limited in edition and numbered. Sophie paid the exhibit no notice. Instead she took a moment to collect her thoughts, consider her options. The commotion at the centre of the room was echoing behind her closely followed by the screams and shouts filling the hall. It piqued her curiosity as to who was pursuing her. Without thought she stepped out from behind the stand and looked down the corridor she'd just travelled. Immediately she retracted herself, regretting her inquisitiveness.

"Quick! I saw something!"

Sophie made for the exit just a short distance to the back of stand '13', noting from a glance that it was secured from the inside with a push bar, a light box above showing a green stick man running through a white door, the legend emblazoned alongside: FIRE EXIT.

"We've found her!" barked one of the men in black, raising a rifle to take aim, seeing the heat signature silhouette before she disappeared at the end of the row. He was followed by the rest of his team who Sophie could hear running hard after her.

Sophie surged forward, thrust the opening bar down hard on the exit door, and burst out into the bright afternoon sunshine, startling a couple of women walking around the side of the building, one dropping an ice-cream she had been enjoying, the other eliciting an involuntary scream.

Parallel with the building ran a road that led to the grounds' exit gate. A rank of black taxi cabs lay in wait, offering no solution for Sophie. Instead she sprinted past them towards a copse of trees that bordered the hospital grounds, only too aware she had very few seconds before her pursuers had her in their sights.

The exit door she'd moments earlier cannoned from burst open a second time, spewing out the squad of black attired men, the leader marching to the head of the group issuing orders in a fearsome bellow. The two women who were barely over their initial fright, balked and yelped in fear at the sight of these newcomers; their clothing, their weapons, the way they talked and the way they walked eradiating an air of foreboding, menacing and ominous.

Sophie leapt to relative safety behind an ancient oak and watched the twelve men in black fan out and begin what they'd started to realise was going to be a fruitless task. Beyond the cover of the trees, Sophie patiently made her way out of the hospital grounds, slowly at first and almost at once coming close to danger. A pair of armed men walked out ahead of her, their backs thankfully turned. She stooped out of sight for a few moments until the way was clear, then with a huge sigh, she slipped through the exit gate and made her way to her father's pre-arranged meeting point, the sound of emergency vehicles approaching from the distance and a number of people milling about like zombies in a *George A. Romero* film. The *Whisper of Persia,* momentarily forgotten, was concealed tightly within a fisted hand.

She could not deny that the whole experience had been terrifying. She had been anxious before smashing the glass case in gallery A5. She had been equally scared during the actual heist, and further petrified as she made her escape. Those feelings and more were unabated even now as she pulled away from any real risk of capture. But in spite of the gut-wrenching, stomach-churning, nauseating fear some other perception infiltrated her consciousness.

As the first police car whizzed past, Sophie realised what it was she felt. She recognised it from the days of high jinks when tying the bus passenger's shoe laces together and during other daring escapades whereby she used her invisibility to carry out pranks and mischief.

It was unmistakeable...?

Not quite.

Mesmerising...?

No.

Then it came to her. It was, quite simply, *exhilarating.* Her whole body thrummed from the elation; she almost peed from the excitement. It was almost bordering addictive.

Should being *naughty* really make you feel so good? She tried to put it from her mind as she closed in on her father's meeting place.

CHAPTER THIRTY-FOUR

TOM KAPLAN

THE WAREHOUSE WAS SITUATED within a large industrial estate on the outskirts of Norwich in a place called Wroxham.

The vast estate covered a very large area and was home to a variety of industries, warehouses and offices. An aerial view of the business park on *Google Maps* would look like any of a multitude of similar development areas constructed throughout the westernised world.

Tom's driver had driven him around the site, home to a multitude of businesses: two large wine merchants, a *DHL* distribution depot, a car valet and cleaning business, tyre fitters (for large vehicles, trucks and trailers), a book printer, a compact disc manufacturer, a cash and carry food wholesaler, an import/export freight forwarding agent, a bank's administration centre and a large call centre belonging to an insurance company that ran an annoying advertising campaign on the television – obviously not the one with the delightful meerkat. Tom *liked* those ones. There were countless other industries and businesses represented operating from unmarked warehouses, their plain white or silver/grey facades bereft of signage or corporate trademarks.

For twenty-four hours, Tom, his driver and Bravo Team had watched and waited patiently. He recalled how, last night, as the overhead light faded fast, it became obvious that the Jennings (father or daughter) were not going to be mounting a rescue mission that night. He'd started to doubt the reliability of the intelligence that had pinpointed the warehouse as the location of where the mother had been taken. To think he'd been willing to stake his wealth on this being the place where George would mount an attack. But his contact at the control centre reassured him that the intelligence was good; this was the place where Harriet was being held. This would be where the Jennings would come.

Eventually.

He sighed theatrically. He didn't have the stamina for long haul stakeouts. With little sleep, a stiff neck and a lack of caffeine, his mood was edging from surly to seriously aggravated.

The silver *Audi* was parked outside a warehouse round the corner. It was the same car analysts at the control centre had followed from Seabrook Road, spying from overhead satellite surveillance two men carrying the prone form of a woman from the boot of the *Audi* into the warehouse. Another man had mysteriously appeared from the rear of the vehicle, his identity was not known and the satellite imagery did nothing to enhance it; he'd followed them into the windowless building. Analysts back in the control centre later reported that 'mystery man' had departed in a *BMW Z4 Roadster* – this was forty-five minutes before Bravo Team had pulled up, hot and itchy, twitchy fingers on assault rifle triggers waiting for their orders. They were pumped for action, disappointed from the letdown of Willoughby Rising but excited by the prospect that confronted them.

A glance at his watch now confirmed the time was nearing 5:00 p.m. He'd barely moved position within the *Bentley* in twenty-four hours. Despite the luxury of the car, comfort had departed the previous night. He started to wonder whether deep vein thrombosis was a possibility, immediately feeling an ache in the lower part of his legs from constant disuse. A nagging pain in his chest worried him that he was about to have a heart attack. He tried to take his mind off his discomfort, absently considering inane things.

Once July was over, he surmised, *it wouldn't be long before the days became noticeably shorter. Then the long, gloomy winter.*

He sighed again. His thoughts weren't helping. How much longer could they wait? A couple of hours? Another day? A week?

It would be in one of the unmarked buildings that they would find Harriet Jennings and those who had taken her, Kaplan pondered. He reached down to his mobile and phoned Bravo Team's leader, connecting instantly before the ringtone had sounded.

"Y'ello," Wyatt spoke abruptly, still peeved about an earlier conversation they'd had.

"What's your status?"

"Bravo Team are still in place sir, a little ways back; waiting YOUR further instruction." Wyatt's response was so sharp you could shave the hairs off a spider's leg.

Kaplan reflected on his previous conversations. Two in particular. The one from the evening before had been civil and spirits were high. Action seemed imminent and success was just an order away. His *Bentley* had still been moving, traversing the industrial estate for its second time having been unable to locate his team anywhere on site. Bravo Team were good. He hadn't seen any vehicles that stood out or gave indication that a stakeout was taking place – and that was saying something as most of the industrial estate was quiet, its working hoards and visiting customers having retired for the day. Very few cars were parked and most car parks were empty.

"Where are you?" he'd asked.

"A little south of the last group of unmarked warehouses – after the cash and carry and PB's Car Valet. There's a pink VW Beetle parked out front – no other cars. You can't miss it. We are parked opposite along the road."

The location the Bravo Team leader had indicated was towards the end of the industrial park. Kaplan's driver took instructions and drove patiently around the site, passing one or two business vehicles spaced a good distance apart; a *Royal Mail* van on a late collection; a *DHL* transit, with its instinctive red and yellow insignia, on its way back to the depot.

Rounding a corner, Tom Kaplan spotted the pink *VW Beetle* first. Despite the diminishing light it stood out like a clown's red nose at a funeral service. A moment later and the black *Bentley Mulsanne* the CEO of Kaplan Ratcliff was seated in parked up behind two white transit vans. They were a safe distance from the location, close enough for surveillance purposes and far enough to avoid detection.

Comings and goings had been limited with just the one notable exception (since *mysterious man* had vacated the warehouse); Wyatt had informed Tom Kaplan that a convoy of black transit vans had driven into the car park, pulled up alongside the building and after ten minutes drove off again - not without collecting a passenger. Through a pair of binoculars, Wyatt had identified the passenger as *Brayden Scott*.

With two of Harriet's abductors now gone, debate had raged between Wyatt and Kaplan Ratcliff's CEO as to how they ought to proceed. Their angry voices volleyed over a mobile phone connection could be heard outside through the thin steel walls of their vehicles. Wyatt had been keen on storming the warehouse and taking Harriet for themselves. *"She'd be leverage for us,"* he'd argued. *"They are ill defended and ill prepared for an attack."*

"No," Kaplan had said simply but firmly. *"We stick with their plan. They no doubt are keeping her hostage as a trade for the Jennings girl. Once the exchange has taken place we will make our move. No sooner. No later."* Wyatt had been vocal in his disagreement. Kaplan had ended the dispute by disconnecting his mobile. The decision was final. It was a decision he would later regret.

Returning to the present, Kaplan spoke into his mobile again. "Okay Wyatt, won't be much longer," he hoped. "Over and out."

On hearing the subdued sound of the radio broadcasting the news, Kaplan asked his driver to turn the volume up. A female newsreader filled the car's interior:

"...armed men stormed a London antiques festival, causing a stir in London today. Reports indicate a robbery took place and eyewitness accounts suggest the armed men were part of an active response unit, though it would appear very little was stolen and no one was seen fleeing from the scene. So far the gallery and the police have declined to comment as their investigations continue." The reporter was replaced by the voice of a young man – an eyewitness – whose testimony sounded fanciful and akin to a Hollywood movie. He sounded excited and spoke with a whiny, nasally voice.

"...it was scary. One minute I was sitting peacefully minding my own when armed men burst out of the building and started charging forward like they were searching for something or someone. Sure, the door opened before them, but no one came out... It was like they were searching for a ghost or something..."

The newscaster moved forward to another story, spouting words of death and doom affecting a few or the many... Afghanistan, Syria, Israel, or some such place... Kaplan lost interest, his thoughts still on the first news piece. There was no reason for him to consider this news item but something bugged him. It was what the eyewitness had said:

...it was like they were searching for a ghost or something...

He couldn't help wonder if this news piece was significant or not. Before he could consider it further his mobile phone started to ring again.

Snatching it up, Kaplan snapped testily. "What?!"

It was Wyatt in the lead vehicle.

"I thought you might be interested to learn that there's been activity at the warehouse." Earlier frustrations in his voice now gone.

"Yes?" renewed enthusiasm in Kaplan's voice. "Go on..."

"A vehicle has just pulled up. You'll never guess who climbed out?"

"Don't tell me, Elvis Presley?" Kaplan spoke in a heavily sarcastic tone. He had caught sight of the *BMW Z4 Roadster* sports car moments earlier as it had passed but had given it little thought as he'd listened to the news on the radio.

"Don't be silly, sir. He's in Vegas," he chuckled. *"No, someone more recently dead, closer to home."*

"Wyatt, the suspense is killing me."

"Dominic Schilling," he blurted. *"Without any doubt, it was him; looked very much alive and well, though a little worse for wear, sir."*

Kaplan fell silent for a moment, and then spoke aloud the thought that would be in everybody's minds. "How is it possible? His body was found burnt to a crisp in his car yesterday afternoon? Hasn't there been formal identification yet?"

"My guess is he wanted everyone to think that he was dead, sir."

"You're a genius, Wyatt. We clearly aren't paying you enough. You should get yourself on *Mastermind* or something...."

The sarcasm was lost on Bravo Team's leader. *"D'you think so? I always fancied having a go at Who Wants to be a Millionaire."*

Kaplan disconnected the call and closed his eyes.

"Are you okay, sir?" Kaplan's chauffeur was watching his boss through the reflection of the rear-view mirror.

"I'm just tired, Alfie," he replied. "I need sleep, a hot dinner and a bottle of *Domaine Romanée-Conti*. I'll be all right once this is over..."

If this is ever over, he thought to himself.

CHAPTER THIRTY-FIVE

GEORGE

FEELING HER SLIP AWAY from him filled him with a sense of dread and foreboding. The worst feeling of letting go most parents felt was when chaperoning their offspring to school on their very first day or helping them pack their effects as they embark on a new life moving away from home. How many fathers stood by as their daughter embarked on a criminal activity?

Not many good ones, he reflected.

George felt useless and exposed standing so close to where Sophie was about to attempt the theft of the *Whisper of Persia*. He glanced down at the brochure, folded over to the page that showed the diamond itself in view. He couldn't deny that the precious stone was stunning in its cut. He still couldn't understand why Dominic would want it so much?

And taking his wife as leverage to get it didn't make much sense, either. The only conclusion George count hazard was that Dominic had become unhinged.

He wished he'd been properly prepared for this mission. He would have preferred to have had communication devices, earphones and mouthpieces so that he could know where Sophie was and what she was doing. Be able to help if ever there were any problems. Be a second pair of eyes and ears.

Instead he had to second-guess what she was doing, where she was, and hope that she stuck to the plan and achieved the less than desired goal.

After five minutes, ill at ease, George turned his back to the entrance of *Masterpiece London Art and Antiques Fair*, and started to walk along the road that headed towards the hospital exit. The only cars that seemed to use the road were the black taxis, of which nine were lined up parallel with the hospital building now falling back behind him.

Five minutes later still, the sound which George had been waiting for, the shrill, discordant jangle of alarm bells, distant for the space between him and the exhibition hall, though sounding loud enough to warn all in and around the grounds that something bad had happened. Rather than alarm those in the vicinity, all it did was evoke curiosity. Like iron filings to a magnet, masses of people started forward to the beacon of sound, roused by the commotion. The same people would run to an erupting volcano rather than flee it. George was always astonished by how insanely senseless the majority of people were these days.

Barely a second had passed when the screech of tyres sounded from the near distance and a moment later the first of two black transit vans followed it, turning sharply round the corner, entering into the hospital grounds sending pedestrians crossing the road sprawling to safety.

George raised the brochure up to face level and hid behind the momentary shield, his eyes peering over the top at the passing vehicles.

Although the van's occupants were paying little notice to the people walking around, or to George for that matter, he was able to see into the front of the vehicles as they passed and what he saw churned his stomach.

Men clothed in black, ocular contraptions strapped to their heads and the telltale sign of a weapon hanging over each and every passenger's shoulder. George was under no illusion that this was anything but a response to Sophie's attempted theft.

But how could they get here so soon?

George watched the two vans advance fast towards the entrance of the exhibition hall, tyres screeching further as they came to a halt just short of the start of the red carpet that led to where two attendants had barricaded the entranceway. Almost synchronised, the side doors of the transits slid open and men wearing uniform black outfits, body armour, night vision/heat seeking goggles and carrying rifles, jumped out and started forward towards the entrance. With the drivers and the two passengers from the front of each transit, there were twelve men in total.

"It's a setup," George intoned. It had to be. Watching the squad of armed men enter the building and the screams of alarm descend, he felt like a General watching a battle from afar, waiting anxiously for the outcome.

Two minutes that seemed like a lifetime passed and George watched soldiers spill out from one of the fire exits from the furthest corner of the building. The black garbed men fanned out and began pushing forward, heads turning from side-to-side, scanning, searching, their guns held ahead like metal detectors, muzzles pointed low.

"Good girl." George turned away and headed in the direction of Chelsea's Embankment Gardens, heading back to their starting place, but more specifically back to the rendezvous point.

"I got it," was all she said when finally she appeared next to him almost an hour later. Well, appeared was not exactly correct. She was invisible still and grabbed her father's attention by placing a hand onto his right knee and giving it a squeeze.

He had been frantically clasping and unclasping his hands,

nervously rubbing the hairs on the back of his arms and rocking back and forth like he had some sort of mental disorder. In a way, he did. He couldn't be right in the head to allow his daughter to embark on such a fanciful scheme, regardless of what was at stake. He had thought something had gone awry, believed that his special daughter had been captured, the whole scheme just a ploy to ambush her during an elaborate and daring diamond heist.

"Miss me?" Sophie startled him. Even with the physical contact, he hadn't registered her presence.

"I thought... I thought... I'd lost you," George stammered, turning to the vacant space where he knew his daughter was now sitting.

George heard her swallow. "Here," softly, this was all she said in reply. He felt invisible hands prise open one of his palms. The diamond from the folded page of his brochure appeared in the centre of his hand as if by magic. Heavier than he'd imagined and the size of a kiwi fruit, it felt precious and clean, the stunningly cut multifaceted faces glinting in the late afternoon sunshine. It was more beautiful than any one could imagine.

"I'm guessing those goons turning up *wasn't* by accident?" Sophie didn't do anything to mask the agitation in her voice. Still slightly out of breath from running, she'd quickly conquered her anxiety that had laboured inside her as she sought an escape route, replacing it with anger at the duplicity of the diamond heist.

Still reeling from the events, George was just pleased to hear Sophie's voice. He wrapped his hand round the large diamond and turned in her direction.

"Thank God you're okay."

Sophie took a deep breath and exhaled, calming herself. "I have to admit. It was a little exciting..." George noted the smile in her voice.

"I'm sorry. I shouldn't have agreed to you going in there… so stupid!"

"Hey. It's fine. I'm fine. We're fine. Besides, what choice did we have?"

"There's always a choice, Sophie..." George looked down at his clenched hand. What had gone on? Clearly, Dominic had set them up, the theft of the diamond a refined plan aimed at getting Sophie out in the open. It was obvious the men garbed in black were pre-arranged. Who turns up wearing night/thermal vision goggles unless you expected to need them?

But why such a scheme?

"Here, take this. Put it somewhere safe." George handed the diamond back to Sophie, the stone disappearing within her grasp. She would stow it in her backpack at the earliest opportunity, then somewhere safe for future use. For now, she returned it to her pocket.

George retrieved the crumpled scrap of paper that Dominic had handed to him earlier, unfolding it to reveal the telephone number that he'd been instructed to ring on completion of the mission. His mobile appeared from deep within a trouser pocket.

"What are you doing?" Sophie was slightly concerned. She absently placed a hand on her father's arm, stilling him from raising the phone. "Don't," she said.

"I think we need some answers." He started to key in the number that appeared on the slip of crumpled paper. "Besides, they still have your mother…" George placed the handset to his ear listening to the ringing tone. After fifteen rings he started to doubt that it was ever going to get answered. Then, almost taking him by surprise, Dominic's unmistakeable voice filled the void.

"Yea, 'ello?"

George found that his voice had betrayed him and that he was momentarily struck dumb.

"George? Is that you?"

Galvanised, George responded without thought, almost spitting his words: "Why d'you set us up you son of a bitch?!"

"George, go easy. Calm down. Remember who you are talking to here. Has it slipped your memory, I still have your wife?"

George exhaled theatrically, closed his eyes and attempted to compose himself. An image of his traumatised wife sprung to mind. Strangely, it helped calm him.

"It was never about the diamond, was it?"

Dominic chuckled. *"Truthfully, George? Not at first. But you know what, the more I looked at it, the more I was captivated, like. Sure, we wanted to draw the girl out in the open – what better way than to put her talent to the test – but I also fell in love with that diamond. So, for me at least it was about the diamond, but first and foremost you've guessed the rest right."*

"What about my wife?"

"She's still alive. For today at least. All depends on whether I get what I want... whether she remains that way."

"What do you want?"

"Now that's the spirit, George. That's the thing I like about you." He trailed off momentarily. *"Yes... quick to the punch line."*

George was growing tired of the conversation. "Dominic, just cut out the bull. I'm growing a beard here." He failed to mask his frustration.

"I'm giving you tonight off. Get some rest. Meet me tomorrow at Whipsnade Zoo at 10:00 a.m. at the lemurs' enclosure. You can get up close and personal with them. I love those critters..." he trailed off, and then remembered himself. *"It will be busy, so it should give us both reassurance that there'll be no nonsense. We will do an exchange – Sophie and the diamond for your wife."*

"Do you honestly expect me to do this?"

Dominic chuckled again. *"We thought you might say that. So we've taken out some more insurance, you know how it is these days George. It's a recession; you need to cover all your assets."* His tone became serious. *"Did you think we wouldn't know about Theodore White? He has a lovely home and a stunning wife, mmmm. Your kids looked like they enjoyed playing in the back garden today with the twins."*

"Dominic! I swear if anything happens to them..."

"George, George, George. You know what you have to do. They will be okay... at least until tomorrow. It's up to you. I'll see you at the zoo. Don't be late," with that he terminated the call.

George slunk back on the park bench, a look of dejection on his face. He dropped the mobile phone where it clattered next to him.

"Dad?"

George shook his head in what looked like defeat. It all seemed like it was hopeless. He was out of words; the spirit in his fight had now waned into extinction. Despite the still warm late afternoon sunshine, George looked to have come over ice-cold, appearing whiter than Casper.

"Dad? What did he say?"

"They know where Meredith, Charlie and Stanley are. They are using them – and your mother – to make me give them what they want. But I... *I can't give them what they want.* I won't!" He closed his eyes, feeling moisture welling up behind the lids. He was at a loss and totally aghast at what he was being forced to do. His family was everything to him.

"Dad, the way I see it is you don't have any choice."

"What are you saying?"

"Isn't it obvious?"

"I can't trade you for them. You are too... *important.*"

"Dad, I wasn't thinking of that... though if it comes to it... No, what if we balance things a bit differently, level the playing field?"

"Go on," he urged, his curiosity aroused.

"If Dominic didn't have any hostages, do you think he would be a little annoyed?"

"More than a little I'd say."

"Then that's where we'll start. Of course, I am assuming I'm not the only one with a GPS tracker stuck inside my brain."

"You know about that?" he was surprised and wore the expression.

"I didn't until just now..."

"Actually Sophie..." he started, then thought better than to be drawn into discussing it. "The others have theirs strapped on. Less evasive..."

CHAPTER THIRTY-SIX

EMILY

THE WATCH WAS DAINTY and delicately clung to Emily's wrist. Ryan had bought it for her last birthday and she cherished it, not that it was very valuable or anything special to look at. Just a simple *Accurist* wrist watch, mother of pearl dial, sparkling stones encrusted in a tennis bracelet. He probably bought it from *Argos*.

She glanced at it now as she waited in her car outside the hotel situated in Harlow, an hour's drive from the command centre.

10:19 p.m.

She had been waiting for nearly half an hour at the location that Richard Cullum (*Ricky* to his friends) had given her.

Leaving the command centre had been relatively easy. Having worked more than her contracted hours she made her excuses citing exhaustion, a microwave meal and a date with a rerun of *Friends* (*The One Where Monica Sings*) beckoning her home. Samuel hadn't lifted an eyelid, in fact his eyes hadn't strayed from the laptop computer open in front of him; he had no plans to go home – not whilst Tom Kaplan and Bravo Team were undertaking a mission that by rights should have been his. He'd cared little that they'd been on stakeout for over twenty-four hours now.

Emily noted that Cullum was four minutes late. She hated delays, detested waiting. If there was one thing that irked her most in a person, it was poor punctuality.

Cullum's initial response to Emily's assertion that Ryan was still alive was to end the call – no warning, just...!

Emily was left cradling the handset listening to electronic silence. A minute after that abrupt moment, the phone began to ring and Emily flicked the connect button on the base unit, not expecting the security officer. *Okay* he said. *Meet me at the Park Inn in Harlow at ten-fifteen*. She hadn't given a verbal nod or anything before electronic silence filled her left ear once again. Cullum was gone before he could change his mind.

That seemed like a lifetime ago.

A couple more minutes passed before the white *Mercedes* van pulled into the hotel's car park, slowly edging closer, then turning to park up beside her silver *Vauxhall Astra*.

The driver of the *Mercedes* climbed out of the van. Although hidden in shadow she could make out that the large frame, broad shoulders and hulking appearance belonged to Ricky Cullum. He walked round the front of the van and approached the *Astra* as though reluctant. He was slow and deliberate.

Emily pressed the button that opened the window electronically, allowing it to wind down a couple of inches as the security man approached, just enough to hear and be heard. She watched him amble over. He was much cleaner than he'd been the last time she had seen him and dressed casually in shiny blue tracksuit bottoms and an *Adidas* collared T-shirt.

"Miss Porter," he said by way of greeting. He didn't look happy to be there. Actually, he wasn't. He was missing *Top Gear* on the telly and had forgotten to *Tivo* it.

Cutting out the pleasantries, Emily proceeded directly to questioning. "Where's Ryan?" she demanded. "What have you done with him?"

All confidence winded from him, Cullum looked down at his feet as though ashamed. "He's safe Miss Porter."

"I want to see him."

"It's not a good idea," he replied, looking up. "It's not safe for him... and it's not safe for me."

"I don't care. I need to know what he meant to gain from helping them. Why he felt he..." she trailed off, unable to stop herself from crying, "...why he couldn't trust me." It was almost a whisper.

Richard Cullum – Ricky to his friends – shook his head not knowing how to respond. He was never comfortable with people crying so did what he always did when confronted with such people. He turned and walked back to his van.

"Wait!" Emily pleaded. "Don't go..." She opened the car door and clambered after the security guard. "Don't go... not without giving me something. Anything!"

Cullum ignored the young woman, retreating to the comfort of the driver's seat of the *Mercedes* van. He closed the door behind him and keyed the ignition. The engine of the vehicle roared into life. Emily, following fast around the front of the vehicle, thumped the *Mercedes'* door, the bang loud but causing no damage.

"WHY!" she screamed. "WHY COME IF YOU ARE NOT GOING TO TELL ME SOMETHING?!"

From behind the transit a dark figure emerged dressed in grey cotton trousers, white shirt (open at the collar), and a loose tie, dressed how she'd grown accustomed over the years. Emily hadn't noticed him as her attention and anger was still aimed at Cullum who noisily shifted the van into gear. Emily smacked the *Mercedes'* door a second time with the flat of her hand, agitated further by the fact that the security guard had set the vehicle in motion heedless to her protests, the *Mercedes* slowly moving backwards accompanied by a warbling reversing alarm.

Emily made to follow – and stopped, her path surprisingly blocked by someone she hadn't expected.

"Hello Em." He had managed to creep up on her without sound or warning. Too preoccupied by her anger at Cullum, Emily had failed to notice the man approach despite him now standing right next to her.

"Ryan!" Surprise and shock overwhelmed her, soon to be replaced by relief and joy. "You're here!"

"I'm sorry kid." Ryan said. He reached the young woman he considered his daughter and drew her into an embrace. Emily wrapped her arms about him in reply. "I'm so sorry."

Behind them, Ricky Cullum had straightened up the van and was preparing to go. Ryan acknowledged him with a subtle wave. Cullum just smiled and then drove off.

"What's going on?" she asked anxiously, pulling away from him. "I need to know. I need answers."

"Spies like us always do," he chuckled. "Em, it's a long story," he replied. "Have you eaten?"

"Not since breakfast." She returned to her car, removing the *Gucci Hobo* handbag, closing the window and then locking the *Vauxhall* with a quick thumb press to the electronic key.

"Then we shall talk over supper." Ryan took the hand of the woman who replaced him as Assistant Intelligence Officer and led her towards the hotel in which he had a room booked for the night.

Walking through the reception area and crossing to the bar aroused strange looks – some suspicious, others jealous – but no one approached or challenged them.

In the bar Ryan ordered drinks and toasted sandwiches and they settled down in a quiet corner away from prying eyes or loose ears. The bar was practically empty with just one lonely businessman sitting a good distance away on the other side of the room working on a laptop and the barman busying himself behind the bar refilling shelves with stock. Soft music played through speakers built into the ceiling, instrumental versions of classic pop songs from the eighties.

"Well?" Emily had taken a sip from her drink – a large wine spritzer – and was impatient to learn the truth.

Ryan had a pint of *John Smiths* bitter, from which he took a deep mouthful. "Where to begin," he started, wiping his mouth with the back of his hand. "I suppose you want to know why I've been warning George Jennings."

"Amongst other things."

"Yes, I'm sure. But to appreciate my position, I think you should understand how it all began."

Emily was puzzled. "All what began?"

"CHAMELEON, and what any of this has to do with me."

"Okay," she was confused but willing to just ride it out. She took another sip from her glass.

"But first, tell me. Is George and his family all right?"

Emily shrugged. "Tom Kaplan has been running things, but so far they have eluded him. Of course, that's likely to change soon enough." Emily recounted the events from when Ryan had left off, describing in great detail the twists and turns that had befell the corporation and the trials and misfortunes that had affected the Jennings family. It took her less than five minutes to update the older man, during which he had taken mouthful after mouthful of *John Smiths,* practically finishing it. Just a white frothy residue lay at the bottom of the glass. After she finished her account Ryan took a moment to consider the grave situation. He found it hard to think so ordered a second drink with a wave of his hand. It sometimes helped to clear his head.

"We have no time to waste," Ryan said after taking another deep pull from the new pint the barman had just placed in front of him. "Do you have your phone?"

"Of course," Emily replied with a snort.

"Can I borrow it?"

"Where's yours?"

"Mine? One was confiscated," she knew this, it was on her desk back in the operation centre. She'd been tasked with unlocking its secrets. "The other... ran out of battery."

Emily reached into her *Gucci Hobo* bag and retrieved her *Samsung Galaxy*. She handed the phone to Ryan who quickly dialled a number remembered from the day before. The speaker volume was quite loud and despite the hand piece being pressed against Ryan's ear Emily could hear the ringing tone almost as clear as if it were held against the side of her face.

"Hello?" The voice was tinny and electronic. Ryan also recognised it as George Jennings, who he'd last spoken to the day before.

"Hello George."

For a moment George was quiet except for his breathing, deep, fast – as though he'd been running; then he spoke. *"Ryan?"* he asked incredulously.

"Listen George, things have moved up a notch since we last spoke. I don't have time to explain but when we meet we will have a long chat."

"Ryan, I can't talk," Ryan heard through the earpiece. *"I'll call you after..."*

"After? After what? Where are you George? Are you all right?"

"I've located my wife. I'm about to get her back."

"Wait! George, tell me you're not at the warehouse?" he sounded desperate. "Agents are staking it out, waiting. They've anticipated your steps. Tom Kaplan knows you are going to go there."

"Ryan, it's too late. I'm already inside."

CHAPTER THIRTY-SEVEN

TOM KAPLAN

IT WAS NOW 9:32 p.m. and night was fast approaching. It was fairly dull now and one or two street lamps were on around the industrial estate, but many were turned off – a council initiative to save money. Everywhere was doing it, Kaplan pondered. Some councils even turned off the street lighting at midnight, a move that angered residents – especially those who travelled to and from home after dark at such a late (or early) hour. One of the lamps stood on the corner of the road ahead. Even without it he was just able to make out the *Audi Q7* parked where it had been since before he and Bravo Team had arrived. There were half a dozen other cars parked in close proximity – none were George's familiar blue *Peugeot 207*.

An hour passed without incident. Kaplan had resorted to answering emails on his *Blackberry*. The eight men sitting patiently in the two white vans ahead did nothing but wait, committed and professional.

The glamorous life of a field agent – 85% of the time was spent sitting and waiting around, 10% was training and just 5% was out in the great wide world actually doing something. To the workshy it offered a dream vocation.

Jack Wyatt in the front of the lead transit, night vision binoculars pressed against his eyes, had a clear view of the warehouse. Having been on site for over twenty-four hours now he had seen every vehicle

– coming and going – and was earlier excited as he'd reported that one of their own agents had appeared at the doorstep.

Dominic Schilling. Wyatt smiled. With the great Dominic Schilling's defection came opportunities. He couldn't mask the feeling of anticipation that his thoughts of grandeur produced.

Other than Schilling and Brayden Scott, there had been little other activity in all the hours keeping watch, and because of the design of the building (it contained no windows and just one entrance door and an 'up and over' garage door) there was no way to observe the enterprise that occurred within.

Since Schilling earlier that evening, no other vehicles had been seen coming or going; no other people entering or leaving – it was going to be a long, long night. The radio was on, the volume low. Nothing but mindless drivel was prattled by the DJ, replaced occasionally with a tune from a singer or a manufactured band, normally the latest fad created by Simon Cowell and his *X Factor*. Had the stakeout taken place a month later Wyatt mused, there'd probably have been football commentary on.

Wyatt was wishing he'd ordered takeout food to take his mind off the boredom. It wasn't too late. A *pizza*, he thought. *Or* maybe *Chinese*. To tell the truth he wasn't fussy with what he ate. Having dined on rat and cockroaches whilst stranded on a mission once, he ate anything without complaint or reason. It's surprising what one would eat when there was little choice or even less option and you were starving hungry. Some, he knew, had been known to resort to cannibalism – Wyatt had been fortunate never to have considered this tribulation.

As 10:00 p.m. passed, Tom Kaplan was beginning to have some doubts as to whether George was ever going to show up. It was rare, but he had been wrong before when it came to predicting the movements of others. He couldn't claim to being psychic but he'd had more than his fair share of luck over the years.

He stifled a yawn. It had been a long day and he wasn't getting any younger. At sixty-six years, though in good health, his face was beginning to show the strain of heading a multinational company – especially one that, from time to time, carried out nefarious activities in the pursuit of success. He was not afraid to make the decisions that would keep weaker willed men awake at night.

"I'm so tired, Alfie," the CEO said loud enough for his driver to hear, breaking the uncomfortable silence that ordinarily blanketed them. The driver had been half-asleep, his eyes closed as he'd fancied himself somewhere else – imagined pictures danced within his mind, of exotic locations and holidays never to be enjoyed. He snapped his eyes open.

"Do you want me to take you home, sir?" the driver asked hopefully in a soft Scottish accent, knowing too well that the answer would be no.

Kaplan snorted a "humpf," in reply and returned to his emails – mostly to delete them. Somehow he'd been bombed with thousands of unsolicited spam messages.

Half an hour further passed and the belief that nothing was going to happen was in all their heads, the thought having infected them all like a virulent disease, so absorbing that it had started to siphon off their attention.

In the lead transit van the radio prattle had given way to incessant techno dance music. Wyatt wanted to turn it off but one or two of the lads in the back of the van were head banging to it, if that was at all possible.

It was due to the inertia tied in with hunger and sheer boredom that they all failed to see the silhouette of a figure approach the warehouse from the furthest side, steeped in darkness and careful in his advance; they missed completely the drama of the man they'd been staking the warehouse out for, promptly disappearing into the hidden unknown that was beyond the now open single entrance door.

CHAPTER THIRTY-EIGHT
GEORGE

THE JENNINGS TROUPE WERE travelling once again in abstract silence since being reunited back at Grandpa Theo's house. One hour earlier, George and a now visible Sophie had said nothing of the day's turn of events, traumatic, exhilarating or otherwise; both wearing the long faces of train wreck survivors, and their grim expressions had spoken volumes as they'd appeared at the front door and crossed the threshold.

"Dad!" Stanley had charged into his father's arms as though he were greeting a man who'd just returned from a six-month tour of duty in Afghanistan. Meredith and Charlie were in the background watching television.

"Any news on Harry?" Theo dared to ask, noting the pained look upon the man's face.

He shook his head. "I'll get her back. By the time the day's over, she'll be here. With us. That I promise."

George had spoken those words forty-five minutes earlier. Without explanation he'd told Theo that his family wasn't safe with him any longer, that their hideout had been compromised.

"How do you know?" Harry's father had asked, imploringly. He had only just gotten to know his grandkids and was loath to see them disappear from his life so suddenly.

"By the fact that there's a silver van parked across the road. They've had you under surveillance."

Theo crossed to the window and peered out. He could just make out a silver van parked on the other side of the road. A look of horror stretched across his face.

"Don't worry, they can't do us any harm. Not now," George almost smiled. "They won't be doing surveillance work for the rest of our lives."

"George? What have you done?"

"Only what was necessary to save your daughter."

"Who are you people?"

The conversation had then turned casual and Theo had filled George in on what the kids had been up to during George and Sophie's absence. It was the only way they were able to distract themselves from the terrible reality. Once conversation had run dry, George took his cue and announced it was time to leave.

"You will see your grandkids again, and your daughter. I promise." Theo nodded, appreciating the sentiment. Deep down he knew that he couldn't trust the man who'd married his daughter. George didn't know it, but his promise would only be partially realised.

Once again, squashed back within the *Peugeot*, George had driven his family away from what had initially been perceived as 'safety' and took them towards what was most likely to be the most dangerous place of all for them. Talk about jumping out of the pan into the fire.

No one had commented on the silver van parked across from Theo's house. Meredith had heard her father mention something about it to her Grandad but hadn't heard the full conversation. Only George and Sophie knew that the two occupants of the van lay in a tangled heap in the back with their throats cut. George had been quick and brutal, using the folding knife that Sophie had earlier that day employed with great success to smash the glass display case and steal the *Whisper of Persia*. Although it was a different side to which Sophie was accustomed to, she hadn't questioned her father regarding this. Extreme measures were sometimes needed in extreme circumstances.

A glance at the *Nexus* continued to pulse Harriet's location. After an hour of driving, George had stopped the car in a location half a mile from where the GPS signal was being transmitted, parking up on what appeared to be a disused lane that led to a dead end or an acre of desolate farmland – it was hard to tell owing to the full dark. Although it was a clear night and the sky looked more crowded with stars than normal, it seemed very *Cimmerian* and little by the way of natural light was pouring down from the heavens to unmask the territory.

"Listen kids, I need you to remain here whilst we go and get your mum."

"Don't go!" whined Charlie. He hadn't gotten over the abandoned feeling from yesterday.

"It's safer here. Meredith will look after you." Charlie glanced down to his broken arm recalling that Meredith had been 'looking after him' at the time he fell from the crab-apple tree. "We'll be back before you know it Charlie," he tried to soothe; then to them all, "Keep down low and try and get some sleep. It's likely to be a long night." He turned to Sophie in the passenger seat: "Are you ready?" George removed the tablet from the dashboard.

"You made me ready, remember? Are you?" she countered.

"No," he replied, honestly.

Climbing out of the car, closing the doors behind them and moving to the rear of the *Peugeot*, George opened the boot and reached into the holdall nestled between a first aid kit and a *Thermos* cool bag. Standing beside him Sophie watched in silence. It was darker than she'd ever known it and the small bulb built into the side of the car's boot afforded little illumination.

Using his hands he found what he was looking for. Military style night vision goggles with integrated heat sensor (which he strapped to his face) to replace the smaller, leisure glasses that were apt to fall off; two handguns (one *Beretta*, the other a *Smith and Wesson*); a large torch (which he flashed on and off); and a hunting knife (like *Crocodile Dundee's*) in scabbard, which he clipped to his belt. All of this, plus three smoke grenades, he placed into a small canvas backpack already half-full with useful items (including a bottle of water, a small first aid pack and some tools he almost never left home without).

"Can I help you with anything?" Sophie asked sarcastically, having raised an eyebrow on seeing the various items going into George's bag.

"Here. Take these." George handed Sophie a smoke grenade, three glow sticks and, as an afterthought, the syringe of *Profonol* which he'd appropriated back at Willoughby Rising. "You never know when these things might come in handy."

Slamming a full magazine clip into the *Beretta* and then chambering a round, George took comfort from the feel of the cold metal object in his hands.

"You look like you've done this before..." Sophie's quizzical look was lost beneath the gloom of the night.

Ignoring her, he said: "Now I'm ready."

"I guess I'd better change," Sophie muttered.

"A change is as good as a rest, they say."

"Ha ha." Sophie tensed up and closed her eyes. Her forehead furrowed as she focused all her attention on the transformation that would return her to the state she was born into. Surprisingly, it took less time to complete, in contrast to returning back into visible form. Worryingly, George's antidote was becoming less effective with each and every dose.

With Sophie invisible, father and daughter walked the half mile in silence. Using the *Nexus* George had been able to pinpoint a path that would take them directly to the warehouse via a back route that required an amble through a field of wheat and across a narrow stream. Despite getting wet feet, it outstripped the chance of being noticed had they advanced towards the warehouse using the busier, neon lit A and B roads.

It took them less than twelve minutes to arrive on the outskirts of their destination, the gap between Harriet's signal on the *Nexus*' application and them almost gone. Ahead, an industrial estate cluttered with warehouses and office blocks of varying sizes stretched to either side. Taking the indirect approach had one negative. The warehouse was obstructed by a twelve-foot-high barbed perimeter fence that stretched for as far as the pair could see.

"Here, hold this." George handed the torch to Sophie. The item disappeared in her grasp but the beam of light continued its milky-white swath ahead of her – appearing to any witnesses as though a small ball of light was hovering alongside the man, like some kind of *David Copperfield* trick.

Having anticipated a fence would at some point block their progress, George pulled the small tan backpack off his shoulder and reached in blindly. Sophie aimed the torch at her father's hands, illuminating the item as it emerged from the bag.

Wire cutters.

"Ta-dah!" George exclaimed playfully, showing the useful tool off.

Through the night vision goggles George could see the dumbfounded look upon Sophie's face, almost seeing a twinkle of amusement in her eyes. She mouthed the word: *Really*?

"I never leave home without them," he said to the quietly voiced question and squeezed the spring tensioned handles, making the cutters do a little scissor action, cutting thin air. With little time to waste, George turned his back on his daughter and proceeded to cut the wire mesh fencing, snipping a hole wide enough for large conjoined twins to climb through, quickly pushing the discarded section to one side so not to get entangled or cause further obstacle. On the other side of the fence he could see the back of the warehouse – somewhere within his wife languished, perhaps beaten, perhaps tortured, maybe (he tried to discard the thought) dead... for what?

To get to him, that's what.

His Harriet, the woman he loved above all others, was trapped and held captive by one or more hostiles just a short distance ahead. He had no idea what he was about to face, how many he would have to confront and what opposition they would make. He'd recently fired a gun for the first time in over fifteen years; would he have to use it again?

Misinterpreting her father's hesitance for fear or reluctance, Sophie took charge. Crouching next to him, she placed a hand on George's shoulder and spoke with an assertive tone: "There's no time to think dad. Come, let's go and get your wife." Without waiting, she crawled through the gap in the fence. George replaced the wire cutters back in the backpack, tossed it onto his shoulder and followed the young woman.

A moment later they were standing at the side of the building hidden deep within shadow. Very few lampposts were lit, which served them well. A halogen security light was on at the front of the building, along with a solitary lamppost; both afforded just enough light across the small car park adjacent to the warehouse to assist any who wanted to access their vehicles.

George counted four cars parked up, including the *Audi* that had been used by his wife's abductors who'd stowed her unconscious in the boot.

"Are you ready?"

In truth, George felt sick. His mouth felt dry and it felt like his heart had grown claws and was trying to tear its way out up his throat. "As I'll ever be," he replied unconvincingly.

"I will go first and open the door."

"Soph, it's dangerous."

"Shhh. You forget, no one can see me without those," Sophie tapped George's goggles with her left index finger. "Besides, if the door is locked I am better skilled at breaking in." Not waiting for further protest, Sophie was running towards what she believed was the entranceway, first passing the large 'up and over' garage door, then stopping as she came to the only visible door that allowed entrance. Next to the door was some sort of combination lock. A nine digit keypad confronted her.

"True," George uttered under his breath but he knew he wouldn't be the only one wearing these. Back at Willoughby Rising, Kaplan Ratcliff's man had been wearing a pair. And in London earlier that day, the men in black jumping out of the two vans came equipped with similar garb. The people they were up against were serious and meant business. By definition, their choice of ocular apparatus also spoke volumes as to who they were truly after.

On closer inspection and with some careful probing, Sophie noted that the security lock was not functional; the keypad was not illuminated (it should have been backlit by a soft lime-green hue) and pressing any of the keys, in any order or sequence had no affect or consequence. Slightly perturbed she tried the door handle, not expecting much – and almost jumped a mile from surprise at finding it unlocked.

"Whoa," she exclaimed, completely perplexed. This was too good to be true, most likely deliberate; she didn't think anything further of it. Sometimes the simplest solution was the least expected. She opened the door a couple of inches and tentatively, she peered in. The corridor beyond was lit by a single fluorescent towards the end – it gave enough light to penetrate the gloom closest to the door, but not enough to highlight anyone's presence beyond it. A quick scan showed the corridor itself was empty. Turning to face her father, Sophie signalled for him – a quick flash (on/off) of the torch, indicating the way was clear.

George jogged from his place of cover towards the door now held ajar.

"That was easy," he said in disbelief. It was a short distance but surprisingly he was out of breath. Seldom did he believe in luck but often recited the phrase: 'never look a gift horse in the mouth'. He didn't know exactly where the phrase came from but knew it meant not to be ungrateful when receiving a gift.

"You think?"

"Come, let's see if we can find your mother." Using the tablet, George zoomed in on the pulsating dot. The map expanded until nothing of the surrounding area remained – just a faint outline of the warehouse's schematic. The GPS signal continued to pulse, indicating she was located in a small room deep within the warehouse.

Entering the building, Sophie took the *Nexus* and led the way. Whilst she'd waited the short time for her father to join her she'd reached into her backpack and removed the gun she'd taken from the Alpha Team agent back at the flat; in its place she left the torch – the flat in Chelsea now seemed like a whole lifetime ago.

With the tablet computer directing her forward, she held the gun in her right hand, pointing ahead. The warehouse door swung closed behind them making more noise than George had wished. The clatter echoed in the dingy corridor. Sophie glared back at him.

"Sorry," he mouthed.

About half the length of the passage George felt a vibration within his trouser pocket.

His mobile phone.

He'd earlier had the good sense to turn off the ringtone – even so, the buzz of the vibration setting was loud enough for any close by to hear. He glanced at the display for indication as to who the caller was. The ID was withheld. He accepted the call and pressed the handset against his ear and listened.

"Hello?" he tried to speak softly but the acoustics in the warehouse corridor were superb and his voice was resounding.

"*Hello George.*"

George was quiet. He recognised the voice from earlier. "Ryan?" He said it incredulously.

Sophie looked back over her shoulder towards her father. She was anxious. She couldn't pinpoint what it was but something didn't feel right. Her father's voice was adding weight to her unease, carrying as it was like a klaxon in a football stadium; she feared it wouldn't be long before their presence was discovered.

George listened to the caller whose part of the conversation was too faint for Sophie to hear.

"*Listen George, things have moved up a notch since we last spoke. I don't have time to explain but when we meet we will have a long chat.*" *And some...* he thought, his mind flitting to images of Clara.

"Ryan, I can't talk. I'll call you after..."

"*After? After what? Where are you George? Are you all right?*"

"I've located my wife. I'm about to get her back."

"*Wait! George, tell me you're not at the warehouse?*" he sounded desperate. "*Agents are staking it out, waiting. They've anticipated your steps. Tom Kaplan knows you are going to go there.*"

"Ryan, it's too late. I'm already inside."

It was just then that the discordant sound of a *whoop* intermingled with a *jangle* started to clang and siren throughout the warehouse. George ended the call with Ryan and without thinking, dropped it back into a trouser pocket.

"Well, I guess the element of surprise is now gone!" George shouted over the cacophony of alarm sounds.

"You think!" yelled Sophie back over her shoulder. They arrived at the end of the corridor above which the single fluorescent bulb burned. The door that barred further progress was secured with a similar device to that placed, though inactive, on the external door – only this one was in full operation. A red light indicated that the door was securely locked. Only the correct combination would allow further progress.

"Is that going to be a problem?" George queried, pointing at the combination lock with the barrel of his gun.

"Only to a locksmith. Step back a bit!" Sophie raised her weapon and discharged three carefully aimed shots, the bullets pulverising the control panel, sending sparks, electronic components and door fragments up and about, the shorting electrics caused the overhead fluorescent bulb to flicker on and off as auxiliary power kicked in. Further damage resulted in the splintering of the wooden frame around the door handle and where, she guessed, the securing bolt was positioned within.

Walking forward, Sophie pushed the door gently, allowing it to swing slowly inwards. The handle on the other side was loose and fell, clanging to the well-polished white tiled floor. She glanced at the *Nexus*. "The signal is coming from a small room at the end of the corridor that leads from this one." She spoke loud enough to be heard over the din of the constant siren that threatened to deafen them.

"Where is everybody?" George had expected some resistance as soon as the alarm had started to whoop around them. He had placed a hand to the ear nearest to the alarm positioned high up the wall; still blaring, the ringing would continue to sound deep inside his head for many hours after.

"I wish this thing had radar," she indicated the tablet.

"Huh, that's a nice idea *Ellen Ripley*. That would make things too easy." The *Alien* movie nod was lost on Sophie who'd never even heard of the film, its three sequels or even the two spinoff *Alien/Predator* movies.

"Easier than *this*?" Something was wrong. The feeling had intensified and had nothing to do with the alarms being triggered. She couldn't help thinking that maybe they were expected and that they'd unwittingly stepped into a hornet's nest.

"Don't worry; I should be able to see the heat signatures of anyone ahead through my eyepiece. You're not the only one I can make visible, remember."

Together they slowly advanced towards the end of the corridor where a T-junction met them. A couple of doors on either side had been met with resistance (George tried one or two on passing) and knowing that Harriet was not behind them they knew not to waste further ammo.

"According to this, mum is down here." Sophie announced, waving the tablet slightly and nodding her head towards the left. Further progress was barred by another door. This one had a narrow pane of glass in the centre allowing sight of the corridor beyond.

"Great; another security door." George made to fire his gun.

"Wait! The light is green!" Sophie didn't like this one little bit. She moved in front of her father without thinking and was opening the door before he had taken his finger off the trigger.

He exhaled intensely. He had been that close to putting a bullet in his daughter's back. George held back a moment to recompose himself.

"That's odd," Sophie muttered as the security door gently closed behind her. She walked ahead, oblivious to her father lagging behind.

"Wait up!" George called out and reached for the door handle. As he pushed down to open it the light on the keypad switched from green and began to burn bright red. A bolt sounded sharply, locking the door – barring any further movement.

"Sophie!" George thumped the door with the heel of his hand. He made an adjustment to the goggles allowing him to read heat through walls and other obstacles and was momentarily relieved to see his daughter returning back to him.

"Dad, why didn't you follow me?" Slightly muffled by the door separating them.

"I... I... I don't know. I was momentarily sidetracked. Stop fussing."

"Why did it lock?"

George could barely hear her.

Why indeed had it locked?

"I will force the door like the other. Step back a short ways..."

Sophie ran back a few feet and waited.

George stepped back and levelled the gun, firing three shots.

BANG! BANG! BANG!

Two bullets destroyed the keypad, smashing the lock indicator lamps and sending sparks once again flying; the ricochet of the other bullet bounced to the side and punched a three-inch hole into the ceiling. A cloud of plaster dust descended like snowflakes. Unlike the previous door and frame, this one did not splinter. He tried the handle, pushing it down. There was little resistance but the door did not open. The lock was bolted fast. Peering in close and running a finger along the door frame's edge he felt its cold, smooth surface. It was solid metal.

George cursed, slamming a hand against the door, utterly dejected. Looking through the pane of glass he saw Sophie had returned on the other side, her face pressed up to the window peering through.

"What are we going to do?" Through the thermo goggles, George read his daughter's lips rather than hearing her words; the alarms still continued to shrill, seeming louder as though building to a crescendo.

"Hold on," he had an idea. "I'll shoot out the glass. Maybe you can climb through. Take cover." George aimed the *Beretta* again and squeezed off two rounds in quick succession.

BANG! BANG!

The glass did not break; instead two crystallised, perfectly circular discs appeared within the window. Evidently, it was bullet-resistant.

"Damn it!" George spat, thumping the toughened glass with the heel of his weapon, futilely. Dispirited, he accepted Sophie would need to find another way.

"Go get your mother," the words were muffled but Sophie could just hear them. "I will try and find another way in, but if not... meet me by the hole in the fence!" George was shouting over the constant noise that by now everyone on the industrial estate would have heard.

Sophie acknowledged her father with a nod and a mouthed "okay," before turning in the direction of the room where her mother's GPS tracker continued to transmit her location.

"Be careful," George said knowing that she would not have heard him. With the goggles he was able to watch his daughter through the door and beyond. So far there were no other signs of life. The significance of this did not register.

With one last look he turned his back on his daughter to make his way back out of the warehouse. His intention was to locate an alternative way in – there had to be a fire exit somewhere. Legally, where large buildings are concerned, you couldn't run a business without more than one escape route; two was the expected minimum.

No longer needing the goggles he flipped the lens up so that he could see normally, an action that he would shortly regret.

At the security door that Sophie had forced, George hastily pushed it open, not thinking about being careful or taking precautions.

Instead, he came face to face with three heavily armed men waiting in the corridor beneath the single fluorescent tube that lit the entire passage to the exit. Still not thinking, George raised his weapon and aimed the gun at the lead man. Before he was completely through the door, obscured by his body, his other hand had pulled out his mobile phone and tossed it backward into the corridor behind him. It bounced harmlessly, the clatter inaudible over the noise of the alarms.

"Drop your weapon!" the lead figure bellowed, his own weapon, a laser-guided rifle, brought to bear on the man who'd just entered the passageway, a red dot of light shining in and out of George's right eye, settling on a spot to the centre of his head just above the thermal night vision goggles.

"Don't shoot!" George loosened his grip on the *Beretta* and allowed it to twirl around his index finger harmlessly. He crouched down and lowered the weapon to the floor. He thought about the smoke grenades in his backpack, wishing they were near to hand. The knife at his belt was totally useless.

The front door to the warehouse burst open and in came a tall, heavyset man wearing light grey trousers, black shoes and a white shirt. His jaw line was chiselled and he looked too handsome to belong to anything away from a movie studio, perhaps the lead in a *romcom* or an *action* feature, the type that yielded a collection of action figures and a plethora of different outfits. He walked purposefully towards the back of the three armed men and George, who had returned to standing after discarding his weapon. He raised his hands in surrender.

"Well, well, well. George Jennings, what a pleasure." Speaking with an American accent, the newcomer had walked ahead of the armed goons so that he was just a foot away from George. Bending down he picked up the *Beretta* and stood up. He studied the weapon for a moment before releasing the magazine clip, placing it into his trouser pocket. He placed the gun into the waistband of his trousers.

"Who are you?" George spat the question angry at his capture. "What have you done with my wife?"

"George, George, George… I thought you'd remember me." Brayden removed the thermal goggles from George's head and unclipped the scabbard securing the knife at his waist. "After all, it's not been *that* long since training… though I may have had longer hair back then."

CHAPTER THIRTY-NINE
TOM KAPLAN

THE KLAXON ALARM WHOOPED and warbled suddenly, filling the night's silence with a harshness that initially startled the waiting Bravo Team in their two vans and Tom Kaplan, in his *Bentley*. Together, through their inertia, they had all been guilty of 'taking one's eye off the ball', having failed to see the obvious intruder enter the warehouse just a short distance away, the shadows and encroaching darkness not entirely concealing his advancement.

Tom once again opened a line of communication with Bravo's team leader. "What's happening?" he barked, simultaneously looking out through the tinted glass of the offside window in the hope of seeing the cause of the commotion at the warehouse.

Jack Wyatt was peering through binoculars towards the warehouse, the security lighting and the single lit lamppost providing just about enough luminance to see. He focused on the entrance. It looked undisturbed, but that didn't mean anything. Using the binoculars he searched all around the building. He shook his head. It was useless. They'd been caught napping.

"*Nothing that I can tell, sir,*" he replied, sheepishly.

"You mean you missed him," Kaplan spat.

"*It could just be a test...*"

A *DHL* van sped through the industrial estate, a moment later passing the *Bentley* and Bravo Team's two nondescript white vans, disturbed air buffeting their vehicles to rock slightly. Shocking them further, tyres screeched as the van tore into the car park being observed, a hubcap detaching from the front wheel and bouncing across the road to crash harmlessly against a set of large wheelie bins stationed ahead by the side of the road a short distance away.

The *DHL* van came to a halt outside the warehouse.

"*Hel-lo,*" Jack intoned to himself, refocusing his binoculars on the vehicle. He watched the back door of the bright yellow van burst open and three heavily armed men dressed in dark clothing jump out. From the front of the vehicle a smartly dressed man climbed down from the passenger seat. He spoke to the three armed men, clearly the man with the power, calling the shots. The Bravo Team leader recognised him from the mug shots sent to his phone earlier. The man's photo had not done him any justice. He looked every bit like the all-American jock often seen gracing the TV or silver screen, chiselled good looks, cropped sandy-blond hair and an outfit that could easily have been tailored for James Bond.

"Tell me you are seeing this?"

Wyatt sighed. "*I am sir,*" he replied. "*Looks like the welcoming party has arrived.*"

"Is that..."

"*The American. Brayden Scott..., yes it is sir.*"

"What are they doing?"

"*Nothing, yet; appears they are just waiting around.*"

Indeed, the armed men kitted out in black and Brayden Scott were just standing around a short distance from the warehouse entrance, looking casual. Between talking to the men, Brayden was turning away to talk some more into a mouth piece Wyatt had spotted attached to the collar of his shirt. Further scrutiny highlighted an earpiece snugly placed in his left ear.

"*What are your orders?*" asked Wyatt of his superior seated in the car two vehicles back.

Kaplan was quick to respond. "We watch… and we wait. You will know when it is time to act."

A couple of minutes passed and the sound of a muffled –

BANG!

– sounded over the din of ringing sirens.

A moment later Wyatt watched the American speak further to the three heavily armed men, making a number of hand movements, gesticulating directions, no doubt backing up verbal instructions. Even without hearing what was said, Wyatt could tell by the sign language that they were about to go in. Brayden held up a hand displaying three fingers. Wyatt guessed the American was carrying out a countdown, confirmed when he started closing his hand one finger at a time.

"*They're going in*," the Bravo Leader said, sounding like an amateur commentating a swimming competition. The three heavily armed men entered the warehouse. Brayden Scott hung back watching his associates disappear into the building. He walked to the driver of the van and spoke briefly with him through the rolled down side window. He indicated something and for a split-second appeared to look directly at Wyatt.

"Okay Jack; prepare your men. There are two ways this is going to play out. They are either going to capture whoever it was who triggered the security hullabaloo. Or, they will end up like Alpha Team this morning – either way, we go in and clean up the mess. Synchronise your watches and begin countdown to two minutes."

In the lead van, Jack Wyatt orchestrated the synchronising of watches between him and the seven other men, all wearing identical chronometers, sitting in the two white vehicles parked up across from the warehouse. Timepieces began to count down from two minutes.

"*Okay, ladies*," started Wyatt, "*you know the drill. When it gets down to zero we go in. Tag' em and bag' em gentlemen. Oorah*!" No one repeated the Bravo Leader's war cry which made him feel (and look) stupid. His team shared disparaging looks, shook their heads in embarrassment or smirked at their leader's behaviour.

A glance through the binoculars saw the American agent head into the warehouse. It was now just a matter of waiting out the final minute and thirty seconds.

On the horizon, in the night sky, a bright light fast approached from the east. Wyatt noticed it but gave it no serious thought – just a helicopter, probably the police tracking a joy rider wreaking havoc along the highway or an air ambulance on its way to the Norfolk and Norwich University hospital.

What he didn't notice was the convoy of black vans that had appeared in the road behind him, their headlights off, their movement slow and deliberate. They had manoeuvred stealthily and strategically to block off the entire road.

Four vans in all.

Almost in a blur the side doors of the vans flew open, spewing forth a mini army of heavily armed personnel, all dressed similarly to those who'd moments earlier entered the warehouse, clearly members of the same organisation. They formed a line as they advanced on the three vehicles parked to the side of the road, *M16* rifles aimed ahead in battle ready pose, fingers caressing triggers. Submerged in shadow, they crept up on their unwitting targets. Wyatt and his team, oblivious to the danger, were too busy mentally preparing and plotting their mission to notice that they were being stalked like the prey of a pack of black-backed jackals.

CHAPTER FORTY

SOPHIE

SOPHIE HAD RELUCTANTLY TURNED her back on her father, feeling his eyes on her invisible back as she ran deeper into the warehouse towards the small room from which the GPS signal continued its transmission. Had she known that he was about to be taken captive she may have abandoned the mission, instead focusing her attention on breaking open the barrier that had separated them. Instead she continued forward, her weapon drawn, her mother almost in touching distance. In the corner of the corridor, just below the ceiling on the left side, a small surveillance camera monitored the hallway, oblivious to her advance. Being invisible had its advantages.

The intruder alarm, a blaring horn filling the corridor, continued its discordant cry, reverberating loudly within her head, threatening to rupture her eardrums. So loud, the alarm would continue to echo inside her head and haunt her dreams for many weeks after.

Outside the room from which the *Nexus* had guided her, the signal pulsed stronger, leaving her in no doubt that the transmitter – and her mother – were within. She tried the door but obviously it was locked. *Why wouldn't it be?* A swipe card reader was affixed to the wall to the right of the door. A small LED lamp glowed red, signifying a confirmation that it in deed was locked. A glance around the corridor indicated half a dozen other doors were all secured by the same method, except for one.

Across the narrow hall was a room with a swipe card reader that glowed green. She moved stealthily to it and without pause or hesitation kicked the door open.

The door catapulted back revealing a startled man, in his fifties, round-of-belly, and balding with a white dressing attached to his head. He was sitting behind a cluttered desk that stretched along the wall, an array of CCTV screens flickering black and white images in front of him. The room was no larger than a store cupboard or utility room.

Although Sophie could see him, Mitch Youngs was not wearing suitable eyewear to see *her*, so it was a further shock to feel the butt of an invisible gun connect with the side of his head, the force of which knocked him sideways – he slumped over the desk in a heap, his elbow connecting with the empty soup cup, knocking it off the desk to shatter on the floor.

Considering the wall of monitors, Sophie focused on the one which paraded her mother. The others that were on displayed sections of empty corridors. The room in which her mother was secured was brilliant white and sparsely furnished. Her mother was pacing, agitated. Oblivious to the sirens beyond her room, her distress was essentially due to her confinement.

"Okay mother, I'm coming. Let's get you home." Slipping the handgun into the waistband of her trousers, Sophie looked for a way to unlock the door to her mother's cell. There were no obvious buttons to press to override the door locks. She kept searching.

Around the unconscious man's neck was a royal blue lanyard attached to which was a security pass card, the face of the man outward facing. Without disturbing the man further, Sophie pulled the lanyard out from under him and slipped the card out from its holder. She briefly studied the card, reading the man's identification credentials:

Mitch L Youngs. Central Intelligence Agency.

The photograph was unflattering. The image looked like it had been taken on a pathologist's table, the face appearing lifeless; Mitch's eyes were closed and his skin tone and complexion were ashen and gaunt. Not wasting any further time she left the CCTV room and crossed the corridor back to the door behind which she knew her mother was being detained. No longer needing the *Nexus*, she switched it off and placed it into her backpack.

A swipe of the card through the card reading slot turned the LED lamp from red to green in an instant, the bolt securing the door retracting with a 'click'. She laid her hand on the door handle. It was refreshingly cool to the touch. She applied pressure and almost held her breath.

The door opened and she stepped into the holding cell.

Harriet Jennings was on the other side of the room as Sophie entered, her back to the door. When she heard the click of the door, she'd jerked round to confront the newcomer, but there was no one to face – just an empty void where she knew there ought to be someone.

"Hello mother," said Sophie, swiftly adding: "I know our last meet up didn't go so well..." She was recalling her birthday back in April when they'd last hooked up; when Harriet had balked at Sophie's appearance, aghast at how swiftly she'd grown - Harriet had turned and fled without so much as a birthday greeting. "...but I don't hold it against you."

The room was soundproofed so with the door now open Harriet became aware of the security alarm blaring from the corridor beyond where she knew Sophie was standing, although she couldn't see her. She said nothing in acknowledgement. In truth, she'd barely heard Sophie over the din of the alarms.

"I hope you don't mind me coming to get you out?"

Stunned, Harriet shook her head. When she found the ability to speak, all she could muster was:

"Where's your father?" she almost shouted it to be heard.

Before Sophie could answer, silence and darkness descended upon them without warning. The searing bright fluorescents above ceased to burn and the sirens that were so deafening came to a sudden end. The instant silence hurt Sophie's ears more than the clamorous sounds that she felt had announced her and her father's presence.

Someone somewhere had cut the power – intentionally or not. So sheer was the blanket of darkness, Sophie felt an overwhelming fear that she had gone blind. Now, not only could anyone not see *her*, she was no longer able to see *them*.

"What's happening?" Harriet whimpered fearfully.

Sophie took a moment to reply, carefully removing the backpack off her shoulder and unfastening it.

"I can't be sure, but I think someone has deliberately cut the electric power to try and make themselves appear invisible. Levelling the playing field at a guess."

Sophie was aware of her mother shuffling towards her. Before the lights had cut out she'd noticed the injuries – mostly superficial, but the haematoma on her left leg looked nasty, the swelling no doubt causing some difficulty with movement.

"What are we to do?"

Sophie reached into the backpack and pulled out some items that her father had given her to carry back at the car less than an hour before.

"We give ourselves an advantage," she said, cracking one of the glow sticks she'd removed from the backpack, passing the chemiluminescent green stick to her mother, immediately washing the room with an effulgent green glow that provided enough light to be able to see. In her hand she held the large torch that she'd earlier used to signal her father the way had been clear at the entrance of the warehouse. She switched it on, the sudden brilliance of the halogen bulb washing the room in a dazzling reflective intensity, almost submerging the glow stick in gloom.

“Sophie, look out!” It was instinctive for she could not see exactly where in the room her daughter was occupying, though she had to be close – the room wasn’t that big to offer up many places to stand.

Beneath the reflected glow of the torchlight and the crack of the glow stick, not only was the total darkness penetrated and the ability to see restored, it had revealed the dark silhouette of a man, his face hidden beneath deep shadow, lurking at the entrance to the small room. In his hand he held a pistol, the muzzle aimed at the back of Sophie’s head.

CHAPTER FORTY-ONE
GEORGE

"PUT THIS ON."

The American tossed George a black hood that looked and felt like velvet and indicated for him to put it on over his head, his voice just audible over the still ear-splitting peal of alarms that continued to deafen from all around. The expression he wore was one of satisfaction.

George complied, immediately feeling claustrophobic from the closeness of the soft cotton material draped across his face and obstructing his airways (despite allowing him to breathe through the material unhindered). Posing no threat, one of the heavily armed men grabbed George by the shoulder, proceeding heavy-handedly to manipulate his captive's arms behind his back, forcing a pair of cuffs onto his hands. Now overtly subdued, George was guided forward down the dingy corridor, its one illuminated fluorescent seeming to lighten the passage to the entrance door less intensely – perhaps dulled by the number of bodies filling the narrow passage or a reduction in power drained by the alarms that rattled their brains.

"Where are you taking me?!" George demanded, speaking loudly whilst walking blindly ahead, one of the armed goons shoving him forward in instant reply, causing him to stumble and almost lose balance. Resistance, he knew was pointless (unless he wanted to fall on his nose and likely break it, he thought).

Brayden offered a steadying hand which George was unable to see to accept. Seeing that he had recovered his balance he answered the question cryptically. "Oh, somewhere quiet for us to have a little 'heart to heart' George. We're going to get to know each other *real* good. PLUS, there's someone back home who's itching to see you again."

They closed in on the exit door.

"What about my wife? What's going to happen to her?"

"You don't need to worry about that anymore George. We have no further use for her… not now we have *you*."

"What're you going to do with her?" persisted the cowled man.

At the entrance/exit to the warehouse, Brayden readied to leave, hand poised on the door handle. He turned to the captured man. "It all depends on your cooperation George. It's all down to you as to whether you get to see your lovely Harriet again," adding as further emphasis, "Really, it's totally up to you."

Before opening the door, Brayden talked into the mouthpiece of his radio. "Are we good to go?"

The small voice in his ear (too low for George to hear) replied with the message, as he'd expected: "*Affirmative. Extraction detail is awaiting your arrival at RAF Mildenhall.*"

"Excellent!" he said exuberantly.

"*Your flight is due for takeoff around zero-one-hundred hours, maybe sooner depending on airspace.*"

"Good."

Opening the door, Brayden's senses became awash with sounds and sights not normally present at the Norfolk industrial estate. A Black Hawk helicopter hovered above the road, a more familiar sight on the battlefields in Kandahar or Mogadishu, a spotlight from its underside aimed towards a line of three parked vehicles, the noise from its rotors deafeningly loud, competing with the still warbling sirens from the warehouse, dust and litter being fanned and gusted about from the air current produced.

A group of men had been herded into the corner of the car park and were lying on their faces, six armed security personnel standing sentinel above them. One of the men lying down – the oldest – stood up and made a run for cover towards the left of the car park.

"Stop!" warned one of the guards, turning his weapon, a hand already nursing its trigger.

Not looking back, the man ignored the demand and ran towards the side of the warehouse (where George had waited whilst Sophie had tried the door). A volley of bullets from an automatic rifle, loud but easily obscured by the cacophony of other noises, peppered his back and halted his progress, his legs flailing out from beneath him as he dived in forced cover to the concrete; his last breath exhaled from his lungs like the air escaping from a half-inflated balloon.

The driver of the *DHL* van was standing at the rear of his vehicle, the doors still open from when Brayden had arrived.

Brayden shook his head in disappointment at what he'd just witnessed. He'd given strict orders: no fatalities! How difficult was it to follow orders?

"I want that soldier's name!" he demanded from someone in command close by. He had needed to shout to be heard. He turned to the van driver. "Okay Spencer, let's get us out of here."

The driver ushered George into the back of the van as Brayden headed to the front of the vehicle. The three heavily armed men followed George in before the doors were closed behind them, sitting either side of the hooded man in a flesh sandwich.

From the passenger seat, having belted himself in, Brayden was holding his mobile phone having dialled his partner. The ring tone continued for an elongated period before going to voicemail. Brayden sighed. It wasn't unusual for the older man to ignore his calls, probably still vexed at Brayden's recent promotion. He flung the handset down into the recess within the van's door. He'd only wanted to tell Mitch to end Harriet's interrogation and to clear out now the compound had been compromised. Stupid old fool!

The driver climbed in beside him. "You all right?"

"Yeah…" he sighed. "Let's go. We've got what we came for."

"What about the girl?"

Brayden shrugged. "I'll leave her to Dominic. Win or lose, it doesn't matter, we've got the next best thing back there," Brayden indicated behind him with a backward jerk of his head. "We'll get *Daddy* to make us one of our own."

The driver started the *DHL* van's engine and drove forward out of the industrial estate just as the warehouse behind fell silent and the halogen light above the entrance door went out. Brayden didn't care to notice. It was no longer of any interest.

Taking a series of roads that would lead to the A11, the *Black Hawk* helicopter followed low in the sky above, its spotlight lighting the *DHL* van like a *West End* or *Broadway* stage performer.

Extractions of VIPs and figures of National Interest were something the Americans were notorious for. They'd also earned a reputation for botching them. But not this time. The plan had been simple. Draw George and Sophie Jennings out into the open, separate them and grab the asset. Dominic, following his old Kaplan Ratcliff programming, assumed that it was Sophie who was being sought, and as such had set about a number of schemes designed in her capture (all doomed to fail, Brayden mused). All they accomplished was to force George into an act of desperation, thereafter playing nicely into Brayden's hands. Once Harriet was in their possession, George's rescue attempt was a foregone conclusion. The timing of it made more assured by Dominic's hostage exchange ploy – Brayden knew George would not have waited, wishing to play out his own advantage. Old training on George's part was hard to forget.

The truth of the matter, it was always George they'd wanted. The Deputy Director of the CIA had been quite specific.

Sophie was expendable – she was too *domesticated*, too... *girlie*. Her hormones would get the better of her; her invisibility and her arsenal of tricks just made her a ticking time bomb. Brayden had suggested taking her out of the equation, a proposal that his superiors had rebuked. Alive, they said, George would be more willing and malleable; dead, who's to say what he might be capable of. He certainly wouldn't be cooperative in any way, shape or form.

An hour later Brayden would be escorting George up a flight of mobile airplane steps into a *Boeing C-17 Globemaster III*, and hitching a ride on the empty cargo plane; the destination:

Langley Air Force Base, Virginia, USA.

CHAPTER FORTY-TWO

SOPHIE

"LADIES..."

The silhouette walked into view to reveal a man who was familiar to Harriet. More than familiar. Not only did she recognise him beneath the subdued torchlight, its beacon bouncing off the wall closest to her to illuminate the room, she recognised his voice. He was the security agent employed at Kaplan Ratcliff, her family's pursuer for more than two years, the man she'd last seen at the roadside by his wrecked *Mercedes* the day before. He had allied himself with the two Americans who'd been keeping her hostage for over twenty-four hours; the *maniac* who'd driven her off Seabrook Road and nearly killed her and Charlie.

With her back to him, feeling the man's eyes boring invisible holes into her, Sophie slowly raised her arms up in surrender, the torch beam rising to the ceiling. Dominic had come prepared and looked at them through thermal goggles, the pistol aimed carefully at the young woman's back.

"I guess you and your father weren't keen on a trade for mother dear. Shame. I like a happy ending." Dominic levelled the pistol, aiming past Sophie's torso and pressed the trigger:

BANG!

In the silence the gun's discharge was thunderous. The pistol fired its deadly load and hit Harriet square in the chest, knocking her backwards, the glow stick falling to the floor and rolling under the table. She collapsed against the far wall and dropped to the floor in a heap, moaning and crying, raising a bloodied hand as an ineffective shield.

"Nooooooo," screamed Sophie. Before her mother had hit the floor, Sophie was whirling round and flicking the lid off the syringe, the second of two items she'd pulled from her backpack. Concealed within her right hand and with barely a second flashing by from the muzzle explosion of Dominic's gun, Sophie had advanced on the man just standing ahead of the room's entrance, aiming the torch into his face, hoping to disorientate him. Almost in slow motion, Dominic brought the pistol round to train on the girl angling for him. Before he was able to fix on his target and depress the trigger, Sophie had propelled him back against the wall by the door with her full weight, dropping the torch to land hard, its beam flickering on and off as though suffering from a loose connection, her left hand thrusting his gun arm up, forcing the weapon to aim harmlessly away, though he still held it tightly in his grip. Before he was able to regain composure or fight further, Sophie brought what Dominic thought was a fisted hand down against his nape. He flinched at the sudden bee-sting of pain that lanced his neck, Sophie depressing the plunger at the same time the needle pierced his skin, injecting the *Profonol* originally destined for her, into the man's circulatory system, consciousness deserting him without expectation and little warning.

As Dominic quickly blacked out, Sophie released her grip on the man's gun arm and stepped back. The gun clattered to the floor, beating Dominic's descent. He collapsed to the tiles with a heavy thud a moment after.

Before running to where her mother was, Sophie retrieved the torch (still flickering) and slapped it hard with the heel of her hand. The flickering stopped. She aimed the torch's beam towards her mother and examined her wound. Still lying on the floor, an inky-dark stain was spreading fast across the front of her blouse. The bullet had penetrated just below Harriet's right clavicle, shredding a hole through the loose fitting garment. On close inspection, Sophie could see that there was no exit wound – the bullet was still inside her mother's body. What she didn't know was it was travelling slowly towards her heart. She applied pressure, momentarily stemming the flow of blood that dribbled from the wound.

"Here, wear these. It'll help you see me." Sophie slipped the special glasses from her backpack and placed them on the bridge of her mother's nose.

"I need to get you out of here." Sophie helped her mother to her feet. The older woman screamed from the pain tearing at her chest and the lesser pain in her left leg.

"Ahhh, no.... no, I... I... I can't!" she wailed.

"I'm not leaving you here. We'll find dad and we'll be all right."

Reluctantly, Harriet pulled herself up and shuffled forward, Sophie shouldering her weight, an arm draped around her neck. On passing the table, Sophie awkwardly replaced the backpack onto her other shoulder and half-carried her mother out of the room, the torch held in her only free hand, Harriet's glow stick forgotten, its soft incandescence suffused beneath the table. Though invisible in Sophie's hand, the torch magically lit the way. Neither of them cared to look at Dominic lying on the floor just to the left of the door. It took all of Sophie's resolve not to put a bullet in the man who'd been dogging her family for over two years and who'd earlier coerced her into committing a crime. An image of the diamond sprung to mind. It was still stowed in her backpack. She dismissed the thought, it served no purpose.

Sophie led her mother out of the cell in which she'd been held captive for more than a day and took her back in the direction that she had arrived. Though the door at the end of the corridor had been locked, refusing her father entrance and thus barring his progress, the cutting of the power had disarmed the electronic locking mechanism causing it to fail. It now opened effortlessly with a gentle shove.

Before exiting the corridor, Sophie peered through the glass panel towards the hallway beyond. As she'd expected her father was no longer there. She guessed he had gone in search of another way in.

Sophie opened the door and stepped through, dragging her mother in with her. Despite her genetically increased strength, carrying her mother around for too long was going to prove exhausting. On the other side of the door, she could see the first security barrier at the end of the corridor, the door she knew was unlocked earlier from the three bullets blasted at the keypad lock. Before it, the torch highlighted something small and black laying on the tiled corridor floor a short way from the exit point. It almost glowed on the polished marble effect flooring.

Sophie trudged slowly towards the object, her mother increasingly weighing her down. With less than four feet from the discarded item, Sophie could see that the object was a mobile phone. She recognised it as her father's.

"What's wrong?" Harriet, in too much pain to notice, or care, hadn't spotted the electronic device lying abandoned on the floor ahead. She had gauged something was amiss by the way Sophie had slowed to a standstill.

"Wait here a second." Sophie propped her mother up against the wall and crouched down to retrieve the mobile handset. She aimed the torch upon the mobile, checking it over; alarm immediately filled her head.

Harriet looked at her daughter anxiously, unable to read Sophie's look of dread or understand what was causing the holdup.

"It's dad's..." she stood up, pocketing the communication device. "He left it for us."

"Something's wrong," Harriet murmured, answering her earlier question.

Sophie ignored her. "Come, let's get out of here." Once again, the girl helped her mother forward, half-carrying and half-dragging her the short distance to the last internal door.

As George had done previously, she took little or no care as she passed through the final barrier; only unlike George there was no armed muscle on the other side waiting in ambush. Now in the final corridor that led to the outside world, Sophie could make out the din of helicopter rotors and vehicle engines revving from outside the building. There were a few shouts but nothing discernible. Once again leaving her mother propped up against a wall, she ran to the door and pushed it open a crack, peering out into the darkness beyond. The lack of the halogen light rendered the car park almost in unearthly blackness.

"What's happening?!" Harriet shouted from behind, barely heard over the harsh noises that lambasted Sophie's eardrums.

It took Sophie just a moment to take in the commotion that played ahead of her; the *DHL* van disappearing out of the car park; the Black Hawk helicopter hovering low; the group of men surrounded by what looked like half a dozen armed soldiers; the convoy of black vans parked up a short distance away.

"WHAT IS IT SOPHIE?!" Harriet had laboured from where Sophie had left her and was now behind her daughter, a note of agitation in her voice. She demanded a response to her question.

The girl allowed the door to gently close, blocking out the tableau outside. She turned to face her mother, her look grave. "It's not safe here. We're surrounded. And they've got dad."

"Can't you go after them? Aren't you programmed to do that?"

"I'm not a machine, mum," she said, half-laughing in a derisive fashion. The *DHL* van was by now gone and soon followed by the helicopter. The turmoil on Sophie's face was palpable. On her own she could have made after the *DHL* van unseen and released her father with a variable degree of success. Anchored down by her injured mother, who wasn't blessed – if you could call it that – with invisibility, she had no hope. Plus there were the children to think about, hiding within the relative safety of her father's car, parked down an isolated, dark, rarely used dirt track half a mile away.

The klaxon of the security alarms began ringing again and the fluorescent at the end of the hall behind them flickered on as power in the warehouse was restored. A bang and echo of a door resounded from somewhere behind them.

Someone (*Dominic*?) was coming. But that wasn't possible, was it?

"I think this is the proverbial 'rock and a hard place'," Sophie said, opening the door a crack. Not much had changed since before, though Sophie could still hear the chopper beating in the near distance. She switched off the torch and tucked it back into the backpack.

"I think we are going to have to make a run for it." Without further hesitation, she flung the door open, "Come, now!" she exclaimed, dragging her mother out to the left of the building, hoping to find cover beyond the luminance of the now-blazing security light and the lamppost – both seeming much brighter than before. Harriet winced with every footfall, but persevered. Through sheer will and adrenaline, she managed to quicken her pace. As luck would have it, even without Sophie's transparent ability, Harriet got out of the warehouse unseen, the armed men too preoccupied with their captives to notice; they were now ordering them to their feet and leading them away towards their black convoy.

At the front of the warehouse Mitch Youngs had appeared, his face flustered. In one hand he held a revolver whilst the other nursed the swelling from where Sophie had clobbered him to the side of his head, adding to the injuries his skull had already sustained.

"Did you see the woman?" Mitch shouted across to the troupe of armed men shepherding Kaplan's Bravo Team towards one of the white vans still parked from their earlier failed stakeout. Tom Kaplan's lifeless body had been carried to it moments earlier. One of the armed men shook his head. Mitch swore and then kicked the warehouse door.

Sophie laid a hand on her mother's arm. "Come, let's go. There are three kids desperate to see you," she whispered.

"What about George?"

What to do about George? It sounded like the opening line to a musical number from a stage show by *Stephen Sondheim*. Sophie wanted to go after him but that wouldn't have been what he would have wanted. It would jeopardise everything and put his family at immense risk. Besides, Harriet was hurt, and hurt real bad.

She tried a reassuring smile. "We'll go get the kids first, get you to a hospital and then track him like we tracked you." Sophie knew George wore a GPS tracker. It hung from his gold chain like a pendant, attached for Sophie's benefit; reassurance for when he was late home after splitting his time with his first family. Harriet's ankle bracelet had been instrumental in finding her, so the fact that George had been taken did not overly concern her.

Harriet smiled back. "I agree with all but one thing. No hospital. Uh-uh," she shook her head firmly. "Look where taking Charlie to the hospital yesterday got us..."

Sophie didn't argue. Silently they skirted around parked vehicles and edged to the furthest side of the warehouse. Hidden, they trudged the full length of the building until they eventually came to the hole that George had cut in the wire fence.

Unobserved, still half-carrying Harriet, Sophie retraced the steps taken for the half mile return journey to the car, the torch retrieved from her backpack lighting the precarious way. Owing to Harriet's injury, the trip back took twice as long, it wasn't until twenty minutes after leaving the warehouse mother and daughter finally found themselves sitting in the front of the *Peugeot.*

"We'll get you to a hospital," asserted Sophie, ignoring her mother's earlier protest, masking her annoyance at not being able to give immediate chase to her father's abductors.

In the rear seats Meredith, Stanley and Charlie were huddled together like a family of rodents, fast asleep, one or two snores filling the night air. They looked too peaceful considering all that they'd been through.

Harriet glanced at her children and shook her head. "No. I told you, no hospital. Patch me up, I'll be fine. Let's go and get your father."

Sophie knew that her mother had lost a lot of blood. The right thing to do would be to get her to a hospital, anything else was just sheer folly.

Instead of arguing she heard herself say: "This is madness..."

"What are you waiting for?" Harriet hissed.

Sophie hurried out of the car heading for the boot where she had earlier seen her father's first aid kit.

CHAPTER FORTY-THREE

RYAN

IT WAS CLOSE TO midnight when Emily had made her excuses to leave. Ryan had suggested she take a room in the hotel but she feared that staying here would complicate things further. Ryan was very much alive, much to her relief. During the hour or so that had passed since speaking to George, the former Assistant Intelligence Officer had made it clear that he intended to help protect Sophie where possible, even though he had no affinity towards the man he directly held responsible for the death of his daughter.

He'd asked Emily outright if he could rely on her to help him. She hadn't hesitated when she had said with sincere confidence, yes.

"You see, Emily. Sophie meant a lot to Clara, more than you'd believe; more than I wanted to know. Days before she died in the explosion she called me and made me promise that I would keep an eye on Sophie. The fact that this infant was *different* to any other child did not come into it. She said she would tell me why one day… but then the so called 'accident' happened." Ryan had gone quiet then, his thoughts drifting off. Emily didn't press him and that conversation came to an abrupt, unfinished conclusion.

Emily could see from Ryan's face that there was more; the man, her mentor, her assumed father, had not divulged all regarding Sophie and Clara.

Despite George's proposal to call back, he hadn't done thus far.

That had been over an hour ago and with every minute that ticked by Ryan felt more apprehensive.

Impatience and persistence had led him to call George's phone a series of times, but each attempt went immediately to voicemail. The most recent effort had been five minutes before Emily had stood up to go. Ryan had been agitated and although she shared his concern it was getting late and she would be expected in the command centre early the following day. She knew that any sign out of the ordinary or act of dissent could result in a jar appearing in the Director's office – only instead of a decoy (as Ryan's was), she feared she wouldn't be so lucky.

"I will speak to you tomorrow," she said, following up with a gentle kiss to the side of his cheek, the sort reserved for close family members or performed by Italians and the French.

Or for fathers.

Emily had called for a taxi and the driver had been waiting patiently in the black cab outside the hotel's main entrance, the engine idling. He'd been waiting for nearly ten minutes and had started the clock early.

"Be careful," Ryan called after her, receiving an admonishing look for his troubles and genuine attempt at concern.

When the young woman had disappeared inside the taxi, Ryan pressed the redial button on Emily's phone having persuaded her to lend it to him. The phone rang a couple of times before the call was connected, startling him. He almost dropped the mobile in his excitement.

"*Hello*?" A young female voice tickled his eardrum. Momentarily he thought he'd dialled the wrong number, finding his tongue tied in knots. "*Hello? Who is this*?"

"Um… is George there?" Ryan suddenly felt nervous. *Pull yourself together Ryan*, he berated.

"*Who is this*?" the question was more insistent in tone, slightly agitated.

"Sophie, is that you? It's Ryan… I spoke with George earlier."

"*Ryan*? *You're the one who's been calling my father*?"

"Can I speak with him?" Ryan persisted.

"*Afraid not. Something's gone wrong. Very wrong. They got him Ryan, the CIA or something; took him whilst we were rescuing my mum. They got those others you warned us about too.*"

"Others? What, Tom Kaplan and his love hearts band?" Ryan sounded incredulous. "Oh Jeez."

"*Ryan, I'm tracking my father. Currently he is still on the move; the vehicle is moving fast on the A11 heading for Thetford.*"

Ryan went silent, considering Sophie's words for a moment, assimilating the information.

"*Ryan, are you still there*?"

"Yes, just thinking. It's not Thetford they're taking him," he finally said. "Sophie, I think they are heading towards one of the US airbases – either Mildenhall or Lakenheath. Both are accessible via the A11."

"*What are you suggesting*?" Sophie asked anxiously.

"I believe the CIA are taking your father to a military installation – probably to interrogate him. You've proven their safe houses aren't much cop, so it's off to a place where five thousand soldiers are in situ itching for some action – can't get more secure than that."

"*Great.*"

"Of course, our cousins from across the pond haven't had to contend with someone of your… let's say, ability."

"*I guess they'll soon get their chance*," Sophie replied nonchalantly.

"Be careful Sophie," Ryan warned earnestly, the pang of fear in his voice overlooked by the teen. On disconnecting he ordered another drink which he quickly followed with another, hoping to dispel the fear and nerves that had taken him by surprise.

Retiring to bed wasn't an option despite the barkeep insisting that he finish his drink as the hotel's bar was now closed. A glance at his watch told Ryan that it was nearing 1:00 a.m., and although he'd been drinking constantly for three hours the alcohol had done little to numb his senses or still his disposition.

Heeding the barkeep's request, Ryan wandered out of the bar area, passing the reception desk that during the day would be manned by three personnel but at night kept just the one person on hand for any late arrivals or urgent room service calls.

Ryan continued left towards three dormant elevators. His room was located on the third floor – room 305 – so he took the lift for the relatively short ride. Despite the proximity, the lift ascended slowly; the soft muzak filling the elevator car did little to affect his mood. Above the door an electronic display indicated each floor it passed in bright red numerals: *1... 2... 3...*

DING!

The doors slid open and Ryan stepped out and drifted quietly to his room. The electronic key card slipped in and out of the lock and the mechanism securing the door clicked audibly in tandem with the lime-green indicator on the door handle. Ryan pushed down on the handle and entered the room.

The door closed behind him and locked with a click as he crossed to the bed that filled the centre of the room. Although a nice hotel, the rooms were very basic, the décor in need of some updating. His room contained very little other than a bed, a chair and small table, tea making facilities, mini bar, and a TV. Despite the late hour and the fact that he'd been awake since before 5:00 a.m. the previous morning, Ryan did not feel the slightest bit tired.

He sat down on the bed and removed the mobile Emily had

loaned him. He looked at the screen saver – an image of a small caramel coloured dog, Emily's Cairn terrier, filling the whole screen, its tongue lolling out as if licking thin air. He hated that dog, yappy little thing – he was more a cat lover. Dogs did as was bidden – cats on the other hand had a mind of their own – you had to earn their loyalty.

It had been more than an hour since he'd spoken to Sophie on the phone. A quick *Google* search on the phone's browser had indicated the journey between Norwich and either of the US airbases in Suffolk took a little less than an hour to reach. Ryan had started to wonder at what was transpiring. Surely they had reached the place where the CIA had taken George?

Not being able to sleep, Ryan needed something to calm his nerves. From the mini bar he helped himself to a miniature bottle of vodka, twisted the cap and upended the contents into his mouth, grimacing from the strong neat alcohol. It was the heightened anxiety that made him reach for another miniature a moment later, this time a whisky.

Were he to still have access to Kaplan Ratcliff's command centre, he would have been roosted behind his desk observing things, manipulating satellite spies in the sky and orchestrating operations that would give him complete visuals on what was going on for a hand in George's rescue.

Not knowing and not being involved was worse than being blind, thought Ryan, now lying on top of his bed.

The *Samsung Galaxy* on the bedside table started to ring. Ryan reached for it, noting the caller was anonymous.

He cleared his throat with a stifled cough then accepted the call.

"Hello?" His voice sounded hoarse.

"*Ryan... I need help*!" Sophie started to cry. She sounded distant. "*Dad's gone*," she sobbed, barely whispering: "*and I think...*" she trailed off momentarily. "*I think... my mum... is dead*."

The former Assistant Intelligence Officer sat up from his bed too fast, his head beginning to spin – a combination of moving too quickly and the effects of alcohol disorientating him.

"What?" his voice sharp and thick with concern.

"*Tell me what to do, Ryan*," Sophie whined. "*I don't know what to do...*"

Almost at a loss for words Ryan spoke the only sound advice anyone could give in this, or any desperate situation. "Sophie, whatever you do: don't panic..."

CHAPTER FORTY-FOUR

HARRIET

HARRIET HAD INSISTED THAT she was okay to drive despite the searing pain that ripped through her chest, tears running freely from the corners of her eyes, hidden behind the glasses which allowed her to see her daughter. There was a grimace permanently affixed to her lips, making her jaw ache. Sophie had poured iodine onto the wound and pressed wadding against the hole to staunch the blood flow, securing it into place with surgical tape and wrapping a bandage diagonally from her left shoulder to below Harriet's right armpit. It did little to stop the bleeding; Sophie could tell this straight away by how quick the wadding had darkened crimson. In the absence of a hospital, this was the best she could do. She knew it wasn't nearly enough.

"You really need to go to a hospital, mum," Sophie had urged, her look pleading. Harriet had grunted, saying nothing but answering the young woman by starting the *Peugeot*'s engine and putting it into gear.

Thankful that the roads were empty, Harriet floored the accelerator and they bombed up the A11, the speedometer dial hovering between eighty and ninety mph, speeding past signs and turnings for Wymondham, Attleborough and Thetford with barely a glance, focus constantly on the moving red dot on the tablet computer that Sophie had slipped from the backpack and was now holding.

Despite the speed of the vehicle the three young passengers in the back did not stir. Sophie was thankful that they'd slept through their mother's whimpers and cries of pain as she'd dressed the gunshot wound. No child should see their mother in such distress – and certainly not the extent of her injuries or the amount of blood.

"How far?" Harriet asked through gritted teeth, overtaking a slow moving fuel tanker.

"About ten miles," Sophie judged from the map. Having been monitoring the dot since returning to the parked vehicle she had guessed the van carrying George was travelling vastly slower than they were, especially as they'd closed the gap between them almost by half in the thirty-five minutes of driving.

"They are still too far ahead. It would be easier if we could get to them before they arrive at a US airbase."

"Are you sure we would have a chance against that helicopter? I'm guessing it's not hauling blanks."

"I thought you were trained to do anything?" Harriet said, unable to mask her sarcasm. Neither of them dwelled on the fact, but it didn't seem possible that this had been the longest the pair of them had spent together since Sophie had been born.

"I must have been absent the day they taught light armed combat against military aircraft," Sophie replied tersely.

The rest of the journey was driven in silence, punctuated by Charlie's slight snoring and the occasional uttered recoil from when his broken arm became disturbed from a jolt.

For the next twenty minutes they drove along an empty road allowing Harriet to squeeze the *207* to speed closer to one-hundred mph. The road was straight so posed little danger, though Sophie couldn't mask her unease, a hand gripping the entry and exit assist handle above the door as though it could slow the vehicle down or help in the event of a collision.

At the end of the A11, across the roundabout, Harriet took the third exit, the A1101 turning. Signposted as the Bury Road.

"Dad's GPS beacon has stopped moving," Sophie broke the uncomfortable silence. "They've taken him to RAF Mildenhall."

"That figures. It's closer than Lakenheath. How long?"

Sophie judged less than nine minutes.

Harriet steered her husband's car right onto Queens Way that became West Row Road, a distance just short of two miles, before taking a sharp right that took them past Wamil Road. Despite it being dark and badly lit, the airbase could be seen ahead, a series of red lights atop guidance beacons marking a path amongst runway lighting for any landing aircraft. A number of large buildings filled the horizon – aircraft hangers, office buildings and other military installations all subdued, deep in camouflaging shadow.

"Turn left ahead," directed Sophie. "We're nearly there."

Harriet drove a little further before bringing the vehicle to a sharp, sudden halt. The way ahead, about one-hundred meters, was blocked by a security barrier that was controlled by armed soldiers sitting within a small guard's office. She killed the headlights, hoping to evade detection.

"I guess it was naïve to think we could just drive in and get your father," Harriet said, miserably. "Now what do we do?"

Sophie was staring at the *Nexus*' seven-inch screen. Using her fingers, she zoomed in closer to the GPS dot, bringing up the faint layout of the surrounding base, the long airfield that stretched across the centre of the map zooming out of the picture.

"It looks like they are outside and moving on foot."

"Where are they taking him?"

Zooming out of the map slightly Sophie could see that the course George was moving was northwards, towards the airfield.

Sophie considered the scene, her brain assimilating the facts. It wasn't difficult – in fact, it was quite obvious. Why else would you go to an airfield?

"They are taking him to an aircraft," Sophie stated. "We're out of time." Sophie unbuckled her seatbelt and clambered out of the car.

"What are you doing? Don't do anything rash!" appealed Harriet, struggling to get out of the car, going after the young woman, the darkness almost concealing her.

"What do you care?" The two women stared at each other for a moment before Sophie turned to face the entrance to the airbase. "I'm going in to get your husband back. Drive somewhere close by and just wait."

"Can't I help?" implored Harriet. She had limped after her daughter and blocked what she thought was Sophie's path.

"You forget... you'd be seen. I have a better chance of success on my own." Sophie sidestepped her mother and walked towards the security barrier. The soldiers guarding the entrance could be seen through the glass window of a small brick building that overlooked the road leading in. They were oblivious to her advance – one fixated on a small colour television that was broadcasting an NFL football match (*Baltimore Ravens* versus *San Francisco 49rs* – the game would end thirty-four - thirty-one respectively), the other guard deeply engrossed with a book (*American Sniper* by ex-Navy Seal *Chris Kyle* - it had been made into a film starring Bradley Cooper).

"Wait!" Harriet was stooping in front of the *Peugeot*, looking after her daughter who was now two or three meters ahead of her.

Sophie stopped and looked back over her shoulder. "I'm still here."

For a second Harriet didn't have the voice to say the words she wanted to say. As the old saying went, *the cat had got her tongue.*

Sophie shrugged and made ready to continue, half-turning away.

"I'm sorry Sophie," Harriet finally said, halting her.

"For what?"

"For everything... but mostly... for not being your mother."

Sophie shuffled on her feet, momentarily thrown off course. She walked back to her mother and pulled her into an embrace, wrapping her arms about the older woman's back and shoulders. She didn't care about the pain or discomfort she was causing her, or the blood that was staining her invisible clothing. For a long moment they stayed clinched together until Sophie finally pulled away. She sniffed and tried to disguise the fact that a few tears had loosened from her eyes. Harriet used a thumb to dry some away herself.

"We'll talk when I get back. I promise," Sophie said before hurrying off towards the security barrier.

"No we won't," Harriet whispered to herself a moment later. She closed her eyes and half-staggered, half-limped back to the car.

CHAPTER FORTY-FIVE
BRAYDEN

RAF Mildenhall had been in the hands of the Americans since 1950, a consequence of the Soviet Union threat and the 1950 invasion of South Korea by Communist forces. Before this time it had played an active and integral part to Britain's war effort against the Germans in World War II, involved in most of the RAF Bomber Command's many offensives against Germany. In fact, on the day Britain and France declared war, three days after Germany invaded Poland, three *Wellington* aircraft from Mildenhall were despatched to bomb the German naval fleet at Wilhelmshaven.

The *DHL* van turned a sharp right off West Row Road, drove a short distance before turning left onto a road simply known as The Street. Above their heads the *Black Hawk* helicopter continued its escort, the bright spotlight chasing a circular swath of brightness that illuminated the van's progress. As the driver took the vehicle closer to the base, the security office and barrier station now in view, two soldiers appeared from within and stood to the right of the driver's side of the road, hands massaging triggers on *M4* assault rifles.

The driver brought the van to a halt and flashed his ID card. Brayden flashed his identification within a gatefold wallet from his side of the vehicle, though the armed guard paid it little notice.

"You're expected. Private Lawrence is waiting just through there in a Jeep," the guard indicated a short distance beyond the barrier, through a pair of electric gates and a short way from a visitor's parking area. "Follow him; he'll take you to the waiting aircraft on the taxiway."

"Thank you," Brayden said, putting away his ID. The security barrier ascended, allowing access to the *DHL* van. The driver put the vehicle back into motion and entered RAF Mildenhall. The barrier quickly descended as soon as the van was through, then the electric gates slowly opened granting final entrance. The *Black Hawk* helicopter, having completed its mission, turned off its spotlight and took off towards a different direction, climbing higher into the full dark sky.

Within the airbase it took less than thirty seconds to find the chaperon Private Lawrence, his Jeep swinging out in front of them as they turned into the visitor's area. A hand snaked out through the side window and waved for them to follow.

Three minutes later they were stopped a short distance from the taxiway, Brayden had climbed from the passenger seat of the van and wandered around to the side, slapping the heel of his right hand against the door. A moment later and the door slid open. Two of the three armed security men jumped out, the third stood behind the captured George Jennings, whom was shoved forward heavily into the open. Brayden pinched the black velvet hood off his head and guided him forward. The *Boeing C-17 Globemaster III* was parked on the taxiway, a metal staircase formed from opening its door downward led up to a passenger entrance. By and large the *Globemaster III* was a cargo plane, but there was room for several passengers. Often used to accompany the President of the United States on domestic and foreign engagements, carrying the Presidential Limousine and security detachment, there were occasions when it was used to carry the President himself, but not often. Air Force One was preferable.

"This way George," Brayden took his arm and guided him gently forward. The three security guards flanked them as they headed towards the airplane, its four turbofan engines whirring; a thrumming noise accompanying them from within.

"Where are you taking me?" George pleaded. He tried to stop walking but Brayden had him by the arm and dragged him along easily.

"I'm taking you home, George." The entrance to the cargo plane was just twelve-feet away.

"If that was so, you need only have asked. Why the spectacle... all this *razzmatazz*?"

"Just following orders, George. You know how it is..."

Before George could protest or struggle further one of the armed security men overzealously raised the butt of his rifle and clobbered him against the side of the head; the other two men walking close by leapt forward to help steady George from falling to the macadam, carrying his slumped figure up the metal staircase into the hulking body of the *Boeing* aircraft.

"He wasn't to be harmed!" shouted Brayden at the offending soldier, climbing up the metal staircase after him.

Satisfied all travellers were safely inside and strapped into their seats, a member of the flight crew activated the switch to close the door and radioed up to the pilot, giving the go-ahead to takeoff.

CHAPTER FORTY-SIX

SOPHIE

GLANCING OVER HER SHOULDER, Sophie could no longer see her mother or the outline of the *Peugeot*, so deeply concealing was the darkness that blanketed the surrounding area. She sighed and tried to put her mother's injury to the back of her mind. It was bad, she knew that, but how bad she didn't want to consider.

She moved forward ten yards and came to within a foot of the access point to Mildenhall's USAF base.

Unheard and unobserved Sophie stooped under the barrier and walked past the security booth and barrier station. A quick peek into the small office indicated that the two men on guard duty were preoccupied with their leisure activities (one still reading, the other continuing to watch television), not expecting further visitors or disturbances of any kind. It was close to 2:00 a.m. and the nightshift were settling down having been extraordinarily busy with the late arrival of the CIA agent, his cohorts and his classified cargo.

Nothing else was expected.

Sophie considered the electric gates that barred her way further into the airbase. Standing twelve-feet high, the obstacle would pose a problem to most chancers fancying a way into the airbase fortress.

Not for Sophie.

The fence posed little problem to someone of her abilities. For safety she placed the *Nexus* tablet into her backpack and secured it to her shoulders. Still within her bag were the handgun, several magazines of ammo and smoke grenades. She hoped not to have to use any of them.

Taking a run up, Sophie leapt up the twin gates, a hinge allowing her left foot leverage and some additional boost. With ease and agility she found herself at the top of the closed gates. Scissoring her limbs over the apex, she was momentarily perched on the narrow metal edge, her bottom pressed against cold steel, her legs dangling over the side. The gates juddered under her weight but made little noticeable sound. Composing and preparing her body for a fall and with feline finesse she allowed herself to drop to the ground on the other side. Also like a cat, but with knees bent to absorb the shock, she landed on her feet.

Crouching low she looked behind for any signs that her assault on the gates and her subsequent descent had alerted the guards to her presence. Counting ten heartbeats she allowed confidence to steel her forward.

Whilst walking she retrieved the *Nexus* once again from her backpack and used it to track her father. The red dot was no longer moving and indicated his whereabouts somewhere towards the centre of the base, near to the airfield. She returned the tablet computer back. A glance to her right indicated a well lit area beyond a number of large buildings and aircraft hangers. As Sophie started to run in its direction, the sound of an aircraft's engine whirring echoed around the base, invading the night's silence, penetrating her thoughts and planting a seed of anxiety within her.

Unable to rid herself of negative thoughts, she pushed herself harder, lengthening her strides so that she could reduce the space deficit between herself and the place where she believed her father to be.

Running through a gap between hangers, Sophie burst through to the runway area and laid her eyes on the aircraft responsible for the noise levels. She saw the *DHL* van parked a short distance away, the driver in situ behind the wheel, and an army Jeep that was tearing away from the area at the rear of the aircraft heading towards some more buildings and what were sleeping quarters. A glance at the *Boeing C-17 Globemaster III* indicated that it was making ready for flight. The stairs/door that had allowed access was being retracted. The whirr of the gigantic aircraft's engines began to roar louder, the sound deafening and threatening to burst her eardrums.

Sophie knew what it all meant – what it fundamentally meant for her father.

"Noooooo!" Her appeal went unheard over the building roar of the *Boeing*'s four turbines.

Though her chest was now burning from the exertion and the lack of oxygen intake – she didn't allow herself to falter, not even when the wheels on the *Boeing* began to move, first slowly, the aircraft rolling forward, and then faster as the four turbofan engines began to thunder, emitting even greater noise as they powered up for the takeoff.

She continued running towards the plane. Despite the genetic modifications to her endurance and strength, physically she was beginning to flag and no matter how much she willed it her legs were never capable of matching the acceleration of an aircraft building up speed for takeoff.

"Dad!" she bellowed, her voice inaudible over the noise of the *Boeing*. She was now running alongside the 173-feet of craft, though the cargo plane was now taking the lead and moving away from her fast.

Sophie ran for a few meters more despite the futile effort until the *Boeing C-17 Globemaster III* left the runway, its nose aimed heavenward, ascending into the night sky.

Out of breath, out of luck and out of ideas, Sophie stopped, collapsing to her knees in a heap. Unbidden and without use she started to cry.

She felt desperate and utterly hopeless.

Although her emotions were supposed to have been genetically eradicated, George had persisted in retaining them for the sake of humanity (and for personal reasons). In truth, it was Sophie's only weakness.

Sophie watched the plane as it climbed ever higher, now just a dark shadow and a handful of navigational and positional lights barely visible in the sky, putting further distance between herself and her father.

"Dad..." she implored. *What do I do?*

It was over, she had failed him.

Her father was gone, taken for whatever hostile purpose – questioning, torture, imprisonment, *death*?

Who knew?

Whatever the purpose, he was no longer on hand to provide for his family, keep them safe and offer them shelter. Less significantly in the scheme of things, he was no longer able to help her – the only person qualified who could possibly fix her invisibility and make her normal.

When she could no longer see the *Boeing* aeroplane or hear the drone of its four engines, Sophie picked herself up from the tarmac and walked slowly, disconsolately, back to where her mum would be waiting expectantly – just an entrance gate and a security barrier manned by two armed soldiers standing in her way.

CHAPTER FORTY-SEVEN

BRAVO

THE WHITE VAN HAD screamed to a halt in the centre of the road outside the modern office building, the driver, disguised behind a balaclava, jumped out and ran to a nondescript black van that had led the way. He opened the door and leapt into the passenger seat, not securing the door behind him before the vehicle hurtled off in getaway mode.

From inside the abandoned white vehicle muffled noises and occasional thumps against the interior walls, deliberate and necessary – trying to gain notice, urging assistance, pleading for help. Not the everyday sounds one would expect on a commercial London street.

At such a late (or early) hour – after three in the morning – no one would hear the restrained, somewhat muffled distress signals, and although the van was parked conspicuously and deliberately in the centre of the road - an obstruction for other road users - no one would be bothered or inconvenienced for a while yet.

In fact it wasn't until 4.08 a.m. that the van and its subdued disquieted inhabitants were discovered.

An early riser walking to work saw the van's strange parking place and on hearing the commotion, had dialled 999.

Ten minutes later a police car had parked up silently behind the van, blue lights flashing self-importantly; two uniformed men clambering out and walking the perimeter of the vehicle slowly and carefully, one peering into the driver's side. He noted the keys were still in the ignition.

A thumping noise came from the interior of the van, alerting policeman number two, who hastened to the rear of the vehicle.

"Hello?" policeman number two had his hand on the door handle.

"Wait, Shaun," policeman number one was hurrying around from the front. "This doesn't feel right."

"There's someone inside," said policeman number two matter-of-factly.

"Perhaps we should get backup."

From inside the van a stifled cry for help could be heard:

"*Hrmmmpppppp*!!"

"Quick, get it open."

Policeman number two pulled the door open and gasped. Policeman number one had crept up and was standing by his side. "Good God," he said, reaching for his radio. "Despatch, this is eight-five-two-one requesting backup and medical assistance. We have multiple victims cuffed and subdued, do you copy?"

"Eight-five-two-one, this is despatch. Can you clarify, over?"

"Despatch, I can't elaborate any more than that. I need assistance right away."

"Eight-five-two-one, standby; backup and medical teams are on their way, over."

Within the back of the white van, crammed together with barely a hair's breadth between them, seven men were tied together, their hands restrained using nylon zip tie cuffs, their mouths duct-taped shut. An eighth man was lying at the back of the van hidden from immediate view; his face turned away, his body inert. Unlike his colleagues he needed no further method of restraint.

One of the men had been constantly head butting the inside wall of the van in what had been a fruitless attempt at gaining notice – his face was drenched in sticky crimson from a gash at his temple. Two of the other six men were unconscious through lack of oxygen.

Policeman number two had climbed into the back of the van and was pulling duct tape from the mouth of the first subdued victim.

"What on earth's gone on in there?" policeman number one was peering in from behind.

"Looks like one hell-u-va party," said policeman number two, the duct-tape almost peeled free from the first victim. The man beneath him started to weep uncontrollably. "It's okay. You're safe now," he soothed. "Tell me what happened."

CHAPTER FORTY-EIGHT
RYAN

"TELL ME WHAT TO *do, Ryan*," Sophie whined. "*I don't know what to do...*"

When Ryan had finished listening to the full account of Sophie's failed rescue attempt he slumped back onto his pillow. For the whole conversation he'd been lying sprawled out across his bed. It was like a nightmare that his body refused to wake from.

"*Ryan? What should I do?*"

It was around the same time the white van parked outside the Kaplan Ratcliff control centre was being discovered by the police. Ryan gave Sophie's question a moment's consideration. The situation was a terrible mess. But he owed it to Clara to help her.

Clara.

The time was closing in on the moment when he would have to come clean with George's daughter. Things weren't all that they seemed – and let's face it, things were far from being ordinary when it involved Sophie Jennings.

"Are you sure Harriet..." *is dead?*

"*I... I can't find a pulse,*" she paused. "*She's not breathing. She's cold to the touch...*" By the breaks in dialogue Ryan assumed she was checking her mother's vitals as she spoke. "*After all we've done we've failed to save her...*" she sobbed.

"Okay, Sophie. Okay." Using his free hand he rubbed at his eyes trying to wake himself. "I'll tell you what I want you to do." In truth,

Ryan didn't have any idea what she was going to do. Before he had formed a response words started to spill from his lips: "I want you and your family to go somewhere safe. I know someone who will be able to help. Someone your father once knew."

In a small, childlike voice, Sophie said: "*Can we trust him*?"

"More than me I'd wager," Ryan harrumphed, clearing his throat. "Sophie, are you able to drive?"

"*Are you asking me whether I have a licence*? *Technically, I'm not yet three-years-old*."

"No, I'm asking whether you *know* how to drive?"

"*I can drive, just not very well*." Sophie said haughtily.

"I guess you have that in common with most of the British population. I will text you a postcode once I hang-up, use it in your Sat Nav and call me when you get there. It's somewhere safe, somewhere secret. For that reason I will give you the exact location only when you arrive."

"*Okay. What about my mother*?" she almost whispered.

"I'm so sorry, Sophie, there's nothing for it; you are going to have to leave her behind."

"*We were going to have a talk when I got back. She said she was sorry… and now dad is gone…*" she trailed off in a flood of tears, grief overwhelming her.

"Sophie… Do as I've said, follow the postcode I'm going to give you. Don't give up, your brothers and sister need you. You need to stay alive. Trust me, together we'll get your father back. I promise."

Unable to bear the sobbing any further, Ryan disconnected the call and allowed the mobile to drop to the bed beside him.

"Poor kid," he muttered, taking a deep breath. He sighed emphatically. *What a colossal mess!*

After a minute Ryan retrieved Emily's phone, tapped through the path of icons to the text function and keyed in the postcode he wanted Sophie to head to. He pressed the send button and waited for the sent report, which came seconds later.

With little time to spare, Ryan freshened himself up, changed his clothes and readied himself for a long drive. Sleep wasn't going to come anyway, so the change of scenery would be a blessing. He intended to be in Devon to meet and greet Sophie, her brothers and her sister when they arrived.

Three hours into the journey, the news that Tom Kaplan was dead filtered through to him during a news report.

Things just kept getting better and better.

CHAPTER FORTY-NINE

SOPHIE

IF LOSING HER FATHER hadn't been difficult enough, finding her mother lying face down at the side of the road next to the car with no pulse, and clearly beyond help was more devastating.

Using her father's mobile phone, she'd returned one of the missed calls highlighted on the phone's call history, calling the man who'd been contacting her father periodically over the past twenty-four hours, seemingly to warn him like some sort of guardian angel.

"Ryan... I need help!" Sophie was crying. "Dad's gone," she sobbed, barely whispering: "and I think... I think... my mum... is dead."

The truth was, her mum WAS dead and the only help her father's guardian angel could offer was to leave the woman who'd brought her into the world behind, discard her like an emptied crisp packet as though she meant nothing, a piece of used rubbish.

Sophie was kneeling beside the dead woman. When checking her vital signs, she'd rolled her onto her back. Now she was holding her head in her arms. "I'm sorry mum," she said, whispering: "I wish you'd allowed me to know you."

A couple of teardrops fell onto her mother's face and slid a trail down the dirt that besmirched her cheeks. Sophie leaned over and kissed her mother gently on the mouth. Her lips were still warm even though the rest of her felt cold. "Goodbye," she said softly before lowering her head back to the road's surface.

Dawn was threatening to break as Sophie walked to the back of the *Peugeot* and reached into the boot for her medicine. Using two vials of serum, she jet injected the antidote into her arm and waited for it to take immediate effect. A moment later she was fully visible. She closed the boot of the car and made the mistake of walking to the passenger side door. Realising her error, she walked round the front of the car, passing her mother lying to the side of the road next to the driver's side, tried to ignore her bloodied body, and climbed into the vehicle, feeling strange seated behind the steering wheel.

Starting the car's engine, Sophie nervously put the vehicle into gear and turned the car around, using heavy feet on the pedals which caused the car to jut, jerk and kangaroo forward, the motion disturbing the sleeping children in the back.

It wasn't long before Meredith stretched and yawned. Noticing Sophie in the driving seat, she asked: "Where's mum?"

With a dry mouth, Sophie shook her head. "She wasn't there," she lied, unable to admit the truth that their mother was now dead and lying discarded by the side of the road behind them.

The drive was taking its toll on the children sitting in the back and on Sophie in the driving seat. The unlicensed driver was battling fatigue having had no sleep in over twenty-four hours. With just a couple of essential food, toilet and exercise stops breaking the tedium – the longest sojourn being for an hour for breakfast at a beaten down roadside rest stop along the M4 – a shabby looking burger van that promised everything under a minute, including gastroenteritis – they'd been travelling for just over four hours. The July weather continued to be glorious with temperatures exceeding 26°C being forecast. Some patches of cloud offered the occasional respite from the sun, but too infrequent to make the journey comfortable.

Sophie, with less than three years of actual living experience, thought it could have been the hottest summer on record, but the Met Office could only generously indicate a slight variance on previous years, not yet willing to give global warming much credence.

Stuck inside a car devoid of air conditioning, all four of the travellers were road weary, uncomfortably hot and growing more irritable by the mile. Bickering between Stanley and Meredith had been filling the air making the travelling even less pleasurable.

Ryan's text had given a postcode starting EX22, indicating an address somewhere in Devon, 310 miles far south from the American airbase, to the west of where Sophie had failed to rescue her father. His GPS tracking signal had grown weaker then flickered off once the aircraft in which he had been stowed had passed out of range. The tablet which Sophie had been watching constantly since George had been captured – now close to being out of battery – was now being used for satellite navigation purposes. It was on the seat next to her, only slightly distracting. She checked it every so often, nervously driving towards Ryan's destination.

After six hours and thirty-eight minutes, the signpost of Holsworthy welcomed them, and the Sat Nav's female voice announced immediately after, in a clipped, clear, annunciation:

"You have reached your destination."

Sophie continued to drive until a parking spot presented itself. She pulled in and turned off the ignition, turning to look over her shoulder at the three kids cramped in the back.

"I'm going to make a call. Please be quiet," she said tiredly.

"Where are we?" asked Stanley ignoring the driver.

"I want to go home," whined Charlie.

Sophie picked up George's pay-as-you-go phone (which she'd

stored in the door's recess) and called Ryan. A couple of rings later and the familiar sound of the older man's voice spoke into her ear.

"Sophie... I guess you've made it okay. Were you followed?"

Automatically Sophie peered over her shoulder and looked past her two brothers and sister, gazing through the rear windscreen.

She couldn't be sure but she answered confidently. "No, no one followed. I'm certain of it."

"Good. Then I won't delay you any longer." Before ending the call, Ryan gave Sophie the rest of the postcode which she keyed into the tablet. After a moment waiting for the gadget to calculate the revised route, its female voice filled the car again with new instructions that would take less than eight minutes to navigate to.

Sophie restarted the engine and the car set forward with a slight jerk. Directed onto the A388, they followed each left and each right until coming to a smaller place called Wimble. The Sat Nav guided them onto a road that was surrounded by fields on either side with just the occasional house or landmark, eventually indicating a left turn that winded up a dusty, seldom used track. A small house, hidden beyond a row of trees marked the end of the journey, the Sat-Nav announcing that the destination had been reached just seconds earlier.

The *Peugeot* drew into the grounds and came to a stop behind a black *VW Golf*, tyres crunching gravel and crushing stones.

"Are we here?" Stanley asked crisply. On reflection, for the most part the kids had been quiet, it was just from time to time that they had argued, and like most children with ages of four, six and nine (respectively), bickering at the best (and worst) of times, was expected.

"It appears so," said Sophie slowly.

"Finally," grumbled Meredith under her breath.

"Is dad here?" Stanley unfastened his seatbelt. Sophie ignored the boy and climbed out of the car, relieved at the opportunity to stretch her legs. She propelled the door closed behind her.

The small cottage-like house had an old white door made from solid oak, the paint flaking and blistered in places, a look that matched the wooden window frames. The building had ivy growing up its brickwork and looked like it sorely needed a bit of TLC and a whole heap of maintenance. As Sophie walked round the front of her father's car the front door creaked open and a tall man who appeared in his late-forties stepped out.

Sophie could hear the children in the rear of the car squabbling as they too disembarked from the vehicle.

The tall man, his face swollen and bruised, took a few steps forward, and then stopped, taking in the sight of Sophie and the three children.

"I guess you are Sophie," Ryan started, his look at first concerned but quickly taking on a surprised, almost amazed expression, one which Sophie mistook for shock at how she appeared. It was the face she often saw staring back at her in the mirror, seeing the sudden changes to her features as her body genetically, unethically, altered at a superimposed speed. "You look a lot like her..." Ryan continued, Sophie stopping just in front of him. "...your mother, I mean."

"If you knew my mother, you knew her better than me," Sophie said sternly, her eyes boring into him. They were granite hard, determined.

Ryan could tell by her look that she wasn't someone to toy with, despite her teenage appearance. It was a look he remembered seeing before, reminiscent to her mothers. "It's uncanny, the likeness," he said solemnly, ignoring her statement.

Sophie sighed. "Shall we go inside?"

"Yes... yes, of course." Ryan became animated, his demeanour and body language sanguine. "This way... come... make yourselves comfortable." He motioned them forward, inviting them in. "You must all be exhausted after such a long journey."

Sophie stayed back and watched the three children walk past her, Meredith walking ahead of the group, with Charlie close and Stanley lagging a short way behind.

"You have no idea." Sophie was the last to enter the old house, just behind Ryan. The door closed of its own accord behind him.

The four guests walked through a narrow hallway and entered a room a short distance into the left.

"Please, take seats. I'll grab us some drinks from the kitchen. Would lemonade be okay?"

Ignoring the question Sophie knew time was of the essence. She didn't want to delay things with simple courtesies or wasteful small talk.

"Ryan, what's going on? Where have they taken my father? Let's not forget... we don't even know who *you* are," sounding petulant. "Who are you?"

Ryan smiled warmly, hoping to defuse the situation. "Please Sophie... you've had a long journey. It's been an ordeal by all accounts, I get that."

"You don't know the half of it..."

"At least let me get you some drinks, the children look parched. Soon enough we can talk."

"All right, Ryan. Have it your way."

"Ice?"

"Just make the damn drinks..." She settled herself into a comfy armchair, ignoring Ryan's admonishing look.

CHAPTER FIFTY

EMILY

THE COMMAND CENTRE WAS abuzz with the triple whammy of Bravo Team's spectacular failure and capture by the CIA, the news that George Jennings had been taken and was now officially missing, and the tragedy of Tom Kaplan's death. Despite this, no one mourned his passing.

Samuel Jackson had been informed of the former and the latter items of news shortly after 6:00 a.m. He was already aware of George's abduction having witnessed it for himself via the spy in the sky – satellite surveillance images had beamed the whole turn of events live onto the large screen taking up the entire wall beneath the mezzanine floor. Once the Americans had him on their base, overhead visuals were lost. His guess was they were going to extract him and take him elsewhere for interrogation… possibly somewhere in the UK, but most likely stateside. Alas, George's trail would now grow cold and he would become a dead-end for the time being.

Just before 8:00 a.m., Emily Porter arrived. Although rested, her sleep had been uneasy and frequently disturbed. Thoughts of Ryan dominated, and the knowledge that he was still alive, though a relief, weighed heavily on her mind. News of the night's events had reached her via her PDA – she wondered how Ryan was feeling having learnt about George. She was unaware of the fate that had befallen Harriet Jennings.

"Mornin' Emily." Samuel was strangely buoyant despite the trilogy of setbacks.

"Director," she acknowledged. "You seem rather chirpy."

"With every cloud there is a silver lining," he replied cryptically, before taking a meandering walk back to his office.

An hour later and the reason for his good humour became apparent. Flanked by two security personnel, Jennifer Ratcliff entered the control room and made her way up to Samuel's office. The two security personnel stood guard at the bottom of the metal stairs.

"What's going on?" Emily asked an analyst on passing. It was Jason, the timid man in his forties who'd been dressed down by the Director just the day earlier. He was walking back from the drinks machine carrying a cup of what looked like turbid water. He'd dispensed fifty pence for what should have been a decaffeinated black coffee but instead reminded her of the time when her toilet had backed-up.

"Word is with Kaplan now dead the silent partner has appointed his daughter to take over the CEO position," he replied. He took a sip from the steaming cup in his hand and winced at the awful taste.

"Samuel's happy."

"Of course; he probably feels like the cat that's just got the cream. They're dating…" Jason winked suggestively.

"That's interesting," said Emily, uninterested.

"Don'tcha think?" Jason walked away, back towards his desk. Before he was out of earshot, Emily spoke a further question.

"What's happening now with George Jennings?"

Jason shrugged. "He's history. The Americans have him. Likely or not we'll never see or hear of him again. Or his body will wash up on some beach somewhere."

"Where does that leave us?"

Jason shrugged again. "I guess it's Jennifer Ratcliff's call. She's all about profit margins and not interested in all this..." he waved a hand theatrically around him at the control room. "But Samuel will probably push to locate the rest of the Jennings with the intention of capturing Sophie. She *is* our property after all..."

"Easier said than done," Emily heard herself say without conviction. She knew that Kaplan Ratcliff had little chance of success whilst she was second in command at the corporation. She would continue where Ryan had left off.

Jason turned away with his hot beverage - if you could call it that - and returned to his desk.

Upstairs, in the office on the mezzanine floor, laughter mingled as Samuel and the new CEO shared a joke.

Emily reached into her bag for her old mobile phone, a pay-as-you-go handset she'd bought from *Tesco* as a spare and which now replaced her regular phone. She left the control room and dialled her *Samsung Galaxy* phone, now in Ryan's possession. She walked the short distance to an empty office, one free from surveillance equipment, closing the door behind her. Two rings on the phone and the line became connected. She closed the blinds on the door, blocking intruding eyes.

"*Hello*?" The voice at the other end sounded tired. Emily guessed that he'd had little sleep also. She was right.

"Ryan, it's Emily. We might have a problem."

"*Add it to the list. I take it you've heard George is gone.*"

"And Tom is dead, yes," Emily replied matter-of-factly.

"*Emily, Harriet is dead also. Caught a bullet during the rescue mission. Sophie is now heading to somewhere safe with the kids.*"

"That's terrible! God...! Those *poor* kids..."

"*I know.*"

"Makes my news insignificant."

"*Go on...*"

"The new CEO is Jennifer Ratcliff," Emily blurted.

Ryan paused at the end of the line. Had Emily been able to see him she would have seen that he'd closed his eyes and was deep in thought. He was trying to think of something positive to come from the situation. The former Assistant Intelligence Officer couldn't think of anything.

Thinking the call had been ended, Emily spoke again: "Ryan?"

"*I'm here. Are you sure Jennifer is the new CEO?*"

"She's with Samuel now."

Ryan's curse was muffled, as though he'd removed the handset from his face. He then spoke with clarity. "*Then we may have a bigger problem.*"

"Why's that?" she quizzed.

"*Jennifer has been dating Samuel Jackson on and off for years. Hell, he's been her 'inside' man since the nineties, and many of his ideas were indirectly hers.*"

"Where's the problem?"

"*Well, on the face of it, there is no problem – except she has a tyrannical determination with all that she does and she's good at reading people.*" Ryan sighed. "*She confronted me once, suggesting she knew that I was 'up to no good'... this was long before I'd committed myself to betraying the corporation. I don't know how, but she sensed it in me. Thankfully she never let slip to Samuel... or if she did, he never believed her. Not at the time.*"

"What could this mean for us... for George and Sophie?" Emily knew the answer but wanted to know that she wasn't alone in her thoughts.

"*Business as usual with no expense spared. Jennifer won't do anything half-arsed. She won't stop until she gets what she wants. AND she always gets what she wants...*"

"Do you believe that?"

"*Emily, our Jennifer Ratcliff is more than just the owner's daughter; she's a greedy, manipulative soulless demon – motivated more by success than hard cash and personal wealth. Embittered by a turbulent childhood and a string of failed relationships. Long term investments aren't a hot topic ever discussed – and though sophisticated intelligence operatives and covert undertakings were never things that excited her, she'll happily entertain them if it will get her what she wants.*" Ryan paused at the other end to take a mouthful of flavoured water. Peach.

"*A word of warning, don't trust anything that woman says. She'll tell you one thing one moment and the next do the complete opposite. As for our friend George – don't expect much advocacy there. They had history a long time ago, in their youth – before Harriet and the kids came along,*" he chuckled slightly, "*so it's rumoured.*" He didn't always heed to gossip but on this occasion the source had been reliable.

"What happened?" she pressed, her phone hand was beginning to get numb from over elevation. She swapped hands.

"*She stabbed him in the back, literally – so it's been said. Yes, their parting ways was less than mutual. I guess a knife between the shoulder blades would have that result.*"

"Jesus…"

"*I guess he never pressed charges as nothing 'official' has been recorded, but I trust the information.*" Ryan paused and sighed again. "*Now the CIA has George and who knows what they are going to do to him and what will happen.*"

"You think Jennifer will abandon him, that all will be lost?"

"*No,*" Ryan said without thought. "*She won't stop until she has him. Or he's dead. There seems to be unfinished business between them. But all's not lost. George still has you and me… so don't give up hope just yet.*"

Emily peered through the glass wall of the office. The corridor was empty. No one had noticed her absence.

"*Listen, Emily. We need to meet up. There's someone I need you to meet; someone who may be able to help.*"

"Okay."

"*I'll call you later. But for now find out what you can about Jennifer's plans and keep your nose clean.*" Bypassing any pleasantries or words of parting, Ryan severed the connection, ending the call.

Emily lowered the mobile from her ear, glanced nervously around the room before peering through a couple of slats of the blinds. She quickly opened the door, stepping out into the deserted corridor. Less than a minute later she was back behind her desk listening to fake laughter as it filtered down from the office at the top of the metal staircase and beginning to plot her next move.

CHAPTER FIFTY ONE

THOMAS

By the time Ryan had finished his account of the events from the previous forty-eight hours, a local pizzeria delivery guy riding a moped with an 'L' plate pulled up in the driveway beside the two parked cars carrying the ordered food in a padded bag. Another man appeared from the side of the house wearing dark jeans and a yellow short-sleeved polo shirt with *Fred Perry* motif. He had cropped brown hair and wore designer spectacles. He approached the delivery man, waving a twenty pound note into his face.

"This should cover it." He spoke deliberately slow with a Scandinavian accent .

"Barely," grunted the delivery guy, scrunching the note up deep into the folds of a pocket and rooting around for some pennies.

The Scandinavian took the three large pizza boxes off the man. "Keep the change," he said. Not waiting for a reply he took them up to the house. He knocked on the door and waited.

A brief moment passed before Ryan opened the door. He nodded confirmation to an unasked question, taking the pizzas from him. On closing the door, the Scandinavian stood in the hallway waiting for the moment, waiting for his cue.

Ryan returned to the living room carrying the three large pizza boxes. *Pepperoni, Hawaiian and Margherita.*

"Get it whilst it's hot," Ryan recommended, lifting out a slice of Pepperoni pizza for himself.

In the corner of the room an old television box the size of a *Mini Cooper*, played a *Disney* movie: *Pocahontas.* Momentarily distracted by food, the trio crowded round the three boxes of pizza and stripped a couple of slices away each, returning to the movie a moment later.

"So, where does that leave us now Ryan?" asked Sophie, helping herself to some pizza. The kids had dived in, oblivious to the continuing conversation.

"Well, I guess we lay low until we have information of your father's whereabouts. We then decide whether or not we go after him."

"What d'you mean 'whether or not'? Of course we are going after him. He's our father!"

"Sophie, it's complicated." Ryan took a mouthful of pizza and continued. "There's someone I'd like for you to meet."

Hearing his cue, the Scandinavian stepped into the living room from the hallway and with a limp, walking purposefully to the centre of the room.

"Sophie, this is Thomas Mundahl."

Thomas Mundahl, where have I heard that name? she thought. A puzzled look appeared on her face as neurons connected in her brain and the image of the man appeared in her mind's eye.

Sophie stood up from where she was sitting and ran to the man. "Tom!" she squealed in excitement, wrapping her arms about his chest and almost off-balancing him. "But how?"

"I guess you thought me dead, little one?" He spoke carefully, over-articulating every word, his accent Norwegian-rich. "Though, not so little anymore," he appraised as she disentangled from him.

Turning to Ryan, Sophie spoke: "But how?" *How did Tom survive?*

Ryan smiled reassuringly. "Thomas survived the explosion that killed Maksim Alekseev, and my daughter, Clara..."

"My dad said they were all dead."

"Yes. George believed it so. George had..." he trailed off for a second, momentarily distracted, before finishing, "...wanted it so."

"I can assure you Sophie that I am not dead. See..." Thomas held out his hands, and turned them palm out then palm inwards, as though this proved everything. He was smiling like a lunatic.

"George wanted them all to be dead, Sophie. Because, I'm sorry to say, George wasn't who he said he was." Ryan took his seat and helped himself to a slice of Hawaiian pizza. "He's been living a lie all this time. As have you..." he shook his head, a look of apology on his face. "You all have."

"I..." Sophie looked confused, almost hurt. "I don't understand. What are you saying?"

"Your father was a spy, Sophie. He worked for the Americans. CIA we think, or NSA; but most likely the CIA in view of their recent involvement with abducting your mother. We didn't want to believe it, but it's true. After the explosion our investigations proved... conclusive."

"You must be mistaken. I know George."

"Why do you think you've been in hiding Sophie, and your family on the run? It was George who blew up the lab. It was George who killed Maksim. It was George who killed my daughter Clara and the others on that hateful day."

"My dad said it was the corporation that did it; he said they wanted the whole team dead once I had been created. They had no use for them anymore... that was why he did what he had to do."

"Think about it Sophie. Why would they want him dead? It doesn't make sense. The team were an asset – you don't kill your star players." Ryan was chewing but the pizza was just going round and round in his mouth. He tossed the half-eaten remnant of the slice back into the box in disdain. All of a sudden he was no longer feeling hungry.

"Sophie, think about it. Doesn't it strike you odd that the Americans found your mother despite her getting away from Kaplan

Ratcliff at the hospital? They were having insider help? Your father. How would they have found her unless they knew where to look?"

Sophie opened her mouth to speak against the accusation and suddenly closed it. She didn't believe this man was right… but he made a convincing point.

"Only George and I knew your mother would be driving down that road," adding as an afterthought, "and, bizarrely, Dominic, of course."

The room was silent whilst the information sunk in. Meredith, Stanley and Charlie had each returned to the pizza boxes for more helpings, their eyes still glued to the television screen, not the least interested in the grownups talk despite it involving their parents.

"Ryan, if what you say is true about my father… why were you helping him?"

The former Assistant Intelligence Officer looked at the young woman and smiled warmly.

"Who said I was helping *him*?"

Sophie looked perplexed. "But your calls, your warnings…"

"My dear Sophie..." he continued to smile, "it wasn't him I was helping. It was you… It was always you… for *Clara*."

Sophie was baffled. *What was he saying?* It was too much information, the overload was barely registering and made little sense.

Ryan felt the urge to unburden his final bombshell.

"Sophie…" Ryan took a deep breath. For a moment he didn't think he would be able to tell her, but then it was out without warning. "My daughter Clara – *not* Harriet – was your biological mother… she," indicating Harriet, "was just the surrogate," he smiled, taking a long pause for the detail to sink in. "Sophie. I am your grandfather…"

CHAPTER FIFTY-TWO

GEORGE

He felt lightheaded and giddy, still subdued from the general anaesthetic that had been injected shortly before the *Boeing C-17 Globemaster III* (prolonging his paralysis having been knocked out with the butt of a rifle shortly before) had started its descent for landing at the Air Force Base at Langley, situated on more than 3,100 acres of land. Unconscious for the landing and subsequent journey, his face was again concealed within the black velvet hood that had first been pulled over him back at the industrial estate just outside Norwich.

Where he was, he didn't know… couldn't even risk a guess. He knew he was no longer in England and basing judgement on the accents of the few people who had been speaking around him he thought it likely that he was in America.

Waking more fully, George shifted around slightly. He was uncomfortable and it took very little time to realise that his hands were still cuffed behind his back and that he had been seated upon a carpeted floor, his legs outstretched ahead of him.

Because he had been put to sleep for a proportion of the journey, he had no concept of time. It could have been a couple of hours since he was at the warehouse with his daughter attempting to rescue his wife, the last time his eyes were free to see the world around him; it could have been literally days… how long *had* he been out for?

A short time had passed when George heard the sound of a door squeak open, the three hinges all protesting in unison to announce the entrance of a visitor (or visitors). It sounded a short distance away. He heard only one set of footfall enter the room. The door closed quietly behind the newcomer, his shoes making whispery noises as they tread softly on the thick, cushioned carpet.

A clatter as if a thick wad of papers or a book smacked the surface of a desk or table, echoed around the room, followed by a creak as weight was lowered onto the surface. George guessed the newcomer was sitting on the table or desk, confirmed by the further metallic/wooden creak as the newly positioned weight shifted, one cheek to the other.

"I'm guessing you've brought me here for a reason." George's throat was dry and the words that escaped his cracked lips were rasped, hoarse and almost whispered. He thought he sounded like an old man.

George detected the sound of the newcomer's feet making further whispery noises as they approached him, then stopped. He sensed the newcomer was standing close by.

A second later and the hood that had obliterated the world around him was swept off his head and tossed aside.

Bright, blinding light lanced into his eyes like twin pokers of searing electricity, stabbing at his pupils. He blanched at the sharp intrusion and tried to turn away, scrunching his eyes closed with minimal effect. Having been in perpetual darkness for longer than he dared imagine, his ocular organs felt lambasted by the sudden incandescence.

"Hello George." The newcomer spoke casually, the voice George recognised but could not place a name to. "You can quit the pretence. You know who I am and why you are here. Would you like a drink?

Some water? Or… something stronger maybe? I have some *Pappy Van Winkle* whiskey in my desk… twenty-three-year reserve."

George was blinking back tears; the glare of light that filtered through the windows that stretched from floor to ceiling along one entire wall was still hurting his eyes. "Please," he croaked. "Water."

The newcomer offered a glass of cold, refreshing water to George's lips and gently poured the liquid into his mouth. George coughed and spluttered and dribbled but then swallowed deeply.

"Good. That's better, hey?" The newcomer took the almost empty glass away and placed it on the desk that was in the room.

With a couple more minutes of blinking furiously, George's vision began to slowly adjust to the room's brightness. The sun was streaming in through the window, three-quarters up the sky. He guessed from its position that the time was closing in on midday. With his eyesight settling he looked about the room in which he was being held captive. Sparsely furnished with just a *Queen Anne* style desk, a leather office chair placed behind it and two small chairs in front, very little else of note filled the room – save for the large stars and stripes flag standing behind the desk. Upon the wall were photographs of former presidents, the most recent, *Avery Harrison* shaking the hand of the man within whose office he now found himself. There were other photographs of the man, the most notable with former governor *Arnold Schwarzenegger*. Also adorning the wall were copies of one or two oil paintings of the sixth President, *John Quincy Adams*, the originals of which hang in the Department of State's drawing room.

George, hands still restrained behind his back turned his attention on the man who'd recently entered the room, who'd removed the obstruction from over his head and who'd kindly given him water. He was in his early forties with a square jaw line, a good crop of hair that was styled like *Tom Cruise* in *War of the Worlds* and a physique that took too many hours in the gym to maintain – a fact which attested to the reason why he was single and long-divorced. Also like *Tom Cruise* he had a good set of pristine white teeth that shimmered in the sunlight. Perched on the *Queen Anne*'s edge, he looked like a politician rather than a senior CIA officer.

George started to smile as recognition darted across his face, the smile turning to laughter at the absurdity of the situation.

"Milo you rabid dog! Get these cuffs off me!" George's throat was still hoarse but his voice was slightly recovered, his mood vastly improved.

Milo Calland smiled. "Hello my old friend," he said mildly, crossing silently through the deep pile of the carpet to where George was still sitting. He crouched down and leaned over the man's shoulder, reaching for the cuffs and deftly unlocking one. He gave the key to George to finish off the job. George unlocked the second cuff and allowed them to drop to the carpet.

"Why the theatrics Milo? We had a deal." George stood up unsteadily and tried walking about a bit to get the blood re-circulating. His feet were numb and his arms, shoulders and hands were a bit stiff from being restrained for so long.

"We *did* have a deal. That was two years ago. We waited. We waited. We waited. We waited some more; we just didn't think you were ever going to come in."

"I did leak some information," George offered in defence.

"Only *after* we contacted you."

"Milo... I had my family to think about. I couldn't just leave them. We were being hounded."

"And the girl?" Milo was now sitting behind his desk. "When were you going to give her up?"

George sat down in one of the small chairs in front of Milo and looked down disconcertedly. "Sophie wasn't part of the deal," he said quietly, pausing to look up forlornly. "I was never going to give her up to you or to anyone; just the technology, the research... nothing more."

Milo sighed. "Very well, for old time's sake I'll let that pass. But I do hope you remember who your allegiance is to, George. We invested a lot of time and money in you... now is the time for a return on capital and we expect a lot of interest."

"You'll get it Milo. You'll get it. As soon as I know that my family is safe I will give you what you want."

Milo smiled reassuringly. "Your family is safe, you have my word on that but we are out of time. D'you remember the old recruitment posters with the catchphrase emblazoned across: *Uncle Sam Needs You*?"

An image of a white haired, white goatee bearded man in a blue white top hat emblazoned with white stars, blue suit jacket and a red dickie bow tie, flashed in his mind.

"Well, the time is now. We need you George; we need your genetically engineered super soldiers in our war against terrorism... our enemies grow stronger by the day, we need them more now than ever before.

"Because George, ever since nine-eleven we've been losing the war against terror. For every *Bin Laden* or *Saddam Hussein* or *Muammar Gaddafi* there's a hundred other fanatics coming up through the ranks taking their place; like weeds in a field of corn trying to poison the crop. I want to rip out those weeds and I don't want them to see us coming."

George frowned. Milo was laying it on too thick for his comfort. He was torn between his conscience and his duty. Despite masquerading as a Brit since the early nineties, George Jennings *was* American, born and raised. He sighed theatrically. "I'll do this for you... on one condition."

"You're not in a good position to negotiate George," Milo cautioned, "but I'm listening."

"When my job is done I want out. I want you to return me to my family – no ifs, buts or maybes."

"Is that all?"

"And..."

Milo raised his eyebrows quizzically.

"... new identities for me and my family – when it's over, we want to disappear. No more running – if that's not too much to ask for?"

"Just give me my super soldiers, George... then I'll consider giving you what you want."

CHAPTER FIFTY-THREE

SOPHIE

SOPHIE HAD STORMED OUT of the room, crashed out of the house through the front door and slammed it behind her. She'd walked to the side of the building and sat down on some grass, her back to the house, knees drawn to her chest. She rocked back and forth as she tried to make sense of the information Ryan had announced. In her hand she held the *Whisper of Persia*, quietly comforting as she passed it from one hand to another, back and forth, back and forth, the stolen item strangely soothing, helping her to think. That had been nearly ten minutes ago. Despite being deep in thought she'd heard Thomas creep up on her. Her hearing was spectacularly powerful.

"What's that you got there?" The Scandinavian had grown concerned and had thought to consol her should she need it.

Ignoring the question, Sophie spoke brusquely. "Ryan could be lying. How do I know he's telling the truth? Who do we trust?"

Thomas shrugged, sitting next to her. "I accused Ryan of being wrong… when I first found out," he spoke with his thick Norwegian accent. "Your father and I had been friends for a number of years, we'd gone to university together, so like you I was sceptical. Ryan gave me this. He said it was proof." He handed Sophie a photograph. It was a bit crumpled, a little old, a bit dog-eared around the edges but it was clear as a sunlit vista. George in US military uniform, peaked hat, a hand pressed to his forehead in formal salute.

Sophie wiped her moist eyes with the back of a hand.

"Apparently, Ryan unearthed this shortly after the lab was blown up. He found it in George's locker... amongst other things."

"It could've been photoshopped."

"That's what I said. Ryan just laughed at me. I could see in his eyes that what I had suggested was ludicrous and not the case," he paused, taking a minute. "No, your father – my *friend* – has been living a double life. Unfortunately, all that we know of him is a lie."

"Why would he do such a thing? He loved us and protected us."

"I don't doubt that he cared for his family, for your mother, your brothers and sister... for you. As for his motives, I can only guess that he meant to steal the research from Kaplan Ratcliff, destroy what we had and kill whoever was capable of replicating what we had achieved. Only, he failed in his attempt at killing me. Not that I came away totally unscathed." Thomas made a fist and knock knocked the top of his outer left leg. A hollow wooden sound followed each tap, three in all. "Prosthetic. Still, better that than being dead, yes?"

Sophie nodded, going quiet. For a couple of minutes the only sound was a pair of *wood warblers*, unseen within a copse of trees, their alternating, high-pitched trill increasing in tempo that lasted for a couple of seconds (*pit-pit-pitpitpitpt-t-t-ttt*), then changed to a series of piping notes that descended in their timbre (*piüü-piüü-piüü*).

"I guess I see why Ryan would say we had to choose whether or not to go after him," Sophie broke the silence. "It's a tough call, but even though he may have done some terrible things, I still love him. He's still my dad."

"True," said Thomas. "You can choose your friends, but not your family. But he's also responsible for the death of your biological mother, who loved you dearly. Whether we go after him as a friend or foe, he should be held accountable, at least for that."

Thomas stood up to leave, taking a couple of tentative steps. He stopped; his back to Sophie. He was facing in the direction of the front of the house. He balled his fists. "I'm sorry Sophie... I don't think I can forgive him for what he did to Clara. I'll leave you now to play with your... trinket." Thomas walked back to the house not giving the diamond a second thought and closed the door behind him.

"I guess... I will have to find you on my own," she spoke low, to herself, hardly audible at all. The diamond she tossed from one hand to another, back and forth, back and forth, a souvenir from a different time. She couldn't deny the adrenalin and the adventure of the heist had been very exhilarating. It didn't seem possible that it had been only yesterday – it felt like longer. She lifted the jewel up to the sky and looked through the cut stone, at the prism of light bouncing within. She wished she felt more than the gut-wrenching sadness at the loss of her surrogate mother and now, seemingly, her father.

Maybe sensing her distress the wood warblers ceased their song, allowing an eerie silence to settle around her. There wasn't even a whisper of a breeze to rustle the leaves or tickle the blue spires of the *monkshood* plants, strangely grown in abundance around the borders of the garden despite their toxicity, their beautiful hooded blossoms belying the potential hazard to any who were to accidentally ingest any parts of them.

Sophie paid them little notice, instead making the most of the peace and solitude to consider all she had been through during the previous forty-eight hours, all that she'd discovered during this time, and finally all that she hoped and now intended to do.

She could never foretell when the dream would come. Sometimes it haunted her every night for a fortnight, plaguing her like a remembered reality of an event long ago gone but too harrowing to ever forget; then her nights would go uninterrupted for long periods conjuring the illusion that she'd grown out of it, that she could sleep normally without fear and not knowing what – and *if* – the hidden message portent.

It had been many months since her mind last teleported her back to the events that had occurred that October ... as always it started off in her room; she'd be carrying *Flopsy* and the deep, resonant klaxon of the emergency alarms screaming warnings from the corridor beyond the locked door, the smell of smoke, at first slight, growing thick in the air. The tableau would play out the scene in vivid high definition detail. Although playing in full within her mind, when waking she'd only remember the final scene from this particular part of the drama:

"*We're leaving*?" Sophie was inside her father's car and sobbing. She could hear her sobs and, like all the times before, she was scared. More than that, she was petrified. She'd never left the confines of the now-burning building before. This was the first time she'd set foot outside, and she was equally new to sitting inside a motor vehicle.

Her father didn't reply. Instead George closed the car's door and jogged a short distance out of the car park onto the main road that serviced the biochemical research centre and other industrialised buildings peppered along the route. Across the road was a bus shelter, and more specifically to George, a black waste bin standing sentinel alongside it, cemented into the pavement, its opening like a large, wide letterbox. No one was standing at the shelter as George approached the bin.

Sophie observed her father take a quick look from side to side and then a nervous backwards glance, ensuring no one was watching, momentarily catching her eye before darting away, now refocused on the task at hand; he pulled a small, weighty object from beneath the dirty white lab coat he wore and hastily posted it into the bin.

From inside the car, Sophie had watched, her eyes fixating on the object that her father was disposing.

The shock of seeing the item stifled her whimpering. For a moment her brain could not (*would not?*) decipher what her eyes were seeing, blotting out the item like a carefully placed pixellation - like that used to censor nudity in pictures appearing in family-friendly publications or the faces of the innocent in video replays of crimes being broadcast to mainstream television.

This was the point when Sophie's innate defence mechanism - or call it her *subconscious* - kicked in, slapping her invisibly awake. But this time things were different.

Ordinarily the dream would dissipate at this point and she would find herself back in bed, sitting upright, coated in sweat and almost sick from fear, the sudden adrenalin rush causing her heart to beat so fast it hurt her chest, threatening to split her in two.

Unlike before, the picture show continued; furthermore, the pixellation blotting her view of the item her father was just about to dispose of shifted, allowing her to see the item for what it was...

The knowledge her brain had shielded her from was not just what the item was her father had disposed of; it was shielding her from the truth that only a few hours earlier Ryan had announced it in such a way, all that was missing was the *'Dun, Dun, Duuuun'* drama sound bite.

It was a handgun.

As the weapon dropped out of sight, George Jennings turned away from the bin and jogged hurriedly back to the car, a look of relief on his face followed up with an easy smile.

Sophie awoke at that precise moment, not with a start or abruptly like all the times before, but gradually, serenely, peacefully, her heart beating normally, her breathing was shallow and no sweat dripped from her brow or matted her hair. Re-closing her eyes she could still see her father smiling in her mind.

"It was always a handgun," she whispered to herself. "I was afraid of the truth. It wasn't the dream that I was so afraid of; it was knowing what my father had done that so terrified me, which I didn't want to accept..." Even without the photograph she knew Ryan had been telling the truth. She sighed mournfully, shaking her head, succumbing to the dark realisation.

Whatever his reason, her father was a spy and a murderer.

But, no matter what, he *was* still her father.

Sophie lay back down on the bed, closed her eyes and started to think.

CHAPTER FIFTY-FOUR

RYAN

WITH OVER FIVE HOURS of driving and just an hour's break (the pizza dinner back in the cottage outside Bude, just a memory), Ryan found himself sitting in the bar area once again within the hotel in Harlow, the same seat he'd kept warm the previous night and early hours of the morning, a pint of *John Smiths* and a whiskey chaser placed in front of him, a plate with the remnants of a mixed grill meat platter placed to the side of it (the fried tomato, half a dozen anaemic chips, the fat from a gammon steak and the bone off a pork chop, all swimming in a millimetre of grease) and Emily's mobile phone barely in between, momentarily forgotten.

Emily had been waiting for him when he'd arrived, concern on her face. "Where have you been?"

Ryan had called her two hours earlier saying they needed to talk: *urgently.* Emily had left the command centre immediately without explanation or hesitation around three o'clock and had been sitting in the hotel's reception area for over an hour. During the wait she'd managed to read two magazines, a newspaper and a couple of brochures, all laid out for hospitality and waiting patrons.

Not allowing time to go to his room to freshen up, Ryan smiled reassuringly and kissed Emily on the cheek. Without speaking he gestured for the woman to join him in the bar area. Despite Ryan's assertion that they meet *urgently*, the topic that Emily most wanted to discuss did not take place until after the former Assistant Intelligence Officer had eaten his meal and downed a full pint of *John Smiths.* Instead conversation had centred on the comings and goings of Kaplan Ratcliff's Director, and the information gleaned from within the corporation's security division.

"Our information is sketchy at best," Emily had started. "After the events of last night leading to the death of Tom Kaplan, Jennifer Ratcliff ordered an immediate enquiry as to what went wrong. She's suspended all operations associated with CHAMELEON *and* the Jennings family for the time being. Despite this, news has been filtering through all day from our spy network and field operatives… and I've been a little resourceful." Emily paused to reflect on that day's events. "A woman matching Harriet Jennings' description was found dead outside the Mildenhall airbase, though it's not being treated as suspicious..."

"And so the cover-up begins..." Ryan interrupted. "I'm guessing the Americans are responsible for that." He flagged for the barman to bring him another pint of beer.

Emily continued: "Two bodies were found in a van parked outside of a house in Norfolk, both had their throats cut and found laid out in the back, both were professionally hit, both American and both claimed by the US embassy for processing…"

"And ditto my last comment..."

"Quite," said Emily. "And, this is amusing; a number of tabloid newspapers are reporting that 'the invisible man' stole a diamond worth millions from an art and antiques exhibition yesterday – caused quite a stir, though alcohol is being largely blamed... and heat stroke."

"Who'd ever believe in such a thing as the 'invisible man'," Ryan chortled. He took another mouthful of *John Smiths.*

"The secret is safe for now," concluded Emily.

"Anything else?"

"Oh, I've been demoted – something to do with recruitment procedures and union interference, ya-da, ya-da, ya-da. Jennifer restored me to my former role without batting an eyelid or an apology. I tended my resignation forthwith and escorted off the premises swiftly after."

"And now we are in this alone..." said Ryan, deep in regret.

"What's going on Ryan? I take it you're still in contact with Little Miss Sunshine?"

"I'm sorry to hear about you losing my old job," started Ryan. "Maybe parting from Kaplan Ratcliff is for the best..."

"Quit stalling. You called me out here to discuss something urgent. It's been a long day and I'm tired. Now talk."

Ryan reached for the whiskey chaser and downed it whole, wincing from the taste and the after burn.

"Well, things have gone a little awry," he said, proceeding to tell Emily everything, and more, of what he knew. He detailed George's capture in full, his whereabouts now unknown (though likely America); he spoke of Harriet's roadside death, as outlined by Sophie (a note of sadness in his voice); he mentioned the arranged meeting in Devon with Sophie, the Jennings children and Thomas Mundahl (no, he's not dead!); and revealed George Jennings' true identity – that all his actions, the sabotage of the laboratory, the deaths of all those people, including Ryan's daughter, were designed to steal research for the Americans, cover up his nefarious deeds and limit the chance of replicating his work.

"You see Emily, George is CIA. I guess the Americans knew about the type of research we were developing long before he turned up and at the turn of the century saw to it to recruit an up-and-coming biochemical geneticist who would carry on with his research and studies whilst his true vocation lay dormant, waiting for his calling – like a terrorist cell. Who's to blame the Americans for wanting the

CHAMELEON research and an invisible soldier of their own? What I don't understand is why George didn't just disappear to America after sabotaging the laboratory? Instead he goes on the run – from us, and seemingly from them as well... for a while, at least."

"Perhaps his conscience couldn't allow it," suggested Emily, sweeping a hand through her hair. "He probably considered the technology too great a weapon for any one country to possess, so did what he thought best. Destroy the research... only he couldn't complete it fully – that would have required him to kill his daughter Sophie too."

Ryan shook his head. "Something doesn't add up though."

"What's that?"

"The CIA aided by Dominic Schilling intercepted Harriet and her son on the Seabrook Road. Only George and I knew she would be there precisely at that time."

"Someone informed them?" Emily looked puzzled.

Ryan smiled, nodding, "Not someone. George did."

"But why? Why the cloak-and-dagger?"

Ryan shrugged. "Probably an attempt to retain his false identity, for the sake of his family. In fact, it still is intact. Only I knew the truth. I discovered this photograph," Ryan handed Emily the same photo Thomas had earlier shown Sophie. "I found it in George's locker after the explosion." Emily studied the young uniformed man in the picture. "I decided to keep the information to myself. Thought it might be useful one day and help get me closer to him."

"Why?" Emily handed the photo back.

"So I could pay him back for Clara, of course. Pay him back with interest," he replied, his tone hard. "Now the son of a bitch has gone." Ryan scrunched up the photograph into a ball and dropped it onto the plate amongst the leftovers, to float on the puddle of grease.

Emily reached out to her father figure and took his hand. Through her eyes she conveyed she knew his pain, understood his anger and the desire for vengeance. She held onto him for a couple of minutes before letting go.

"What do we do now?" she asked softly.

"Honestly?" Ryan shrugged. "Sophie wants to go after him, to get him back. Part of me wants to go too… but my motives are different. I don't think I can trust myself. I'd rather see him lying face down in a ditch somewhere."

"In that case, maybe I should go with her instead. I'm due a vacation and I now have all the time in the world."

"Maybe," Ryan considered, bouncing the idea around his head. "Maybe, but first there's something I need you to do."

EPILOGUE

GEORGE

DEEP BELOW THE SCORCHED ground within a large, desolate area of desert eighty-three miles north-northwest of Las Vegas, in an area of America listed as Area 51, a large laboratory the size of two Wembley football stadiums was spread out with various machines, scientific apparatus and what appeared to be hundreds of large translucent polyethylene bags filled with liquid, suspended in racks of five hanging hammock-like atop of one and other with just a couple of inches gap between each. Tubes and wires were connected to each bag, an electronic console flashing and flickering data was situated alongside every bag, affixed to the rack. There were ten rows, each containing five racks.

Many personnel milled around the facility, dressed in sealed biochemical hazmat suits, some holding clipboards, others wheeling trolleys containing equipment or chemicals.

The one entrance into the laboratory was heavily fortified with three sets of security doors, each manned by two armed guards, all similarly attired. Despite being indoors with the absence of sunlight or bright light they wore matching aviator sunglasses.

At the first security door, having travelled for two minutes within the elevator (at a speed of two mph) down to the laboratory, George swiped his security card and placed his right eye level with the scanner screen, a small ten-inch monitor to the left of the steel door.

A moment later a green line of light slowly coasted across the screen and took a retinal image which it then cross-examined against images stored within the security database. Face recognition images flashed upon the screen flickering at fifty per second. A moment later the small screen flashed up a picture of George Jennings, with the word: MATCH in bright neon green. The door glided open to allow George admittance.

The second and third security doors required vocal recognition and finger and breath analysis, together with further swipes of George's security pass. No chances were being taken.

At each security door the guards stood on either side of George as he underwent clearance, poised to seize at the slightest sign of rejection, hands gently wrapped around the butts of their holstered weapons, at the ready.

When the final door closed behind him, George audibly sighed his relief and made his way to the conference room, an office nestled between a store cupboard and the toilets along a short corridor that ultimately led to the large underground laboratory.

Inside the conference room five men and one woman were sitting behind the large rectangular desk that took up the whole of the centre of the room. All wore military uniforms of varying rank. At the furthest end, to the left, a fifty-inch screen sat at the head of the table. Milo Calland was sitting in his office more than 2,000 miles away – the same office George had found himself in a little less than three weeks earlier.

"George, glad you could make it," a note of sarcasm in Milo's voice.

"Yeah, well... I didn't want to keep you waiting," George replied smugly, taking his seat.

"President Harrison is keen to know how things are progressing. I take it the facilities are as you required."

"Yes... better than expected."

"And the product?"

George looked a little apprehensively at the man on the screen, brushed a hand through his hair and then composed himself. He felt nervous and noted a tinge of fear in his voice when he spoke:

"They are nascent," he said. "I've been successful expediting the programme to phase two – all embryos are growing normally within the pods, all at their expected growth cycles, and all on schedule."

"And the modifications we talked about, George?"

"I've incorporated the emotion inhibitor as you instructed."

"Good."

"What does that mean, exactly?" The woman in the room, Warrant Officer Mary Taylor-Marsh, a tall woman in her mid-fifties, shoulder-length black hair and a face that, for many, would explain her meteoric rise up the Army's ranks, regardless to her ability or work ethic. She spoke with a southern accent.

"Well, simply madam, it means that we have stripped out the bits that get in the way," Milo stepped in, saving George the task of explaining a modification that he'd been dead set against. Milo continued, "Fear... anxiety... love... hate... All – and *any* – feelings that hinder one's ability to function efficiently... all gone."

"So, I guess no women, then?" One of the men in the room, his name not known by George, spoke up, chortling at his own joke. George paid little attention to him.

Also ignoring him, Milo readdressed George. "When can we expect the first delivery from your so called project *GYGES*?"

"In two months... your first 250 soldiers will be ready to begin their training."

One of the other men in the room, the eldest and most senior officer, General Bill Eastman, raised his hand to speak.

"Yes, General," Milo was straightening his tie on the big screen at the end of the table.

"You say 'first 250', how many more are there to be?"

"Well, General," Milo replied with a smile, "just ask the question: how many soldiers, including Army, Navy, Air Force, Marines, Coast Guard and reserves, does the US have now? Your conservative guess?"

"Conservative guess, " he shrugged, "two-and-a-half million."

Milo crossed his arms and looked each person around the table in the eyes, ending on George Jennings. He then smiled and nodded, almost as though he had answered the question verbally.

George turned away, suddenly engulfed in shame and guilt. He looked down at the desk, focused on a smudge of black ink worked into the mahogany surface and closed his eyes, wondering whether the nightmare for him was over... or whether it had only just begun.

What have I done? he pondered.

Beyond the corridor behind the office, through a final set of security doors (these only requiring an electronic pass key to open), the laboratory; ten rows of racks laden with large polyethylene pods filled with liquid and... and something moving inside each of them.

A small foetal hand, barely formed, pressed against the inside wall of one of the pods, causing the plastic to bulge outwards. A moment later the hand was quickly pulled back, as though stung by a nettle or burnt by a naked flame... only to be replaced by an indistinct face, its small, dainty nose distending the pod's translucent wall much like the hand seconds earlier. Though obscured by the pod's hazy barrier, one could see that the face was human.

The foetus' eyes popped open and took its first glimpse of the world.

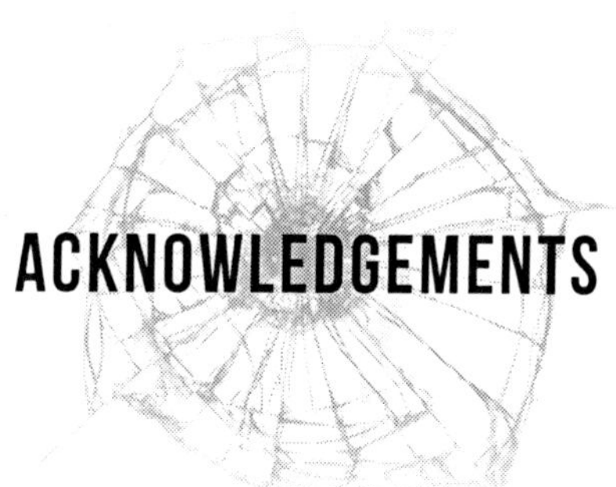

ACKNOWLEDGEMENTS

Gratitude and thanks are extended to the following people who assisted in some way or another, great and small, with the production of this book.

First and foremost my editor Laura Ling who has been on board since the inception of The Girl in the Mirror (I so hate your red pen!), and been a sounding board for many of my ups and downs (even if you were playing the world's smallest volin!) for a long time.

My troupe of beta readers: Lynne & Paul Cotton, Darren Staff, Martin Kendray, Kelly Tinsey, Sonia Jennings, Terry Gould, Louise Ruse and my wife, Beth Gould. Each of you had a part in shaping this story, ultimately improving Sophie's journey into print.

And to those of you who have taken a chance and bought this book, I take a bow to you. I always had you in mind when I first sat down to begin writing this series. It's a lonely business, being an author, but it's made bearable knowing that someone, somewhere, has read this book. Without you, there is no point.

ABOUT THE AUTHOR

PHILIP J GOULD was born in Ipswich in 1974, and still lives in Suffolk with his wife Beth, and three children, Rebecca, Sophie and Matthew. At an early age he discovered a vivid imagination and an affection for the written word. Leaving school at sixteen, he went onto work in shipping and insurance, and is also a qualified personal fitness trainer. He quit the day job in 2012 to develop his career as an author and to spend more time with his family. His first book was *The Book of Alternative Records*, first published in 2004 by Metro Publishing Ltd.

Be the first to hear news and read exclusive content on the official website:
www.philipjgould.com

Join the official Facebook page:
www.facebook.com/philipjgouldbooks

Follow Philip on Twitter @philipjgould

Lightning Source UK Ltd.
Milton Keynes UK
UKOW01f1803050916

282281UK00001B/29/P